W9-BRJ-276

"I haven't seen that steady of a hand in a long time," Shane said. "You have a gift, Miss O'Toole."

Her shoulders stiffened at his compliment and some unknown emotion flashed in her eyes.

"I—I do?"

"Yes."

"I…" She lifted her chin. "Thank you."

Her uncertain manner was replaced by a quiet dignity.

For a moment the foundation of everything Shane thought rocked under him. He was a healer, called by God to treat the sick, a man others turned to in times of need. He did not rely on anyone.

No human, at any rate. Only the divine.

Then again, he'd never met a woman who made him want to admit he might be weary of standing helplessly by as his patients struggled with illnesses that far too often resulted in death.

For the first time in his life, a woman—a fancy, overdressed, far-too-beautiful stranger—made Shane want to share a few of his burdens with another person.

"Miss O'Toole, what I ask is highly respectable," Shane continued. "Would you consider working as my assistant?"

Renee Ryan
and
Janet Lee Barton

Loving Bella

&

Somewhere to Call Home

 HARLEQUIN® LOVE INSPIRED®CLASSICS

If you purchased this book without a cover you should be aware
that this book is stolen property. It was reported as "unsold and
destroyed" to the publisher, and neither the author nor the
publisher has received any payment for this "stripped book."

 LOVE INSPIRED BOOKS

Recycling programs
for this product may
not exist in your area.

ISBN-13: 978-1-335-45464-5

Loving Bella & Somewhere to Call Home

Copyright © 2019 by Harlequin Books S.A.

Loving Bella
First published in 2010. This edition published in 2019.
Copyright © 2010 by Renee Halverson

Somewhere to Call Home
First published in 2012. This edition published in 2019.
Copyright © 2012 by Janet Lee Barton

All rights reserved. Except for use in any review, the reproduction
or utilization of this work in whole or in part in any form by any
electronic, mechanical or other means, now known or hereafter
invented, including xerography, photocopying and recording, or in
any information storage or retrieval system, is forbidden without
the written permission of the editorial office, Love Inspired Books,
195 Broadway, New York, NY 10007 U.S.A.

This is a work of fiction. Names, characters, places and incidents are
either the product of the author's imagination or are used fictitiously, and
any resemblance to actual persons, living or dead, business establishments,
events or locales is entirely coincidental.

This edition published by arrangement with Love Inspired Books.

® and TM are trademarks of Love Inspired Books, used under license.
Trademarks indicated with ® are registered in the United States Patent
and Trademark Office, the Canadian Intellectual Property Office and in
other countries.

www.Harlequin.com

Printed in U.S.A.

CONTENTS

Renee Ryan grew up in a Florida beach town where she learned to surf, sort of. With a degree from FSU, she explored career opportunities at a Florida theme park and a modeling agency and even taught high school economics. She currently lives with her husband in Nebraska, and many have mistaken their overweight cat for a small bear. You may contact Renee at reneeryan.com, on Facebook or on Twitter, @reneeryanbooks.

Visit the Author Profile page at Harlequin.com.

LOVING BELLA

Renee Ryan

Brethren, I count not myself to have apprehended: but this one thing I do, forgetting those things which are behind, and reaching forth unto those things which are before.
—*Philippians* 3:13

To my father, Dr. Augustus Emmet Anderson, Jr.
This one's for you, Daddy!

Prologue

Isabella O'Toole's life swept from one tragedy to another. And she loved every dramatic, heartwrenching moment. Singing opera, as her mother once said, was in her blood. No matter the setting or situation, Bella always wept for her doomed heroines.

Tonight, however, there was an added layer of emotion that had nothing to do with tragedy. The sensation left Bella with a dull headache and unusually raw emotions.

He was here. In the audience. Watching her—*only her*—with the intense stare that never failed to steal her breath away.

The moment the curtain made its final descent her first impulse was to run to her dressing room and prepare for his visit. But that would be self-indulgent, a trait she disliked in others and thoroughly despised in herself. Somehow, she found the patience to offer congratulations to her fellow cast members with a genuine smile on her lips.

Still, in the back of her mind she was well-aware that he beckoned and there was little time left to prepare. She offered a quick hug to her understudy, and began the brief journey to her dressing room. Much to her amusement, she caught herself nearly running by the time she arrived at her destination. So much for dignity and grace under pressure.

With an impatient shove, Bella shut the door behind her and leaned against the sturdy wood. Thoughts of William filled her mind. Her heart pounded, her hands shook.

Conflicting emotions tangled inside one another, threatening to overwhelm her. Despite the joy of seeing William again, she was still on edge after playing Isolde. No matter how many times Bella sang the shifting chords in the final aria, the music rent every bit of emotion from her. She was exhausted.

Trying to force calm into her thinking, she breathed in and out. Tonight was too special, too important to allow grief for a fictional heroine's lost love to engulf her.

At last, the drumming in her heart shifted and she looked around the room.

Her refuge.

The one place solely hers, where she morphed herself from Bella O'Toole, youngest in the famous O'Toole acting family, into the most acclaimed opera singer of her day. With grace and comfort in mind, she'd decorated her small space by paying close attention to details and fuss. Intricate lace, fresh flowers and soft, cushiony furniture created a tone that was warm, feminine and fashionable.

To add a touch of glamour, Bella only used candles,

preferring the soft golden glow and warm scent of the wax to the bleak ambiance provided by modern gas lamps. Perhaps she did have her moments of self-indulgence. But she tried to contain them to these small facets of her life instead of giving rein to the wild emotions that sometimes seized her.

Pushing from the door, Bella ran her finger along the edges of her makeup table, across the rims of the various jars of creams and rouge. Tools of her trade. Where she donned the mask of her characters and became the tragic heroines only found in the opera.

She spun in a circle and let dreams fill her head. Dreams of what life would be like if William proposed to her at last. Unlike the characters she portrayed, her love story would have a happy ending.

The charming, handsome viscount had been persistent in his pursuit of her over these last two months, often pushing for favors they both knew she would not give him until their wedding night. She was afraid, afraid he would come to mean more to her than she could handle. Afraid she would forget her moral upbringing and allow emotion to overpower her good sense. He already drew feelings out of her that no one else had.

In truth, his polished sophistication troubled her. Although she'd been raised in the theater, traveling with her famous parents and talented siblings across continents, she wasn't as worldly as Lord Crawley. Her parents had sheltered her from the uglier side of their profession. Reginald and Patience O'Toole had raised their children with Christian values and a strong knowledge of Scripture.

Bella often felt much younger than her twenty-four

years. She missed her family. Especially now, when she desperately needed someone to talk to about her handsome viscount. Her mother or brother, Beau, would know what words to use to settle her unease, or rather what Scripture.

Oh, Lord, she prayed, *guide me.*

Whatever happens, conduct yourselves in a manner worthy of the gospel of Christ. Then, I will know you stand firm....

The words from Paul to the Philippians gave her confidence. Changing out of her costume would give her more. Bella bit back a sigh. With unsteady fingers, she quickly shed Isolde's medieval costume and changed into the dress she'd worn to the theater. The locket William had given her hung beneath the lace collar, warming her skin and reminding Bella of the viscount's deep affection, a tangible symbol of his love for her.

Sighing, she removed her stage makeup and laced up her boots. There was nothing left to do but wait.

As if on cue, the expected knock came at the door.

In spite of her efforts to remain calm and mature, a jittery surge of excitement tickled the base of her spine and she fingered the locket. "Enter," she said on a breathy whisper.

The door swung open. Bella's pulse drummed in her ears as her gaze connected with the man she loved. William Gordon. Lord Crawley. As she drank in the sight of her viscount immaculately dressed in black tails, she tried to look past the title and straight to the man.

He was tall and lean, his face aristocratic with a strong cut of cheekbones under deep-set blue eyes. Even the stark white of his shirt set off his dark good looks.

An unhurried smile drifted along his lips and he

reached out his hand to her. Her pulse tripped, slowed to a near stop then quickened again. Tossing her head back, she started toward him.

He shut the door with a jab of his elbow and then lifted a single eyebrow at her.

Alone. They were all alone. Her stomach rolled over itself, but Bella continued forward. The click of her heels echoed across the parquet floor.

William was so appealing she wanted to rush her steps. She restrained herself. A moment like this required confident, liquid grace.

Tenderness and genuine appreciation mingled in his gaze before he covered his reaction with an unreadable expression. Her heart leapt to her throat and stuck. William Gordon was always kind, generous, quick-witted and charming. The sort of man a woman waited all her life to find. But he was also a man filled with hidden depths. And staring at her now, with such intensity, she realized he had a suggestion of danger about him.

With that thought, her steps slowed. She stopped a foot away from him and placed her palm in his.

"My beautiful, talented Bella," he said, lifting her hand to his lips. "You were magnificent this evening."

A jolt of impatience whipped through her at his standard compliment, but Bella hid the emotion behind a dazzling smile. Pleasantries first, sincerity later. That was their pattern. "Thank you, William."

He stared at her for a long moment, saying nothing. Seconds ticked by with only the sound of their breathing filling the barren silence. Bella's lack of experience with men made her unsure how to fill the awkward moment.

Searching for a clue as to how to proceed, she stared into his handsome face. A sudden gust of wind threw open the window behind her, blowing out the candles closest to her. Shadows filled half the room, concealing William's face. She thought she saw a flicker of something different in his eyes, something a little dark. A little unsettling.

A shiver iced across her skin and she felt the first stirrings of concern. Drawing her bottom lip between her teeth, she wheeled around, shut the window and quickly relit the candles. As she moved through the room, she reminded herself that this was her William. She knew him well. The realization settled her nerves.

"Where would you like to dine this evening?" His gaze shifted to the divan as he strolled toward her. "Or would you prefer to stay in?"

Bella looked around her dressing room. She eyed the soft lighting, breathed in the scent of a spring garden, noted the many pillows strewn on the divan. From a certain perspective one might mistakenly believe she'd prepared for something…illicit.

"I think we should go out," she said, flashing him a bright smile. "Celebrate my magnificent performance."

She'd hoped to make him laugh but his face remained impassive, and his shoulders stiffened. He drew her close to him and took both her hands in his.

"Tonight could be very special for us, my dear."

The sleepy charm in his manner pulled her a step closer.

He tightened his fingers around hers and commanded her gaze. "A beginning, if you will."

In spite of his pleasant tone, Bella couldn't shake the notion that something strange was creeping into their conversation, something sordid. She withdrew one hand and then another. "I—"

"Let us drop these pretenses at last." He shoved shaking fingers through his hair and started pacing along the edge of the Venetian rug. "You are too good for the theater."

He took her elbow and steered her to the divan.

Unsure of his motives, she slid away from him and perched against her dressing table instead.

"I have always dreamed of more," she said, her voice sounding as tentative as she felt. Where was this leading?

He opened his mouth to speak, then clamped his jaw shut as though he was considering his next words carefully. His breath came out in a ragged sigh. She feared his next words would define their fate and she wasn't sure she wanted to know the outcome.

At last, he nodded as if he'd come to some decision, rubbed his hand across his mouth and resumed his pacing. "It's good you want something other than the theater."

The satisfaction that shone in his eyes was at odds with the tenseness in his movements. She'd never seen him quite so edgy. "William?"

"Let me provide for you properly," he blurted while never missing a step. "In the style and comfort you deserve."

His words staggered her and she found she had to clutch the side of her makeup table to steady herself. "Are you asking for my hand?" she asked, but she feared she already knew the answer.

He stopped pacing, turned to look at her with a frown marring his brow. "Marriage? You thought I came to offer marriage?"

His voice held genuine shock, as though the notion

had never crossed his mind. She had to fight a wave of hysteria as she stared at him.

"You said you loved me," she said at last, touching the hidden locket with her fingertip.

He rushed to her, knelt at her feet and clasped her hands in his again. "I do love you, Bella." His breathing came in hard, shallow spurts. "It is why I offer my protection. It is the greatest gift I have to give."

He was no longer the suave viscount, but a man too desperate to have his way to remember his rank. The thought brought her no comfort, no hope. Only anguish.

She pressed her lips together to keep from sobbing and closed her eyes. Her heart pounded in her ears. "You think that little of me, of us, that you would make me your mistress?"

He squeezed her hands gently. "Look at me," he coaxed with his low, soothing baritone back in place.

She didn't think she had the courage, yet she forced open her eyes. The sincerity in his returning gaze gave her hope.

She held her breath.

"You deserve better than marriage, my love. I would never relegate you to the role of wife. It's nothing more than a gilded cage."

She lowered her eyes and said nothing, knowing no response was necessary. Very carefully, very slowly, she pulled her hands from his and straightened. He stood, as well.

"As an opera singer, I am not good enough to become your wife." She tilted her head to stare at him. "Is that what you are saying, William?"

"I love you too much to imprison you." He rose to his full height and continued. "As my mistress, you would have certain freedoms my wife could never have. I would give you a notice of carte blanche. You will never again incur a debt and will live a life of complete luxury."

The haughty tone of his words conflicted with the desperation she saw in his gaze. He looked so young, staring at her with those startling blue eyes. So sincere. As though he'd just offered her the most precious gift in the world.

"Yet, you don't love me enough to marry me."

He clasped his hands behind his back and drew in a long breath. "I already have a wife."

Bella gasped and her hand clutched at her throat. Her fingers brushed the locket which now weighed heavy around her neck. Chills swept across her skin, followed by scorching heat. Unable to speak, she stumbled backward until her spine hit the door leading to freedom. She dropped her gaze to her toes. From the hallway, a beam of light shone like a beacon under the door. She wanted to run from the ramifications she could not yet face, but that would make her a coward. Thus, she found the courage to demand further explanation. "You've pursued me all these months, while already married?"

"What I am offering is far more than marriage." He stood tall, head erect. His stance was full of aristocratic pride but his gaze held a silent plea. "Think of it, Bella, you will be the celebrated mistress of a viscount in his own right."

How could he think he offered her something of value, when it meant the desecration of his wedding vows? These long months of pursuit she'd held him at arm's length, had remained pure, all the while assuming he respected her as very few men respected women in her profession.

She'd been woefully mistaken. He hadn't been court-ing a wife. He'd been seducing a mistress.

She had just enough pride left to be furious at him. "I would like you to leave now."

Rage and anguish, guilt and love tangled in his gaze. "Bella, no, don't make a hasty decision. I love you."

His eyes begged her to believe him, and to her shame, she wanted to do just that. Hadn't she felt his admira-tion, respect and love grow deeper these past weeks? Was this how Bathsheba had felt when King David had pursued her? Was David's love so real and desperate, his arguments so convincing that Bathsheba willingly walked into sin with him?

Bella had never felt pity for the woman who com-mitted such a brazen act of adultery. Until now. Heaven help her, Bella still loved William.

But the emotion shamed her.

Perhaps if she found the strength to walk away she could redeem them both. "I cannot accept your offer, William."

"I will not lose you, Bella. You are my greatest de-sire, I will die without you. I know I can make you happy. You will never want for anything."

Desire? Want? Was that how he defined love? She kept her head lowered to hide the spark of anger. At him. At herself for feeling such sorrow over her loss.

Marriage was sacred. *Therefore, what God has joined together, let no man put asunder.*

"I will not turn into an adulterer this night."

But she knew, in her heart, the deed was already

done. Hadn't Jesus said that the thought alone made her accountable for the sin?

Apparently unaware of her turmoil, William turned his back to her, idly fiddled with the wax on a candle.

"I have pursued you these two months, have I not, with the benefit of nothing more than your smiles?" He sent her a shrewd glance over his shoulder, shifted to face her. "I honored your purity when I could have had any number of mistresses by now. I want you, Bella. The way a man wants a woman."

With each word he spoke, her disgrace grew. The room was suddenly hot, so hot she feared she would faint.

Dry eyes were her only defense. "I cannot become your mistress. I will not."

A range of emotions crossed his face again, more subtle and harder to read. The eyes that locked with hers were sharp and measuring. She knew he was calculating how best to win her. A wager he'd already lost. Bella would not harm an innocent woman.

At that thought, her mind was suddenly clearer. So clear it hurt. The churning in her stomach was humiliation, she knew. But she would survive.

Unfortunately, shame was a bitter taste on her tongue, one she feared would never go away. It helped to remind herself that she was not the victim here. Lord Crawley's wife bore that burden alone.

"Bella," he pleaded.

Their stares locked, held. He was so handsome. And she loved him so much. Even now. Still. Self-directed anger and misery bubbled up, but Bella forced it back with a hard swallow. She had to come up with a plan to get him to leave before she agreed to do something she already knew she'd regret. It was her only hope of salvation. "I need time."

A flicker of hope pulled his lips into a soft smile. "I understand." He drew her hand to his lips. "But make your decision quickly. I have been patient long enough."

It was a caddish remark, but Bella saw genuine emotion in the flash of anxiety that wavered in his eyes. In that moment, Bella realized he loved her. Truly loved her.

Yet, he would never understand her. His upbringing had taught him duty and possession and broken vows. Hers had taught her the sacredness of marriage and loyalty and obedience to Christ, her Lord and Savior.

With that last thought, her humiliation burned deeper.

She knew what she had to do now.

It was only years of training that enabled her to look him in the eyes without breaking into tears, knowing this was the end. "Allow me one day to consider."

He dropped her hand. A smile hinting at his confidence slithered across his lips. "I will return before noon tomorrow."

She nodded. "Tomorrow, then."

A knot twisted in her stomach as she watched him walk out the door. There would be no additional meeting. Her only chance was escape. And she knew just the place to run, a place where William would never dare to follow.

A small victory, to be sure, but hardly an honorable one.

She could only hope with distance and time, absolution would come.

Chapter One

One month later, Denver, Colorado

He couldn't let her leave. Not without a fight. The
spasm of panic shocked him, even as it pounded angry
and insistent through his blood. For a moment—just
one—Dr. Shane Bartlett had to fight the horrible urge
to give in and beg, but he knew any display of emotion
would be his doom.

For the sake of his patients, he had to ignore the
choking sense of dread rising inside him and continue.

Jaw tight, Shane dragged a hand through his hair. If
he was to win her over, persuasion had to be doled out
in degrees of charm and skill.

Putting aside his frustration, Shane forced his heartbeat to slow to the same rhythmic cadence as the tick-
tick-tick coming from the clock on the mantel behind
him.

"Please, Miss Marley," he said, curving a pleasant
smile along the edges of his mouth. "I only ask that you
hold off making a final decision until you hear me out."

Her gaze remained direct and unwavering. But instead of responding right away, she clamped her lips shut and scrunched her forehead into a web of hard, vertical lines.

Shane felt his chest heave. Trying to gauge how best to present his argument, he dropped a glance over the woman in one quick swoop. Dressed in a drab gray dress and equally uninspired shoes, her bland brown hair looked as if it might have corroded onto her head. Her starched collar matched her rigid spine. In fact, she sat so straight and so far back in her chair, Shane was amazed the pattern from the upholstery hadn't tattooed itself to her dress.

When he raised his gaze to meet hers, the cold eyes and pursed lips reminded him of the women he'd encountered throughout his childhood on the streets of New York City.

His instinct was to dismiss her at once. But he owed it to everyone involved to put his own feelings aside and conduct this interview with polite professionalism.

Taking another moment to control his emotions, Shane lowered his chin and scanned the references he held in his hand. He couldn't deny Miss Marley had the nursing experience he needed in an assistant. Her background was without blemish, her training impeccable. But did she have the temperament required for the unique position he offered?

There was one way to find out.

"The Charity House orphans are—"

"Orphans?" Her eyes went narrow and frosty, while her lips curled with pitch-perfect disgust. "You use that term loosely, Dr. Bartlett."

A muscle shifted in his jaw and Shane felt his smile slip.

Let the children come to me, and do not hinder them, for the Kingdom of God belongs to such as these...

At the reminder of Jesus's words, Shane had to fight back a wave of resentment at the woman's sanctimonious attitude.

"Perhaps they are not orphans in the literal sense," he acknowledged with a grim twist of his lips. "However, they are children who—"

She snorted. She actually *snorted* at him. The sound was harsh enough to stop him in midsentence.

"These children." He paused to emphasize his point, but then a dull drumming pounded in his ears and the pattern on the rug at his feet bled into a kaleidoscope of chaotic colors. Shane shook his head and began again. "These *children*...deserve decent medical care like everyone else."

She pierced him with a sharp look and spoke as though she hadn't heard his words. "This is a house for harlots' mistakes." She lifted her nose and looked pointedly around her. "Is it not, Dr. Bartlett?"

Before responding, Shane followed her gaze as it moved beyond the Persian rugs, past the expensive furniture, and straight to the crystal vases filled with fresh-cut flowers. The attention to detail was impossible to miss. Charity House was like no other orphanage in the territory, incomparable in its elegance and style.

And yet, Shane wondered if he'd made a mistake in choosing the mansion's front parlor as the place to conduct his interviews today.

He'd hoped that by showing the candidates the interior of the orphanage they would realize Charity House and its occupants had class and substance. Apparently, instead of unleashing this nursing candidate's compassion, he'd opened her judgment.

Whispered reminders of his own childhood crept forward in his mind. Shane clenched his jaw, refusing to allow this woman to see his growing anger until he had the poisonous emotion under control.

He forced his shoulders to relax.

"Whatever you might think of these children, remember they did not choose their parents," he said, surprised to hear his calm tone when so many ugly emotions churned just under the surface. "As I said before, they deserve equal and fair medical treatment."

He pierced her with a hard look, daring her to argue.

She blinked. Blinked again. Swallowed. Then slowly nodded. "I will concede your point, doctor. However, the children's situation notwithstanding, I am entitled to know about your other patients. What of the mothers still alive, the ones working in the brothels on Market Street?"

Shane held her stare. "I treat them, as well. And anyone else in need. I turn none away."

A sound of outrage slipped from her lips. "Innocent children are one thing, but their mothers are quite another. You did not say in your advertisement that you care for…for…sinners."

Her words were like a solid punch to his gut. How often had he heard similar accusations thrown at his own mother, all because she had chosen to be a wealthy man's mistress?

Memories lurking below the surface bubbled forth, taunting him. Shane's breath turned cold in his lungs under the assault.

Yes, his mother had been a sinner, but she had paid

dearly for her mistakes. She'd died in shame, and there had been nothing Shane could do to stop the tragedy.

He'd been too young, too inexperienced, too—

Another unladylike sniff yanked him back to the present.

"You have nothing else to say to me, doctor?" she asked. "What is your defense for misleading me into thinking this was an ordinary nursing position?" The chill of her tone sat heavy in the room between them.

Shane fought to keep his resentment and anger from taking control of his reason. What had he been thinking, to allow this interview to continue so long?

He could never subject the Charity House children, their mothers, or any of his patients for that matter, to this woman and her...judgment.

He owed it to the memory of his own mother to find a compassionate nurse to assist him in his practice. Was guilt driving him to care for the disenfranchised? Guilt over failing the one woman who had sacrificed her life for him. Or was it true conviction that pushed him to care for the unwanted?

He wasn't sure anymore. Nor was he convinced his motives mattered. His patients, and their care, had to come first.

With his mind made up, Shane rose from his chair and waited until the woman did the same. "Thank you for your time, Miss Marley. I am no longer in need of your services."

He did not offer her his hand.

"You are dismissing *me?*" The woman had the nerve to look mutinous, as though she was being unfairly sent away. "But you need my assistance. You said so yourself at the beginning of this interview."

With each breath he took, his patience wore thinner. "I think it is best we part ways at this juncture."

Gasping, she threw her shoulders back and lifted her chin high in the air. "I'm your last candidate," she said. "You have no one else."

"I am confident God will provide."

"You will regret this," she warned.

Shane met her gaze with an unrelenting glare of his own. "I will not."

He'd never spoken truer words. For although he knew things would get worse before they got better, he also knew he just needed a little more faith, a little more patience. All would work for the best.

With a loud huff, Miss Eugenia Marley skimmed her ice-edged gaze across him, turned on her heel and marched out of the room. Each angry step she took sounded like a hammer hitting unforgiving iron.

Shane stood stock-still, staring straight ahead. He barely flinched when she slammed the door behind her with a loud bang.

For several moments he remained unmoving, looking out the window facing the backyard of Charity House. The wind beat at the glass with an angry fist, sending an unrelenting howl past a crack between the pane and wood casing.

A perfect expression of his own frustration.

There was no one left to interview. Shane could only hope that—

No. He would not waste precious energy on hope. Nor would he worry.

He would trust.

Rolling his shoulders, Shane shoved a hand through his hair and shut his eyes. He let the tension drain from him for a single moment. And then another. And another still. Waiting until his mind cleared enough to focus on prayer.

At last, he whispered, "Lord, I cannot do this alone. Where man fails, I know You excel. I pray You bless my patients with a compassionate woman to assist us."

Opening his eyes, Shane looked around the parlor room of Charity House. At first glance nobody would think this large and fancy mansion housed over forty children with nowhere else to go. Marc and Laney Dupree had created a home filled with compassion and caring, a refuge for the abandoned and unwanted boys and girls no other orphanage would touch.

The Duprees' generosity of spirit humbled Shane and inspired him to expand his own medical practice in the same vein, a practice that was becoming unmanageable for one man.

Trust. He had to trust that God had a plan. The Lord would bring relief in His perfect time.

A deep clearing of a throat jerked Shane out of his reverie. Pivoting at the sound, he locked his gaze with Marc Dupree's concerned expression. Dressed in a brocade vest and matching tie, with his dark hair immaculately combed and face clean shaven, Marc looked more like a banker than the fierce proprietor of an orphanage. But just like Charity House, Shane knew the other man had hidden depths, and was an example of complete integrity.

"Any success?" Marc asked.

Shane shook his head at his friend, and jammed his hands in his pockets. "It appears I've wasted another day with fruitless interviews." He lifted a shoulder in a helpless gesture. "Perhaps—"

A high-pitched scream cut off his words, followed by a round of incomprehensible shouting. Shane's ears pricked when he heard one voice rise above the others. "Somebody find Dr. Shane. Hurry."

Bella pivoted in several directions, searching desperately for the source of the panicked cries tumbling over one another.

Forcing herself to remain calm, she took a deep breath, stood immobile and listened intently. The shouts were coming from behind her.

She spun around and gasped at the sight before her. Chaos had erupted in the massive yard that backed up to her brother's church.

Heart in her throat, Bella lurched forward. Stopped. Frowned.

Hadn't she learned from her recent experience with William that it was better to assess a situation before rushing headlong into the unknown?

Dreadful memories of her last meeting with the viscount slammed through her mind, washing away her concentration. She shook her head violently and gritted her teeth so hard her jaw hurt. Bella knew she should find the source of the disaster unraveling in front of her. Instead, exhaustion, shame and anger at William's betrayal threatened to steal her focus.

No. No, no, no. William would not invade her thoughts today.

Breathe, Bella, breathe.

One heartbeat passed.

And another.

By the third, Bella had taken in the stylish mansion at the opposite end of the yard. The fairy-tale backdrop was at odds with the trouble riding along the stiff mountain breeze. She counted over fifteen children of various sizes colliding into one another. Like waves crashing onto a beach, they plunged toward a common point—a child lying flat on his back.

Bella curled her fingers into fists. Where was the adult in charge?

Tossing her reticule to the ground, she sprinted toward the clump of frightened children. She'd barely taken two steps when a young girl of about ten years of age skidded to a stop at her side. The child had halted so abruptly that her shiny black pigtails swung forward and then landed with a soft thump on her narrow shoulders. Eyes wild and unfocused, her little cupid mouth worked quickly, but no sound came out.

Bella stooped to the girl's height and touched her shoulder. "Deep breaths, sweetie. Take one at a time."

Nodding, the girl gulped in large chunks of air.

"That's it," Bella said. "Now tell me what's happened."

"It's…it's…" She broke off and looked frantically around her.

Bella rolled her shoulders and prayed for patience. "It's…" she prompted in what she hoped was a soothing tone.

"My. Brother. *Ethan*." She pointed to the cluster of children knotted around a small boy lying on the ground. "He hurt his leg. You gotta get Dr. Shane for me."

"Where?"

The girl cocked her head toward the mansion behind her. "Inside."

Bella placed her palm on the child's cheek. "Don't

worry. I'll get him." Rising, she gave the girl's shoulder an encouraging squeeze. "You see to your brother. And whatever you do, make sure he doesn't move until the doctor gets there."

As though she hadn't heard a word Bella said, the child stabbed her gaze back to her brother, over to the large house behind her, then back to her brother again.

"Did you hear me?" Bella asked.

The girl nodded. Gulped. Gulped again. Then finally—*finally*—she lifted her chin and lurched toward the injured boy.

Bella whirled in the direction of the house. At the same moment, two large men exited the backdoor in a run.

Bella faltered in her steps, froze. In her stunned state, she only had time for impressions. Both men were tall. Dark-haired. Broad-shouldered. One was dressed in expensive clothing that would make her flamboyant brother Tyler fall to his knees and weep with envy. The other wore a nondescript white shirt and black pants and carried a small black bag.

Dr. Shane.

The calm in his manner gave Bella such a sense of relief she pressed a hand to her throat and sighed. This man would make everything better.

The young girl changed directions and dashed to the bottom of the porch steps. "Ethan's hurt, Dr. Shane." She grasped his hand and tugged. "You gotta come quick."

The sharp planes of his face tensed and his mouth pressed into a tight line. Yet, he carefully patted the girl on her back. "Don't worry, Molly. I'll take care of him." His smooth baritone was pitched to the perfect level to instill calm. "You concentrate on finding your mother and father and then bring them here."

"Right." Teetering from one foot to the other, arms flailing, the child found her center at last and set off at a terrifying pace.

Focused on his task once more, the doctor lengthened his strides. With each step, his gaze shifted over the scene, taking note of every detail. He measured, assessed. Picked up the pace.

The other man followed hard on his heels.

Negotiating the final few feet, the doctor gently set two of the smaller children to one side and then dropped to his knees. "Marc," he threw over his shoulder. "I need room."

The fancy-dressed man went to work at once. With an authoritative tone and in-charge manner, he organized the children into two work groups. In perfect rhythm they shifted away from the injured boy, picked up toys, balls, shoes and began setting them into neat piles.

They were so purposeful in their task, so obedient, even as the nightmare churned around them, that Bella found herself gaping.

What sort of children were these? And then she remembered her brother's many letters telling her about the unique orphanage that shared the church's backyard. Charity Home. No. Charity House. Yes, that was the name.

Before she could take another look at the mansion-turned-orphanage, the doctor darted his gaze along the perimeter of the yard as though he was searching for something. Or someone. A helper, perhaps? Before

Bella could offer her assistance, his eyes locked on to hers.

Snared in his powerful stare, her lungs constricted. Although she was too far away to make out the individual features of his face, the impact of all that intensity thrown her way had her stepping sharply back.

"You, there," he said, his features twisting into a frown of concentration. "I need your assistance."

Jolted into action, Bella yanked off one glove and then another. "Yes, of course." By the time she'd crossed the yard, she'd tossed her hat to the ground, as well.

The children continued to chatter softly as they made room for the doctor to work. Their voices rose slightly as they began trooping one by one inside the large house but it was all background noise now. Never taking her attention off the boy, Bella knelt beside him and looked into his small, pale face.

Glassy eyes stared back at her. She swallowed down a gasp of surprise. He was so young, no more than four or five, with black curly hair and big brown eyes.

Lord, please ease this child's pain. Use me as your instrument to erase his suffering.

Unsure what to do next, she waited for specific instructions from the doctor. When none came, a shiver of foreboding iced across her skin.

Cautiously, she lifted her gaze. And found herself staring into ocean-blue eyes the exact color as William's.

Unwelcome images swirled through her mind like leaves on a deserted street. Incapable of grasping any one thought before it was replaced by another, her mind drained into a black void of nothingness.

Air clogged in her lungs.

Focus, Bella. Focus, focus, focus.

The doctor must have sensed her internal struggle because his eyes narrowed to inscrutable slits.

Bella quickly lowered her gaze back to the hurt boy. Little Ethan's eyes were ringed with pain. Tears wavered on the edges of his lashes, but he gritted his teeth and released a shaky sigh.

"Oh, you brave little boy." Bella touched his cheek softly then brushed the sweaty hair off his forehead with her fingertips. "You're going to be fine. Just fine."

As though her words gave him permission to give into the pain, the tears spilled from his eyes. "It…it hurts," he gasped, his young voice shaking with anguish. "Real bad."

Bella stroked her hand along his hairline. "I know it does, baby. But the doctor is going to make it better."

Shutting out all thoughts but this small, helpless child, she boldly returned her gaze to the doctor's face. "Isn't that right, Dr. Shane?"

The sun chose that moment to break through a slit in the fast-moving clouds. Big. Hot. Illuminating.

The doctor stared at her for a long, tense moment. This time, Bella couldn't look away. The bold, aristocratic angles of his cheekbones, the finely shaped nose and strong jaw covered with day-old stubble created a handsome portrait any leading man would covet.

Bella blinked.

Slowly—very, *very* slowly—Dr. Shane dropped his gaze to the child. "I'll do my best, Ethan."

The boy let out another shaky sigh. "I know."

Dr. Shane cut his gaze back to Bella. "Let's get to work, shall we?"

His words were more statement than question, but

there was an edge of doubt in his eyes. He was asking her to assist him, daring her perhaps, yet convinced she'd somehow let him down.

Would she? She had no training, no experience. Yet an injured boy needed her.

Lord, give me the courage to do what is needed.

Fortunately, the very moment she ended her prayer, Bella's worries fell away. All that remained was a driving sense of purpose.

She swallowed back the last shreds of uncertainty and boldly held Dr. Shane's gaze. "Tell me what to do."

Chapter Two

Locked inside that startling amber gaze, Shane's thoughts morphed into one undeniable realization. She hadn't hesitated. The woman with the dark, golden curls, flawless features and refined British accent had defied his expectations. Instead of fleeing the unpleasantness of a child's injury, she'd taken her place without question.

Could she be the answer to his prayer?

Wishful thinking at best. It was far too soon to determine if she had the character and necessary qualifications he required in an assistant.

Yet, even now, as she boldly held his gaze, conviction blazed in her eyes. *What eyes. What depth of emotion.*

His heart kicked hard against his ribs, warning him to beware of this woman, this *stranger.*

Lifting a perfectly arched eyebrow at him, she blew out a slow, impatient breath. "I'm ready whenever you are."

It took another few seconds for Shane to empty the overload of thoughts and impressions twining together in his mind. "Tell me where it hurts, Ethan."

The little boy moaned in response, pain twisting his young face. "My…my leg."

"Let's have a look."

Careful to keep his features bland, Shane flicked his gaze past the boy's torso. Shane's first reflex was to pull in a sharp breath. Instead, he detached. Separated emotion from logic. And focused.

The right pant leg had been torn at a jagged, vertical angle. Blood soaked the material, turning the light brown cloth nearly black.

"Don't move, Ethan." He flipped open his medical bag. "I have to cut away the material surrounding the wound."

"Oh…okay."

Shane's chest pinched tight at the sound of the boy's anguish. *Oh, Lord,* he prayed. *Fill me with Your Spirit. Guide my hands and use me as Your instrument for healing.*

With slow, careful movements, Shane set a firm grip on Ethan's thigh, and then looked up at the woman again. "I need you to keep him calm for me."

Eyes wide, she sank her teeth into her lower lip. "How?"

"Hold his hand. Speak to him." Shane lifted a shoulder. "Whatever it takes."

Nodding, she braided her fingers with the boy's. "Ethan. I want you to concentrate on me." She waited for him to turn his head toward her. "That's it. The doctor is going to have a look at your injury. Nothing more."

Ethan sucked in big gulps of air. "I'm scared."

"I know," she said, her voice barely above a whisper. "Me, too."

Shane wanted to tell them both that everything would be fine, but he couldn't make such a promise. Not yet.

"You talk funny," Ethan announced. "I like it."

Shane did, too. The proper British accent suited her.

"Why, thank you, Ethan. I like the way you talk, too." Leaning toward the boy's ear, she asked, "Do you have a favorite song?"

His dark brows pulled together in a frown of concentration. "I…lots… I don't know…maybe… 'Amazing Grace'?"

She smiled her approval. "I like that one, too."

In a low, hushed tone, she began the hymn. Her soft, lilting voice was no piercing soprano as Shane half expected. Rather, she sang with a rich, smoky timbre. Pure velvety warmth. The perfect alto to calm the beast in any man. Or boy.

As Ethan's leg relaxed under Shane's touch, Shane found the restlessness inside him also stopping, pausing. Listening to the beautiful song.

Torn between shock and admiration, Shane shook his head and returned to his work. With quick snips, he cut away the tattered material and pulled it aside to reveal a long, nasty gash running down the side of Ethan's leg. Thankfully, there was no swelling or misshapen bump to indicate a break.

As if on cue, the woman turned her gaze toward the injury, as well. To her credit, her singing never faltered. Nor did she flinch.

Astounding.

Shane had seen trained doctors fail to maintain their reactions so well. Stunned once again by her remarkable behavior, Shane sucked in a lungful of cold mountain air. Who was this woman? He was certain he'd never met her. Then why did he experience recognition when he looked into her eyes?

The sound of approaching footsteps cut off his thoughts.

Stabbing a glance over his shoulder, Shane barked out a set of orders for Marc. "I'm going to move Ethan to the kitchen. I'll need water, clean rags and Laney's sewing kit."

Having experienced his share of injuries, Marc pivoted on his heel and flicked his wrist in the air. "I'm already on it."

"Ethan, before we move you I want to make sure you haven't broken anything."

The boy squeezed his eyes shut, sighed. "I'm ready."

"This might hurt," Shane warned.

At his words, the woman stopped singing. Shane silently willed her to resume her impromptu musical. Instead, she gently stroked the child's hair along his forehead. "I don't think I've ever met a braver boy than you, and I've been all over the world."

Ethan cracked open one eye and then the other. "You have? Wh…where?"

Her expression never changed nor did her rhythmic stroking of his hair. "Lots of places."

"Tell me. Tell me," he demanded with little-boy earnestness.

"Let's see." She tapped her chin with a fingertip. "Paris. London. Ro—"

"London?" Ethan tried to sit up, but she gently pushed him back down.

"I've always wanted to go to London," he declared. "To see the Tower and all."

Both grinning, they began a lengthy discussion of the infamous prison.

While Ethan babbled, Shane took the opportunity to check for broken bones. "Tell me if it hurts when I press on your leg."

"What's your name?" Ethan asked once he wound down his list of reasons for seeing the Tower of London.

Eager to hear her response himself, Shane turned an ear in their direction and ran his hand across Ethan's leg.

"I'm Bella," she declared.

Italian for beautiful. The name suited her. Shane moved his fingers along the boy's kneecap.

"Bella," Ethan said, his face scrunched in confusion. "I've never heard that name before."

She released a tinkling laugh, the sound as clear and musical as her singing. "It's short for Isabella."

Holding back a grin at the look of adoration in the young boy's eyes, Shane moved to the calf.

"Actually," she said. "My full name is Isabella Constance O'Toole, but you can call me Bella."

Ethan jerked.

Shane froze. "Did I hurt you?"

Ethan ignored the question. "*O'Toole?* That's Pastor Beau's last name."

Laughing again, she gave the boy a dazzling smile. "I know. He's my brother."

Shane took a quick pull of air into his lungs. Of course she was the reverend's sister. The similarity was hard to miss, now that he looked. They had the same golden hair, same tawny eyes, same memorable, aristocratic features. Perhaps that explained the odd sense of recognition every time their eyes met.

Shane finished his exam by searching for any obstruction or object lodged in the wound. Satisfied at last, he hopped to his feet and lifted the boy in his arms. "Let's get you inside."

"Don't leave me, Miss Bella." Struggling, Ethan reached out his hands to her.

"Not to worry, Ethan." She rose and closed her fingers over his. "I'm not going anywhere. You're my priority right now."

A burning throb knotted in Shane's stomach. There was a time in his life when he would have given anything to hear those same words uttered directly at him.

Closing his mind to the unwelcome thought, Shane repositioned the boy in his arms. Without being told, Miss O'Toole grabbed his medical bag and stuffed the scissors inside.

The three of them entered the kitchen, Miss O'Toole leading the way. Shane shouldered the door shut behind them and then took a cursory look around.

The room was empty. Unusual for this time of day. But before Shane could speculate further, Marc entered with an armful of clean linens and set them on the center counter.

"Where's your wife?" Shane asked.

Marc shot him an apologetic glance. "Laney and Mrs. Smythe went shopping for supplies. And Megan is upstairs organizing the children for naptime." He began rolling up his sleeves. "That leaves me as your only helper at the moment."

"And Miss Bella, too," Ethan added.

"And Miss Bella, too," Shane said without looking at the woman. He found looking at her distracted him.

Setting Ethan on the counter, he picked up a cloth off the pile Marc had set down.

Using the clean water out of the bucket, Shane washed the blood from Ethan's wound, revealing good news and bad. The good news—the cut was indeed free of any debris. But the bad news was as disheartening as Shane had feared. The large gash would need stitching to close the wound.

A crash from upstairs had all three adults jumping. Marc shook his head in resignation. "I better check on that." He turned to Miss O'Toole, who was standing slightly back but within eyeshot of Ethan. "Looks like you'll have to assist Shane without me."

She stepped forward, her gaze filled with fierce determination. "Of course. I'll do whatever is needed."

Marc smiled at her, a look of relief filling his features. "Thank you." He leaned over Ethan, touched the boy's arm. "Hang tough, little man. No doubt your parents will be here soon. In the meantime, Dr. Shane and Miss Bella are going to fix you up."

Ethan's lower lip quivered. "Okay."

After sharing a quick look with Shane, Marc left the room.

Miss O'Toole smiled after him. "Nice man," she muttered.

Shane swallowed back a surprising kick of jealousy and rummaged through Laney's sewing kit for a needle and thread. "Can you sew, Miss O'Toole?"

His voice must have come out harder than he'd planned because she took a sharp step back, and eyed him with a healthy dose of wariness. "I've been sewing my own costumes since I was twelve."

"Good. I'll need you to stitch the wound for me." He spoke over her shocked gasp. "You'll make individual stitches, knotting and cutting them off one at a time before beginning the next."

She slid a quick glance at the angry wound. Shivered. "Can't you do it?"

If only he could. But he knew the procedure would be painful, painful enough that Ethan would need holding down. "I'll have to…keep him still."

Her eyes widened in instant understanding. *"Oh."*

Shane closed his fingers over hers. The unexpected warmth that spread from her palm to his had him quickly releasing her. "I'll talk you through it," he promised.

She nodded, flexed the hand he'd just held. Nodded again. "All right, then."

Ethan whimpered at her declaration. "Will it hurt, Miss Bella?"

Sighing, she trailed the back of her fingertips down his cheek. "A little, but I'll work as quickly as possible."

"Fine." Ethan squeezed his eyes shut once again and took a deep, shaky breath. "Do what you must." The adult words were completely at odds with the childish hiccupping that followed.

Shane passed the needle and thread to Miss O'Toole. With slow, deliberate movements, he placed one hand on Ethan's shoulder and the other on the thigh of the boy's injured leg. For now, he kept his touch light, and would only increase the pressure when needed.

After threading the needle, she leaned forward and placed a kiss on the boy's head. The lingering scent of jasmine and sandalwood brought a vague memory dancing on the edges of Shane's mind.

He shut it down.

Miss O'Toole met his gaze with honest trepidation in her eyes. No coyness. No pretend confidence.

Shane gave her a heartening smile. "Let's begin."

Bella's hands might be shaking, her heart might be pounding faster than a series of half notes, but she was getting the job done as quickly as she could.

"Only one more to go," the doctor encouraged. "You're doing fine."

She appreciated his support, more than he probably knew. This task went far beyond her capabilities. But prayer and this man's precise instructions had gotten her through the worst.

Gritting her teeth, she tied off the final knot. "There." She released her breath and placed her hand on Ethan's shoulder. "All done."

"That…" The little boy's bottom lip quivered. "Wasn't so bad." The tear tracks down his face told a different story.

The realization that she'd hurt a child, in spite of the necessity, weighed heavy in her throat, making her breath come in ragged pants.

Seeking reinforcement, or at least a nod of approval, she glanced at the doctor. But he wasn't paying attention to her. Head lowered, he blotted the remaining blood off Ethan's skin and then wrapped a series of plasters and strips of linen over the wound. It wasn't until he finished the task that he looked at her directly.

She sucked in a quick breath of air. The eyes that stared back at her were a deep, troubled blue.

What sort of inner strength did it take to administer necessary healing, even when it caused such pain? Certainly, it had to be a difficult life. Lonely, even. She felt a sudden urge to offer some show of compassion, give a kind word at least. But the doctor turned away and began cleaning up the mess they'd made.

Needing to do something, *anything* but stare at the man's rigid back, she whisked Ethan into her arms. Holding him tightly against her, she paced to the back corner of the kitchen and began humming the aria from *Tristan and Isolde*.

Ethan sniffled, then wiped his nose on her shoulder. "That really hurt, Miss Bella."

"I know, darling," she said. "But you were very, very brave."

He clung harder to her neck. "I don't ever want you to do that again."

A shudder ran through her and she tightened her hold. "Me neither. I'd rather—"

The door flew open with a bang. Bella spun toward the noise.

Two adults, one male, one female, spilled into the kitchen. The young girl from the yard trailed closely behind. Hidden in the shadows, Bella cast the three a quick, assessing look.

The man was tall, broad-shouldered and ominous-looking with his dark hair, dark eyes and dark-stubbled jaw. A tin star was pinned to his chest, making him look every bit the terrifying Wild West lawman of legend. The woman was smaller, softer, her coal-black hair and blue eyes a grown-up version of the girl clutching her hand.

Clearly, this was Ethan's family. All three—mother, father, sister—wore identical expressions of concern.

Patting Ethan's back, Bella moved out of the shadows.

The woman's eyes landed on the boy first. "Oh, baby," she cried. "My poor baby."

Ethan twisted toward the voice. "Mama."

He nearly launched himself out of Bella's arms. The momentum from his struggles flung them both forward. Bella half handed, half dropped the squirming child into his mother's ready embrace.

The lawman moved just as quickly as Ethan had. Jaw tight, gaze locked with his wife's, he patted the boy on the back and whispered his own words of affection. For a tense moment, all thoughts and attention were on the sniffling little boy. Even his sister added her own soft words, patting the boy's back like her father did.

Once Ethan's sobs died down to sniffing hiccups, the father lowered his hand and leveled a hard glare on the doctor.

"What happened?"

His tone came out harsh, unrelenting, a father demanding a full accounting of his son's accident. Clearly, this man protected his own.

In clipped, short sentences, the doctor sketched out the details of the boy's injury. He ended with an explanation of Bella's role in caring for the child. "Miss O'Toole was good enough to step forward and sew the wound shut."

A pall of silence filled the room as all eyes turned toward her.

Unsure what to say, Bella simply stared back.

The little girl found her voice first. "Daddy, Daddy. She's the one I told you about, the one in the church's backyard."

He raised a questioning brow at Bella.

A dozen responses ran through her mind, but none

seemed quite right. Bella curled her fingertips into her skirt and swallowed. Facing this stern, upset father was far harder than walking on stage in front of a hostile theater audience.

She had no experience to draw from.

As though sensing her unease, Dr. Shane caught her eye and gave her a quick, approving smile. Her stomach performed a perfect roll, and she found the confidence to speak. "I was very proud of your son," she said, careful to keep her voice from quivering. "He didn't kick out once."

Both parents smiled at her then. And to her surprise, she saw no judgment in their eyes. No condemnation. Just genuine appreciation. "Thank you, Miss—" The woman shook her head. "I'm sorry, but I didn't catch your name."

"It's Bella. Bella O'Toole." At the instant recognition in their eyes, Bella opened her mouth to explain but Ethan beat her to it.

"She's Pastor Beau's sister," he said with a look of pride in his eyes, as though he didn't often know something the others didn't.

At the news, the woman flashed a dazzling smile at Bella, a smile brilliant enough to reach the back row in any theater. "That's lovely. We think very highly of your brother."

"Yes, we do," the husband agreed.

The look of admiration in all their eyes told its own story. Who would have thought her brother, the only member of her family who had denied his place on the stage, would become so popular, so well-loved without ever singing a note or reciting a fictional phrase.

Because he was Beau. A man of solid, Christian

integrity who ministered to the lost and hurting—the shamed.

People like Bella herself.

A wave of melancholy crashed through her. She suddenly wanted—*no, needed*—to see her big brother. Now.

But she couldn't leave yet. Could she?

Ethan's father stepped forward, ending her quandary. "I'm Trey Scott." He pointed to the woman standing closely behind him. "This is my wife, Katherine. You already know Ethan." He swiveled halfway around and pulled the girl closer. "And this is our daughter, Molly."

Tugging the child with him, he moved back to his wife's side.

Bella's heart ached at the picture the four made. Standing there like that, staring at her with such gratitude in their eyes, such peace and contentment in spite of Ethan's injury, they made a beautiful family.

Sadness, sorrow and a bone-deep sense of loss overwhelmed her all at once. She had dreamed of starting her own family—with William. But the viscount was living that dream with another woman.

Bella's heart broke a little more at the thought.

As though sensing her shift in mood, the little girl rushed forward and gripped Bella's hand. "Are you all right?" she asked. "You look like you're about to cry."

Bella angled her head to stare into the guileless face. "I... I'm fine."

But she lied. She wasn't fine. She hadn't been fine since she'd escaped London and William's ugly proposal.

Clicking her tongue, Katherine handed Ethan to her husband. The next thing Bella knew she was being pulled into the other woman's embrace. "Thank you," she whispered. "Thank you for taking care of my son."

Bella tried not to cling, but for one black moment she thought she might break down and cry. If she gave in to the urge, she might never stop.

At last, Katherine pushed back.

"I hope you will be staying in Denver awhile," she said.

No, Bella thought, as she took a farther step away from all that suffocating kindness. She didn't want to stay here with these nice people. She didn't deserve to stay. She wanted to run. And never look back. But where would she go? There were already too many secrets, and too many regrets that had followed her from London. Surely, they would follow her wherever she went.

"I'm here for an extended stay," she said once she had command over her voice again. Which, all things considered, was as truthful as she could be at the moment.

Katherine eyed her for a long moment, then nodded. "Good. I think you need to be here."

She spoke with such certainty, such compassion, Bella's hand flew to her throat. Her fingertips caught against the pendant William had given her, reminding her of her shame.

Why hadn't she thrown away the necklace?

As soon as the question arose, the answer came. Because the heavy pendant was a reminder of how close she'd come to committing adultery and how far she'd walked from her faith. Until her sins were washed clean, *if* they were washed clean, she would continue to wear the incriminating necklace.

As though mocking her, the wind scratched at the window with clawlike strokes. Bella wanted to rush into the raw air, wanted to feel the hard slap of sobering cold against her skin.

Her breaths started coming shorter, faster, harder.

To her horror, and in front of these kind people, Bella stood on the brink of panic.

Dr. Shane cleared his throat, saving her from making a fool of herself. With extraordinary patience, he waited until he had everyone's attention—including hers—before he began a litany of instructions needed to keep the boy's wound clean and infection free.

Bella tried to listen. Truly, she tried. But all the pain of the last month, all the nerves of the last few moments tangled into a tight knot in the pit of her stomach.

At last, the doctor finished his list of instructions and then turned his attention to her. "Miss O'Toole."

Bella bristled at the abrupt tone, ready to do battle, until she noted the hint of vulnerability in his gaze.

"Yes?"

He ran his hand through his hair. A gesture he clearly repeated often, if the messy edges were any indication. Instead of making him look foolish, the mussed hair added a hint of boyish charm to his otherwise too-handsome features.

"Miss O'Toole," he repeated. "Am I to understand you are in Denver for an indefinite period of time?"

He sounded so formal. So distant and cold. But there was a hint of desperation in his tone, as well, and thus she found the courage to answer his question with complete honesty. "You are correct in your assumption."

The sincerity in his gaze gave her renewed hope.

But then he spoke. And condemned her all over again. "I have a proposition for you. One I pray you will consider with the utmost care."

Chapter Three

At last.

Shane had found a capable woman to assist him in his practice. But instead of feeling a sense of relief, a burst of unease pounded through his veins.

Miss O'Toole's face had gone dead white. She remained frozen in place, staring at him with ill-cocealed horror.

Had she misunderstood his intentions?

Shane rubbed a finger over his temple and fought down a second wave of uncertainty.

Grabbing a quick breath of air, he began again. "What I meant to say is…thank you. You did a fine job with Ethan today."

Her hand rose to her throat. She fiddled with the golden pendant around her neck while her gaze flitted around the kitchen, landing on nothing in particular.

Was she listening to him?

"We're all very grateful," Trey added with one of his rare smiles directed solely at her.

Unfortunately, the magnanimous gesture was lost on

Miss O'Toole. She blinked rapidly now, sending the first glitter of tears wiggling along her long, spiky lashes.

Confused and terrified. Those were the words that came to mind as Shane tried to unravel her odd reaction to his request.

In truth, he sympathized.

He was battling his own sense of bewilderment, as though he, too, was on the cusp of diving into something beautiful and *terrible*.

"I haven't seen that steady of a hand in a long time," he continued. "You have a gift, Miss O'Toole."

Her shoulders stiffened at his compliment and some unknown emotion flashed in her eyes. Discomfort? Pleasure? Something else entirely? "I… I do?"

"Yes."

"I…" She lifted her chin, pulled in a composing breath. "Thank you."

Her uncertain manner was replaced by a quiet dignity.

Something inside Shane threatened to snap.

How could he want to protect the woman one moment and wish to rest in her strength the next?

Rest in her strength?

For a moment, the foundation of everything Shane thought rocked under him. He was a healer, called by God to treat the sick, a man others turned to in time of need. He did not rely on anyone.

No human, at any rate. Only the divine.

Then again, he'd never met a woman who made him want to release some of his tight control, to admit he might be weary of standing helplessly by as his patients struggled with illnesses that far too often resulted in death.

For the first time in his life, a woman—*a fancy, overdressed, far too beautiful stranger*—made Shane want to share a little of his burdens with another person.

What did that say about him? About his faith in God as his only guide and one true hope?

"Miss O'Toole, I have an offer I would like to present you, a *job* offer," he hastened to add when she sucked in her breath a second time at his words. "What I ask is highly respectable."

Glancing from Trey's amused expression to Katherine's pitiful shaking of her head, Shane shifted his stance and continued. "Would you consider working as my assistant?"

Instead of answering him, she looked at Katherine who tossed her palms in the air and shrugged. The gesture seemed to say: who can understand what men really want from us women?

They shared a smile of feminine understanding. Or maybe it was a grimace. Either way, a thousand words passed between them, words no mere man could hope to understand.

There was another long pause, during which Miss O'Toole released a sigh and turned back.

"You want me to be your assistant, nothing else?" Her eyes narrowed with suspicion.

Shane shoved a hand through his hair. "Nothing else, I assure you."

She blinked at him, opened her mouth, closed it again. And so the staring began again.

What was wrong with the woman?

Clearing his throat, Trey resettled Ethan in his arms and glanced at his wife. "I think we should leave these two to their discussion."

The marshal's suggestion was innocent enough, but the casual alertness of his posture said he'd been listening to every word spoken, and a few unspoken, as well.

Nodding, Katherine murmured something Shane didn't quite catch before she turned to Molly. "Come on, Moll." She plucked one of her daughter's pigtails. "Let's get Ethan home and in bed."

"But it's still daylight," the little boy whined as he struggled in his father's arms. "I want to stay and play with the kids."

Kicking with remarkable strength, his face was a contorted mixture of childish rebellion and youthful disappointment.

"You've had a bad time of it, baby." Katherine reached out in silent command to her husband. Trey handed the boy over with the patience of a man used to obliging his wife's wishes.

As they made the exchange, Shane marveled at the silent harmony between Trey and Katherine Scott. The couple had created a happy, tight-knit family out of impossible odds. If Shane ever doubted God's ability to heal the wounded and bring about good from tragedy, all he had to do was look at this unified family for proof.

"Please, let me stay." Ethan's voice squeaked along the edge of a loud sob.

"You need to rest for a while, little man," Trey said in a placating tone with a firm hand on the boy's back. "Then we'll see how you feel."

He shot his wife a challenging look over Ethan's head. "Isn't that right, darling?"

"We'll discuss it, *after* his nap," she said, her voice no less formidable for its soft tone.

A stalemate began.

But as was often the case, the ruthless lawman who could intimidate murdering outlaws without flinching capitulated under his wife's unyielding stare. "Whatever you say, dear."

Katherine gave her husband a pleased smile. "I knew you'd see things my way."

"What can I say?" Trey returned the look with another long, intent stare. "I'm an accommodating man."

She giggled. She actually giggled. This, from the same woman who ruled her schoolroom with iron-clad structure.

Shane tried not to gape.

Molly rolled her gaze to the ceiling and groaned.

Silently agreeing with the girl, Shane handed Trey a roll of linen bandages. "Use these to wrap the leg once you've cleaned his wound in the morning. I'll be by to check on him in the afternoon."

"Right."

Before the Scott family filed out, Miss O'Toole summoned a brisk air of confidence and said, "Let me know if there's anything I can do, as well."

"We will," Trey answered for them all. "And thank you again, Miss O'Toole. For everything." One side of his mouth kicked up and he gave her a gallant bow, one more suited for a ballroom back east than a well-worn kitchen.

"It was my pleasure." She dropped her gaze to Molly, touched the girl's shoulder. "You were very brave today."

The little girl flushed. "He's my brother."

Miss O'Toole squeezed the child's shoulder in understanding then dropped her hand. Sighing, she walked over to Ethan and rubbed his back. There was such tenderness in her hands, such sweetness in her smile Shane found himself as riveted as Ethan appeared to be.

"Will you come see me, too, Miss Bella?" the boy asked. "With Dr. Shane?"

"I'll do my best."

Katherine patted Ethan's bottom. "All right, folks, enough stalling. Let's go." She touched Bella's arm and smiled. "Thank you again."

One by one the Scott family trooped out the backdoor with Ethan waving enthusiastically over his mother's head.

Once the door banged shut, Shane was far too aware of the silence as Miss O'Toole turned back to face him.

Their gazes locked with a force that nearly flattened him. In that moment, he forgot about steady hands and compassionate hearts and all the other reasons he'd decided Miss O'Toole would do nicely in the role of assistant.

He had one clear goal now: to convince this woman to work with him, by his side, for as long as possible.

What if she says no?

Desperation at the thought came so strong, so quick, Shane staggered back a step.

Cocking her head, Miss O'Toole pulled her eyebrows into a delicate frown. "I'm afraid I don't quite understand what you're asking of me."

Shane started forward, hesitated, shoved a hand through his hair. "It's quite simple. My practice is growing faster than I can keep up. I'm in need of someone to assist me in—"

"No, no." She waved her hand in a vague gesture. "I understand that part. What I don't quite fathom is why me?"

A ripple of unease slipped down his throat. Blunt honesty was the only way now. Shane stuffed his hands in his pockets and rocked back on his heels. "I started this practice to provide medical care for the women and children no other doctor would touch. It's—"

"Yes, yes, my brother told me about Charity House and the unique children living here. I also know some aren't actually orphans." Her chin lifted. "I have a good idea of the sort of patients you see."

He ignored how the sunlight streaming in from the window shone off her hair, how it twinkled in her gingerbread eyes. But he could not ignore the relief he experienced at her words. She knew all about Charity House, every squalid detail. And yet, she wasn't running in the opposite direction.

This could only be an answer to prayer.

Thank You, Lord.

"Life is difficult for the defenseless ones in this world," he said. "Regardless of life choices, everyone deserves medical care."

"All the more reason to make sure you hire the right person."

"I believe I am."

She wrapped her arms around her waist. "I still don't understand why you want me?"

Her voice was steady, but there was something in her gaze that told him his answer was far more important than merely convincing her she was the right person for the temporary position.

She needed reassurance.

He wouldn't have thought that of her. But whatever secret she harbored—and yes, she held a dark secret in her heart—it had destroyed a portion of her confidence.

A small, still voice told him to go forth with faith. "Perhaps I don't know everything about you, but remember I witnessed you in action today. You never hesitated, you followed directions precisely. You're Pastor O'Toole's sister. And you—"

Before he could expand further, the backdoor swung open and in strode the very man he'd just mentioned.

Unfortunately, Reverend Beauregard O'Toole's face was twisted in alarm. "Where is she?" he demanded, drilling his gaze into Shane. "I heard my sister is here but I don't believe it."

With each word the preacher spoke Miss O'Toole took a step back, nearly blending into the shadows of the outer edges of the kitchen. Her tawny eyes became like soiled glass, completely concealing her emotions.

With growing curiosity, Shane watched her odd retreat.

Following Shane's gaze with his own, Beau swung around and caught sight of his sister. "Bella?" He moved in her direction. "Bella! It is you."

"Beau." She took a tentative step forward, two back, another forward, then rushed across the kitchen floor and flung herself into his arms. "Oh, Beau. I've missed you."

Wrapping her tightly in his arms, he patted her back much like a parent would a child. "Ah, Bella," he said. "It's been too long."

She sniffed, buried her face against his shoulder.

After countless seconds, Beau pulled back and very slowly, *very* carefully set her away from him. He studied her face a moment longer, then frowned. "What's happened?"

She gripped the pendant around her neck and tapped

her collarbone lightly with her fist. "Nothing's happened," she said, her voice nonchalant. *Too nonchalant.*

Beau folded his arms over his chest. "Try again, little sister."

She dropped her gaze to her toes and dug the tip of her boot into a slat in the wood floor. "Can't a girl visit her brother and meet his new wife without there being a reason?"

Shane sighed. Whatever had brought Bella O'Toole to Denver she wasn't going to share the details with her brother anytime soon. Pity, that. Shane knew from personal experience the unholy tragedies that grew out of hidden secrets.

"No, Bella." Beau gently clutched his sister by the shoulders. "A woman does not travel halfway around the world to see her brother without a reason. Not when she's on tour in Europe." He placed a finger under her chin and applied pressure. "Not when she's been given the role of a lifetime."

Chin up, she glanced desperately at Shane out of the corners of her eyes. He lifted a shoulder in a helpless gesture. In return, her face took on a look of feminine determination, the personification of "watch this."

Shane's stomach did a fast roll.

Unconsciously regal, she crossed the kitchen and stood next to Shane, shoulder to shoulder, in a show of solidarity. *Take that big brother,* her stance said. *It's us against you.*

Shane's stomach did another, faster roll.

Right. He was in the thick of it now, caught in the middle of a sibling squabble full of dynamics he didn't fully understand.

Miss O'Toole slid him a quicksilver grin, took a deep breath.

Shane braced for impact.

"As of today," she said on a breezy whisper, turning those remarkable eyes onto her brother. "I no longer sing opera."

The dramatic lilt of her voice made Shane visibly cringe. A scene was in the making.

Thankfully, as a member of a famous acting family, Beauregard O'Toole had seen his share of female theatrics. And like any big brother worth his salt, he didn't seem overly impressed with his sister's performance.

"Just like that. No more opera." His tone flattened. "One day in Denver and you quit your life's calling."

With elegant movements, she reached out, took a deep breath and smoothed a loose strand of hair off her face. "Who said singing opera is my life's calling?" she asked.

Beau's eyes narrowed to thin slits. "You did. In every letter you've written since you turned twelve years old."

Ah, the rare valid point in the midst of female illogic. A point, Shane noted, that Miss O'Toole completely disregarded with an unladylike sniff. "As of today," she wrapped her arm through Shane's, "I'm a nurse."

Beau sucked in a breath. "You're a *what?*"

"A. Nurse," she said through clenched teeth.

"Assistant, actually," Shane muttered.

Both O'Tooles glared at him.

"There's a difference," Shane pointed out, his voice sounding defensive even to his own ears. "A rather large difference," he added with more confidence as he untangled his arm from Miss O'Toole's.

"You hired Bella?" Beau's gaze cut through Shane like a scalpel. "Have you gone mad?"

Shane glanced at the woman standing beside him, noted the hidden desperation behind her false bravado. For whatever reason, she needed this job—he knew it as sure as he knew his own name—and Shane Bartlett was a fool for a woman in need.

No matter what that meant to his friendship with Beau, no matter how ill-thought out the idea was, Shane was going to hire Bella O'Toole as his new assistant.

"Apparently." He blew out a frustrated hiss. "Insanity is indeed one of my more stellar traits."

Chapter Four

Alone at last in her brother's house, belongings long since stowed in the guest bedroom, Bella stood in the small, beautifully decorated parlor. Ignoring the lace curtains, the rose-print wallpaper and stylish furniture, she placed her hand on the windowpane, leaned her forehead on the cool glass and simply looked at the scenery beyond.

The slow ticking from the clock on the mantel soothed her nerves. She found herself slowing her breathing to match the rhythmic cadence.

She hadn't expected to find Beau settled in the middle of a wealthy neighborhood. He'd written in great detail of his decision to build a church that would be directly connected to an orphanage for prostitutes' mistakes. He'd told of his wife's support, both financial and emotional, throughout the entire building project. But his letters had failed to do justice to the fairy-tale world in which they'd settled.

And not just the large homes of expensive brick, manicured lawns and attention to detail.

Bella had never seen a sky so blue. So clear.

The mountains in the distance marched in a row, looking like sentinels on duty, safeguarding all who moved in their shadows. Puffy white clouds weaved along the top peaks, creating a sheer downy blanket of added beauty.

Bringing her gaze closer to Beau's home, she took in trees of all shapes and sizes lining the lane between the church and Charity House's front door. The afternoon breeze swirled fallen leaves into a tapestry of shifting shapes and rich colors of autumn.

Switching to the window on her right, Bella eyed the yard that connected the church to Charity House. The children were at play again. Now that the drama of Ethan's injury was hours old, the fun had resumed.

Some of the more active boys played a hearty game of tag. Others climbed trees. Some of the girls sat in a small group, tying miniature bonnets on their dolls' heads. All in all, the children looked healthy, happy, and well-cared for.

But Bella had seen the anguish in their eyes, the sense of aloneness that they all shared. She had seen the look that both connected them to one another and yet kept them painfully separate. There was an underlying sense of dishonor and disconnection that they didn't think anyone else could understand.

Oh, but Bella understood all too well. She knew the loneliness that was brought on by shame, the inability to connect to people she'd once adored. Even her brother seemed a foreigner to her now. He was too much a man of Christian integrity. Surely he would see through her facade if she allowed him to look too closely. So she wouldn't allow him to look. Ever.

The sound of approaching footsteps halted her

thoughts. The hint of authority in the steps told her Beau had returned for round three of their argument.

Bella took a fortifying pull of air into her lungs as her brother joined her.

She pointed to his wrinkled forehead. "If you don't watch out, that line will become permanent."

His scowl deepened. "You can't seriously be considering Shane's offer."

Bella scrunched her face in an identical expression and tried to ignore the fact that her brother looked well. The brute. Happy, too. The hint of contentment in his gold eyes belied his abrupt words with her, as though his shock and anger could do nothing to dispel the joy that was a part of his life, a part of who he was in Christ.

Why did Beau have to be so...*good?*

"Help me to understand, Bella." He scratched his chin in frustration. "Why do you want to do this? And why now?"

She didn't like his tone, but it was the familiar clenched jaw and narrowed eyes that had her bristling. It was the same expression all her brothers gave her when they were about to lecture her over some serious—in their mind only—offense.

Well, she might be the youngest of six. *And* the only female. But she wasn't a child anymore. "Beauregard O'Toole, you might be older by nine years, and you might have an education from a renowned university and equally impressive seminary, but that does not make you an expert on everything."

"I don't need to be an expert to know you aren't a trained nurse. And, I might also point out, that whine in your voice makes you sound twelve. Hardly the way to go about convincing me of your maturity."

"Don't be so dramatic."

"Me?"

She made a face at him. "Dr. Shane only needs me on a temporary basis. He's not even paying me."

"He's what?"

"Oh, he offered," she said, careful to keep her voice from quivering. "But I refused to hear of it. I don't need the money."

Which had only been a portion of the reason for her refusing the man's offer of a salary. The true reason had been connected to her sense of shame, her sin. Perhaps by volunteering her services for free she could do penance for her blunder with William.

William. So much regret there. Such humiliation. Even now, a month after their disastrous last meeting, she inwardly recoiled at how far she'd walked away from her Christian upbringing. How close she'd come to destroying a family.

How had she been so foolish?

Lord, how do I get past this? How do I make atonement?

Beau touched her arm. "Bella, what aren't you telling me?"

She lowered her gaze. What would he think if he knew the real reason she'd fled London? "Beau, don't. Please don't ask."

Thankfully, Hannah, Beau's wife, walked into the room with the sort of grace any lead actress would envy. Even knowing of her renown, Bella was a little awestruck at the woman's mere presence. She was...stunning. Unforgettable.

It was no wonder she had earned enough prominence on the stage and consequently sufficient money to walk away a wealthy woman after only five years of treading the boards.

With a swoop, her startling green gaze landed on her husband for only a second before swiveling back to Bella. "Beauregard, introduce me to your sister."

He blew out a frustrated breath, but then walked over to his wife and covered her hands with his. For a brief moment, the two shared a connection that went beyond words, similar to the one Bella had seen pass between Trey and Katherine Scott.

And similar to the Scotts, these two were not only in love they actually seemed to like each other. Bella had never thought marriage could include both love and affection, at least not outside her parents' marriage. She'd always assumed Patience and Reginald O'Toole had been lucky.

Luckier, at least, than she would ever be.

Perhaps that was why she had been so willing to believe William's lies. To convince herself what they had was love. Oh, there had been happiness between them, but also an inexplicable awkwardness. Pain, but hope, as well. But there had never truly been ease between them. And certainly nothing warm.

She'd never realized that until now.

And she felt more the fool because of it.

Smiling, Beau kissed his wife on the nose then turned back to Bella. Unfortunately, his worried scowl returned as soon as he spoke again. "Hannah, I would like you to meet Isabella Constance O'Toole, my baby sister."

"*Younger* sister," Bella corrected.

Hannah gave her a serene smile. Could anyone look lovelier? She was outwardly beautiful, yes, with her waterfall of raven curls, creamy skin and big green eyes, but this woman also had an internal light that was impossible to miss. The Spirit dwelling within her made her radiant. And like Katherine Scott, Hannah had no qualms over tugging Bella into a tight embrace.

Panic gnawed at her but Bella tried not to struggle free.

Why were the women connected with Charity House so kind? So understanding?

Bella wanted to hate them both. She *needed* to hate them both. For their inner goodness, if nothing else. In stark comparison to Hannah and Katherine, Bella felt dirty.

And yet, she yearned. Yearned for something she'd never had in her life. She yearned for sisters.

As though reading her mind, Hannah whispered in her ear. "Welcome, sister."

Bella forced down a sob and tried to pull away.

Hannah's grip tightened. "Whatever pain you're running from, I pray we can offer you a safe haven in which to heal."

Bella quit fighting.

How did Hannah know of her troubles? Had Beau used his preacher eyes to see into her sin and thus alerted his wife?

As ridiculous as the notion seemed, Bella pulled away from Hannah to check for sure. Looking into the other woman's uncomplicated gaze, Bella realized Beau had said nothing. Hannah knew Bella had been scarred because Hannah was a woman.

And just like that, Bella had a sister.

The next morning, a vicious wind thrashed off the mountains in bone-chilling gusts. Shane hunched his shoulders against the driving cold and hurried down Market Street toward the rented rooms that housed his medical practice.

A sharp gust kicked up, whipping Shane's coat tightly around him. Blowing into his cupped palms, he quickened his pace.

Autumn mornings like these, when the temperature dropped, reminded him that living in Colorado came with a cost. Given the alternative, Shane was comfortable with his choice.

Squinting toward the ground, he maneuvered around piles of frozen mud and crossed the threshold of 35 Market Street.

With a solid yank, he shut the door behind him. Warm air enveloped him at once, while outside the wind battered angry fists against the building.

As he waited for his eyes to adjust to the inky stillness of the room, Shane took a deep breath. The sharp scent of iodine filled his lungs. He was in his world now, a world of medicine and science, his personal sanctum of healing.

His vision cleared at last, and he moved farther into the room. With each step his heels clicked across the wooden floor, the sound echoing off the walls. The weak morning sun speared thin fingers of light along his path, providing enough illumination for Shane to work.

Preparing for a long day of visitations, he opened his portable medical bag and took a quick accounting of his supplies. Setting aside the heating iron and tourniquet, he checked the number of sponges and plasters. As he expected after Ethan's accident, Shane was low on bandages. He would order more from the medical supplier in New Brunswick.

Satisfied with his inventory, he replaced the instruments he'd cleaned last night into the small surgery box that was housed inside the larger bag. Stethoscope, scissors, lance, forceps and cutting knife. All necessary tools of his trade.

Clasping the bag shut, Shane circled his gaze around his domain. The room was small, sparse, but serviceable enough.

One day, God willing, he would expand to a larger building.

For now, he had the basics.

A long table positioned in the middle of the room cut his realm in half. Shelves containing books and vials of medicines in powder, liquid and pill form lined the south wall. Two cots sat empty on the north end of the room. The linens would need changing, the wool blankets and pillows airing out. A simple enough task for his new assistant.

His. New. Assistant. The thought made him smile.

Isabella. Constance. O'Toole. The name made him pause.

Shane let out a breath. A very heavy breath.

What had possessed him to hire Bella O'Toole, the sister of a trusted friend?

Evidently, the woman had scrambled his brains. What else explained his trip into insanity? Of course, in his own defense, he'd been awed by her resolve and her undeniable strength under pressure.

Did that mean she belonged in his world, even on a temporary basis?

Yesterday, he'd thought so.

Hadn't he seen past the dazzling beauty, straight to the vulnerable woman underneath?

One thing was certain, Bella O'Toole was a contradiction of strength and innocence. She was also, undoubtedly, hiding a terrible secret.

She'd probably end up more trouble than she was worth.

That thought brought on a painful memory of another woman. His mother—long since dead—was never far from his mind, even after all these years.

Shane tried to suppress the unwanted memories, but they prodded and poked at him, making him feel as helpless and vulnerable as he had at sixteen.

His mother had lived a wretched life, her painful last years the worst. Amanda Bartlett had chosen to become the adored mistress of a wealthy New York businessman. At first, there had been flowers, candy and lots of money. But when Peter Ford's visits ceased, Shane had been forced to watch his once-glorious mother shrink into a sick, embittered, hopeless shell of a woman. And when the money and all hope had run out, he'd been forced to watch her die.

As Shane had held her lifeless body in his young arms, he had vowed to seek revenge on the man responsible. He'd never fully succeeded. And when Ford had failed to father another son, Shane had thrown the scoundrel's offer of legitimacy back in his face and had come to Denver to practice medicine.

What had started as revenge had turned into important work, a calling direct from God. If nothing else, Shane was in a position to prevent women like his mother from dying without a decent chance to beat their illness.

And now, Bella O'Toole, with her secretive eyes and hidden pain, had agreed to stand by his side.

A relieved sigh shuddered through him.

God had brought an answer to his prayers in the form of an unlikely vessel.

Of course, Miss O'Toole hadn't seen all of his patients, nor where they lived. Today would be her first real test.

Eager to get started, Shane finished organizing his supplies and left his office without a backward glance.

Once outside, the cold air frosted his breath and he tightened his coat at the collar. At this time of morning, the streets were relatively deserted. The only sound came from the squeak of a milk wagon's wheels muted in the stiff ruts of the weathered road. He looked to the sky, took a moment to watch the clouds collide into one another in an aggressive, almost hostile manner.

Denver was a world apart from the dingy neighborhood of his youth. Shane didn't live in an especially nice part of the mile-high town, yet even here, one block off a continuous row of brothels and saloons, the filth seemed cleaner than it had on the streets of New York City.

Setting out toward Charity House, Shane lifted his head and instantly realized he wasn't alone on the wooden-slatted sidewalk. A tall figure strode in his direction, bearing down hard. And with each purposeful step, Beauregard O'Toole looked less like a compassionate preacher and more an overprotective big brother.

His face scrunched into a frown, Beau stopped a scarce two feet in front of Shane. His jaw was set at a rock-hard angle as he said, "Just the man I came to see."

Shane couldn't fault the hard tone. If Miss O'Toole had been his own sister he'd feel the same urge to protect.

"Beau." Shane nodded, bracing for the fight that was riding between them on the pounding wind. "I don't need to guess why you're here."

The wind shifted, crashed over them.

Both men held their ground.

"Bella can *not* be your assistant."

Shane's breath turned hot in his lungs. The monumental consequences of losing her so soon struck him like a blow to his gut, hitting like a heavy, leaden weight. "Did she send you to say that?"

"I sent myself. In spite of my arguments, she's bent on this new direction in her life." The frustration in the man's eyes confirmed the truth of his words. "Since she's stubborn as a mule, you need to be the clear thinker here."

"I see." Shane tried to keep his tone mild, but his answer sounded a little too gleeful, even over the howling blasts of air. He erased all emotion from his expression and added, "Perhaps we should have this discussion out of the cold."

Beau gave him a long look before nodding in agreement. "Lead the way."

Neither spoke as Shane retraced his steps and unlocked the door to his office.

He directed Beau to enter ahead of him.

The set of the other man's jaw alerted Shane that the conversation was far from over. Absently, he shoved at his hair. Frustration. Guilt. He didn't have room for either.

Nevertheless, he would hear his friend out. They had a history of working well together. While Shane at-

tended to a patient's physical health, Beau ministered to
the spiritual. With God guiding their hands and words,
they made a powerful team.

Circling the room, Beau paused to scrub a hand over
his face. "You can't hire Bella," he repeated through
clenched teeth. "She's not a nurse. She's an opera
singer."

Shane bristled. He found himself caught between defending his decision and honoring his friendship with
this man. "According to your sister, she has taken a self-
imposed sabbatical."

Beau rolled his shoulders, then sighed. "There's more
to the story. Something's wrong. I don't like that she
showed up, tight-lipped and unannounced."

Ah. Miss O'Toole had yet to explain herself to her
brother. Oddly enough, Shane wasn't surprised. "And
that's your only concern? That she's hiding something
from you?"

Closing his eyes, Beau shook his head. "You have to
understand, Bella isn't like most women."

Remembering the courage she'd displayed with
Ethan, the compassion in her manner, the instant display of rebellion when Beau had first shown up, Shane
gave an ironic lift of his eyebrows. "Well, that certainly
needed clearing up."

Beau's lips twitched but instead of responding right
away, he walked to a row of books and ran a finger
along the spines.

Shane gauged the mood in the room and decided on a
tactic. The brother might not hear his words, but surely
the preacher would. "I remember you telling me once
that if a man waits to be certain of a course of action,

he's sure to be too late. Those were your exact words. I know. I wrote them down."

Beau's shoulders stiffened before he spun on his heel to glare at Shane. "I was referring to God's Will for *your* life."

Shane allowed himself a tight smile of satisfaction. "Precisely."

Beau crossed his arms over his chest. Genuine concern fell across his face. "Bella has never lived in the real world. Her whole life has been about make-believe and fantasy. She doesn't understand anything outside the theater."

Studying his friend's expression closely, Shane leaned a shoulder against the wall. Again, he appealed to the preacher and not the brother. "The most unlikely people can demonstrate courage. And given her lack of experience, perhaps it's time Miss O'Toole left the opera for a while."

"Don't misunderstand me. I'm glad she's left. In fact, I'm relieved. At least, in theory." Beau started pacing through the room, slapping a fist against his thigh as he walked. "We both know the perils of *that* life."

Shane nodded gravely. The Denver brothels were filled with women who had failed on the stage. Whether due to lack of talent or disappearing youth, far too many women had nowhere else to go and no hope of gaining respectable employment.

"It's whatever drove Bella to leave the opera that worries me," Beau continued. "Something terrible happened to her in London."

Why deny the truth? Shane, too, believed something bad had happened to Miss O'Toole. But instead of concern at the thought, certainty filled him. The woman was meant to be here, in Denver, assisting him instead of singing opera. There was something else happening here, something bigger than any of them understood.

Something from God.

All along, Shane had assumed Miss O'Toole had been led to him by the Lord in order to assist in his practice. But maybe—*maybe*—she'd been brought to Shane for a bigger reason.

One he couldn't comprehend just yet, and probably wasn't supposed to. As Beau often said when he was thinking like a preacher and not a worried brother, it all came down to walking in faith.

"Perhaps this is just what your sister needs," Shane suggested. "A safe environment to spread her wings and—"

"Safe?" Beau stopped pacing to glare in Shane's direction. "She'll spend her days in brothels, saloons and mining camps."

Shane took exception. "Places where people are still people. The same places, I might remind you, you and your wife inhabit daily. If Hannah can do it, surely your sister can, as well."

"Hannah's different. She's strong."

"Your sister is strong, too."

"Hannah isn't alone."

"Your sister won't be either." Shane pushed from the wall and stood tall, unbending in his conviction. *"I'll* be with her."

Clearly unimpressed with the bold declaration, Beau turned away and started pacing again, muttering under his breath. "How will she survive once her money runs out?"

Rage shot up, threatened to linger, but Shane

squashed it back. "This from you? A preacher well-versed in the Bible? Jesus told his disciples not to worry. 'Look at the birds in the air; they do not sow or reap or store away in barns, and yet your heavenly father feeds them.'"

Eyes blinking in shock, Beau responded with a tiny, rather hapless nod, but Shane continued before the other man could speak. "Rest assured, my friend. This situation is only temporary. And, let's face it, your sister may not make it through the week."

The thought left Shane a little sick, for reasons he refused to explore.

"Oh, she'll last." Beau sank onto a hard-backed, wooden chair and released a frustrated puff of air. "Once Bella gets something in her mind, there's no stopping her."

"Good to know." For a moment, *just one,* Shane allowed his heart to soar with possibilities beyond a simple working relationship. Stunned by the direction of his thoughts, he quickly shut down the notion. "In the meantime, I assure you I plan to continue interviewing qualified candidates."

Beau stared at him for a long, measuring moment. Shane remained unmoving under his friend's scrutiny.

At last, Beau nodded. "Fair enough." Looking far more at ease now, he stretched out his long legs and crossed them at the ankles. "What's on your schedule today?"

"I'll be making visitations all afternoon," Shane said.

Beau leaned forward and rested his elbows on his knees. "Is Lizzie one of those…visitations?"

"Of course. After I retrieve your sister, Mattie's brothel will be our first stop."

"Is that a fact?" A twinkle of amusement entered Beau's eyes. "Do you expect Mattie to show up during said visit?"

Shane grinned at last. "When doesn't the woman make her presence known, dramatic entrance and all?"

"Dr. Bartlett, I believe I owe you an apology." A slow grin spread across the preacher's lips. "Clearly, I underestimated you."

"You aren't the first."

"Bella won't know what hit her."

"That is the general idea."

Beau pushed out of the chair and walked over to slap Shane on the back. "You are either very brave, my friend, or very, *very* stupid."

Shane's smile disappeared. "Maybe both."

Beau chuckled. "Time will tell."

And that, Shane thought, was exactly what he feared most.

Chapter Five

Before the sun had fully risen, Bella faced her first dilemma of the day. She had no idea what a nurse wore while attending patients. If her experience with Ethan Scott was any indication, the work would be messy.

That meant silk was out. Satin, too. Definitely no ruffles or lace.

A quick rummage through her trunks sent a wave of distress rippling through her. Sighing, Bella rubbed a finger across her temple. Maybe she should have thought this through better.

She had nothing appropriate to wear. Which only made her more convicted to pursue this new course for her life. As her mother always said, "If it comes too easy, it's simply not worth doing."

Perhaps her new sister-in-law would have a solution.

Shoving her feet into slippers, Bella wrapped her dressing gown tightly around her and went in search of Hannah.

Out in the hallway, her gaze tracked everywhere, past the wallpaper, the rugs, the wood floors underneath, the lone chair halfway down the corridor. Nothing looked familiar. Bella spun to her left and then to her right.

She couldn't seem to get her bearings.

Beau's house wasn't all that large but it wasn't small either. Hannah had given her a tour of the home last night. Navigating the two stories had seemed easy enough. But this morning, Bella was hopelessly lost. Understandable, she supposed. She'd only spent a hand-ful of days in a real home. Her childhood had consisted of makeshift beds either backstage or in a temporary flat.

Focus, Bella. Focus.

Choosing a direction at random, she set out. She hadn't gone far when she stopped midstep and inhaled deeply.

The smells.

Yes, the smells were different here. Clove, cinnamon, coffee, the lingering scent of food mixed with lemon oil. It was all so very pleasant. So heartwarming. A slice of the kind of life she'd secretly dreamed of and only now just realized how much.

A deep longing for something—something *more*—rose up, threatened to linger, but she fought the disturb-ing emotion back with a hard swallow.

William's necklace weighed heavy around her neck, a bold reminder that she'd failed her first real test as a woman. The urge to yank off the offensive talisman burned, but she would not touch the necklace. She would *not*.

Needing to think a moment, Bella collapsed against the wall and closed her eyes. Pure and simple, she was a fraud. She was no more a nurse than she was a pure-hearted woman.

Yet no one need know of her deception, did they? She was a trained performer, after all, schooled from childhood to take on varied roles. How hard could it be to pretend innocence?

The key, of course, would be to keep her mouth shut. Little talking meant few revelations. Yes, yes, that was it. *Silence.*

Mouth pressed in a firm line, she fumbled from the wall, and resumed her search for the perfect dress to wear on this first day of her atoning.

The sound of—was that retching?—stopped her cold.

Bella spun on her heel.

"Hannah?"

There was a pause, followed by a series of coughs and sniffles. "We're in here," came a weak voice.

Bella rushed in the direction of the voice. When she got to the end of the hall, she halted at the sight of her sister-in-law crumbled on the floor of the washroom, her head pressed in the lap of a tiny, unusual-looking old woman.

Mavis. This had to be Hannah's adopted grandmother.

Bella thought Beau had been exaggerating when he'd told her about the woman. But Mavis's hair was indeed white as fresh-fallen snow and it did shoot out in wild waves from every direction. Her age was indeterminate, and her clothing bright. A bawdy old girl, as Bella's brother Tyler would call her. Unconventional in every way. And long past the days of innocence.

No wonder Hannah adored the woman.

And it was obvious Mavis loved Hannah in return.

Her thin, gnarled fingers petted Hannah's head in slow, gentle strokes. "Deep breaths, baby girl." Her voice was as hard and raspy as Beau had described. "It'll pass."

From her seat on the floor, Mavis looked up at Bella and grinned. "Don't take no brains to tell you're Pastor Beau's sister."

Waving a limp hand in Bella's general direction, Hannah took a shaky breath. "Bella, meet Mavis. Mavis, Bella."

Casting the older woman a quick nod of acknowledgment, Bella dropped to her knees and lifted Hannah's tangled mass of ebony curls. "What can I do to help you?"

Hannah lifted her head, dropped it just as quickly. "Don't look so frightened, Bella dear." She swiped the back of her hand across her mouth and struggled to sit up. "I'm fine now, really."

Clearly, Hannah exaggerated. The edges around her mouth were pulled tight with tension and her face was leached of color.

Bella exchanged a concerned glance with Mavis. "You don't look fine," she said for them both.

"I will be in a moment." She took several slow, full gulps of air. "It'll pass. Once the baby grows bigger."

Bella shifted her weight from her knees to her heels. The very edge of excitement and fear had her rocking back and forth. "How long has this been going on?"

"A few days now." Hannah grinned in spite of her misery. But then her eyes glazed over and she bent over herself.

Mavis lifted the pot by her feet just in time.

Hannah finished with a series of dry heaves.

"Lay your head back down in my lap," Mavis

ordered, gently pulling until Hannah obeyed the command.

Once settled again, Hannah's hair fell forward, curtaining half her face.

Unsure how to proceed, Bella asked, "Does Beau know yet?"

Surely he would have told Bella. Wouldn't he? Maybe not. He'd been awfully angry with her when he'd gone to bed last night.

"I wanted to make sure before I told him," Hannah said.

Bella felt very young and very inexperienced, but if she was going to work as a doctor's assistant she better know such things. "How…how do you make sure?"

With a shaky hand, Hannah shoved the hair off her face, glanced at the full bedpan near Mavis's crossed feet. "I think it's safe to say God has blessed us with child."

"Oh, Hannah. I'm so happy for you."

Bella reached out and smoothed her fingers across her sister-in-law's forehead. She wanted to connect with this woman, to become her friend, as well as her sister, but something in Bella refused to soften, something dark warned her to keep her distance. "When is the blessed day?" she asked in a whisper.

"In about seven months."

Seven months. So soon. So far away.

"Will you tell Beau soon?"

A smile played at the edges of Hannah's lips. "As soon as he returns from his errand in town."

"He'll be pleased," Mavis announced, lifting her chin to a jaunty, I-know-these-things angle.

"Yes. Yes, he will." Hannah sat up again, blinked several times. Slowly, the color returned to her cheeks.

Bella sighed at the sight of Beau's pregnant wife. Bittersweet tears welled in her own eyes. She dashed them away with a single swipe. But, truthfully, she'd rarely seen such a look of contentment on another woman's face, had never thought such joy possible.

Surely, she wasn't jealous was she?

"This is truly a blessing from God," Mavis said with such conviction, Bella gave the older woman a closer inspection. She didn't look like a believing Christian. In truth, she had the hard, craggy exterior of someone who had lived a difficult life.

Ah, but Bella had already learned a person's exterior was no indication of the inner heart.

"It is a blessing." Hannah squeezed Mavis's hand. "And I pray, God willing, our child looks just like my husband."

Bella sighed again. No matter which parent it took after, the child would be beautiful. And not to mention he, *or she,* would be the first grandchild in the O'Toole family.

Bella's parents would want to know the happy news.

They would want to be present for the child's birth. And if Bella was still living in Denver, there would be questions. More like a full-blown interrogation.

Oh, no. No, no, no. Bella could bear anything but one of her mother's "concerned" lectures, the ones that always began with, "If you would have listened to me in the first place."

That settled it, then. Bella would be long departed before her parents arrived. She had less than seven months to figure out her next step.

When the time came, she'd be glad to go. She bit down on her lip.

Wouldn't she?

Why did she feel the loss already? Why did she sense leaving this place, this town, *these people* would bring on far more regret than anything she'd left behind in London?

Shane waited for his new assistant in the O'Toole's front parlor. A quick glance around the tiny room revealed Hannah's handiwork. She'd decorated with an overabundance of frills and lace. But instead of feeling too feminine, the fancy decor created a warm, comforting sense of home.

At ten, he'd tried to create something similar for his mother. But his efforts had been pitiful, a small lace doily the only thing he could afford to give his mother the day she'd turned thirty, the first of many birthdays Peter Ford had missed.

Forcing down a surge of restlessness, Shane took another, slower study of the room. Framed photographs of the famous O'Tooles covered all four green walls. Playbills, clippings and newspaper reviews filled two entire tables, all clear evidence that Beau and Hannah O'Toole cared deeply for their relatives.

What would it be like, Shane wondered, to be a member of such a large and loving family?

A dark, wistful longing he hadn't experienced since childhood speared through his heart, leaving a vague sense of dissatisfaction. Disgusted with himself—*with the unexpected emotion*—Shane remained very still and forced his mind clear.

He had no room in his life for dreams abandoned

years ago. His patients depended on his sole dedication to the science of medicine. Logic, reason and hard work, yes, those were the three fundamentals of his life.

The distant sound of light, airy footsteps hailed Miss O'Toole's impending entrance. Shane shook himself out of his troubled musings. By the time his assistant joined him, he had successfully buried all thought, save one. They had a busy day ahead of them.

"Here I am," she said in her lilting accent, her arms outstretched as if to present herself for his inspection.

Turning slightly, Shane brought his gaze in direct line with Bella O'Toole. His eyes loitered on her face. *So many secrets buried in that beautiful head.*

The thought did nothing to ease his foul mood.

Pulling her bottom lip between her teeth, she lowered her hands to her hips. "Are you ready to begin our new alliance?"

New alliance? A swelling of something he couldn't quite identify streamed through his resolve to think logically. Was it doubt? Or something more complex?

Needing a moment to collect his thoughts, Shane studied Miss O'Toole's chosen ensemble for the day. She'd dressed in a simple blue dress, rather nondescript, but she'd covered it with a bright purple apron with red patches sewn haphazardly across the hem. The dress alone was acceptable enough, but the apron added an entirely different quality to the overall look, bordering on the ugly.

He did a quick estimate of Miss O'Toole's height and weight and figured she'd borrowed the two garments from Mavis Tierney. No wonder the dress and apron clashed so completely.

Suppressing a grin, Shane moved his gaze back to Miss O'Toole's face.

She wore her hair down, the golden locks cascading in a riot of curls down her back. She'd pulled the thick mane off her face with a black ribbon, tied with a large bow on top. She should look silly.

She looked…incredible.

Rendered momentarily speechless, Shane lowered his gaze for a final pass, and stopped dead at her shoes, or rather her fancy, thin-heeled *slippers*.

His brows dived into a scowl. "Those won't do."

He hadn't realized how harsh his tone sounded until her eyes widened in response. She looked shocked, offended perhaps, but she quickly covered the emotion with a pleasant, almost vacant look in her eyes. "Well, they're all I have."

Her flat tone gave nothing away, nor did her eyes.

How could the woman hide her thoughts so quickly and so completely? He puzzled over the question until he remembered she was a trained actress, an opera singer of the first order who made her living pretending to be someone she was not.

Like any man dealing with a woman he didn't understand, Shane took a fortifying breath and prepared for the inevitable battle ahead.

"We'll take care of finding you appropriate footwear in town," he said, using his mildest tone in hopes of forestalling any argument on her part. "We'll get you a pair of shoes that will be warmer and more comfortable and—"

"Whatever you say."

"—better suited for trekking through ice and mud." *Whatever you say?* He blinked.

"Did you just agree with me, Miss O'Toole?"

Tucking a loose strand of hair beneath the black ribbon, she lifted a careless shoulder. "You would know better than I what sort of shoes I should wear."

And just like that, she threw him off balance. *Again.* This time with her complete cooperation. Would this woman never stop surprising him?

"Right, then." He cleared the shock out of his voice and turned all business. "Let's be off."

Feeling more hopeful than he had in months, Shane helped Miss O'Toole with her coat and then stepped back while she tugged on the matching hat and gloves.

Once outside, Shane gripped her elbow carefully and assisted her into his small, but serviceable buggy.

She wiggled and shifted and squirmed until she finally settled herself on the cushioned seat. Only then did she turn her head and smile down at him.

Shane's pulse kicked hard in his chest. The sight of all that beauty aimed solely at him was like a swift punch to his gut.

He quickly broke eye contact and made his way to the other side of the carriage and climbed aboard. With mechanical movements, he snapped the reins and clicked his tongue.

His horse set out at a slow, easy gait.

Focused on the passing scenery, Miss O'Toole remained silent during the ride into town. Shane took the opportunity to slip covert glances in her direction. Her wool coat was the color of a Colorado pine and set off her creamy skin to perfection. With her honey, sun-kissed curls pouring past her shoulders she looked almost imaginary. A storybook princess brought to life.

But she was real. Very real. Her scent gave her away.

She smelled of sweet perfume, like fresh jasmine, all pleasant and inviting.

Shane smiled.

Without warning, she turned her head, and Shane found his lips slipping into a frown. Imprisoned in those remarkable tawny eyes the dark, wistful longing he'd experienced in the parlor returned, somehow stronger, and with enough force to yank the breath out of his lungs.

He tightened his hands on the reins and forced his attention back to the road. It took every ounce of his willpower not to look at her again.

You do not need this sort of trouble, he warned himself. *It's dangerous, imprudent and reckless. Very reckless.*

Then again...

Perhaps Shane was thinking too hard, allowing a pretty face to complicate a simple matter. Perhaps all he needed was a little distance from the woman sitting entirely too close to him.

With that in mind, he turned his thoughts to the day's schedule and scrutinized the road with careful attention.

The rhythmic turning of the wheels mingling with his horse's steady gait hypnotized him until Shane had no idea how much time elapsed. Surely, no more than ten minutes.

At last, he drew the carriage to a stop in the alleyway between Mattie's brothel and the Smoking Horse Saloon.

This was it, their first real test as doctor and temporary assistant.

He let out a slow breath of tension, shoved his fingers through his hair and tugged at the ends.

In a matter of minutes, Shane would discover what Miss O'Toole was actually made of. And for both their sakes, as well as his patients', he prayed she was up for the tasks that lay ahead.

Chapter Six

Truly? Bella squinted into the muted, gray light. He'd *truly* brought her to a filthy, stinky, back alley in the heart of a derelict part of town?

There had to be some mistake.

Why would the man direct them straight to a dead end and simply sit there without speaking?

Swallowing her confusion, Bella covered her nose against the stench of garbage and stale liquor. She shot her gaze in all directions. Unfortunately, the jagged rooftops swallowed the sunlight and blue sky above, casting dark, ominous shadows over them. She could only make out a scant few details such as dirt, dirt and, oh, right, *more dirt*.

Confusion giving way to frustration, she glanced at the good doctor for some clue to this unusual turn of events. He simply stared at her. Blinking, staring, grinning, frowning? She couldn't tell. Shadows, long and deep, concealed his features entirely.

Well, of course. Why make this easy for her?

In spite of a hot surge of rebellion, Bella scooted a little closer to the man, casting her gaze to the right and back to the left again. She didn't particularly like the dark.

And, uh, were the walls closing in on them by chance?

Stifling a gasp, Bella quickly lowered her gaze to the ground that...was...*moving*.

Moving?

One explanation came to mind.

Rats.

In spite of the calm horse at the end of the reins and the equally calm man beside her, the street was teaming with hideous rodents, their sharp little fang teeth waiting for a fresh ankle to bite.

She tried to pretend she was on the stage with a packed audience. She failed. And all at once Bella surrendered to abject terror. "Do...do you see that?" She jabbed her finger toward the ground.

"See what?"

"R...r-r-r...r-r-r-rats! Everywhere." She clawed at his sleeve. She hated rats worse than the dark.

He gave her hand a condescending pat. "They're more afraid of you than you are of them. Give it a moment more and they'll scurry away."

"No. You...you...you d-d-don't understand." She yanked hard on his arm, pulling at him until his ear came close enough for her to speak in a loud whisper. "I hate rats!"

One by one, he slowly untangled her fingers from his sleeve and chuckled. "I should think you've seen enough of the little black creatures in your life. Aren't they a staple backstage of most theaters?"

The man had a point, a rather large point. But Bella

was not in the mood to concede anything to the unfeeling, overly calm beast. "Ssss… So?"

"So," he said with the same practiced patience he'd used on Ethan yesterday. "I should think you've had plenty of time to get over any phobia you might have incurred through the years. You must know they won't hurt you."

They won't hurt you? Was the man insane? "Rats bite."

"Has one bitten you before?" he asked, his voice filled with genuine worry.

Oh, right, *now* he showed concern. When it was too, too late.

Bella jerked her chin. "That is not the point."

"Has a rat bitten you in the past?" he asked again, his tone growing softer and his hand patting with less condescension.

"*No.* But, at the risk of stating the obvious, I… I… I am wearing slippers."

"Right. I forgot." The man sounded entirely too passive, almost gleeful in the face of her panic.

Something bigger was going on here, bigger than rat teeth searching for Bella flesh. And just like that, she knew. Beau's terribly important meeting this morning made perfect sense now.

This little trip down rat alley was a test.

One the horse was passing, one the doctor was passing and one Bella had every intention of passing, as well.

Just give her a moment.

Once she started breathing again she'd have her fear under control. Oh, sure, her hands were shaking uncontrollably. And her heart was pounding a fast tempo against her ribs. But she would not submit easily.

Lord, empower me with the courage to do Your work today, regardless of the black furry challenges You've set before me.

"While we're waiting for our new friends to find a hiding place," Dr. Shane began in a matter-of-fact tone, "I should take this opportunity to warn you about what's to come."

"Of course," she said, waiting silently for him to proceed. *Anything* to get her mind off sharp, pointy fangs.

Turning her head slightly, she considered the doctor more carefully now that her eyes were adjusting to the shadows. In the dim light, his features had taken on a series of sharp angles and well-defined planes. His eyes were the color of polished pewter.

Unfortunately, the look he cast her was completely impersonal, as though he'd slid an invisible shutter across his features.

Bella swallowed a sudden urge to cry. She wished she could understand what was going on in that complicated mind of his.

"Our first patient is Lizzie." He shifted away from her and set the brake. "She's suffering from consumption, as many of her kind do." The sorrow in his eyes told her there was more to the story than he was revealing.

"Her kind?" she asked.

His head rotated back in her direction. An inner struggle was written across his face. "Prostitutes. Lizzie earns her living by accepting favors from men."

A gust of cold, misty air swept through the alley at his proclamation. Bella shivered.

"We're at a brothel?" she asked, trying to hide her terrible fascination at the notion.

"Yes."

Bella studied the two buildings on either side of her, silently wondering which establishment was their destination.

As though sensing her unspoken question, Dr. Shane pointed to his left. "It's that one."

Cocking her head in fierce concentration, she eyed the sooty brick and mortar. "I see."

She felt rather than saw him take a deep breath. "You are not shocked?"

"Of course not."

Well, maybe a little. But she pitched her voice to a confident level. "I *am* a woman of the world, after all. In fact, I have sung the lead in the opera *La Traviata*."

She hoped her rapid blinking didn't belie her bold words. She might have sung the notes of a doomed prostitute, but she'd never fully understood the tragic Camille's choices. Her performance had suffered, resulting in the worst reviews of her life.

"Did you enjoy playing the ill-fated courtesan?"

"The story was quite sad," she said. Then sighed. "I always wished she'd have accepted her young suitor's love and simply left..." She cleared her throat. "That life."

That life.

The very same life William had offered her.

Of its own volition, her hand reached for the locket around her neck. She spread her fingers across her collarbone and let out another sigh. If she was honest with herself, she'd admit she'd left London out of fear, not moral conviction. Eventually, she'd have given in to

William's vows of love, just as the fictional Camille had done over and over again with her various suitors.

Bella hadn't believed in her own inner strength, hadn't believed she had the character to turn away from her temptation and the sin that came with it.

So she'd run.

She was still running.

"Brace yourself, Miss O'Toole. The play glosses over the harsh reality of a woman dying of consumption."

She tossed her head back and scoffed at him. "You needn't worry about me. I've seen my share of ugliness in the world. I will not be shocked."

Oh, but she would be. She was sure of it, yet not for the obvious reasons. She sensed, down to the bottom of her slippers, that she would find a kindred spirit in Lizzie, the prostitute.

And that, Bella thought miserably, told the true state of her wretched sinner's soul.

Stepping quickly to the ground, Shane studied the area surrounding his feet. Confident the last remaining rat had fled, he proceeded to Miss O'Toole's side of the carriage.

"Ready to start our day?" he asked in what he hoped was a pleasant enough voice, one that would soothe away the majority of her fears.

At her wide-eyed stare, a thread of discomfort wiggled through his conscience. Perhaps he should have brought her to the front door after all. Perhaps his scheme to toss her immediately into the thick of things wasn't as well-thought out as he'd told himself.

Unfortunately, it was too late for second guesses.

What was done was done. He'd simply have to do his best to protect her from this point forward.

Inching toward the edge of her seat, she squeezed her eyes shut a moment then said, "I suppose I'm as ready as I'll ever be."

Shane stifled a smile at the muffled squeak in her voice, the one she was trying so hard to hide behind a brilliant smile.

Oh, she was a brave one. He'd give her that.

In spite of the fact that her eyes brimmed with mistrust and she glared at the ground around his feet, Shane knew Miss O'Toole would exit the buggy. Eventually.

He wished she'd lift her head and look at him, though. She would only make herself miserable if she continued searching for rats—especially since there was a high possibility she'd find one. Or twelve.

Well, rodents or not, they had a schedule to keep.

Stretching out his hand, he waited patiently for her to gather her courage.

Still glaring at his feet, she took a fortifying breath, boldly placed her palm into his and finally looked him directly in the eye.

An unmistakable scratching noise filled the silence.

Her face drained of color.

He opened his mouth to make some inane comment about nothing to fear, he would protect her from the big bad rats, but words failed him. "I..." He broke off, wrapped his hand tighter around hers and gave an encouraging squeeze.

She gripped him back with equal intensity.

He should release her. No doubt about it. And yet, Shane clutched her fingers as though she was the most important thing ever to come across his path.

Lord, what's happening here?

Struggling for air, he drew her slowly to the ground. Only after she found her balance did he release her hand.

This was going to be one very long day.

"After you," he said.

"Right."

To his amusement, she set out at a slow, careful pace, tiptoeing as though she could escape notice one baby step at a time. He allowed a slow smile to spread across his lips.

The woman was anything but dull.

And her rat phobia was oddly charming.

Still grinning at Miss O'Toole's wretched attempt to avoid detection, Shane lifted his medical bag and took off after her.

Thankfully, no furry creature dared tread in their path thus far. Pulling alongside her, Shane gripped Miss O'Toole's elbow and led her to the backdoor of the brothel.

With each step he silently reviewed the prescribed plan in his mind. In spite of his previous doubts, he knew it was important to stay the course this morning. Everyone, especially their patients, depended on Miss O'Toole fulfilling her appointed duties without hesitation just as she'd done yesterday with Ethan.

No matter what they came across today, Shane would not gloss over any portion of the work that lay ahead. If Miss O'Toole was to remain as his assistant for any length of time, she needed to understand exactly what a brothel looked like from behind the scenes. No false sheen. No glamour. Just the harsh reality of shame and early death.

Standing on the back doorstep, Shane considered his assistant's nervous profile before knocking. Regardless of her "woman of the world" platitudes, she was in for a shock this morning.

But it was Shane who received the biggest surprise when the door swung open and a young woman stared at him from the other side of the threshold.

Two thoughts came to mind. The girl couldn't be more than fifteen, and he'd never seen her before. She was well-dressed, and unbelievably attractive with her brown hair, blue eyes and light brown skin. Even more startling, innocence radiated out of her.

But there could be only one reason for her presence in the brothel at this time of day. She was one of Mattie's newest girls, another casualty of the harsh western frontier.

Which made no sense.

Unlike most madams in the territory, Mattie Silks had her own unique set of standards. She had never hired anyone this young before.

Unaware of his thoughts, the girl's gaze flitted from him to Miss O'Toole and back to him again.

"May I help you?" she asked in a voice just above a squeak, sounding much like Miss O'Toole had when she'd discovered the alley's rodent problem.

Shane stepped forward. "I'm Dr. Bartlett. Would you please inform Miss Silks I have arrived?"

The girl's gaze dropped to the medical bag in his hand. "Oh. Yes, of course."

The relief in her young voice made Shane smile. She was not one of Mattie's girls. Yet.

But how long would that hold true? Had Mattie relaxed her standards for this beautiful child?

Watching the young woman pivot and then walk out of the room with guileless elegance, Shane shuddered at the inevitable tragedy her life would become if something wasn't done soon.

Yet, what could he do?

He would alert Pastor Beau of her existence. Surely, the preacher would know what course of action to take next.

Feeling a bit more hopeful, Shane dragged an unsteady hand through his hair and offered up a silent prayer. *Lord, You are the Great Protector. I pray You keep that young girl from falling into the sin of this house.*

"You don't think she's—" Miss O'Toole let out an audible breath. "You know. A…a…"

"No."

She turned to look at him.

Their gazes locked.

Held.

Held.

"You are sure of this?"

"Completely."

Her brows drew into a delicate frown and she angled her head in confusion. "But how do you know?"

"I know."

Her left eyebrow lifted a fraction closer to her hairline, giving her a slightly wounded look. "You can simply look at someone and know that sort of thing?"

Realizing his answer was important to her, and not quite understanding how he knew or why, he nodded slowly, never taking his eyes off her stricken face. "Sometimes."

"Oh." Her voice came out steady enough, but anguish was written all over her features.

If the question of a young girl's innocence could distress the woman this much, what would happen when she actually followed Shane upstairs and witnessed the ugly realities of life in a brothel?

She thought playing the part of a doomed courtesan gave her an understanding of the world inside these walls. But there was no glamour to be found here.

And suddenly, as sure as he knew his own name, Shane didn't want to subject this fine, Christian woman to the dark world upstairs. Not yet.

In fact, he *never* wanted to watch this bright, young opera singer lose her innocence simply because she agreed to assist him when no one else had the courage or the character.

For some inexplicable reason, Shane desperately needed Miss O'Toole to keep her fantasies intact. He needed to believe there were people who still had such illusions. And most of all, he needed physical proof that there were people living in this world free of pain, death and complicated life choices.

"Wait for me in the carriage," he said in an unbending tone.

Her face took on the stubborn edge Shane was beginning to recognize. And dread.

"No."

"Miss O'Toole—"

"I will not leave your side before I've had a chance to prove myself. *I will not.*"

Stunned at the relief her words brought him, Shane lifted a hand to her, dropped it just as quickly. This was not about him. "It is for your own good. You shouldn't see—"

"Don't do this. Please. Not now." She placed a gentle, yet firm grip on his arm. "I promise you, I will be quite fine."

And perhaps she would.

But would Shane?

Chapter Seven

Much to her shock and against all effort to the contrary, tears invaded Bella's eyes. She would not buckle under Dr. Shane's misguided attempt to protect her. She would *not*.

Refusing to look at him until she had her emotions under control, Bella called upon the familiar breathing technique she used to calm her nerves. In. Out. In. Out.

In...

Out...

But no matter how slowly she breathed, she could not seem to get her thoughts under control. What if this man could see into her heart and know what was there? Hadn't he said he knew the young girl was innocent? Could he also know Bella was not, at least not in her heart?

Still a bit unsteady, she continued breathing deeply. She was being ridiculous. It didn't matter what Dr. Shane thought of her. God had given her this chance to atone for her sin with William.

The urge to wrap her fingers around the locket came

strong, but Bella balled her hand into a tight fist and cast a quick glance at Dr. Shane.

He appeared lost in his own thoughts, looking toward the ceiling with grave interest.

Perhaps he was impatient to begin his day.

Or maybe there was something else on his mind.

Before Bella could contemplate further, the beautiful child returned.

"I am to tell you to proceed directly to Miss Lizzie's room. My…" She let her words trail off, cringing with obvious embarrassment at some unplanned slip of the tongue. "That is, *Miss Silks* said she will join you in a moment."

The doctor nodded. "Thank you, Miss…"

"Annabeth."

His lips cracked into a smile. Warm. Accessible. The man certainly had his share of charm.

"Thank you, Miss Annabeth," he said. "You may tell Mattie that I've set off for Lizzie's room with my new assistant in tow."

Smiling at his choice of words, Bella followed her employer through a pair of swinging doors. She glanced over her shoulder in time to witness Annabeth retreating in the opposite direction.

Bella paused. "I wonder why she isn't at Charity House with other young girls her age."

"That's a question I plan to ask Mattie as soon as the opportunity arises," he ground out.

Understanding his frustration, Bella remained silent as they made their way through the lower level of the brothel.

A sickening dread crept through her stomach but

she refused to flinch, not at the hideous decor or the stale odor of cigar smoke mingled with cheap perfume.

In truth, the interior wasn't as bad as she'd expected. It was worse. *Much worse.*

Bella had never seen such an ill-staged setting, not even in her early days of playing smaller, seedier venues. The gaudy red-velvet furniture stood in stark contrast to the gold filigree wallpaper, lamps and tables. A trio of fake-looking Oriental rugs covered the wood flooring. Vulgar paintings hung on the walls, their bold colors and shocking themes made Bella think she was walking inside a cliché.

Really, Miss Silks, must you be so obvious?

More disturbed than she cared to admit, Bella inched closer to the doctor, nearly nipping his heels with her toes.

A winding staircase took them upstairs to a long hallway with five doors along both walls. The carpet on this floor was much shabbier, a floral print long since faded.

There was a sense of neglect up here, as though the madam had spent her time, effort and money decorating the lower level—for what it was worth.

But how had Miss Silks decorated the individual rooms?

Bella had her answer as soon as the doctor opened the third door on their right.

The smell hit her first. Musty, sour, rank. As she closed the door behind them, she decided she actually missed the rancid back alleyway. Rats and all.

Squinting into the darkened room, she waited for her vision to clear before stepping forward. The ragged curtains and threadbare furnishings brought one word to mind. *Forgotten.*

Dr. Shane set his bag on a chair near the bed and began unbuttoning his coat.

Bella did the same.

"Good morning, Lizzie," he said in a low voice, placing his coat across the foot of the bed.

Setting her coat next to Dr. Shane's, Bella followed his gaze to the shriveled, pale form lying in the large bed in the center of the room.

While the doctor rummaged in his bag, Bella studied the poor woman. It was impossible to determine her age. Her long, black hair hung in dirty tangles and her face was pinched into a grimace of pain.

Much as the downstairs looked like a poorly constructed theater set, Lizzie looked like an actress bent on playing herself yet failing to bring genuine enthusiasm to the role.

A wave of sympathy crested. Bella couldn't take her eyes off the pitiful sight of the worn-out woman.

Unaware of her morbid fascination, Dr. Shane wrapped a stethoscope around his neck and pivoted back to his patient. With practiced movements, he took Lizzie's limp hand in his and pressed two fingers against her wrist. After a minute, he released her and touched her brow.

Riveted, Bella stared at the doctor's fingers as they made a rhythmic sweep across Lizzie's forehead. The elegant gesture reminded Bella of an artist's expert stroke across a canvas.

And yet, it was the compassion in his manner that struck the strongest chord within her. Bella stood in awe. What depth of character he had, to look past the sin and straight into this poor woman's tortured heart.

This man was a true model of Christian integrity.

"How are you feeling today?" he asked his patient.

"Not so good," she croaked.

He patted her hand. "We'll try to make it better."

His tone was so gentle, so patient, Bella nearly wept. She desperately wanted someone—anyone—*him*—to show her that same careful consideration.

If only she could leave her memories of William behind. Perhaps then…

Then, what?

What did she want from Dr. Shane?

As though sensing her inspection, he turned his gaze to meet hers. But his eyes were filled with an inner sadness, not curiosity.

At the sight of his unguarded despair, Bella's thoughts of herself disappeared. She had a compelling urge to rush to him, to ease his pain somehow.

Just as she moved forward, Lizzie began coughing. Bella switched directions.

Acting on pure instinct, she moved in behind Lizzie and lifted her head to a less awkward angle. "There, now," she soothed. "Take your time."

She continued to speak softly, practically chattering, until she sensed the doctor watching her again.

Compelled by some silent nudge inside her, she lifted her gaze to his and found that his eyes were no longer sad. They were filled with a mixture of surprise and gratitude.

Her breath backed up in her lungs.

No theater review had ever brought such instant pleasure.

Without a word, he handed her a clean handkerchief and cocked his head toward Lizzie. Understanding his silent command, Bella placed the cloth against the woman's lips and wiped.

"You poor dear," she whispered, never taking her eyes off the doctor.

He held her stare, silent a moment, and then stepped forward. "I'll take it from here."

Nodding, Bella lowered Lizzie's head to the pillow and moved out of his way.

He reached out and squeezed her hand as she passed by him. "Thank you."

Choked with emotion, she simply nodded.

In that moment, Bella realized why he had brought her to the brothel first thing this morning. He hadn't wanted to test her, rather he'd wanted to warn her that this job would be hard, both physically and emotionally, and it would require a level of courage Bella wasn't sure she had.

Just then, Jesus's words to his disciples came to mind. *I tell you the truth, whatever you did for the least of these brothers of mine, you did for Me.*

This work was vastly important for the Kingdom. And Dr. Shane had asked her to share in it with him.

Her very soul trembled at the implication.

Singing opera might have brought a moment's enjoyment to others, perhaps even a brief respite in a complicated world, but this—this caring for the sick—was infinitely more significant than memorizing an aria or hitting a difficult note.

"Miss O'Toole, would you be so kind as to hand me the elixir in the clear bottle on your left?"

Determined to prove herself invaluable, she fixed her mind on the task at hand. "Of course."

Just as she made her way around the bed, the door swung open with a bang.

Bella spun around at the noise.

"What is the meaning of this outrage?" said an angry female voice from the shadows.

Dr. Shane blew out a frustrated breath and cast his gaze to the heavens. "Not now. Please, Lord, not now."

He quickly lowered his head and shot Bella a pained expression. "Brace yourself."

With another deep inhale, he swiveled toward the woman who now stood silhouetted in the dim lighting from the hallway.

"Miss Silks," he began with forced patience. "I am attending Lizzie at the moment. Please be so kind as to wait outside until I call for you."

In spite of the doctor's request, the woman swept boldly into the room. Each step she took was calculated, carefully placed and used for absolute effect. Bella should know. She'd trained for years to avoid making such an obvious entrance.

Dr. Shane muttered something under his breath, but Bella was too busy watching Mattie Silks to decipher his meaning.

With her gold satin dress, matching gloves and overtight bodice, the woman was a complete caricature of herself. She might have been a great beauty once, but the icy glare, unnatural blond hair and overplucked eyebrows made her look hard now, almost manly.

Her sharp gaze arced through the room, halted a moment on the ill woman in the bed. Bella thought she saw a show of compassion in the depths of those inflexible blue eyes but the moment passed and Bella found herself on the receiving end of an unbending glare.

Well, Bella had spent too many years fighting her way to the top of her profession to let an amateur intimidate her with such transparent tactics.

Slanting her own challenging glance in the woman's direction, Bella drew herself to her full height and locked gazes with the surly madam.

Mattie bristled.

Bella smiled. Sweetly.

Wrathful sparks flew between them like sabers.

"Who are you?" Mattie demanded. Her voice came out gravelly, as though she had only just awakened from a fitful sleep or had yet to go to bed for the night.

Judging from the attire, Bella decided on the latter.

She also decided the rude question warranted no response from her.

"I asked you a question, girl."

Casting himself in the role of protector—the dear man—Dr. Shane released a low growl, moved around the bed and positioned his large body between Bella and the indignant madam.

"This is my new assistant," he said, gently shifting Bella farther behind him. "And I would ask you not to bother her as she is in the midst of performing duties for me."

He was playing his part to perfection, all the way down to the fierce scowl on his face. How…sweet.

And completely unnecessary.

Squaring her shoulders, Bella brushed around her gentle lion.

"I assure you, I am only here to assist Dr. Shane in his daily tasks, Miss Silks. Nothing more." Might as well make *that* perfectly clear.

Mattie ran her gaze all the way down to Bella's toes

and back up, stopping at a few spots along the way on the return journey.

"That hideous attire does not fool me." Mattie waved a hand between them. "You are no nurse. And you look familiar. Did Emma Bradley send you?"

Bella cocked her head at the odd direction of their conversation. "Emma who?"

"Don't play ignorant." Mattie pointed a finger at Bella and shook it. "Emma Bradley is my fiercest competitor, as you well know."

Lizzie chose that moment to cough up a lung.

Bella made a face at the madam and quickly rushed to attend her patient. As she'd done before, she moved in behind the sick woman and lifted her thin shoulders off the bed.

Concern written on his face, Dr. Shane touched Lizzie's forehead with his fingertips. "She's hot."

"Is that normal?" Bella asked.

He gave a slight, almost imperceptible shake of his head. But when he spoke he used the calm baritone she was beginning to think of as his "doctor" voice. "Don't worry, Lizzie. I have some medicine that will ease your suffering."

The moment he stepped back, Mattie Silks rushed forward. She grabbed his shoulder and forced him to turn until he was facing her again.

"I demand to know who this girl is." She narrowed her eyes at Bella like a woman plotting murder. "Tell me now, or I'll have Jack throw the both of you out on your ears."

Dr. Shane ignored the verbal threat and simply shook his head at the obnoxious woman. "Mattie, as usual, you're overreacting. Miss Bella is my assistant." His lips pulled into a mocking grin. "And since you asked so nicely, her full name is Isabella Constance… *O'Toole*."

"O'Toole?" Her eyes flicked over Bella in disbelief. "As in Beauregard O'Toole?"

"Correct. My assistant is the reverend's sister."

Mattie tapped a finger against her chin. "His sister, you say?"

Dr. Shane blessed her with a mild shrug, as though he had all the time in the world to prove his point.

Still tapping her chin, Mattie studied Bella through narrowed eyelids.

"Well, then. That's *new* information." She heaved a dramatic sigh and waved a dismissive gesture in Bella's general direction. "Carry on."

Without further comment, Mattie Silks spun on her heel and left the room.

Bella blinked at the spot the infamous madam had previously occupied. "What just happened?"

"Mattie Silks happened," came the doctor's droll response.

She turned her head to look at him. For a moment, they simply stared at one another in silent camaraderie.

"Is that right," she said at last.

"The woman is an event unto herself," he added with a sardonic grin spreading across his lips.

"That's one way of putting it," Bella muttered.

He chuckled. "Miss Silks will grow on you. In time."

"Grow on me?" Bella shuddered at the thought. "Might I remind you, doctor, that mold, pestilence and all kinds of hideous diseases *grow* on people."

His lips twitched, but he maintained his composure

like the true gentleman he was. "At least the drama has passed for now."

Bella failed to agree with that inaccurate statement. In her estimation, the drama had only just begun.

Chapter Eight

Sunday morning brought cold, icy rain and the perfect reason to sleep in. Unfortunately, Bella could not indulge in such luxury. Beau would expect her to attend church with the rest of the family. He'd probably insist she sit in the front pew with Hannah and Mavis. Which, of course, would bring speculation from the rest of the congregation.

Bella would have to explain her unexpected visit and new position as Dr. Shane's assistant. All with a pleasant smile on her face.

"Oh, Lord, please. Not yet." Her heart gave two hard knocks. "I'm not ready."

Flopping on her back, Bella clasped the locket around her neck with a tight fist and stared at the tiled ceiling. The rain continued its steady scratching against the window in an unbroken knot of gloom and doom.

All the while, one question kept gnawing at her. Why couldn't she fully repent of her mistake with William and allow God to heal her broken heart?

Sudden tears blurred her vision, making it impossible to decipher the patterns swirling above her.

Bella desperately wanted to become the good Christian woman she'd been before William had entered her life. But she didn't know how.

Bella yanked the covers over her head and sorted through the bigger dilemma confronting her this morning.

How could she walk into the Lord's House and face her Heavenly Father knowing sin still lived in her heart?

Familiar guilt came hard and fast. She rolled over and buried her head under the pillow. She'd nearly destroyed a marriage. Not that she'd known at the time. But she should have. All the signs had been there. William's elusive schedule, for one. Always available at night, never present during the day.

Because she'd wanted to believe in William's love for her, Bella had stubbornly refused to see the truth. And didn't that make her as guilty as her viscount? Yes, and thus she wore his necklace as a reminder.

Bella burrowed deeper under the covers and tried to think up a reason to skip church.

Perhaps she could pretend illness.

Sitting up, she tested out a cough, tried for a sniffle. No good.

Beau would know she was faking and call her bluff, perhaps even summon Dr. Shane. No. Out of the question. Pretending illness was not an option. Shane Bartlett could not think ill of her. Bella would not allow it.

She punched air into the feather pillow. "What to do. What to do."

Perhaps she could claim she had another engagement. But where?

And with whom?

It would have to be someone who wouldn't be attending church this morning. Someone who wouldn't ask too many questions. A woman with her own hidden secrets. Yes, of course. That was it.

With Lizzie's pale, thin face in mind, Bella tossed the covers off her legs and quickly dressed for the day. While she was lacing up her boots, a firm knock came at her door.

Beau.

On full alert, Bella set her chin at a stubborn angle and rose. "Come in."

Smiling, Beau stuck his head into the room. He smiled. Broadly. "Ah, good. You're up."

She spun in a circle. "And dressed, too."

His smile widened. One look at that boyish grin and Bella knew Hannah had told him the news of his impending fatherhood at last. For a moment, Bella simply stared at her brother with wistfulness. At the sight of all that joy, she felt strangely unmoored, disoriented.

Left out.

Now…really…when had she grown so selfish?

Disgusted with the direction of her own thoughts, Bella forced an answering smile across her lips. "You're certainly happy this morning." She knew her voice sounded too sharp, too bitter, so she struggled to lighten her tone. "May I ask the cause?"

He leaned a shoulder against the doorjamb, his gaze filling with satisfaction. "God has blessed me more than I can fathom."

She waited for the rest.

"I'm going to be a father."

With those simple, heartfelt words, Bella's own concerns faded and she rushed to hug him. "Oh, Beau. I'm so pleased." And she was. Her brother deserved a happy family of his own. With a wife who adored him.

But now that Bella was sheltered in his arms, a deep sadness warred against her pleasure. With the conflicting emotions battling inside her, she clung a little longer than usual.

"You'll make a great father," she whispered, tears slipping along her lashes.

"Ah, Bella." He pulled back and wiped an errant tear away with his thumb. "I hate to see you so sad."

Good, solid Beau. He always worried about others first, never himself. Why did he have to be so good?

"I'm happy for you and Hannah," she said. "Truly. I am." But the loneliness was too loud in her voice, too thick and obvious for her words to ring true.

"Bella. Bella." Beau exhaled slowly. "I can't help you if you won't tell me what happened in London."

"I just needed a break," she said. "Nothing more."

"There's more." He dropped his gaze over her, shook his head. "But I know you well enough to know you won't reveal the full story until you're ready."

Relieved he wasn't going to force her to confide her secret, Bella hugged him once again. And tried not to sob into his shirt.

He patted her head like he had when she was little, and then set her at arm's length. "Church begins in less than an hour. Come eat and we'll be off."

Here it was. The moment of truth. "I… I won't be there." Her gaze chased around the room, landing everywhere but on Beau. "I have to see a patient this morning."

His gaze turned direct, making him look like a man

who knew when people were lying to him. "Where are you seeing this patient?"

Dropping her gaze to the toe of her boot, Bella bit down on her lip. "Mattie's."

"You're going to a brothel?"

Bella jerked her chin at him. "Yes."

"Now?"

"No one visits prostitutes on Sunday mornings. It's time someone did, for all the right reasons."

She knew she sounded bitter. Well, she *felt* bitter. Memories of William's indecent proposal poked at her. Women like Lizzie—like Bella—like all of Mattie's girls—were good enough for an evening's entertainment, but never good enough for respectable marriage proposals.

"I see."

"No, you don't."

Beau sighed. Heavily. "Then explain it to me, Bella. Help me to understand why you would choose to spend Sunday morning at a brothel rather than in worship."

Bella lifted a careless shoulder. "Don't make this more complicated than it is. Lizzie needs me." She reached to her bedside table. "And look, I'm bringing my Bible."

Beau's eyes went dark and turbulent, reminding Bella that her brother might be a compassionate preacher but he wasn't stupid. "A very realistic prop, little sister."

"How dare you."

"Am I wrong?"

It was her turn to sigh. Heavily. "Not completely. But Lizzie does need me."

"Fine, Bella. Have it your way." Annoyance spiked

his voice to a lower octave than usual. "I won't force you to come to church."

"Thank you."

"And I suppose some good will come of this." Beau crossed his arms over his chest and held her gaze. "There's no better cure for despondency than caring for the sick."

Disappointment had Bella biting down on her lip. It was obvious Beau didn't understand her motives for avoiding church. How could he? He'd never veered from the godly path the Lord had set before him. Not once.

How could a man who always made the right decision ever understand Bella's shame? Her regret?

It would seem her ugly little secret must remain hidden inside her forever. Unfortunately, no peace came with the realization, no triumph. Just bone-weary loneliness. And a strong sense she was making another mistake. This one larger than the first, and far more life altering.

Heavy-hearted, and from a safe distance, Bella watched Lizzie struggle for every breath. With each labored intake, Bella found herself sucking air into her own lungs with the same sporadic rhythm. Before meeting this woman, she would never have believed anyone could live through such agony.

How could Shane Bartlett confront such misery, day in and day out, with no end in sight? Because he was strong and good and anointed by God to heal the sick.

Realizing how much she was growing to admire the man, Bella pressed a hand to her throat. Dr. Shane was drawing feelings out of her no one—not even William—had before.

Fear began unfurling in her heart. Oh, no. No, no. Bella would not fall for another man. Not now. Not like this. Not so soon. She had to be careful this time. She had to be smart, and in control.

The first step was to focus on the reason she'd come to Mattie's in the first place.

Poor, poor Lizzie.

The illness was clearly taking its toll. The woman looked exhausted, her faded green eyes hopeless, as though she'd long ago given up on ever leading a happy, normal life.

Had Lizzie left her dreams behind, or had her dreams failed her somewhere along the way?

Would Bella become this woman one day if she didn't take care?

After covering her face with a cloth like Dr. Shane had taught her, Bella wrung out a rag from the washbasin and scooted toward the edge of the bed. She placed the wet rag onto Lizzie's forehead.

"There," she said. "That should help relieve some of the heat."

Lizzie relaxed into her pillow and sighed. "Thank you, Miss O'Toole."

"Call me Bella."

A hint of a smile crossed the sick woman's lips. "Thank you, Bella."

Smiling, Bella picked up the woman's hand and gripped it between her own. Words of encouragement seemed trite, yet she didn't know Lizzie well enough to discuss anything of real importance.

Perhaps she should start small. "Does Lizzie stand for Elizabeth?" she asked.

"It does. I…" Lizzie struggled through a breath, and

then another before continuing in a stilted tone. "I chose it after my favorite literary character, Elizabeth Bennett."

Pleasure swamped Bella at the declaration. The Jane Austen story was one of her favorites. Feeling a genuine connection now, she gave Lizzie's hand an affectionate squeeze and quoted the famous first line from *Pride and Prejudice.* "It is a truth universally acknowledged, that a single man in possession of a good fortune, must be in want of a wife."

Lizzie didn't actually grin in response, but her eyes crinkled at the edges.

"If I were to find a copy of the book, would you like me to read it to you?" Bella asked.

"I..." Lizzie's chin trembled. "Oh, yes. Please."

Heart hammering, Bella felt a rush of excitement. At last, she had found a way to offer comfort to this sad woman. "I will search out a copy this very afternoon."

Lizzie looked especially pleased, but then her gaze flicked to the doorway and her eyes widened.

Bella looked over her shoulder, caught sight of Mattie Silks standing in the doorway. "Good day, Miss Silks," she said without moving away from Lizzie.

The madam's eyebrows lifted at a proud angle. "Good day, Miss O'Toole."

Sighing, Bella rubbed a finger over her temple and wished she had a quick, pithy remark that would send the disturbing woman on her way.

Seconds ticked by before Mattie sailed into the room and lowered her gaze to Lizzie's face. The sorrow in the madam's eyes made her appear less harsh, accessible even. There could be no doubt she cared for this woman.

"I have a copy of *Pride and Prejudice* in my parlor," she said as she continued to stare at Lizzie's limp form.

Despite the hostility they'd shared at their first meeting, Bella wasn't prepared to alienate the madam completely. Not for Lizzie's sake, at any rate. "Would it be a bother if I asked to borrow the book, Miss Silks?"

Shifting away from the bed, Mattie regarded her with a long, serious expression. She remained silent so long, Bella feared the woman would refuse her request but then she said, "Come with me."

Bella shared a quick look with Lizzie when Mattie turned on her heels and left the room without a second glance.

"I'll be right back," Bella called over her shoulder.

Trotting to catch up, she uncovered her face and fell into step with the madam. A cold draft swept through the hallway, bringing the oddly pleasant scent of jasmine and musk. She hadn't expected that. Bella shivered in spite of herself and crossed her arms around her middle.

Mattie chose that moment to break the silence. "I would have expected a preacher's sister to be in church on a Sunday morning."

Bella ignored the feminine triumph in the madam's eyes and pretended grave interest in the crown molding running along the ceiling of the hallway. "I wanted to visit some of my new patients at a more leisurely pace. Sunday morning can be a lonely time if one cannot leave the bed."

"And yet the doctor feels the need to go to church."

Bella made a noncommittal sound. Why start an argument when they were getting on so well?

To her credit, the madam continued the rest of their

trek without speaking again. In blessed silence, she led Bella down a back stairwell, past the kitchen and inside a small parlor.

As expected, the decor was as gaudy as the rest of the brothel. Yet there was a sense of homeyness here that transcended the tacky red and gold furnishings, as though this room was meant for the madam's private use only.

Best of all, shelves lined an entire wall and were filled with books from top to bottom.

Who would have thought Mattie Silks was a reader?

She eyed Bella with a speculative glance. "Are you an actress or a singer or both?"

Bella took immediate offense at the blunt question. "You aren't much for small talk, are you, Miss Silks?"

With unexpected grace, Mattie lowered herself into a wingback chair and crossed her legs at the knees. "You carry yourself with great confidence, Miss O'Toole, especially for one so young. You must have trained all your life."

Surprised by the compliment, Bella found herself unable to do more than stare at the woman as she tried to understand the odd change in Mattie's behavior. She was different here, in this room, almost pleasant.

"I am an opera singer," Bella said in answer.

"Are you any good?" Mattie asked, swinging her foot to some unheard beat.

No one had ever asked Bella that question outright. Oddly enough, she found Mattie's interrogation refreshing, and thus decided to answer with complete honesty.

"The Lord has blessed me with a gift, Miss Silks. One I do not take lightly. Already I am winning lead roles from singers twice my age. If I continue to train and no damage comes to my voice, I will become the premiere opera singer of our day."

Mattie nodded. "Then you must continue to train."

"It's not that simple."

"Why not?"

How could Bella explain to this woman that if she continued to perform in the world she'd just escaped, she might well become some man's mistress?

Her experience with William had opened her eyes to the only type of man she would attract. If she didn't leave the stage, she might sacrifice her soul, her very salvation, for her dreams. When the singing was over she would be just another Lizzie, only in a more comfortable cage.

And yet, singing opera was all she knew.

"I believe God has a different plan for me now."

Oh, Lord, please let that be true. Please, please, please.

Mattie looked at her oddly but didn't respond. Just as the silence grew uncomfortable, the madam shook her head sadly and rose from her chair.

With a flowing gait, she ambled over to the shelves, pulled out a book and handed the thin volume to Bella.

Bella slowly opened the cover. From the worn binding and curled pages she could see the novel had been read often.

"It's my favorite, too." Mattie touched Bella's hand. "I find great comfort in the happy ending."

Bella locked gazes with the older woman and a startling sense of understanding passed between them. The connection should have been disturbing, should have been terrifying, but it wasn't.

Had Bella found a kindred spirit in the notorious madam?

Perhaps underneath their individual professions, underneath their different life choices, Mattie Silks and Bella O'Toole were more alike than any would believe.

But did that make them objects of pity or women destined to become friends?

Chapter Nine

Just as Beau had suggested, Shane found his errant assistant hiding out in Lizzie's bedroom. He tried not to be disappointed, but he couldn't ignore the fact that Miss O'Toole had chosen to spend Sunday morning in a brothel instead of church.

Leaning against the doorjamb, he studied the mysterious woman who seemed to surprise him at every turn. She certainly made a pretty picture, perched gracefully on a chair next to the bed. Her head was bent over a book. And as she read aloud, her soft, lilting accent imparted a whimsical mood in the otherwise austere room.

Shifting his focus to Lizzie, Shane marveled at the change in his patient. With her eyes half-closed, she looked the most peaceful he'd seen her in weeks.

Out of the corner of his eye, he caught a flutter of material and realized there was a third occupant. Mattie Silks sat in a chair on the other side of the bed, holding herself serenely, pleasantly. Quietly!

Shane blinked.

At the sight of the three most unlikely women sitting

together, an eerie sense of déjà vu whipped through him. In their own way, each reminded him of his mother.

Lizzie was the woman his mother had become in her final months. Worn out, sick, beyond all reasonable hope.

Mattie was the woman his mother might have become had she lived. A woman who had outlasted the mistakes of her youth and now did what she thought she had to do to survive the harsh world around her.

Lastly, there was Miss O'Toole. Despite the seemingly innocent picture she presented to the world, she reminded him of the mother from his youth. Beautiful, full of promise, the personification of possibilities. And just like his mother, Shane sensed Miss O'Toole was one bad choice away from a dark, dismal future.

Which was absurd, and probably a case of bad lighting. Bella O'Toole was the daughter of solid Christian parents and the sister of a dedicated preacher. She was nothing like Amanda Bartlett.

Yet…what did Shane really know about the woman he'd hired to assist him?

Was she ministering to Lizzie out of charity, as it would seem on the surface? Or had some other motive brought her here today, something less respectable? Something unthinkable.

A muscle locked in his jaw.

Pushing from the doorway, he cleared his throat and stepped into the room.

Miss O'Toole lifted her gaze from the page. At the same moment, a rogue sunbeam kissed the top of her head, casting a thousand shades of gold in its wake.

Shane froze. All thought evaporated into a black void.

Seemingly caught in the same trance, Miss O'Toole

held his glance. After a moment, however, her gaze softened, warmed. And his pulse scrambled.

How could a simple look hold such power?

Slowly, distant sounds broke through his mind, piece by piece: the rocking of a chair, the ticking of a clock, his own shattered breathing.

And *still* he stared.

Blushing, Miss O'Toole lowered her gaze. She stumbled over a sentence, sighed and then closed the book. "Dr. Shane, we weren't expecting to see you this afternoon."

When her gaze met his again he found the connection between his brain and his mouth had disappeared.

With a rustle of skirts, Mattie sprang to her feet, drawing his attention away from Miss O'Toole at last.

"What a pleasant surprise…doctor." Her tone said otherwise.

"Mattie," he replied on an equally flat note. From the calculating gleam in her eyes, Shane knew better than to engage the madam in further conversation.

Of course, what he did—or did not do—hardly mattered. This was Mattie Silks. Nothing on his part could deter her once she'd resolved to have a bit of fun at his expense.

Swishing her hips in a telling manner, she made her way across the room straight to him. "Dare I hope this is a social call?" she asked. "Have you admitted to your loneliness at long last?"

Shane frowned. Mattie had asked him that question often enough. He usually had a witty comeback that shut her up. But he would not play her game today, especially in front of the other women. "I am here to see to my patient, Miss Silks. As always."

She seemed to accept his response, but then he made a fundamental mistake. He glanced at Miss O'Toole.

Mattie, of course, followed his gaze.

Eyes narrowed, she measured. Calculated. Then flipped him a knowing smile. "So it's like that, is it?"

Swallowing back a hasty response, Shane forced a bland expression on his face.

"I came to fetch Miss O'Toole, as well." His tone came out lower and deadlier than he had planned. "Her brother is worried about her."

Smirking, Mattie placed a well-manicured hand on his arm and relaxed into a hip-thrusting pose. "Now, doctor, why the pretense? We both know *you* were the one worried about our lovely opera singer."

He glared at the talons wrapped around his arm. When she didn't release him right away, he moved out of reach. "Don't be obvious, Mattie. It does you no credit."

"Me?" She laughed. A short, tinkling, terrible sound of glee. "Maybe you should glance at your face in the mirror over there," she pointed her thumb over her right shoulder, "and see what 'obvious' really looks like."

Shane pressed his lips into a flat line. "I'm warning you. Don't start. Not today."

"And I'm warning you." Mattie's eyes hardened. "Remember who you're dealing with, *doctor*."

Shane opened his mouth to end the childish battle but was interrupted by Miss O'Toole's soft sigh. "Dr. Shane. Please…" Her voice flowed into another sigh.

Shane switched his full attention to her and waited for the rest.

"I…that is…" She quickly cast her eyes to the book in her lap, chipped at the binding with her fingernail.

"Please be so kind as to tell my brother there is no need to worry. As you can see, I am quite well."

Shane saw no such thing.

Not only was Miss O'Toole keeping company with a notorious madam, he'd caught the quick slice of shame in her eyes before she'd lowered her gaze. The gesture reminded him that Bella O'Toole was more than his friend's innocent sister, more than his competent assistant. She was a woman harboring a secret, one she refused to reveal to her brother or anyone else.

An ugly thought occurred to him. Had Miss O'Toole shared her worries with Mattie Silks or even Lizzie?

Frustration reared, and something darker, uglier, but he fought back the troubling emotions. What did it matter who Miss O'Toole shared her secret with? He had enough to worry about without adding a beautiful, wounded opera singer to the long list of people who needed him.

But, in this, Shane knew he lied to himself. He *wanted* this woman to turn to him. He wanted to be her confidant, her *only* confidant. The strength of the wish nearly knocked him to his knees. He felt the shock in his gut. *In his heart.*

Needing to return to familiar ground, he cleared his mind of all thought save one. "I'd like to examine Lizzie now."

Miss O'Toole rose. "Of course. Miss Silks was on her way out when you arrived." She shot Mattie a pleading look. "Weren't you?"

The madam stared at her for several seconds. A silent message passed between them and then, wonder of wonders, Mattie slowly nodded. "Of course. I'll leave you to your business."

Without looking at Lizzie or Shane, Mattie retrieved the book from Miss O'Toole and headed for the door. Stopping at the threshold, she looked back over her shoulder. "Bella?"

"Yes?"

"You may borrow this anytime you wish." She waved the book above her head. "You know where to find it."

"I certainly do. And thank you. It's a very kind offer." A genuine smile spread across Miss O'Toole's lips. "One I plan to accept often."

Mattie appeared ready to say more but she snapped her head around and left the room without another word.

At this odd interaction between the unlikely pair, a jolt of alarm spread through Shane. Mattie might have a soft spot deep, deep, deep, *deep* in her heart, but she was also a shrewd businesswoman, ruthless to the point of cruelty when she wanted something. Or someone.

Was she befriending Miss O'Toole for her own end?

Shane didn't have time to contemplate that awful thought before the door clicked shut, and Miss O'Toole turned into his assistant once again.

"You'll be glad to know Lizzie's feeling much better today." She removed the compress from their patient's forehead and dipped it in the bowl next to the bed. "Aren't you, dear?"

Lizzie smiled up at her. "Much."

Recognizing Miss O'Toole's closed expression, Shane held on to his questions—for now—and moved deeper into the room. With a flick of his wrist, he shed his coat. After rolling up his sleeves, he took Lizzie's wrist in one hand and pulled out his watch with the other.

All business now, he counted the heartbeats, pleased

to discover her pulse thumped strongly against his fingertips. Her coloring was good today, less ashy, and her face wasn't as drawn as usual. For a brief moment, he allowed himself to believe she might recover. At least long enough to change the condition of her soul, if not her body.

Healing the sick was what Shane had been called to do, especially women with nowhere else to turn for medical care. But their salvation mattered more. If he could afford them enough time to resolve their relationship with God then he'd fulfilled one of his purposes in life.

Unfortunately, he'd never known his mother's heart, or whether she'd turned to Jesus in her final moments of life. He'd been too young and too caught up in his bitterness toward his father to care enough to pursue the matter. He hadn't even prayed for her soul. For that alone, he'd failed her.

He would not fail the others.

With that thought, he caught Miss O'Toole's eye.

She was staring at him, her gaze full of concern, as though she could read his troubled thoughts.

A reflex to share the pain of his distress came fast. His eyes stung from the effort to form his thoughts into words. Just as he started to speak, he was hit by a wall of common sense and kept his mouth shut.

He had to remember Miss O'Toole's presence in his life was temporary. All too soon she would leave for London or New York or some other world stage miles away from Colorado.

Unlike his mother, Shane would not fall for someone out of reach. He ignored the small whisper in his head that suggested it might be too late.

* * *

"Dr. Bartlett, you left your coat," Bella called after his retreating back.

He turned to look at her with an absent expression on his face. "What coat?"

She waved the garment in her hand. "This one."

"Ah." He gave her a sheepish grin. "That one."

With clipped steps, he returned to her side.

As she helped him shrug into his coat, a wave of fondness crashed over her and she had to resist the urge to smooth the dark fabric across his broad shoulders. Balling her hands into fists, she followed him out of Lizzie's room and down the long hallway that led to the front stairwell.

Walking silently next to the doctor, Bella realized she had learned a few truths about the man in their week-long acquaintance. Although brilliant, he spoke to his patients in a way that made them feel accepted, and heard. He was truly a compassionate healer who also carried the burden of his patients' pain in his heart, even if he refused to acknowledge that fact out loud.

In spite of the distance he kept between him and the rest of the world, she saw his goodness, his integrity.

And the more time she spent around Shane Bartlett, the more she wondered what it would be like to share the healthy give and take of a relationship with a godly man. She was sure it would be nothing like her involvement with William.

Lord Crawley had offered her protection and worldly luxury. But he'd never offered himself. Or his life.

How had Bella missed that?

Easy enough. She'd been dazzled by William's dark

masculine beauty, by his well-timed compliments, and by her own love for him.

But, truly, how could she have loved such a man? When wonderful, decent men like Shane Bartlett existed in the world. She cast him a quick glance, then sighed at the truth that flashed through her mind.

She wasn't good enough for men like Shane.

She'd accepted William's suit because deep down she'd sensed the awful truth about herself. She had deserved nothing better than what William had offered.

Swallowing back a rising sob, she followed the doctor down the steep stairwell. Perhaps her lack of goodness explained her affinity for Mattie Silks and Lizzie. In their company she felt less sinful by comparison. Oh, she knew she was deluding herself. There was no hierarchy of sin in the Lord's eyes. All sin was wrong and led to separation from God. But knowing a thing and believing it were two separate matters.

Drawing close to the main floor, she looked around her, desperate to rid herself of her depressing thoughts. Unfortunately, the gaudiness and sour smells matched the ugliness of her soul. Would she ever be cleansed of her sins? Was she destined to live a life as black as her soul, like the women who conducted their business here?

Her eyes filled with tears and she nearly collided into Dr. Shane as he drew to a sudden stop.

"Oh." She stepped away too quickly and fell backward, landing on the bottom step.

"Miss O'Toole." The concern in the doctor's voice made her feel...worse.

He offered her his hand. "My apologies."

For a tense moment she stared at his outstretched fingers. This competent, compassionate man was simply offering her his assistance, nothing more. Why, then, did she sense he was asking her a question? And that her answer mattered.

No, she was being overly dramatic. An unpleasant character trait she was only just discovering about herself.

Gathering her courage, she placed her hand in his, palm to palm. As his fingers closed over hers, a sense of calm rippled through her.

Staring into her eyes, he pulled her to her feet, blinked and then quickly released her hand. His gaze, however, stayed locked firmly with hers, as it had in Lizzie's room. And just like earlier, all that intensity directed at Bella made her feel wrapped in safety.

It was an uncomfortable, thoroughly wonderful sensation.

"Are you all right?" He shoved at his hair, leaving a few ends sticking out when he pulled his hand away. "You appear upset."

If only he knew the half of it. "I am quite well," she said with enough over-the-top enthusiasm to make her sound like a rank amateur.

Disgusted with her inability to tap into her usual poise around this man, she took a step back, forced her gaze to a spot on the tip of her shoes. "I always find it hard to leave Lizzie."

He placed a finger under her chin and applied gentle pressure until she looked at him again.

"Why is that?" he asked, his voice soothing. He was in full doctor mode, but there was something more personal in his eyes. For the first time since leaving London, Bella wanted to confess all. To him. *Only him.*

Would he understand? Or would he pity her? Once he knew her secret, would he shove her into a different category of women and quit looking at her as if she mattered, truly mattered?

Bella couldn't bear the possibility of this man thinking less of her. That, she realized, would be far worse than what William had done to her.

"Miss O'Toole," he urged. "Tell me why you find it hard to leave Lizzie."

She took note of his patient expression and was suddenly frightened. And oddly hopeful. Confused. And so very, very sad. "I... I don't want her to be alone."

Which was true enough.

"She has a house full of women around her."

Which was also true. And completely beside the point. "It's not the same. They don't understand her."

"And you do?"

Pressing her hands palm to palm, she threaded her fingers tightly together. "Yes."

He reached out, laid a hand on her shoulder. "Are you trying to save her soul?"

He was so handsome, so pure-minded that she answered with complete honesty. "No. I am far from qualified."

"No one is qualified," he said gently. "As your own brother has said often enough, we humans plant the seeds. God does the rest."

At the utter conviction in his voice, Bella clasped the necklace around her throat and whispered, "Perhaps I have no seed to plant."

He stared at her so long that Bella was sure he could see straight into her soul. "Give it time."

Bella sighed. "Yes, of course."

But she feared time was running out for her. If she didn't atone for her sin soon she might never be able to come back into the fold. And where would that leave her then?

Chapter Ten

Several mornings later, Bella stood alone in Beau and Hannah's kitchen. Having slept poorly, her steps were sluggish as she headed to the window overlooking the backyard.

A misty fog slithered along the frozen ground, twisting around the base of each tree. A patch of pearly gray light hit the branches above declaring that a new day dawned. But Bella found no joy in the promise of a fresh morning.

Cold air slipped its icy fingers through a seam between glass and casement. Bella shivered. Familiar tension knotted along her spine. Seeking relief, she closed her eyes and clasped her hands together. *Dear Heavenly Father—*

She cut herself off, desperately searching for the right words to pray. None came. She could confess her sin for the thousandth time, but it wouldn't take away what she'd done. Oh, she knew her God was a forgiving God. She just couldn't seem to forgive herself.

What had Paul said to the Ephesians? Something about forgetting what was behind and straining toward what was ahead. Yet, how could Bella move forward when she couldn't let go of the past?

Opening her eyes, she wrapped her fingers around William's locket and tugged. Hard. As always, she released the necklace before the chain broke.

Hot tears of frustration stung her eyes. What was wrong with her? Why couldn't she remove the wretched piece of jewelry?

Oh, Lord, help me. Guide me.

"Bella?" Hannah's soft voice sliced through her thoughts. "May I join you?"

Bella spun around to face her sister-in-law. "Of… of course."

Hannah glided farther into the room. Thankfully, instead of dragging Bella into a conversation, she held out her hand and produced a sealed letter. "This came for you yesterday." She rolled it in her palm. "It looks important."

At the sight of the expensive paper, Bella sucked in a tight breath. One glance was all it took for her to recognize William's seal. Her entire body turned ice-cold. She needed to sit, but she gathered her courage and accepted the letter with trembling fingers before her legs collapsed and she dropped into a nearby chair.

She'd half dreaded, half hoped this day would come, the day William recognized his mistake and called her back to him. But now that he had found her, Bella felt nothing. Wanted nothing. *Believed* nothing.

Nothing. Nothing. Nothing.

With little worry lines forming between her eyebrows, Hannah stooped in front of her and rested her hand on Bella's knee. "I see I was right not to show this to your brother."

Bella nodded, gulped in a ragged breath.

"It's from a man." Hannah said the words as a statement.

Unable to answer, Bella could only stare at her sister-in-law. She needed more control, less confusion. But her mind refused to cooperate.

"Is he the reason you left London?"

Biting her bottom lip, Bella studied the red seal with the viscount's family crest pressed into the wax. "I... I... I don't know how he found me."

"He?"

The muscles in her stomach quivered. "William Gordon, Lord Crawley."

"A suitor?"

"Yes." Bella rubbed a shaky palm along the top of her thigh, shuttered. "No. Not in the way you would think."

Tugging one of Bella's hands into hers, Hannah spoke very softly. "Bella, whatever has happened, whatever he did to you, you can tell me."

Bella fought back tears, a useless indulgence when control was needed. She wanted to rail, to pound her fists in the air. She sighed instead. "You wouldn't understand."

"You might be surprised." Hannah kept her voice low. "For years I traveled with an acting troupe. Your brother, Tyler, was one of the more notorious members. Thanks to his example alone, I've seen my share of shocking behavior." She gave Bella an ironic smile. "He did run off with my sister, after all. My *engaged* sister."

Of course. Bella knew the ugly details well enough. The scandal was still a sore subject in her family. Tyler had been wrong to travel alone with Hannah's sister without the benefit of marriage, especially when she was engaged to another man. Tyler meant well, most of the time, but he could be selfish and an unconscionable rogue of the first order. Hannah had seen him at his worst.

Hot shame spread through Bella, shame for what Tyler had done to this woman and her family. No, Bella would not allow Beau's new wife to discover that yet another member of the famous O'Toole family had a sinful heart.

"I'm sorry, Hannah." She drew her hand free. "I… can't."

A look of disappointment spread across the other woman's face. "I won't press. But when you're ready, I'll be here to listen. No judgment. No condemnation."

Shaken by her sister-in-law's kindness, Bella refused to do anything so dramatic as cry.

"I'll leave you to your letter now." Hannah gave her hand one last pat, rose and then left the kitchen with her typical grace.

Alone again, Bella turned the letter over and over in her hand. The monumental significance of William actually finding her here in Colorado was staggering. Frightening.

What could he possibly have to say to her now? Had his circumstances changed? Was he renewing his suit, this time with a more respectable end?

She fingered the locket around her neck. It felt lighter this morning. Surely, a trick of her imagination. After all, nothing had changed. Not for her.

Or had it? An image of Shane Bartlett flitted across her mind. Integrity. Courage. The doctor had both. Lord Crawley had little of either.

If Bella had an ounce of sense, she would toss William's letter in the nearest fire and that would be the end of that.

Unfortunately, Bella was discovering her ratio of sense to senselessness was far out of balance, with senselessness winning hands down.

Read it? Toss it?

She would decide later.

Shoving the paper into the pocket of her apron, she tried to put the matter out of her mind and focus on the day ahead.

Then again…

Perhaps she should read the letter now, just get it over with. Or perhaps she would look at it tonight, when she was alone, with endless hours of solitude stretching before her. Yes, maybe then, when there was no chance of interruption, she would read the words William had sent halfway across the world to her.

Or…maybe not.

Something had happened since Shane had last seen Miss O'Toole, something that put her on edge. She was pleasant enough, on the surface, but the difference was there. In her eyes. If he didn't know better he'd say she had the look his mother always had right before his father made his weekly visit—an odd mixture of hope and dread, melancholy and joy.

With his own emotions still in a tangle from Sunday afternoon, Shane chose to ignore the change in Miss O'Toole. Jaw tight, he stepped aside in order to allow her to enter Charity House ahead of him.

As usual, they were met at the door by Laney Dupree, Marc's wife and co-owner of the orphanage. Her arms were filled with a squirming miniature version of herself.

"Good morning, Laney." Shane reached out and ruffled her young daughter's hair. "Laurette. You're both looking fine this morning."

Laurette pulled her thumb out of her mouth and grinned. But Laney's face scrunched into a frown. "Shane. Miss O'Toole, thank God you've finally arrived."

She lowered her daughter to the ground. Laurette clutched Laney's skirt with one hand and held a doll tight against her chest with the other. Sensing her mother's tense mood, the child adopted an identical expression of worry on her face.

"What is it?" Miss O'Toole asked before Shane had a chance. "What's happened?"

"I don't know, precisely," Laney admitted, her gaze darting between them. "Six of the children came to me yesterday with runny noses and complaining of headaches, nothing we haven't seen before. I kept the lot of them home this morning and sent the rest on to school as usual. But in the last hour, two have grown worse."

By the end of her explanation, Shane was already striding for the stairs. "Did you separate the children from the rest?"

"Last night. I put the boys in the tiger room. The girls are in the castle room." She turned to Miss O'Toole, her eyes serious and worried, her hands wringing together in front of her. "We always try to keep the sick children separate from the rest. Illness can spread quickly."

A thick blanket of tension fell between them, but Miss O'Toole patted Laney's shoulder in a feminine gesture of solidarity. "Makes perfect sense to me."

Shane continued forward, stopped.

"What about the babies?" he asked.

"Megan is with them. She's kept them away from the others since yesterday."

Shane was glad to hear it. And especially grateful they only had two babies in residence at the moment. If illness spread they would be hit the hardest.

Conflicting emotions tugged at him but he shoved them out of his mind. He needed to gather as much information as possible and he needed to do it with a clear head. "Tell me the precise symptoms of each."

"All six have runny nose, coughing, sneezing and sore throats." Laney's tone never varied, her eyes never left his face, but Shane could feel her concern as though she were screaming at him. "Miles and Stacy have progressed to a loss of appetite."

On the surface, the symptoms could mean anything. Various diagnoses were shooting around one another in his mind like moths to light.

A tug on his pant leg broke his concentration and he glanced down.

"Stacy has goo in her eyes," Laurette added gravely. "White goo."

That certainly narrowed down the possibilities. He looked up at Laney again. "Do they feel hot to the touch?"

Laney nodded.

All right then. The symptoms could mean bad colds. But Shane noted that neither Laney nor Laurette showed any signs of illness. Added to the "white goo" description he feared they had another case of measles on their hands. The disease had spread through the orphanage six months ago. Laney, Laurette and half of the children had suffered.

The other half had been spared, Miles and Stacy among them.

Shane turned to Miss O'Toole and asked her a question he should have asked long before now. "What childhood illnesses have you had?"

Urgency made his voice clipped. She didn't seem to mind. "Pox, mumps and measles."

"Good. Then let's go have a look."

One by one they started up the stairs, but Miss O'Toole held up her hand to stop Laney and Laurette. "You two stay here. At least until we know what we're dealing with."

Laney looked prepared to argue, but Miss O'Toole spoke again. "We don't want you and your daughter exposed."

Normally, Shane would have had Laney join him in the sickroom. However, that was before he'd hired an assistant, a very smart assistant who had recognized the larger ramifications before Shane had himself.

"Miss O'Toole is right," he said. "It would be better if you stayed downstairs. For now."

Laney shook her head, started forward.

Miss O'Toole laid a gentle hand on her arm. "I'll bring you a report as soon as we have more information."

Eyebrows slamming together, Laney tried to push forward but Laurette tugged on her hand. "Mama? Why are you so ang-ery?"

An odd sound came out of Laney's mouth, not quite a snort of frustration, not quite a sob.

Laurette popped her thumb in her mouth and whimpered.

With visible effort, Laney cleared her face of all emotion and forced a smile across her lips. "I'm not angry, baby. Just worried."

Laurette gave her a dubious look that had four-year-old doubt written all over it.

Laney closed her eyes and blew out a long sigh. "Why don't you come along and help me make bread for tonight's supper?"

"Really?" The child grinned around her thumb. "You never letted me do that before."

"There's always a first time." Laney lifted the child in her arms and hugged her tightly against her.

Laurette struggled. "You holding too tight."

Sighing, Laney shifted the child in her arms and glanced at Miss O'Toole. "We'll be in the kitchen when you have more to tell me."

Before setting off in the opposite direction, Laney blessed Shane with a sharp glare of warning, as if to say he better remember she was waiting for news.

Shane barely noticed. He was too busy marveling at how Miss O'Toole had taken control of the situation.

Yet again, the woman had surprised him. He was starting to like the sensation. He was starting to like it a lot.

But then she quirked her eyebrow at him. "Let's get to work, shall we?"

Realizing he was staring and feeling like a besotted idiot, he turned slightly to his left and waved her forward. "After you."

She sent him a quick lovely smile as she passed,

but her eyes remained distant. Just as well. There were six miserable children needing his complete attention.

He stared up at the ceiling. Once he focused on his patients, he would be immune to Miss O'Toole's surprises.

He was sure of it.

Of course, as self-deception went, this was one of his best efforts yet.

Chapter Eleven

From the bleak look on Dr. Shane's face, Bella expected a dismal prognosis. Nevertheless, she kept her opinions to herself as she joined him on the examination of each patient. Looking around, she realized she'd never been in this room before.

There were eight beds in all, with an equal number of matching chests of drawers. No expense had been spared. The high-quality design of the furniture spoke of an attention to detail that most orphanages ignored.

Of course, the exquisite furnishings were nothing compared to the murals on the walls. Bella now understood why Laney had referred to this as the castle room. The paintings brought to mind childhood fairy tales and happily-ever-afters. Each scene made Bella want to return to her innocent youth, where dreams still existed, where every boy would grow up to become a courageous knight and every girl a beautiful princess.

Along the top edges of the walls Bible verses had been painted in a glorious, flowing script. She read one from Matthew 19, *Let the children come to me, and do not hinder them.* And another from Isaiah 43, *Fear not, for I have redeemed you. I have summoned you by name.* And her favorite, from Hebrews 13:5, *Never will I leave you; never will I forsake you.*

As she read the Scriptures silently to herself, Bella experienced an overwhelming sense of peace. It was as if God was wrapping His unconditional love around her and cloaking her in His warmth.

Dr. Shane's quick intake of breath had Bella turning her attention to him. He leaned over Kimberly, a girl of thirteen who was normally full of energy and good cheer. This morning, her cheeks looked flushed as she wrestled inside a fitful sleep.

"What can I do to help?" Bella whispered.

"Come closer." His words came out even, but Bella could tell by the slight tensing of his jaw and flare of his nostrils that he was deeply worried.

Bending over for a better look, Bella detected the beginnings of a blotchy rash on Kimberly's face. Stifling a gasp, she glanced at Dr. Shane. By the stress lines around his mouth, it was obvious he didn't like what he saw.

Bella didn't either.

Grim-faced, he nudged the girl awake with a gentle hand to her shoulder.

Kimberly moaned and her lashes fluttered open.

"Hi, there," he said in a serious tone. "I hear you're not feeling well."

"My head hurts. I ache everywhere." She kicked her legs out from under the covers. "And I'm hot. Really hot."

Don't forget cranky, Bella silently added.

Seemingly immune to the teenager's sour mood, Dr. Shane turned her head to the right and brushed a clump of hair behind her ear. "Miss O'Toole. Tell me what you see."

Bella studied the area he indicated. "The skin is red, looks like the rash is spreading."

"It is." He pointed to their patient's neck next. "But it hasn't spread there. Yet."

Dr. Shane turned Kimberly's head back toward him. "How long have you been feeling bad?"

"A couple days." Her eyes filled with tears. "What's wrong with me? Am I going to die?" she whimpered with dramatic emphasis.

An actress in the making. Bella liked her more and more.

Clearly amused by the performance, Dr. Shane smiled. "No, you're not going to die. But I need to check the other girls and boys before I make my final diagnosis."

His hands were so beautiful, Bella thought as she watched him sweep Kimberly's hair back over her ear, so full of healing. Bella wanted to weep, but she didn't understand why.

Surprised by her reaction, she caught her trembling bottom lip between her teeth and followed Dr. Shane to another young girl on the other side of the room.

This one looked decidedly worse. The rash had moved to her neck and she had the infamous "white goo" in her eyes.

After checking behind her ears and studying the eye infection, Dr. Shane sighed. "It's what I feared."

Bella lifted her eyebrows.

"Measles."

The air in her lungs pulsated hot, then cold. "That's highly contagious, isn't it?"

Nodding, he raked both hands through his hair. "The only remedy is bed rest."

"I remember. A bad case whipped through our theater company when I was seven. I was confined to bed for a week." She eyed him carefully. "I'm surprised this hasn't hit the orphanage before now."

"It has. Six months ago. I'll have to retrieve my records to clarify which children contracted the disease last time." He scrutinized the room, his gaze sharp and measuring. "There may be more sick children before the day is out. The symptoms don't usually develop until about a week after a child has been exposed."

A week? "Oh."

He considered Bella with the same measuring look he'd shot around the room. "I'd like you to stay until the contagious period passes. In the meantime, I'll attend our other patients alone."

The panic started at her knees, moved up her spine and ended in a tremble that rattled the tips of her hair. "I…" Bella broke eye contact.

What could she say? That she didn't feel comfortable around the children? That she'd rather spend her time at Mattie's brothel where she couldn't do much damage to souls already tainted?

What would he think of her then?

What did that say about the selfish state of her heart?

Heavenly Father, give me the courage to put these little ones first, and please, please, keep my penchant for making bad decisions from rubbing off on them.

Misunderstanding her anxiety, Dr. Shane touched her hand. "There will be many moments of boredom, I'm sure. Is there anything I can do for you while I'm out? Anything I can bring from your brother's home?"

A little courage? "Nothing. No, wait. There is one thing you can do for me. I…"

"Yes?" he urged when she didn't continue.

Oddly nervous, Bella shifted from one foot to the other. "Will you check on Lizzie, let her know I won't be able to read to her for a while?"

He smiled with his eyes. "Consider it done."

The moment he turned to leave, Bella lowered her gaze back to Stacy. Without looking up, she called after him just as he crossed the threshold. "You forgot your coat."

"How did you know that? You're not even looking at me." His voice sounded both surprised and oddly frustrated, as though he wasn't sure he liked her knowing him so well.

Moving across the room, she lifted a shoulder. "I know because you always forget your coat."

She reached for the garment and held it out of reach when he tried to snatch it away from her. "Allow me."

He glared at her but then slowly stuck out one of his arms. As was becoming their custom, she helped him shrug into the first sleeve and then the next.

When he turned back to face her, she tugged on the lapels and had to fight the urge to reach up and even out his hair where he'd pulled his fingers through the glossy chaos a few too many times.

In truth, the man was a mess. His future wife would have her hands full organizing him on a daily basis. She would have to be patient and kind, smart and fast on her feet. And, most of all, she would have to be willing to share him with his patients.

Did Bella want to be that fortunate woman? Was such a beautiful reality possible?

No. Wishful thinking, at best. After all, the sealed letter in her pocket reminded Bella of her real worth in a man's eyes.

Bella felt the urge to weep again. But this time, she knew exactly why.

After explaining the situation to Laney, Shane's next stop was his office. On his way, he passed the Charity House School, wondering how many children were already sick but weren't showing symptoms.

There wasn't much he could do at this point. His best defense was to gather his records as quickly as possible and return in time to examine the children who had missed the first round of measles.

For now, they were best left at school, away from the sicker ones.

Needing a moment to gather his thoughts, he drew his horse to a stop and studied the school's building. The outside looked like the rest of the mansions in the neighborhood: sturdy, elegant and fashionable.

In seven short years, with diligence and a lot of prayer, Marc and Laney Dupree had created a safe haven within a larger, harsher world of prejudice and hatred. It had begun with Charity House, had expanded to the addition of the school, and now, thanks to Beauregard O'Toole and his gifted wife, there was a church.

God's hand was clearly at work.

And Shane wanted to do his part for the effort. His dream was to add a clinic nearby, perhaps even a connecting shelter for women in trouble. But that would take money. And since most of his patients didn't have the funds to pay for his services, he was far short of an acceptable down payment. God willing, the funding would come one day and then Shane's clinic would become a reality.

Refusing to lose faith, no matter the odds stacked against him, Shane flicked his horse's reins and steered his wagon toward town.

The Rocky Mountains stood on his left, God's handiwork evident in their stark beauty. The cool air felt clean and fresh in his lungs. There was only a slight bite in the breeze today. A good sign. Winter was still a few weeks off.

As he turned onto Market Street, the heavy traffic demanded his complete concentration. Vendors, merchants and horse-drawn carriages formed a labyrinth of chaotic activity.

It was all so familiar. And yet, something felt… wrong. The hair on the back of his neck stood at attention, much as it had when he'd picked up Miss O'Toole this morning and noted her change in mood.

Shane was a man who dealt in facts, not feelings. Thus, he drew his horse to a stop outside his building and willed the sensation to pass.

Climbing down, he grabbed his medical bag and scanned the area. Nothing seemed out of the ordinary. Except…

A tall, brown-haired gentleman, dressed in a well-designed suit stared at him from across the street. Shane hadn't seen that sort of man since his youth, and only when he'd ventured beyond the Bowery to the more expensive neighborhoods of New York.

The man looked like a solicitor, or maybe a big-city banker. Or whatever he was, he certainly didn't belong in Denver.

Bothered that the sight of a stranger could disturb

him so easily and wanting to return to Charity House as quickly as possible, Shane broke into a swift trot to avoid a fast-moving carriage and entered his office with a frown. The room stood empty, the air heavy and stuffy. A good cleaning was long past due but it would have to wait until the crisis at Charity House was under control.

Thoughts of the orphanage reminded Shane of his promise to check on Lizzie for Miss O'Toole.

Gathering the necessary supplies he would need for later, he grabbed the Charity House record book off the shelf and headed out.

Once back on the street, he gazed around him, pleased to discover the man in the stylish city clothes was no longer in the immediate area.

Ten minutes later, Shane only had to knock once before the big double doors of Mattie's brothel swung open. Although too early for any real activity, there were a few men taking their lunch break with the girls.

Before Shane could see what was what, or rather who was who, Mattie sidled up to him, grinning like a tomcat over his next easy prey.

"Well, well. Dr. Shane. Isn't it a little late in the day for you?" She craned her neck to glance around him. "Is your lovely opera singer with you?"

Shane's gut tightened at the calculating glare in her eyes. "There's been a breakout of measles at the orphanage," he said. "*My assistant* is tending the sick children."

"What a good girl. You tell her I asked about her."

When speaking of Miss O'Toole, Mattie had a softness about her around the edges that scared Shane spitless. "Don't try to recruit her."

Mattie tossed her hair over her shoulders and hitched

her hip against his. "Shame on you, doctor, I wouldn't think of such a thing."

Yes, you would. "She's mine, Mattie."

A rush of satisfaction flicked in her eyes. "Is she now?"

"I meant, she's *my* assistant. Leave her alone."

"Right. Right." She bumped her hip against his again. "I know what you meant."

Frustration sent a growl humming in his throat. "I'm here to check on Lizzie."

Mattie's eyes filled with delight. Then she smiled. "She's over there." She waved her hand toward the center of the room.

Shane's stomach dropped. Just as Mattie indicated, Lizzie reclined on a red-velvet divan. Her shaking fingers held a champagne glass none too steady, the golden liquid swishing precariously close to the rim. Worst of all, she was entertaining a gentleman in every wrong sense of the word.

Disgusted, Shane swallowed back a wave of condemnation. He shouldn't be surprised. After all, this wasn't the first time he'd seen a woman on the verge of death one day resort to using her feminine wiles on a customer the next.

But now that the initial shock was wearing off, he rounded on Mattie. "What is Lizzie doing out of bed? Are you that heartless?"

Mattie jerked her chin at him. "Don't blame this on me. She made her choice."

"Did you pressure her?"

"Of course not." Clearly offended, her eyes hardened. "She won't do me any good dead, now will she?"

She was right. But Shane still narrowed his eyes in

warning. "You will see she doesn't overtax herself," he said.

A pall of silence passed between them. "I'm not her keeper. She chooses to be here, Dr. Bartlett. As do the rest of my girls."

Her eyes were blank, almost lifeless, but Shane heard the resignation in the madam's voice, reminding him that desperate circumstances brought women like Lizzie to Mattie's doorstep. The madam offered them an answer to starvation, and for some, even a better life than what they'd experienced before, but that didn't make what she did right.

Prepared to do a little preaching, he opened his mouth but a soft, youthful voice caught his attention and he turned toward the sound. At the sight before him, he sucked in a hard breath. Annabeth, the young girl he and Miss O'Toole had met two weeks ago in Mattie's kitchen, carried a tray of long-stemmed glasses, weaving her way among the clientele. Every few feet she would stop and offer a flute of sparkling liquid to one of Mattie's patrons.

"What's she still doing here?" A burning throb of anger knotted in his throat. "I thought you told Beau she was a distant relative visiting for a week."

Mattie's eyes frosted to a cold, sharp blue. "You leave her out of this."

Their stares locked, clashed, but Shane refused to back down. "Who is she?"

"None of your business."

"She's too young to live in a brothel."

"I know that." She wrapped her arms around her waist in an uncharacteristic display of defensiveness.

"She will return to boarding school as soon as the arrangements are made."

Something in the madam's eyes told Shane this was a personal matter for her, one he should leave alone.

He pushed anyway. "She attends a school back East?"

Mattie's expression closed, and he knew she was through answering his questions. "Let me remind you, Dr. Bartlett, your job is to care for the sick. Nothing more. Forget that, and you won't be allowed in my establishment again."

Her threat sent another burst of anger rolling through him, but he didn't doubt she meant every word. Business always came first for Mattie Silks. And aside from kidnapping Annabeth himself, there wasn't much he could do to help the girl. He had to trust that Mattie spoke the truth.

Shane released a frustrated sigh.

A breakout of disease, a stranger in town that left him feeling uneasy, a battle with a notorious madam over a young girl's fate, clearly, the day was shaping up to be one of his worst in years.

Chapter Twelve

Bella had never felt so helpless in her life. These children, these *innocent* boys and girls were in severe pain and she could do nothing of consequence to ease their suffering.

The letter from William was burning a hole in her pocket, but she didn't dare take it out now. There would be time when she was alone. Perhaps once the children went to sleep she would read what Lord Crawley had to say to her.

In the meantime, she wrung out a rag and brought it to Kimberly's heated forehead. "Does that help any?"

Kimberly closed her eyes and sighed. "A little."

Bella moved through the room and replaced the compresses on the other four girls' foreheads. Now that Dr. Shane had returned from town, he and Bella had decided to split the rooms between them. There hadn't been time to discuss anything else, since four more sick children had been sent home from the school.

According to the doctor's records, there could be another six still to come.

Bella caught a movement in the doorway.

She turned in time to see Dr. Shane motioning her into the hall.

Confused by his sudden appearance, she made her way quickly across the room. The moment she shut the door behind them she noted the lines of fatigue around his mouth and eyes. The man had to be exhausted, living with little sleep and meager wages, yet he never complained. His dedication awed her. Inspired her. Made her want to be a better person.

"You wanted to see me?" she asked.

"How are the girls?"

"Sick, hurting, bored. I'm afraid the bored portion of that equation is making them cranky."

Reaching out, he touched her sleeve and then just as quickly dropped his hand. "We'll get through this. A few days after the rash disappears the contagious period ends and then you will be able to return to your brother's home."

She thought of the two girls that had joined her room this afternoon, neither of which had shown any signs of rashes. "Are you saying you want me to stay here until the threat is over?"

"It's the best solution." He cocked his head at her. "Is there a problem with that?"

"No." Resigned at this point, she merely shook her head. "I was thinking about our other patients."

"I saw Lizzie today."

Bella didn't like the look in his eyes. "You have bad news."

"She's back to work."

Her eyebrows scrunched together at the news. "You don't mean—"

"I'm afraid I do." There was such sadness in his eyes,

such loss, as though the idea of Lizzie returning to work was his own personal failure.

Bella understood completely.

"What a mess," she whispered. "If only I could speak to Mattie."

"It was Lizzie's choice."

"Yes, but—"

"Bella," he said with such gentleness she only half realized he'd used her given name. "The hard reality of life is that some people don't want to be saved. They're happy in their choices."

Why did she sense he was speaking from personal experience? Or had he seen into her heart and was urging her to change her ways?

"I thought she wanted to change." Was she speaking of Lizzie now, or herself? "She—"

"—is a prostitute."

This time, Bella didn't appreciate his harsh honesty. "By profession, maybe. But it's not who she is."

"For some, what they do *is* who they are."

He sounded so certain that tears of frustration filled her eyes. She swiped at them with the back of her hand. "Lizzie's too weak for that kind of life. I have to go to her. I can talk sense into her, I know I can."

He stopped her with a firm grip on her arm. "You've been exposed to measles."

"But I've already had the disease."

"What if you're carrying the virus?" He released her arm. "You could infect Lizzie."

"I—"

With gentle fingers, he touched her cheek. "You know this, Bella."

Closing her eyes, she offered up a swift prayer for

Lizzie's soul but the inability to help her friend left a sour taste in her mouth. "Oh, Shane, I feel so power-less."

He gave her a sad smile. "Now you know how I feel every day of my life. But then, our lack of control leaves us with the choice to open the door to God."

She shook her head at him. "Still…what an awful burden to carry, day in and day out. How do you manage it? All by yourself?"

"I'm not alone, Bella. Not anymore." He tentatively took her hand in his. "God answered my prayers. I have you now."

"Yes." She tightened her grip and smiled when a definite flash of contentment settled on his face. "Yes, you do."

Later that night, Bella waited until her patients had fallen asleep before settling down to read William's letter. The room was silent other than the soft snoring of the girls with stuffy noses.

Restless, Bella rose from her chair and moved to the window. Pressing her forehead against the cool glass, she studied the clear night sky. Black fabric strewn with a thousand diamonds, painted with God's skillful hand. Controlled chaos. Much like her life had become these last few weeks.

But unlike God's perfect masterpiece in the sky, Bella doubted she could hold on to her control much longer. Her secret was burning a hole in her soul, turning her conviction of sin into self-loathing. And her attraction to Shane Bartlett was confusing matters further.

Clutching William's letter in her hand, she could no longer put off the inevitable.

Returning to her chair, her hands shook as she slid a finger under the seal. Her pulse thundered loudly in her ears and she set the letter down in her lap.

What if William renewed his suit?

What if he didn't?

Taking a deep breath, she shifted until light from the moon illuminated the paper, flipped open the letter and read…

My dearest love, my Bella, my heart,

You were very naughty to run away from me. However, I do believe I understand. I am dread-fully sorry for the clumsy way I made my initial offer of protection to you. Come home at once and allow me to renew my suit properly. The ar-rangements are made. All you need do is contact my agent in Denver and you will be on your way home to me.

Yours most affectionately,
William

Come home? Renew his suit? "What of your wife, William? *What of your wife?*" she hissed in the dark-ened room.

A rage so strong, so refined burned in Bella's chest at William's callous arrogance, at his assumption a few words scribbled on fine parchment would change her mind and entice her down a road of sin with him.

How could he expect that of her? How could he?

A knock came at the door just as she crumpled the letter in her fist. Confused by the distraction, she took a deep breath and stared straight ahead. Still a bit disoriented, she looked around her. Blinked. Her gaze landed on Stacy breathing heavily in her bed.

Another knock split through the silence.

Blowing out a heavy sigh, Bella jammed the letter into her pocket and padded silently to the door. Ordering her heartbeat to slow, tucking her rage into a dark corner of her mind, she cleared her features and opened the door a tiny crack.

Shane stood on the other side, carrying a tray with full tea service. The skin beneath his eyes was dark with fatigue yet there was contentment in his gaze. This was a man who knew who he was, a man who understood his purpose in life. He wasn't idle, like William, or confused over right and wrong. Shane Bartlett was good and sure and true.

Staring into his handsome face with those intense blue eyes and disheveled hair, Bella's earlier rage over William's letter shattered into something else entirely. Something far more pleasant. A tinge of hope sprang to life inside her.

She quickly lowered her gaze to the tray he carried. "What is this?" Her voice cracked a bit but he didn't seem to notice.

"You didn't eat much at dinner. I thought you might like some tea before going to bed."

The dear, dear man. Even in his own exhaustion he had thought of her. Again, something pleasant tugged at her heart. Not chaos, not fear, but something more refined, something comfortable and safe.

He smiled at her, a flash of white teeth and sincerity. "I'll set the tray in the upstairs parlor down the hall."

Not wanting to be alone with William's letter, Bella

placed her fingertips on the doctor's forearm. "Will you join me?"

Lowering his gaze to her hand, he stared for a long moment and then nodded slowly. "I suppose it would be all right. As long as we leave the door open."

At the innocent announcement, memories assaulted Bella. Her mind sped back to the months of William's pursuit. She thought of the way he'd always closed the door to her dressing room during their visits. He'd claimed he hadn't wanted to share her with anyone, especially not the other members of her cast and crew. At the time, she'd thought his explanation sweet. Now she saw how dishonorable his actions had been.

She glanced over her shoulder at the girls, saw that they were asleep and slipped out the room. Vanity had her turning back. "I'll only be a moment."

Rushing to the mirror, she took a quick look at herself and cringed. Her hair was a tangled mess atop her head. Her face was lined with worry and exhaustion. William's locket looked cheap against her skin.

No one in London would recognize her. Oddly enough, that didn't seem such a bad thing at the moment. Of course, it would be ridiculous to try to tidy herself at this point. Dr. Shane had already seen her in this state and had agreed to share her tea anyway.

For a moment, a very brief moment, Bella's heart opened and she allowed herself to trust. To believe healing would come in spite of her mistakes.

It was a nice thought to end an otherwise horrendous day.

Chapter Thirteen

Unsure how long his assistant would take to join him, Shane rubbed an impatient hand down his face. The day had been a trying one, but ever since his connection with Miss O'Toole in the hallway he hadn't felt as weary as he might if he had to face this outbreak of measles alone.

There was no denying he and Miss O'Toole worked well together. And yet, he'd be foolish to forget that she held a portion of herself back. Foolish to hope more was growing between them than a healthy give and take of doctor to assistant.

Needing to walk off his uneasy mood, he rose but she joined him in the parlor at the same moment and he sat back down. She looked tired, a bit disheveled, yet incredibly beautiful. He decided she must be glorious on the stage.

Lowering herself in the seat opposite his, she shuffled around the cups on the tea service and began pouring. Her movements were elegant, graceful, but he could tell something was bothering her tonight, more so than usual.

Was he pushing her too hard? Was she having regrets about agreeing to assist him? "Miss O'Toole, are you—"

"I realize I know so little about you, Shane. I can call you Shane, can't I?" She tossed her hair back and stared at him, those big tawny eyes of hers filled with anticipation.

Realizing she wasn't going to talk about herself, not yet at least, he eased back in his chair and nodded. "I believe we've progressed past the customary formalities."

"So, *Shane.* Did you grow up here in Denver?"

He carefully considered how to respond to her question. He went with the short answer. "I'm from back East."

A charming smile spread across her lips. "I knew it."

"Is that right?" She seemed a little too pleased with herself.

"Your accent. Very highbrow. You clearly come from money."

He didn't know whether to laugh or scowl at her incorrect observation. If only she knew the truth of his nefarious beginnings. But instead of sketching out the ugly details of his childhood, he said, "I was given the best education available in this country."

"Oh? Which schools did you attend?" she asked, her eyes filled with simple curiosity.

His heart tripped. For a second he thought of his mother. How she had longed for a better life for him than the one she'd given him in the Bowery. Her death had provided for his future in an unexpected way. "A premiere boarding school at first. Princeton next. Harvard Medical School."

"Ah." Sipping from her cup, she stared at him over the rim. "Do you have any family left back there?"

Unbridled emotions buzzed in his head like angry mosquitoes. He should have expected the question, prepared for it at least. "My mother is dead. She died when I was sixteen."

"I'm so sorry." Holding his gaze with a sympathetic look, she set her cup on the table and clasped her hands in her lap. "I can't imagine losing mine. She's my rock."

Silence hung between them. His mind blurred with complicated sensations, severing his ability to respond.

"Was your mother all you had, then?" she asked.

Shane sucked in a violent breath. Pride battled with weariness. Weariness won. He was tired of holding his past a secret. He needed to share his history. And he needed to share it with this woman. "I have a father and two younger sisters, two *half* sisters."

"I don't understand." She cocked her head at a charming angle. "Are you saying your father remarried?"

He held back a snort of disdain. "No. He only married once." Years of resentment sounded in that single word. "I'm a bas—that is, my father was never married to my mother."

A look of horror filled her eyes. "Does that mean—"

"My mother was a rich man's mistress."

Bella had an instant of pure shock. Her hand flew to her throat and her fingers knotted in the gold chain around her neck. She tugged, but only managed to tangle her hand further around the locket. Cutting through her shock was a quick, primal urge to run.

"I see I've rendered you speechless." His voice was flat, calm, but his eyes told her she'd let him down with her stunned reaction.

He didn't understand. He thought she'd judged him and found him wanting. But he was wrong. So. Very. Wrong.

The thought of this man, this kind, considerate healer, experiencing such a terrible childhood broke her heart. She freed her fingers from William's locket at last and reached to Shane across the small table between them. When he didn't shake her hand off his arm, she asked in a gentle voice. "Did you know your father? Was he part of your life at least?"

He relaxed into her touch, and she could see some of the tension easing from his shoulders. "My father never recognized me. Not in public, anyway."

"Oh, Shane." She squeezed his arm gently. "That must have been hard."

He made a low sound of anger in his throat, but he placed his hand calmly over hers. "When I was young, he came to see my mother weekly. But his visits decreased once I turned ten, stopped altogether when I was fourteen."

Bella had no words. Afraid she would say the wrong thing she rolled her palm against his, clutched tightly and then moved around the table to kneel in front of him.

How could she tell him she had a sick fascination with his tale, a personal interest that went far beyond curiosity?

So many thoughts ran through her mind.

At the time William had made his proposal, she had thought only of his wife as the victim. But what if Bella had accepted his proposition? Would she have had a child, like Shane's mother?

Her heart clenched in her chest. "How did your mother take your father's abandonment?"

"Badly. She died two years later, when I was sixteen." He shook his head. "But in truth, she died in her heart the day his visits stopped."

Words of sympathy seemed inadequate. So she pulled his hand to her face, laid her cheek against his palm.

He didn't register her touch, just stared into the distance. "My father must have heard of her passing because he came three days after her funeral. There'd been no sadness in him at the loss of a woman he'd claimed to have loved. *Love.*" He spat out the word. "Peter Ford didn't know the meaning of the word. He allowed my mother to suffer ridicule, shame and condemnation because of him. That's not love. That's possession."

"Yes." Her fingers curled around his wrist. *"Yes."*

"Instead of sharing his condolences, the man had the nerve to offer to pay for my education." Shane's bitter tone told her he hadn't considered the offer a blessing. Thus, his next words shocked her all the more. "I accepted."

"You…you did?"

"Not out of gratitude." His eyes blazed with distant memories and he pulled his hand away from her face. "I accepted out of revenge."

How could she fault a sixteen-year-old boy his anger? "You were young, Shane."

"There's more."

Still on her knees, she blinked up at him.

"There were…stipulations."

The raw pain in his eyes gripped at her heart. Bella had to help him understand she wasn't judging him. On the contrary, she was judging his father. His mother, even, for her inability to put her son ahead of her love for a wicked man.

A wave of tenderness had her pushing a clump of hair off his forehead. "What did he ask in return for your education?"

"I had to keep silent about my mother and my relationship to my father." His gaze filled with wounded pride. "In the eyes of the school administrators, I was a charity case of the great philanthropist Peter Ford."

"How that must have hurt. I'm so sorry."

"I agreed to the lie. I perpetuated it for my own end." His voice was husky with self-directed anger. She knew all about that particular emotion.

But, unlike her, he was wrong to condemn himself. "You were sixteen, alone and grieving your mother. You were vulnerable. Your father took advantage of that."

His spine went rigid. "I wanted revenge, not an education. In the end, I won."

Understanding dawned. "Instead of staying in New York you came here, to Denver, and opened a practice that caters to women like your mother."

His lips twisted in self-disgust. "A sinful, self-serving response, don't you think?"

"No, Shane. You might not realize it, but the Lord brought you here, not your drive for revenge. Like Paul says in Romans 8, *God works for the good of those who love Him, who have been called according to His purpose.*" She cupped his face in her palms. "No matter how or why you came to Denver, you are living out your purpose for the Kingdom now."

"How can you be so sure? God wants our efforts to be out of a cheerful heart. I can't say that's true of me."

"Oh, but it is." Her affection for him felt so foreign, and yet so right. "You forget. I work alongside you daily. I see your strength of character, your integrity, your love for the lost. It's in everything you do. You save lives, Shane."

"Except my mother's life, she—"

"Your mother chose to love a married man. She chose to believe his lies."

Who better than Bella to understand the woman's delusions? She herself had chosen to believe William's false promises. She'd ignored the signs. She'd only been spared a life like Shane's mother through escape, not strength of character.

Her hand went to the pendant around her neck, her albatross.

"I couldn't save her," he whispered. "I failed my mother."

Bella dropped the locket. "No. Like you said when we were discussing Lizzie, there was nothing you could do. Your mother didn't want to be saved."

But Bella did. Oh, yes, Bella did.

She wanted to break free of William. Somehow, someway, she would find the courage to move forward with her life. If not in her own strength, then with God's help.

Why hadn't she seen the truth sooner? She had to let God take the lead. If her Heavenly Father could place stars in the sky, surely He could guide her through the process of repentance.

Only then would she be worthy of a man of Christian integrity, a man like this compassionate doctor who had turned his drive for revenge into something powerful for God's Kingdom.

Could she be falling for Shane Bartlett? Was that possible when she was still confused over her feelings for William?

As soon as the thought surfaced, Bella realized nothing would come of the situation.

One day Shane would find out about William. He would discover Bella had nearly thrown her life away over a married man, just like his mother had done.

And then he would hate her.

Shane watched the myriad emotions cross Bella's face. He saw understanding, pain, but not pity. How could someone so young and with such a small amount of worldly experience not judge him or his mother?

Because she was special. "I…thank you for listening, Bella. I've never shared that much of my past with anyone."

"No?"

"My half sisters know nothing of me. I was sworn to secrecy and I have kept to that vow."

Her gaze filled with sorrow. "You've carried this burden alone all these years?"

"Yes."

She slid back into her chair, studied his face intently. "Do you think you will ever forgive your father?"

It was a good question, an astute question, one he wrestled with daily. Looking into her intense gaze, he realized his answer mattered to her.

Was she expecting him to make the right decision, the godly one? If so, she was going to be sorely disappointed.

He knew what Jesus taught about forgiveness, had studied the Bible for hours while searching for freedom from his burning resentment. Unfortunately, Shane's hatred for the man who had fathered him ran too deep. And so he answered her question with complete honesty. *"Never."*

She nodded. "I...don't blame you."

Her quick response gave him a sick feeling in the pit of his stomach. And then, an ugly thought reared. Was Bella's secret, the one that made her eyes sad and kept her out of church on Sunday mornings, tied to an illicit association? Had she fallen for a married man? Was she pining for him now?

Shane prayed he was wrong. For both their sakes.

Chapter Fourteen

The quarantine lasted one week. Bella spent her last morning at the orphanage helping the girls dress for school.

Their excitement was so contagious she couldn't bear to stifle their fun. Thus, she allowed face scrubbings to turn into splashing and hair braiding into giggling.

With most of the girls already downstairs, Bella stood behind Stacy and secured a light blue, polka-dot ribbon atop her shiny brown curls. "There," she said, looking at their shared reflections in the mirror. "Perfect."

Getting into the spirit of things, Stacy spun around and twirled the skirt of her green dress. "You mean, perfectly mismatched."

"Precisely."

They giggled together but then Stacy's eyes turned serious and she threw her arms around Bella's neck. "Thank you, Miss Bella. Thank you for everything."

Heart in her throat, Bella hugged the girl tightly against her. "It was my pleasure."

Which was nothing short of the truth. Thanks to her

constant days and nights with the children, Bella had lost her uneasiness around them.

Peering over the top of Stacy's head, Bella eyed one of the Scriptures scrolled along the wall. *Love each other deeply, because love covers over a multitude of sins.*

The verse struck at her core. Love. Thanks to the Charity House orphans, and a certain dedicated doctor, Bella was learning a lot about the elusive emotion. And none of what she discovered remotely resembled what William had callously offered her.

One last squeeze and she released Stacy.

Casting her gaze around the room, her curiosity got the best of her. "Stacy, do you know who painted these walls?"

"I did," said a soft voice from behind them.

Bella whipped around and connected her gaze with a tall blonde standing in the doorway. She'd only met the girl once, but even in that brief exchange Megan had left an impression on Bella. More woman than child, the kind look in her sea-green eyes spoke of a tender heart and a gentle soul.

"You've done a lovely job here." Bella swept her hand in an arc through the room. "Simply exquisite."

"Thank you." Megan smiled, but something sad came and went in her eyes.

Bella recognized that look. The young woman was suffering some sort of loss, but she was putting up a brave front nonetheless.

"You're very talented," Bella added.

Megan lifted a shoulder then focused on Stacy. "Laney sent me to get you. You're late for breakfast. Johnny is already on seconds."

Stacy's face lost a few shades of color. "You don't think we'll run out of food?"

"Of course not." Patting her back, Bella handed the girl her coat. "But that doesn't mean you should dally up here any longer."

Stacy grabbed the garment and rushed into the hallway.

Smiling, Bella turned a circle and tried not to cringe at the mess she and the girls had made. Squaring her shoulders, she began picking up wet towels and blankets. Megan quickly joined her and they worked in silent harmony.

Bella had so many questions she wanted to ask the talented girl. Unsure how to begin, she set a blanket on the edge of a bed and looked at the walls again. "Have you thought of getting further training for your art? At a woman's college, perhaps?"

Megan's mouth opened and closed three times before she finally managed more than a squeak. "I could never leave Charity House."

"Because of money?"

Megan shook her head. "Nothing like that."

Bella took Megan's hand and drew her down on the bed. "I don't know you, and you certainly don't know me, but I must tell you that I think it would be a mistake to ignore your God-given gift."

"It's not that special. I was just having a bit of fun." Megan sat stiffly as she spoke, oblivious to the beautiful world she had created with a vivid imagination and a paint brush.

"Are you afraid?" Bella asked, touching a hand to the girl's shoulder.

Grimacing, Megan stood abruptly. "Of course not."

Bella tugged her back down beside her. "The world isn't as frightening as it seems."

"I know." But she shifted out of Bella's reach and stared at her with eyes a frigid, pale blue.

"Megan, *please,* tell me what's keeping you here."

The girl rose, but didn't move, didn't blink. Bella feared she would stand there frozen forever, but eventually her face crumbled. "I can't... I can't risk losing him."

Bella's heart played a rhythmic beat against her ribs. "Him?" *Please, don't let her say Shane.*

"Logan. Logan Mitchell."

Relief swam in Bella's brain at the unfamiliar name. "I don't think I know him."

Megan twisted her fingers together in front of her. "He used to be Marshal Scott's deputy. He was transferred to the San Francisco office."

"I see."

Megan turned her head away, jaw set. "He will come back for me."

Ah, so Megan was yet another hopeful woman waiting for a man to fulfill his vow. How Bella wanted the girl's trust in Logan Mitchell to be warranted. But she bit her lip and resisted the sympathy building in her. One of them had to be practical. "How do you know he's coming back?"

"Because he promised. And I'll be here when he returns because *I* promised." Megan's sad sweet smile broke Bella's heart.

Such faith. Such blind trust. But at what cost? "Surely Marc and Laney would tell him where you were if you left to pursue your art."

The girl hugged her arms around her waist. "I won't have him misunderstand if I'm not here."

"But you have no idea when he'll return. It could be years."

"Then I'll wait years."

"Oh, Megan." What else could Bella say? The girl was so young, not yet twenty. How could Bella explain the harsh reality of a world she was only discovering herself?

"It was nice talking to you, Miss Bella." Megan looked toward the door as though it were an escape route. "But I need to check on the babies."

Bella didn't try to stop the hasty exit. But as she watched the girl leave the room frustration had her rising from the bed and balling her hands into fists.

Was this the same helpless emotion Shane had experienced as a child? How utterly and completely awful.

Her heart bled for the little boy Shane had been.

Unfortunately, she knew empathy could not change the past. That didn't mean Bella couldn't do something about the future.

Yes, she would do…something. Soon.

She just didn't know what. And she didn't know when. But details like that had never stopped her before.

The air in Shane's office pulsed with the scent of iodine, furniture polish and sulfur. Not particularly pleasant, but the room smelled exactly like a medical office should. Sadly, though, the familiar odors did nothing to calm Shane's restlessness. Ever since he'd revealed the details of his childhood to Bella, he couldn't relax around the woman. Even now, as they worked side by side preparing for their day, he had to tamp down his rambling thoughts.

Problem was, the woman knew too much about him now.

She hadn't spoken of the matter, nor had she tried to encourage further discussion, but for the last week, she'd gone beyond her normal duties. She kept his office tidy, ensured he ate three meals a day and never once allowed him to forget his coat.

Pondering the change in their relationship, Shane dumped a salicylic compound in a medium-size mortar and began mixing a fresh batch of painkillers.

With every few flicks of his wrist he cast a quick glance at Miss O'Toole. Dusting the bookshelves, the only sound she made was her gentle humming. Shane wondered what she was like on stage, singing the lead in some famed opera.

No doubt, she was stunning. Unforgettable.

Displeased with the direction of his thoughts, Shane set the pestle down and raked a hand through his hair, tugging at the ends as though he could yank his thoughts under control with the gesture. He couldn't forget Bella would soon be leaving. The reminder made his gut curl into a tight ball of dread.

Thankfully, a loud knock at the door splintered his musings.

Bella quit humming and settled her velvety eyes on him. "Do you want me to answer that?"

"No. Finish your dusting." He slanted his head toward the bookshelf. "I'll let you know if we have a patient."

She nodded, but instead of returning to her duties, she watched him move across the room.

Hand on the knob, a wave of foreboding washed over him and Shane hesitated, oddly reluctant to admit whoever was waiting on the other side.

Nevertheless, he threw open the door.

Blinking into the bright morning sun, his gaze landed on a complete stranger. Much older than Shane, the man was dressed in a tailored suit, his white hair slicked back in the popular fashion of the day. His small, expressionless eyes put Shane instantly on guard. "May I help you?"

Before the man had a chance to answer, Shane lowered his gaze to the man's hand. He carried a small leather satchel made specifically for holding important documents. Shane had seen an identical case in his father's possession the day he'd come with his offer of education.

"Are you Shane Bartlett?"

"I am." Shane leaned forward to get a better look at the satchel. "And you are?"

"Ronald Wilson. I have come on a matter of grave importance."

Frowning at the melodramatic words, Shane stepped back and allowed the man to enter his office.

Shoulders rigid, Ronald Wilson strode into the room. His gaze swept the small sitting area and stopped on Bella.

Shane stepped between them. "This is my assistant, Miss O'Toole."

The man removed his hat and nodded. "A pleasure, miss."

With her usual politeness, she inclined her head slightly, but then her solemn gaze connected with

Shane's. From the glint in her eyes it was clear she didn't trust the man.

Shane didn't either. Something wasn't right about Ronald Wilson. He was too slick, too polished and he carried the scent of "city" all over him.

Shane slid his hands into his pockets and watched the man walk through his clinic with a confident step. Shane had seen that sort of walk enough to recognize the look of money.

"Are you in need of medical services, Mr. Wilson?"

"No."

A brief pause. Then the man continued his inspection, turning in a half circle before moving to the wall of bookshelves.

Bella came to stand next to Shane. The gesture turned them into a unit, much like the time she'd boldly announced to her brother she was going to be a nurse.

Standing here now, her narrowed eyes never leaving Ronald Wilson, she looked small and fierce and incredibly sweet.

Shane's heart gave a swift kick.

"I don't like this," she whispered. "I don't like *him*."

Mr. Wilson turned at that last part, his stare locking onto Bella. Shane didn't appreciate the light of interest in the other man's eyes. Stepping forward, he shifted Bella behind him.

A look of understanding flashed across the other man's face and he nodded. The respect laden in the simple gesture threw Shane off balance.

"My assistant and I have a busy day ahead of us. Please state your business, sir."

Mr. Wilson gave another quick nod. "Certainly."

He paused, looked at Bella. "Perhaps we should speak alone."

Shane thought he heard a soft growl come from Bella's lips. Of course, he was mistaken. He had to be mistaken. But when she gripped his elbow in a silent request to remain he knew he couldn't deny her.

"She stays."

Mr. Wilson inclined his head. With quick steps, he strode to a table in the middle of the room and set the leather satchel on top. "I'll get straight to the point."

"I would appreciate that."

"I'm afraid there's no easy way to say this." He rested his palms on the table and adopted an expression of sympathy. "Your father is dead."

A long moment passed, and then as if in a nightmare, dark, angry emotions linked together in Shane's mind. Shock, relief, regret, guilt. The violence of his sporadic emotions hit like a punch in his gut, a hard, ruthless punch that stole his ability to take a decent breath of air.

Bella's hand tightened on his arm. "Shane," she whispered. "You should sit. You…"

He didn't hear the rest of her words over his own muddled thoughts. Of all the scenarios he'd expected this morning, the news of his father's death was not one of them.

With quick movements, Bella dragged a stool across the room and then urged him to sit with a hard push to his shoulders.

Knees unbuckling under the surprisingly strong pressure, Shane collapsed into the seat and gazed up at her. She approached him slowly, placed a hand on his cheek. The concern in her eyes was palpable. "It's okay, Shane. Take a moment to accept this."

Shaking his head, Shane glared at the man who had brought this unexpected news. "When did he die?" He held up a hand to prevent the other man from answering right away. "I don't care how, or why, I just need to know when."

"Three months ago."

Three months. Three months and Shane had known nothing, had sensed nothing. That alone spoke of the relationship he'd shared with the man who had sired him.

Hatred, bitterness, rage, a legacy of dark emotions was all that had existed between father and son. But to what end? Peter Ford was dead and Shane would no longer have the opportunity to…to what? Further his revenge? Make amends? Forgive?

How could God forgive a man like Peter Ford? More confounding still, how could Shane?

He forced his emotions to the back of his mind and tried to focus logically on the problem before him.

One question arose. "Why this visit, Mr. Wilson? Why not send a telegram?"

Head bent over the satchel, the man sighed. "I was Peter Ford's personal solicitor. Due to the nature of his business and certain life choices he made in his youth, he wanted complete privacy for a number of matters."

"*Matters?* You mean me and the situation of my birth."

"Yes, Dr. Bartlett. That is precisely what I mean." Eyes still cast down, he flipped open the leather pouch's flap and dug his hand inside. "I have kept track of you through the years on your father's behalf."

The statement could mean a number of things, but the sympathy in Mr. Wilson's eyes eroded any delusion on Shane's part of a father keeping tabs on a beloved son. Whatever the reason Peter Ford had monitored Shane's progress through the years, it had not been out of love.

Shane drew in a sharp breath, jerked his knee up and down in agitation. He relaxed only when Bella's hands smoothed over his hair.

"I still don't understand why you're here now?" he said once he had his control back in place.

"I have come to explain your father's will to you."

"His what?" Shane jumped up so fast the stool went tumbling behind him. Bella's touch to his arm kept him from rushing forward.

"Go on, Mr. Wilson," she said for them both. "Tell us the rest."

"Dr. Bartlett, your father left you everything."

Shane let out a bitter laugh as he batted away the declaration with a contemptuous wave of his hand. "Impossible."

"It's true." The solicitor pushed a mountain of papers toward Shane. "However, there is a stipulation."

"Of course." Shane curled his lip in derision. But then he remembered the others. "My father had a wife, and two daughters. Did he leave his family nothing?"

"My client's wife died several years ago. As for his daughters," Mr. Wilson's eyes turned sad, making Shane wonder what the man's life had been like in constant service for a man like Peter Ford, "they receive nothing of your father's estate."

Nothing? Peter Ford's daughters, daughters raised in the height of privilege, would get nothing from their father? Shane struggled with the ugly realization of their instant poverty, fought to close his heart to what that meant. But he could not. He had two sisters left destitute. What kind of monster had his father been? "How old are they now?"

"Drusilla is fourteen, Elizabeth only ten."

"Who is caring for them? Where are they living? How are they taking this change in their circumstance?" He fired off the questions like bullets from a six-shooter.

Mr. Wilson took a bracing breath of air. "They are residing in my home at present, but not in the style they have previously known. With four daughters of my own, and my largest client dead, I am a man of limited means."

Stunned at yet another unexpected revelation, Shane readjusted his first impression of the man. Of course, now that he was the sole heir of his father's estate, he would have to decide what to do about his sisters. He would…

He would…

A burst of confusion took hold of him. There was too much information coming at him all at once. He needed air, needed a moment to think and organize his thoughts. He started for the door, but Bella stopped him.

"Shane, wait. The stipulation." She gave him a meaningful look. "You have to listen to the rest."

Shane halted, spun to glare at Mr. Wilson. "What is the stipulation?"

"The details are spelled out in your father's will." The solicitor pointed to the pile of papers he'd set on the table. "You should read every page carefully for yourself."

Shane waved a dismissive hand. "Summarize the important points."

Mr. Wilson sighed. "In order to receive your inheritance, you must legally change your name to Ford, return to New York and take on your role as your father's rightful heir."

The air in the room turned cold, heavy, closed.

Shane swallowed. "And if I refuse my inheritance? Will my sisters receive the money in my place?"

Mr. Wilson shook his head. "If you refuse, the entire estate will be sold and the proceeds will be distributed to Harvard Medical School for the sole purpose of research."

Bella gasped. "Are you saying the money won't even go to charitable organizations?"

"Not a penny."

With that simple statement, any remaining hopes Shane might have had about his father's motives disappeared. Peter Ford had been a selfish, cold-blooded man in life, and was proving no better in death. And this time, with one swoop of the pen, the ruthless snake had found a way to control them all from his grave.

Chapter Fifteen

Bella had heard enough, but before she could expel the solicitor, Shane straightened to his full height and forced out a hard breath. "I think you should leave, Mr. Wilson. I need time to sort through everything you've told me."

With each word spoken, Shane held himself rigid, his gaze locked on the solicitor like a hunter eyeing his prey. His breathing wasn't quite steady and he looked upset. Bella went to him, touched his back. No, not upset, she decided. Furious. She could feel the rage in the bunched muscles below her palm.

"Mr. Wilson," she appealed, employing all the charm she could muster under the circumstances. "The doctor is only asking you to allow him the opportunity to study his father's will, as you yourself suggested a moment ago."

The solicitor lifted his left eyebrow the barest fraction but, mercifully, his eyes held a considerable amount of compassion in them. "I suppose a few days will make no difference one way or the other."

"Thank you for your understanding," she said, removing her hand from Shane's shoulder.

A muscle in his jaw flexed as he clenched his teeth. She could tell he was trying to contain his rage but the threads of his control were unraveling with every heartbeat.

With swift movements, Bella helped the solicitor gather his belongings and ushered him toward the door.

Hand poised above the knob, Mr. Wilson peered over his shoulder at Shane. "I will return Tuesday afternoon, if that meets with your satisfaction."

"Tuesday will be fine," he said.

Wanting the man gone, Bella placed a solicitous hand on the man's arm. "I thank you again."

After closing the door with a click, Bella took a long, slow, careful look around her. With so much information to take in, she decided to give Shane another moment to cool his anger. Flexing her fingers, she walked to the table where Shane's copy of the will sat. Unable to relinquish her awful fascination, she stared at the top page but the letters snaked into blurry, incomprehensible lines before her eyes.

Outraged on Shane's behalf, she lifted her gaze to his and found herself confronted with cold disdain. Even knowing his fury was not directed at her, she quickly lowered her head.

He'd held so much bitterness toward his father before this. *How will he find peace now, Lord?*

With legs that felt full of water, she made her way across the room. "Shane?"

Unblinking, he stared over her head. His stone-cold expression worried her. Why wasn't he ranting, yelling, showing some emotion, *any* emotion?

At last, his eyelids tapered to tiny slits. "He never accepted me."

She knew he meant his father. "He's left you his entire estate."

Shane gave one hard shake of his head. "With impossible limitations attached."

"Perhaps he thought he was doing the right thing."

Scowling, he pushed forward. His expression held the regret of a man who knew he would never achieve what he wanted most in life. "I was not a son to him. Even now, he only wants his name to live on through me." He clenched his jaw. "I was never able to earn his love."

In spite of his anger, Bella didn't miss the agony in his eyes, or the pain in his voice. "I don't have any fine words for you. And I don't have any answers. But I can steer you to my mother's favorite verse, one that has held me up in times of despair."

She hurried to the small round table next to one of the sickbeds in the room and retrieved the Bible Shane kept there. Her fingers shaking, she flipped to Isaiah 40 and began to read. "But those who hope in the Lord will renew their strength. They will soar on wings like eagles; they will run and not grow weary, they will walk and not be faint."

Shane furrowed his brow as he joined her. For a long moment he stood next to her, unmoving, while he stared at the page. With an incomprehensible mutter, he took the Bible and concentrated on the passage she indicated with her finger.

Bella waited for him to speak. A dozen platitudes came and went in her mind. *Oh, Lord, if ever there was a time for the right words, this is it. Please guide what I say.*

"Shane, God's love is unfailing and unconditional.

You might not have earned your earthly father's love but you will always have your Heavenly Father's love."

Unflinching, he stared at the page.

She touched his arm. "It's no accident God brought you here. The Lord will use this experience for good. He's been preparing you for a specific assignment all along. Remember, most of the children at Charity House have been abandoned by their fathers, just like you."

And still, he stared at the Bible. The only sign of his turmoil came in the fast ticking of a vein in his neck.

"Shane." She shook his arm. "What would your patients do if you weren't here? You yourself said no other doctor will see them. Who would care for them if not you? God had a plan for you from the start."

Closing his eyes a moment, Shane shut God's Word and returned it to the nightstand. "If I stay…" He pressed a finger to his temple. "What happens to my sisters?"

She gave him an overbright smile. "You could send for them."

"And how would I care for them?" He looked around him in disdain. "I can barely afford these rooms."

"I don't know." She shook her head. "Maybe—"

"Don't you understand?" His eyes hardened. "Peter Ford knew what he was doing when he put that stipulation in his will. He *knew* he was leaving me in an impossible situation."

"I—"

"If I stay here, continue as I always have, I abandon my sisters in the care of a stranger, one who readily admitted his funds are running low. Yet if I return to New York, I abandon my patients here."

Bella had no good argument. She had no answer at

all. He was correct. Completely, utterly, miserably correct. A fresh spurt of defeat tickled her throat, but she would not allow Peter Ford to win that easily. "There's an answer, Shane. God already knows what it is. We just have to pray He'll reveal it to you soon."

After a brooding hesitation, Shane nodded. "Perhaps God does have a plan."

Despite his words, Bella saw the skepticism in his eyes. Shane wasn't agreeing with her. He was appeasing her.

Under the circumstances, there was only one thing left for her to do. She closed her eyes and began praying on his behalf.

At half-past eight the next morning, Bella threw out every lofty ideal she'd spouted to Shane in his office. She might have spoken of the power of prayer and the need to believe God already had a solution, but when it came to her own life she lacked the courageous faith she expected of Shane.

Some Christian she was turning out to be.

Oh, she knew all the right words, had memorized countless Scriptures, but when it came to her own troubles her actions had yet to reflect her beliefs. And as James said, what was faith without deeds?

Unwilling to have a lengthy conversation with Beau this morning, she silently tiptoed to the back door and found herself halting at a soft plea from behind. "Bella, please, don't run away like this."

Bella spun around, her eyes landing on Hannah standing stiffly in the kitchen doorway. Bella opened her mouth to rail at the unsolicited interference, but the genuine concern in her sister-in-law's eyes made the words back up in her throat. "Hannah, I'm not—"

"Don't deny it." Hannah glided closer. "Not to me."

Bella lowered her gaze to her toes. "I *must* check on Lizzie. It's been two weeks since I've been able to spend any time with her." She lifted her gaze. "I fear I've failed her."

"What of your other fear?"

Thanks to years of training, Bella mastered her emotions enough to give her reply without her voice shaking. "I have no other fear."

Brows knit tightly together, Hannah took a few steps forward and held out two more letters. "These came for you last week, the last one just yesterday."

Bella saw the familiar scrawl on the top envelope and backed up as though it were a snake ready to bite. William was her past, yet he was turning out to be her ongoing shame, as well. "I…no, I don't want them. Throw them out."

Flipping over the top letter, Hannah studied the fancy red seal. "He's very persistent."

Bella closed her eyes until the need to shudder passed. Unable to craft a good explanation, she lifted a pleading look to Hannah. "Please. Take them away from me."

Hannah sighed. "I can't. They are addressed to you. *You* must decide what to do with them." She placed the letters in Bella's palm and closed her fingers over the thick stack of papers.

Swamped by her churning emotions, Bella stuffed the offensive letters in her pocket and turned to go.

This time, a light touch to her shoulder stopped her progress.

"Bella."

Bella shrugged her off and pivoted to glare at her sister-in-law. "No. Don't."

Hannah lifted her hand to her hair, shifted a curl off her forehead. "What have I done to make you distrust me?"

Fists clenched, Bella fought back tears. "It's not you, Hannah. It's… You're too good."

Hannah's gaze softened and she gave a short laugh. "Oh, Bella. We all sin and fall short of the glory of God. Even me."

Bella saw the look of genuine sorrow on Hannah's face. Yet what had she done? Said a bad word? Forgotten to pray one morning? Certainly nothing of real consequence, nothing as bad as desecrating a marriage.

"I find that hard to believe." Her tone sounded bitter even to her own ears.

Hannah placed her palms in the air. "All right. We'll leave it a little longer. But, Bella, know this." She tugged her into a tight embrace. "You can trust that I am here to listen whenever you need me."

And with those words, Bella felt worse. She'd been harsh and abrupt with her sister-in-law, yet Hannah still dealt with her in love. The woman personified the Fruit of the Spirit. Hannah would be a trusted confidant, but Bella couldn't find it in her heart to share her secret with her.

"I have to go." She rushed out the door without looking back. She heard Hannah's sigh of defeat right before the door banged shut behind her.

Less than a half hour later, Bella entered Mattie's brothel with determination in her steps. An eerie silence enveloped the main salon, but Bella hardly noticed. She wove her way through the open area, past the divans and chairs that had been full of paying customers the night before.

Instead of feeling out of place in this den of iniquity, Bella felt safe, protected. But whether that was due to the Holy Spirit's indwelling or a guilty conscience she couldn't say for sure.

One thing was certain, though, she understood the women who lived and worked in this house. Perhaps she had a connection with these women because she knew what it felt like to live with the blot of shame.

Deep in thought, Bella ascended the stairwell slowly. At the top of the landing she heard both male and female laughter coming from down the hall. Surely, a customer wouldn't visit this early in the day, not even on a Saturday? Would he?

Uncertain if she wanted to know the answer, Bella padded silently down the hallway and paused outside Lizzie's room. The laughter was coming from just inside.

Undaunted, Bella curled her fingers into a fist and knocked on the door.

The laughter stopped.

She knocked again. "Lizzie, it's me. Bella. I've come to read to you this morning."

No response.

She reached for the knob. "Lizzie? Are you in there?"

"Go away, Bella. I'm…working."

Bella snatched her hand back to her side. Her blood turned to ice. Shane had been right. Lizzie *had* returned to her old ways. "But, Lizzie, I—"

"Why, if it isn't Miss Bella O'Toole herself, just the girl I wanted to see."

Bella swung in the direction of the familiar voice, took a steadying breath. "Hello, Mattie."

Mattie nodded in response. Although still dressed from the night before, the madam's finely sculpted lips were unpainted, making her look less artificial and more approachable.

"Bella, darling, what are you doing up here all alone?"

Surprised at the question, she kept her tone light and friendly. "I was visiting Lizzie. Thought I'd read to her."

Mattie's gaze fused with hers so long Bella shifted under the blunt inspection.

"She wasn't expecting you this morning," Mattie said at last.

Bella's shoulders slumped forward. "I gathered as much."

The madam's eyes narrowed, then she nodded absently, as though she'd come to a conclusion of some sort. "Follow me. I have something to show you."

Oddly enough, as the woman took Bella's hand and tugged her down the hallway, her face held the same compassionate look as Hannah's had earlier. Bella didn't like the expression any better on the madam's round, overly powdered features than she had on her sister-in-law's. Nevertheless, she didn't struggle as Mattie literally dragged her down the back stairs.

Once inside Mattie's private parlor, Bella pulled her hand free. "What is it you wanted to show me?"

"Nothing." Mattie smirked. "I just wanted you out of the area."

Bella made a face. "Are you protecting me? Or Lizzie?"

Before responding, Mattie took her time reclining

into a large, cushioned chair facing the door. "Why, you, of course."

Bella jammed her hands on her hips. "Isn't that a bit out of character, Miss Silks?"

"Perhaps." Mattie rose and ambled over to the bookshelf, pretending grave interest in the titles written on the spines. "Or perhaps I like that arrogant brother of yours and wanted to do him a favor."

"Try again, and this time why don't you play it with a little more feeling."

"Perhaps I simply like and admire you."

Rooted to the spot, Bella blinked in astonishment at the madam's declaration.

Seemingly unaware of the stunned silence, Mattie pulled out a book, studied the title and then put it in a new spot farther down the shelf.

Tapping her foot in impatience, Bella broke the silence between them. "You know, Mattie, I find it necessary to stomp on your illusions concerning me."

Mattie continued running her finger along a row of books. "How so?"

"Let's just say you wouldn't admire me if you really knew me."

"Secrets?" Mattie spun to stare at Bella. "I love secrets. And from one so young. My, oh my, I've struck gold."

Unsure what to make of the madam's strange response, Bella looked down at her hands, and because they refused to stop trembling, she folded them tightly around her waist. "Half your girls are younger than me."

"True. True. But none of them have a caring family to watch over them."

Bella took immediate offense, but refused to show it.

She was Isabella Constance O'Toole. She knew exactly how to portray a woman of the world. Nevertheless, her hands still trembled as she lifted them to smooth her hair. "I'm not a child, Mattie. I've been on my own for two years now."

"So young. And jaded already." Returning to her chair, Mattie sank into the cushions with a soft whoosh. "Are you in trouble, dear?" She lowered her gaze to Bella's stomach.

Bella instinctively clasped her waist. "Of course not."

Mattie simply looked at her.

"All right, yes."

Mattie's eyes widened.

"Not *that* sort of trouble."

A sigh of relief was the madam's only response.

Feeling more than a little moody, Bella threw herself into the chair opposite Mattie's and proceeded to sulk for two entire seconds. But then she stopped herself. She was tired of thinking about William, about his ugly proposal and the newest batch of letters in her pocket. But most of all, she was just plain tired of *thinking*. Her secret was becoming too much to endure alone.

She hadn't been able to confide in Hannah, but Mattie was a woman who had made her share of mistakes. Mattie would understand. She would recognize the darkness inside Bella. Perhaps that explained why she blurted out, "I had a suitor in London."

Mattie chuckled. "I'd wager more than one."

"No, just one. But he was special. A viscount. I… He…" Bella rose, started pacing, halted just as quickly. "I thought he loved me. I thought he wanted to marry me."

Mattie's wise eyes stared into hers. "You were wrong, of course."

"He asked me to be his mistress." Bella buried her face in her hands. "I'm so ashamed. No. *No*. Not ashamed." She dropped her hands and pounded her fists in the air. "I'm angry."

"You gave in to him?" Mattie's question held no judgment, just curiosity. And maybe a little sympathy.

Bella threw herself back into her chair. "No."

"Then why all this anger?"

"I believed his lies, all of them, I never once doubted him, even when it was clear his stories weren't matching up with his actions."

Mattie laughed, a condescending sound that made Bella feel as if she was twelve years old again. "You think you're the first? Women are notoriously foolish in the face of pretty words and false promises. And I'm sure viscounts have their charm."

Bella's frustration rose, probably because she wasn't convincing Mattie of her obvious sin and resulting darkness in her soul. "You don't understand. He was married."

"You're not shocking me, dear." Mattie stretched out her leg and nudged Bella's foot with the toe of her shoe. "Any woman who looks like you is bound to have men fall in love with her. And for most men, marriage is not a deterrent in the face of such beauty."

Unimpressed with Mattie's summation, Bella scoffed at the ridiculous notion. "Marriage is sacred. No matter what anyone says, I know the truth. I ruined a marriage."

"I thought you said you didn't give in to him, so technically—"

"I was tempted. But instead of standing firm in my

convictions, instead of refusing him outright, I ran away. I ran here."

Mattie gave her a funny look, glanced over her head and then released an odd, calculating smile. "Let me see if I have this straight." She tapped a finger against her lips. "A married man asked you to be his mistress but instead of accepting you ran to your brother for safety?"

The calmly spoken words hit Bella like a slap. "Don't you see? That makes me a coward."

"In my estimation," Mattie glanced up again, "that makes you the bravest person I know."

Bella snorted.

Mattie glanced over her head, *again*. "Do you still love this viscount?"

She thought of Shane then, how he treated her with respect and honor. She thought of his patience, his integrity. How he made her feel safe and important, and very, very special. With Shane she was simply Bella, a woman worthy of acceptance for herself. Not Isabella, the famed opera singer worthy of nothing more than a role as mistress in any man's life.

Mattie nudged her foot again. "You haven't answered my question. Do you still love your viscount?"

"I couldn't love a man who thought that little of me."

"That's not an answer."

Shrugging, Bella reached into the front pocket of her skirt. "William has been sending me letters, begging me to return to England and the cozy 'setup' he has planned for us. These latest ones, I can't open them. It would be a betrayal to Sha—" She cut her own words off before she revealed her heart. There were some secrets Bella would never reveal to Mattie, or anyone else.

Tight-lipped, she handed the letters to Mattie. "Will you dispose of them for me?"

Staring at the papers in Bella's outstretched hand, Mattie remained firmly planted in her chair. "I'm confused. Who would you betray by reading those letters?"

"No one." Bella jabbed the envelope in the air between them. "Take them. Please."

At last, Mattie snatched up the letters and leaned back in her chair. "You're a brave girl, Bella O'Toole, but you can't hide your feelings as well as you think."

"What do you mean by that?" Bella snapped. She wasn't in the mood for one of the madam's infamous word games.

"You're in love all right." Mattie wagged the letters at her. "And I'd wager my house the viscount isn't the one holding your heart."

Bella gave a noncommittal shrug. Mattie saw too much. With a little encouragement she would turn Bella's feelings for Shane into something sordid.

Still grinning, Mattie glanced at a spot over Bella's head, again, the fourth time if Bella was counting. Which she was. *What was the madam up to now?*

Sensing they weren't alone anymore, Bella looked over her shoulder and saw Shane standing in the doorway.

Frozen inside her shock, she wanted to howl in outrage and then, *and then,* she wanted to snatch Mattie off her chair and shake her.

It was painfully clear what the ornery madam had been up to with all her questions of love. She had known Shane was standing behind Bella.

Marshaling as much grace as she could, Bella rose and turned to face Shane eye-to-eye. This was not a time for pleasantries, so she moved straight to the point. "How long have you been standing there?"

His stricken expression answered her question. "Long enough."

Chapter Sixteen

Shane didn't know what was worse. To discover Bella was yearning for a man she left behind in London or that she had shared her secret with Mattie Silks.

Either way, his greatest fear was realized. He'd fallen for a woman who longed for another man, just as his mother had pined for Peter Ford his entire childhood. And so the vicious cycle continued.

He turned to leave.

"Shane, wait."

He halted midstep but didn't turn back around. He couldn't look into her eyes now. Not with the knowledge of her love for another man standing between them.

He knew he had no right, but jealousy ran hot in his veins.

"Please." Her voice came out very small, very sad. "Let me explain."

For a maddening second, his heart pounded with expectation. But he gave a one-shoulder shrug and distanced himself from her with a step forward. "You owe me no explanation."

"Oh, but I do." He heard her footsteps approach.

Then her hand touched his back. Her fingers felt like ice through his jacket.

Clearing her throat, Mattie moved to his other side. "I think I'll go check on, oh, I don't know…something."

She brushed past him, turned, then gave him an encouraging look wrapped inside years of experience. "Hear her out," she said, a bit misty-eyed. "You might be surprised what she reveals."

She squeezed his hand then hurried off. Shane could only stare in amazement. An infamous madam playing matchmaker? That was too much even for his open mind.

With great effort he turned on his heel and entered the room. With each step he took, Miss O'Toole backed out of his way. The trepidation in her eyes made him wonder if she was afraid of him, or frightened of what he might say.

Better and better.

"You have nothing to fear from me," he said. "I'm the last person to judge you."

Shame flooded her eyes and she bowed her head. "I never wanted you to know what brought me here."

"You mean…*who.*"

She visibly cringed. "Yes, who." Head down, she shuddered again. "But you must believe me when I say I didn't know he was married."

Neither had Shane's mother known Peter Ford was married, at first. "What do you want me to say to you, Bella?"

Slowly, she lifted her head. Her eyes pleaded with him to understand, to forgive. "Tell me you don't hate me."

How could he? He was so far from that emotion his heart hurt. "I don't hate you."

She released a sigh. "But you think less of me."

Ah, a moment of truth. Dark emotions rose within him, anger so deep, so penetrating it battled with his hope for a future with this woman. Nevertheless, the truth could not be avoided, at least not in his own mind. He'd found a woman that made him want to risk love for the first time in his life. And he feared her heart belonged to another man.

No, he didn't judge her. He judged himself.

When he continued staring at her in silence, she shook her head. "Why are you so stoic? Tell me I'm bad, rant at me, call me a name."

"To what purpose?"

She rushed to him, gripped his hands. He hated how good her hands felt wrapped around his, hated how much he wanted to believe in her.

"I didn't give in to temptation, Shane. I ran. Isn't that worth something?"

"Yes, Bella, it is. But it doesn't matter in the end. All that really matters is what you do in the future." He took a deep breath and braced himself for the most important question of all. "Are you still in love with him?"

"No!"

He didn't believe her. She'd answered too quickly, as his mother had always done when he'd held her head in his lap after she'd spent hours crying over Peter Ford.

He will come. He will come, she chanted over and over again.

He never did.

And then she'd say: it doesn't matter. *I don't love him. I don't love him.*

But she did.

"You don't believe me." Her hand flew to her throat and her fingers fiddled with the pendant around her neck.

Shane's heart went numb. "Did he give you that?"

She dropped the gold chain at once. "Yes, but I—"

Shane lifted a hand to stop the rest of her words. No matter what she said, if she still wore the man's necklace she still cared. "No, Bella, don't continue. I don't want to hear any more. I know. I *know* what this is about." He shut off all emotion. "I think it best I renew my search for a qualified assistant, beginning today."

Her eyes filled with tears. She swiped at them with the back of her wrist. "Are you dismissing me?"

"Yes."

"Have I done a poor job for you?"

"No. You've been competent." *Wonderful. Exemplary. An answer to prayer.*

"Don't hold this against me, Shane. Let me continue as your assistant. At least with your patients in the brothels and mining camps. I know I'm tainted, so I won't go near the Charity House children again."

Is that what she thought? That he was dismissing her because she was soiled? "It's not that, Bella. The children of Charity House have seen much worse in their own mothers."

"Then what is it? Why dismiss me now? You have so much on your mind not to accept my help. You need me to pick up some of the duties so you can work on a solution to your father's stipulation in his will."

His father's will. Shane had nearly forgotten about that ugly little mess. In the span of days, his past had come back to haunt him through both his dead father *and* his dead mother. But it was the hazy memories of his mother's hopeless face that gave him the courage to speak the truth. "You're right. I do need your help, but I can't rely on you indefinitely. Eventually you will leave and return to the stage."

"Please, Shane." She pulled his hand to her face, fitted his palm against her cheek. "Let me continue working with you." Her eyes asked for more from him.

Staring into her beautiful, shattered gaze he knew he would give in to her plea. Not because she asked it of him, but because he couldn't bear to say goodbye to her yet.

In that moment, sadly enough, he understood his mother better. He now realized how the smallest spark of encouragement could make a person act against logic. *I don't love her. I don't love her.*

But he did.

"All right, Bella. I will see you Monday morning as usual." He turned to go, but pivoted back around as a thought occurred to him. "And, Bella, for what it's worth." He paused, hesitant to continue.

"Yes?"

"Temptation is not the same as sin."

Her face crumbled. "Jesus taught that the thought is equal to the act."

"Yes, that's why the thought must be surrendered to the Lord the moment it occurs."

"What are you trying to say?" The flicker of hope in her eyes made him feel strong, powerful. He wanted to ease this woman's pain, a woman who would always love another man. What did that say about him? It said he was more like his mother than he wanted to admit.

"You haven't sinned, Bella." He held her gaze, willing her to hear what he was saying. "Not yet."

The next morning, Bella stood outside the Charity House church. Thanks to a sleepless night, her eyes felt gritty and every muscle in her body ached. But she would not use her physical discomfort as an excuse to avoid God any longer.

She had to stop running. And if she didn't attend church today, she feared she never would.

She fingered the locket around her neck. It felt heavy, like a shackle that couldn't be removed with a simple tug.

Lord, please help me walk through those doors. Help me to put You first today.

Maybe then, once she'd realigned her priorities in the proper order, she would be able to remove her gold-chained albatross. Yes. She was sick of her selfabsorption, sick of allowing William's ugly motives to cause her any more shame. It was time to put her Lord first. Today, she would forget her past, forget her worries over Shane and simply worship her Father in Heaven.

As she began her ascent, each step became more difficult. To an outside observer her slow progress must look ridiculous.

She turned to leave. And came face to face with Shane.

"Going somewhere?"

"No, I… Yes. That is, I…"

"The entrance is facing the other way." His tone was incredibly gentle, the tone he used with his most frightened patients.

Could he read her panic? Did that mean he forgave

her? Could one day make such a difference? Could she possibly think in anything other than a question?

"I—"

"Would you allow me to escort you inside?"

Glory…*glory,* but she saw genuine respect in his eyes, as though he knew how hard it was for her to enter God's House.

"Please."

Smiling, he placed his hand on her elbow and swung her around. With a quick repositioning, he tucked her arm under his and drew her closer to him.

She felt incredibly protected.

Best of all, he was still smiling.

Truly, the man was incredibly handsome when he smiled. The simple gesture softened all those sharp planes and angles. She cast a covert look at him from under her eyelashes. He was dressed in his usual uniform of black pants, black waistcoat and black jacket, but today his hair was pressed down in place. He looked far too handsome for a country doctor. *He'd put any leading man to shame.*

She was so caught up in studying Shane she almost forgot to be nervous about entering God's House. Almost.

The moment their feet crossed the threshold she wavered. He pulled her tighter against him. A show of solidarity, much like she'd done when they'd faced Mr. Wilson together in his office two days ago.

Bella relaxed. A little.

Shane led her to the back pew. As she settled in next to him, she folded her hands in her lap and looked straight forward.

She could do this.

Her hands started to tremble. *How* was she going to do this? Would people be able to read her sin in her eyes?

Did her iniquities show on her face?

Men and women, some familiar, some strangers, nodded at them as they passed by, but none made an attempt to sit in the pew with them.

Surely it wasn't because of her?

As though hearing her thoughts, Shane leaned toward her and spoke in a whisper. "I always sit in the back, in case I have to leave quickly. Part of being a doctor."

"Is that why no one joins you in this pew?"

He looked thoughtful for a moment. "I never thought about it, but yes, I suppose so."

People continued to file down the center aisle and Bella dared to watch the door to see who might show up today. She was quickly rewarded with the sight of the Scott family. Ten-year-old Molly led the way, marching quickly down the aisle, her head held high. Her father rushed after her, probably trying to ensure she didn't do something outrageous in the short distance to their seats.

Bella's father had done the same with her. Little Molly Scott was a girl after Bella's own heart.

Mrs. Scott walked slower, more serenely, with Ethan by her side. The little boy looked at Shane, peered around him and caught sight of Bella. He waved his hand and yelled, "Miss Bella! Hi, Miss Bella."

Bella waved back. "Hello, Ethan."

Over her shoulder, Katherine Scott smiled at Bella, nodded to Shane then stopped. She scooted Ethan forward and told him to join his father.

Satisfied her son was going to obey, she leaned over the adjoining pew and said, "I know this is an unusual time to ask, but would you two care to join us for Sunday dinner today? We haven't really had a chance to thank you for all you've done for Ethan and the Charity House orphans."

Bella sat up straighter. Sunday dinner with the Scott family? She wasn't sure she could take church and the quintessential, perfect family all in one day.

Shane looked to Bella, an encouraging smile on his face. "Do we dare?"

"I don't know. I—"

"Ethan would be devastated if you said no," Mrs. Scott added.

Bella relaxed. "Well, we wouldn't want to disappoint the poor boy."

"Is that a yes?"

Bella nodded slowly. "It's a yes for me."

The other woman lifted a brow at Shane. He grinned at her. She grinned back. Bella's stomach clutched. The two had a connection that she didn't quite understand. It wasn't exactly like brother and sister, but—

"Yes for me, too," Shane said over her thoughts.

Pleasure filled the other woman's eyes. "Wonderful." She swiveled around and continued toward her family.

Once everyone settled into their seats, Beau walked to the front of the church. As one, the congregation stood and opened their hymnals as he directed.

For a moment, Bella closed her eyes and allowed the words to wash over her. By the second stanza, she joined in the song. Immediately, her heart lifted with her voice and she focused all her praise on her good God this glorious day.

Sensing others staring at her, she opened her eyes and noticed the people closest to her sneaking glances her way.

"Am I singing too loudly?" she whispered to Shane.

He shook his head. "No." He squeezed her hand. "You're lovely. I mean…your singing is lovely."

All that intensity and emotion thrown her way gave her encouragement to continue. When the song was done, everyone sat.

Beau caught her eye, smiled and then gave her the big-brother look that meant he was about to challenge her to a dare.

Bella swallowed. *Oh, no, Lord, please no.*

"I have a treat for all of us. My sister has agreed to sing 'Amazing Grace' for us."

"I did no such thing," she muttered.

"You can do this," Shane said softly.

"No, I can't."

"You *need* to do this." He closed his fingers over hers. "Trust God."

Trust. Her breath turned frigid in her lungs. Why was it the big things in life always came down to trust?

Knowing Shane was right, she slowly rose and made her way to the front of the church.

All eyes were on her. Oddly nervous for a woman who had performed before packed houses, she kept her gaze glued to the pulpit straight ahead.

When she arrived at the front, Beau reached for her hand and gave her a triumphant smile full of brotherly love.

Feeling more confident, Bella turned to face the congregation. And then, in an attempt to gain the sisterly upper hand, she muttered a warning. "I will kill you for this."

"You're welcome to try."

"Don't think I won't."

Taking a deep breath, her gaze landed on Hannah's face. Tears spiked her sister-in-law's lashes. Tears of joy, tears of understanding.

Bella swallowed.

Hannah gripped Mavis's hand tightly and the two nodded at Bella with approval. It was the same look she'd seen in Shane's eyes when he'd encouraged her to accept her brother's challenge.

Refusing to look at any more faces, Bella began singing "Amazing Grace." The words flowed out of her memory, out of her soul. And with the declaration of her sinful nature, a sense of well-being filled her.

No more shame. No more guilt. Just a strong desire for repentance.

Shane's words returned to her. Temptation is not the same as sin. Her flesh had been tempted, but Bella had remained obedient to God.

All this time, she had thought she carried the burn of a scar, but she had learned from weeks as Shane's assistant that scars did not come with pain. Only wounds.

She needed to allow God to heal her wound.

And the process began with confession.

When she came to the last stanza she locked her gaze with Shane. His eyes were intense, unblinking and full of awe.

She held his stare and a tear slipped from her eye. Followed by another. After the third, she gave in and allowed the rest to flow down her cheeks.

She sang the last note and a hush came over the

crowd. Through her blurred vision, she looked at their faces. Tears flowed from many of their eyes.

Before she could escape, Beau gripped her in a bear hug. "Well done, Bella. Well done."

"Thank you, Beau," she said softly.

He held a moment longer then released her. "Go back to Shane now."

As Bella made her way down the aisle, her heart felt too big for her chest. *Go back to Shane now.*

She smiled at him with a blush rising in her cheeks. Knowing this man had changed her. And because of him, she no longer wanted to grasp at the past.

Once settled in their pew, she lowered her head, reached up and released the clasp of William's necklace. She balled the locket in her fist and looked back into Shane's eyes.

He blinked at her, lowered his gaze to her hand.

She said nothing, simply set the necklace on the floor and kicked it gently under the pew ahead of her.

Her hand felt light, empty. Until Shane reached out and placed his palm against hers, right in the spot the necklace had occupied earlier.

A sigh lifted from deep within her. She looked into his eyes and saw the forgiveness she'd been craving ever since she'd seen his stricken face in Mattie's parlor.

With his acceptance, she'd taken her first step toward mending the wound William had inflicted on her heart. Now, she must turn to God and trust Him.

As she clung to Shane, fingers twined tightly with his, words were impossible and completely unnecessary. So they sat that way, hand in hand, for the rest of the service.

Chapter Seventeen

By the time Shane led Bella down the church steps, the early-morning breeze had built into a cold, raw wind. One sniff and he could smell the coming snow like a nasty threat. Not a good day for strolling. Thankfully, the Scott's house was a block away.

Huddled inside her wool coat, Bella smiled up at him. Her rosy, wind-chapped cheeks peeked out from beneath her hat, making her look young and healthy. Returning her smile, Shane boldly took her hand in his.

Heads bent together against the wind, they trekked along in companionable silence. Looking up, Shane glanced at the great mountains in the distance. He loved the untamed beauty of the Rockies, but today the compelling scenery held no real interest for him.

He had other, more important, thoughts on his mind.

From the moment he'd escorted Bella into church, Shane had sensed a change between them, a subtle shift toward a daring new future together. When she'd taken off the viscount's necklace, Shane had pressed his hand into hers and had accepted the truth. He was in love with Bella O'Toole.

But what would come of it?

Heart pounding like the wild wind, Shane opened the Scotts' backdoor and stepped aside so Bella could enter the mudroom first. Following closely behind her, a wave of enveloping warmth hit him as he shut the door behind them. Shrugging out of his coat, he helped Bella remove hers and then hung both garments on the wall hooks to his left.

Shane cleared his throat. "After dinner, perhaps we could talk?"

She pulled off her cap and her hair tumbled like a golden waterfall past her shoulders. "I'd like that."

There was so much gratitude, so much relief in her eyes that he realized his initial reaction to her revelations yesterday had hurt her deeply.

He pushed at his hair, started to apologize but was cut off by a delighted squeal.

"Miss Bella!" Ethan Scott launched himself in the air.

Bella swiveled just in time to catch the boy midflight. "Oh. Oh, my." Sounding a little breathless, she lifted the boy higher in her arms. "And how is my favorite four-year-old?"

Ethan's face spread into a brilliant smile. "Happy, now that you're here."

"I'm glad to see you, too." A shaft of sunlight streamed through the window behind her, glittering through her hair like polished gold.

Shane gulped. Looking at Bella O'Toole made his heart hurt.

Oblivious to everything except the woman holding him, Ethan patted her cheek with his palm. "Want to play checkers with me?"

Still smiling, she set the child on the ground and took his hand in hers. "I can't think of a happier way to spend the afternoon."

She looked back at Shane over her shoulder. "Would you mind?"

"I suppose I can spare you for a few minutes. You'll take care of her for me?" He winked at the boy.

Ethan puffed out his little chest. "Of course."

Tripping slightly as Ethan yanked her forward, Bella gave Shane an apologetic smile as she half trotted, half skipped behind her new friend.

At the look of pure adoration in the child's eyes, Shane felt an odd twinge of jealousy. Which made no sense. The boy was nothing more than an infatuated child. Perfectly harmless.

Ashamed of himself, Shane inhaled the smell of a happy home.

He drew in another breath. Apple pie, meat, potatoes. Shane had smelled these same scents at Charity House often enough. But he couldn't recall the welcoming scents in a single childhood memory. The aromas of his youth had been rotting fish, stale liquor, dirt and mold.

Here in Denver, Shane had found freedom from that life. But would his half sisters have a satisfying future, as well? Would they survive under the impossible restrictions of their father's will?

Yes, they would. Shane would see to it himself. Once he figured out a way around the stipulation. He had two days before Mr. Wilson returned. Unfortunately, he had yet to come up with a viable solution that would satisfy everyone involved.

Perhaps Bella had been right. He was thinking too

hard, trying to figure out the solution on his own, instead of allowing God to take control.

Shane cast his glance heavenward and prayed for guidance. *Lord, You have the perfect answer. I pray You reveal it to me in the next two days.*

Molly chose that moment to skip into the mudroom.

"Hi, Dr. Shane. Miss Bella told us you were out here." She planted two tiny fists on narrow hips. "What ya doing staring up at the ceiling like that?" She craned her neck to follow his gaze. "I don't see nothing up there."

"You don't see *anything* up there," Katherine said from the doorway.

Molly pressed her lips into a grumpy line and scowled at her mother. "Do you have to correct me on Sunday, too?"

With affection in her eyes, Katherine tugged on her daughter's braid. "I'm a schoolteacher, darling. It's what I do."

"Well. In that case." Molly gave her a pointed look. "I'm going to find Papa."

"He's in his office," Katherine offered without a hint of insult in her tone.

Molly darted off in the opposite direction. Katherine caught her by the sleeve. "And while you're in there, please inform him Dr. Shane and Miss O'Toole have arrived," she said before releasing her daughter.

Molly tossed a wave over her head.

Katherine sighed. "Honestly, that girl. She's becoming more and more like her father every day. Rash, impetuous, stubborn."

"And you wouldn't have her any other way," Shane reminded her.

Katherine grinned. "No, I wouldn't." She motioned him to join her. "Come in the kitchen with me. Let's talk while I finish rolling out the biscuits."

There was something in her eyes as she spoke, a female cunning that made Shane falter in his steps. Surely he was misreading her intentions. Her request was an innocent invitation to discuss the dismal weather.

He hoped.

With a bracing swallow, Shane entered the Scotts' spacious kitchen just as Katherine rounded the large chopping block in the middle of the room.

"How's Ethan's leg healing?" he asked.

"Other than the scar, you wouldn't know he'd been hurt at all."

"No limping. No—"

"He's fine, Shane." She gave him a curious look, one he couldn't fully decipher. "The wound has completely healed, just like you said it would."

Unsure what that odd look in her eyes meant, Shane pressed the issue. "Are you sure there's no problem with the leg?"

"None."

"Well, then. All right."

Capturing a smile between her teeth, she placed her palms in a pile of flour, grabbed a hunk of dough and began kneading the lump. "Tell me, how's your assistant fairing after the measles outbreak?"

The way Katherine said "your assistant" put Shane on his guard. Clearly, the woman was heading toward an uncomfortable topic, but not understanding her motive, Shane answered the question directly. "Miss O'Toole is handling her duties very well."

"She's been a blessing to you, then."

"Yes."

"Lovely."

Shane didn't like the smirk on Katherine's lips. Every male instinct told him to leave. Get out, now, before he fumbled into a female trap. "What are you about, Katherine? Why all the questions?"

"Just confirming my suspicion."

He narrowed his eyes. "Which is?"

"You've fallen in love with Miss O'Toole."

"No." He quickly responded. "I—"

"Oh, don't deny it. I mean, really, why wouldn't you? She's smart, beautiful and has the voice of a songbird. Clearly, she feels the same toward you. It's in the way she looks at you." Katherine pointed a finger in the air near her own eyes.

Pride, temper, a hundred other messy emotions had him speaking his greatest fear aloud. "I think she might still be in love with another man, a man she left behind in London."

Katherine's eyes widened and her hands stilled over the dough. "Oh." She looked into his eyes a moment longer, and then shook her head. "No. That's not true. You're mistaken."

How could she be so certain? And who was she to have this conversation with him?

"I won't speak about this with you, Katherine. It's not appropriate." His tone took on a harder edge than he'd planned. But in his haste to end the conversation, he'd revealed too much, said too much. And he couldn't take back the words now that they'd been spoken aloud.

"If you won't discuss this with me, then with whom? Lest you forget, doctor, you once proposed to me."

A direct hit. A sucker punch straight at his gut. "That

was a long time ago. And lest *you* forget, you turned me down."

She held his stare.

Shane turned away. Where were the others? Why had they left him alone with Katherine and her incessant questions?

"I wasn't in love with you, Shane," she added. "And you certainly weren't in love with me."

Cringing, Shane knew where she was going now. And he didn't want to dredge up ancient history. "That was a different time, Katherine, a different situation. Molly had just been in a fistfight defending your honor. You were both facing real scandal. The talk had to be stopped before Molly got hurt any more than she already had."

Katherine flicked her wrist at his feeble attempt to defend himself. "I didn't care about the talk. With my mother an infamous madam, I'd faced scandal all my life."

"My offer wasn't solely about you." Shane crossed his arms over his chest and scowled. "I wanted to spare Molly a childhood of whispers. She deserved better than that. *Every* child deserves better than that."

Sighing, Katherine grabbed a towel and wiped the dough off her palms. "Don't misunderstand me. I thought your gesture was sweet."

There had been nothing sweet about his motives at the time. He'd have done anything to prevent an innocent child from living the life he'd suffered. Agitated now, Shane tapped the toe of his shoe on the floor.

"Do you remember what else I told you that day?"

Tap. Tap, tap, tap. "Go on, Katherine, have your say and be done with it."

She shot him a triumphant smile. "I told you that one day you would fall in love and understand why I had to refuse your offer."

Spreading his feet apart, Shane lowered his arms to his sides. "All right. Let's go with your logic for a moment."

She cast a glance to the heavens. "At last."

He ignored her rude outburst. "You refused my proposal because you were in love with another man. Correct?"

Eyes wary, she inclined her head. "I don't think I like your tone."

"You were right."

That caught her unaware. "I… I was?"

"Yes." He clenched his teeth a moment, then relaxed his jaw. "And I promise you this. I will never again make an offer of marriage to a woman who is pining for another man."

He had more pride than that.

Unfortunately, Katherine seemed unimpressed with his declaration. "Oh, now I understand. Because you think there's someone else back in London, you won't pursue Miss O'Toole for yourself."

"Correct." And that should have been the end of it. Except he was conversing with a female, one who liked to talk a subject to death.

"He isn't here, is he?"

Stunned by her boldness, Shane looked at her, blinking hard. Where was she going with this new line of questioning? "No, he's not," he said carefully.

"Well, then, fight for her."

Fight for her? The outrageous idea staggered him and he took a step back.

What if Shane did what Katherine suggested and ultimately failed to win Bella's heart? But what if he failed because he didn't even try?

Heavy in thought, he walked to the window overlooking the Scotts' backyard. Eyes blind to the fierce storm brewing outside, he pondered Katherine's suggestion.

Fight for her...

Laughing loudly, Trey and Molly sauntered into the kitchen.

Shane cut off his thoughts and spun around to face the newcomers. Trey's gaze connected with Shane's and his eyes narrowed to small slits. Grimacing, he turned to his wife. "What did you do to him?"

Lifting a shoulder, she went back to kneading her dough as though they'd been talking about nothing more important than the weather. The woman had gumption, Shane would give her that.

"Katherine?" Trey urged.

"I didn't do anything to him," she murmured.

"Katherine, darling, the poor man looks poleaxed."

She jerked her chin at him. "Oh, all right, I may have pointed out an error or two in his thinking."

Trey clicked his tongue at her. "We had this discussion. You promised no meddling."

"I did no such thing."

"You didn't promise, or you didn't meddle?"

Shane's question precisely.

Grimacing, she pounded her fists into the dough but she kept her lips pressed tightly together.

Trey shook his head at his impossible wife, kissed her straight on the lips then turned back to Shane.

"Come on, my friend. I'm no authority but from that

hunted look in your eyes I'd say you were a man on the verge of escape. Oh, wait." He tapped a finger against his badge. "I *am* an authority on such matters."

"Marshal Scott to the rescue," Shane muttered, only half-joking as he followed hard on the other man's heels.

Later that afternoon, Bella walked silently next to Shane as he escorted her to Hannah and Beau's home. Since the distance between the two houses was only a few short blocks, she decided to enjoy every moment of their time together.

The air was cold and pure, but the threat of heavy snow had passed with the clouds an hour ago. Smiling, she cast her gaze to the clear heavens. She'd never imagined a sky could look that blue.

Lowering her head, she eyed the mansions on her left. The thin blanket of snow on the lawns gave her a sense of homecoming. Bella O'Toole had finally arrived where she belonged.

And, wonder of wonders, there was no stage in sight.

In the last few weeks, something had changed inside her. Something remarkable. It had started with this man walking solemnly beside her and, of course, with his job offer.

She'd always thought of herself as an opera singer. Nothing more and certainly nothing less. But now, she realized how shallow her life had become. Traveling from role to role, she'd grown obsessed with her craft, and had unconsciously turned her art into her idol. She had put her career ahead of her Heavenly Father.

There is no God but one...

Bella bowed her head. *Forgive me, Lord.*

Her mistake with William had come about because

she'd lost sight of her priorities. But instead of confessing and moving forward in victory, she'd allowed shame to eat away at her confidence in Christ. Removing William's locket had been her first real step toward repentance.

And now, free from the viscount at last, she could open her heart to a man who would help her become a better person.

She turned her gaze to Shane. His expression wasn't exactly closed, but it wasn't welcoming either.

He was probably thinking about his current dilemma with his father's will. Mr. Wilson would want his answer in two short days.

How had she forgotten?

"Shane, do you—"

"I was proud—" he said at the same time. Cutting himself off with a chuckle, he continued, "Go ahead, Bella."

"You first."

"All right." He stopped walking.

Bella did the same.

"I want to tell you how proud I was of you in church today."

"I—" She smiled at him. "Thank you."

He gave her a poignant smile and something fluttered in her stomach. He understood. He *knew* that the famous opera singer had been terrified of singing in front of her brother's tiny congregation. "I couldn't have done it without knowing you," she added.

"You're stronger than you think." His expression turned sad, troubled even. "You've been obedient to God in a way most women given the same situation would never have been."

She lowered her gaze to her toes. This was not an easy conversation, especially with a man who had experienced the ugly repercussions of an unholy alliance between a man and his mistress.

If there was to be any relationship with him she had to be honest now, as honest as possible. Honest enough to scare him off. "I ran away, Shane. Who's to say what I would have done had I stayed?"

"Running away, as you put it, took courage, Bella, especially given your feelings for your suitor at the time."

She saw the unspoken question in his eyes and knew her answer would set them on a new path. "I don't love him anymore."

His gaze searched her face for a long moment. Bella held his stare, unflinching under his scrutiny. She had nothing to hide from him.

"Are you sure, Bella? Completely sure?"

"Yes." She put all her feelings, all her emotions into that lone word.

"You've only been here a few months. Can love die that quickly?" There was doubt in his eyes as he spoke.

"What I felt for William wasn't love. I know that now." And what she felt for Shane, the admiration, the respect, the desire to see him happy, was so much truer, deeper and real than her feelings for Lord Crawley had ever been.

"How do you know that, Bella?"

"Because…"

He lifted a single brow, hope flickering in his gaze.

"Because." She placed her hand on his cheek and smiled. "I love you."

Chapter Eighteen

Shane's first instinct was to pull Bella into his arms and swing her round and round with pleasure. She loved him. He loved her. The rest would work itself out. Except life and love didn't always end happy.

Thus, his second instinct was to step back from her declaration.

How could she love him when her heart had yearned for another man until very recently?

His tangled emotions must have shown on his face because Bella lowered her hand from his cheek. "You don't believe me."

She looked so downtrodden, so dejected, that he wanted to deny her words. But he refused to lie. "No. I don't. But Bella, I want to."

She nodded, resignation slumping her shoulders forward. Shane almost felt the need to comfort her. But then her chin shot up and her eyes grew determined. "I'll prove myself to you."

He swallowed back a hasty response. His life had found a perfect tempo with this woman, yet he couldn't trust what they had was real. Why did his past still have such power over him? Why couldn't he forgive his mother and father, and truly live his life for himself?

He looked at Bella then, really looked at her, and tried to separate both of their pasts from the present.

Caution got the best of him. "Bella, you were in love with another man only a few days ago."

Her jaw went rigid and she swallowed hard. "I told you that wasn't love. It was a whim."

The wind kicked up, howling and snapping at them with vicious delight.

"A whim," he said through flat lips.

She opened her mouth, sighed, shook her head. "I understand why you don't believe me. And I realize words alone won't convince you. So you'll have to give me time to show you my feelings are real."

Time? She asked too much of him. How could he spend countless days and nights, working side by side with her, and not fall deeper in love with her? And when she went back to the stage, or to her viscount, or wherever her next *whim* took her, he'd be left behind. Alone. Pining.

"What happens when you return to the stage?" he asked.

She shifted her stance. "Maybe I don't want to return to the stage."

Not return to the stage? She'd been born to sing. "What is this really about, Bella?"

She scowled. "I don't know what you mean."

"Don't you?" He placed his finger under her chin and applied gentle pressure until she looked into his eyes. "People don't change this dramatically in such a short period of time. And even if they did, I heard you today. You would be wasting God's gift if you never sang again."

"How do you know I didn't find my calling today?" Her eyes lit with an inner fire, a sureness he'd never seen in her before. "How do you know I wasn't meant to sing in church, praising God, not on a stage demanding the audience's worship for myself?"

Now she sounded angry. Truly angry. But he couldn't let either of them forget she was young. Her sheltered youth hadn't prepared her for the harsher realities of the world. How could either of them be sure she knew her own mind when less than two months ago she was charging to the top of the opera world, with a viscount pursuing her for his mistress?

"You'll see, Shane, as the days pass I will remain constant."

He would see nothing of the kind. And he knew the exact way to save them both from further pain.

It's the coward's way out, a voice whispered in his head. He ignored the thought as he walked her to the front of her brother's home.

He stopped before taking the first step leading to the porch. "Your services are no longer needed at this time, Miss O'Toole."

"You're dismissing me? *Again?*" Her voice was one of pure outrage, as though no one had ever dared to disagree with her on a matter more than once, much less twice in two days.

Had she been upset by his words, contrite even, Shane might have changed his mind. Instead, he stood his ground. "As of this afternoon, you are no longer my assistant."

Her mouth hung open, then it shut with a determined snap. "We've been through this before."

"Yesterday, to be exact."

Her eyebrows slammed together. Shane could see her mind working through the conversation, coming up with and then discarding several responses. At last, a look of triumph spread across her face.

Shane braced for impact.

"Technically, you can't dismiss me because you don't pay me. I'm a volunteer."

"Not anymore."

She balled her hands into tight fists by her sides. "You are the most stubborn man I know."

"And you're the picture of flexibility." His ironic tone made her frown.

"You will regret this," she warned.

"Probably."

With a blink and a snap of her head, she wrapped her dignity around her like a cloak. "I won't go quietly."

"I'm not at all surprised."

Angry shock leapt into her face. "You need me."

If she only knew how much.

"Please don't do this to me. To us."

He hated that he was hurting her. But he couldn't relent now that he had taken this step. Maybe he needed to prove to her, as much as to himself, that she wouldn't run away from love. Maybe they *both* needed to know her love for Shane was real.

With that thought, he held himself back, folded his emotions further inside himself and fought an overwhelming urge to pull her into his arms and beg her forgiveness.

"Good day, Miss O'Toole." He turned on his heel and left her sputtering after him.

As he walked away, he feared he'd made the biggest mistake of his life. Not only had he turned his back on the woman he loved, he'd just angered a very determined female. One who would not slink away meekly.

Oddly enough, the thought made him smile.

The following morning, Bella begged a ride into town from Beau. Ever the devoted brother, he delivered her to Shane's office at precisely nine o'clock. Of course, the stubborn mule of a doctor was off making his daily visits without her.

Well, she wouldn't allow him to dismiss her so easily. Thankfully, he'd forgotten to retrieve the key he'd given her that first day of work.

She let herself into the office, stood just inside the door inhaling the scent of iodine and sulfur. A sense of rightness filled her. This was where she belonged, with Shane, working by his side.

How far they'd come since the first morning of her employ. No, *she* had come far. Shane had remained the same. Convicted in his beliefs, compassionate, a true man of integrity. On his best day, William was only half the man Shane was on his worst. She'd been dazzled by the viscount. But she loved Shane.

Of course, convincing Shane she knew the difference between the two was going to be a problem. His cruel father and selfish mother had inflicted too much damage to him when he was a boy. And now, Shane didn't believe in his fellow man, or fellow woman, as was the case with Bella.

She trudged to the table and noticed that Peter Ford's

will was where Mr. Wilson had left it. By its position, she realized Shane hadn't read a single page. She ran her finger across the top edge and sighed. How was he going to find a solution when he wouldn't read the stipulation for himself?

Oh, Lord, help Shane.

He deserved an answer that would hurt no one, not even himself. Yet, according to Mr. Wilson, the will was written in such a way as to ensure Shane lived with regrets the rest of his life.

Bella flipped through the pages, not really focusing on the words. She prayed the solicitor was mistaken, he had to be mistaken.

Starting over, Bella carefully read each page. Most of the legal language confused her, but then she came to the stipulation of Shane's inheritance.

"This agreement is contingent on Shane Bartlett practicing medicine in New York City," she read aloud. "If he fails to do so, my complete estate is bequeathed to Harvard Medical School for the sole purpose of research."

There it was, in black ink on white parchment, the stipulation that condemned Shane to a lifetime of regret and guilt. No matter what course he chose, the requirement meant Shane had to move to New York or forfeit his inheritance to his alma mater.

Anger swelled. "No. I'm missing something."

With a fast flip, Bella turned to the last page. The will was dated less than a year ago.

The beast. The nasty, unfeeling beast. Peter Ford must have known about Shane's work in Denver at the time he'd drawn up his will. The old man must have known what he was doing.

And then to leave his own daughters completely without provision? "Nasty, nasty man."

Pounding her fists against her thighs, Bella paced around the room. Surely, there was a way out of the legal restrictions set before Shane.

This agreement is contingent on Shane Bartlett practicing medicine in New York...

Bella stopped pacing and rushed back to the table. *Oh, Lord, is that it? Can it be that simple? Could Peter Ford have been that shortsighted?*

Surely a man of such vast wealth wasn't so bent on getting his own way that he'd miss something so simple.

Bella flipped through the pages frantically.

"Slow down, slow down," she whispered. "Make sure you're correct."

Reading carefully, slowly, taking meticulous care with each line, Bella found Shane's solution.

Oh, Lord, You are a good and gracious God. You really do take care of Yours. Thank You, Lord. Thank You.

She gathered the papers and stuffed them in her satchel. Shane might not believe she loved him. He might not believe she was over William. But he would hear her out this morning.

Oh, yes. Shane Bartlett was in for a little lesson when it came to Bella O'Toole's devotion to him.

And for his sake, he better listen up the first time.

Chapter Nineteen

Shane wanted to believe Bella loved him. But as his feet led him in the direction of her brother's home, he couldn't prevent his skepticism from mounting. Years of boyhood trauma had left him cynical. Thoughts of his youth had Shane's mind wandering back to his mother.

Even now, as a successful adult, his heart yearned for the woman Amanda Bartlett had never been. Her unrequited love for Peter Ford had left her bitter. And because of her resentment, she had abandoned her duties as a mother, imprisoning Shane in a world of poverty and loneliness.

He waited for his anger to rise at the memories deluging him. But all he experienced was an overwhelming sadness. How could he condemn his mother when he himself had fallen into her same trap? He was in love with a woman whose heart was still tangled with another man's.

Caught inside his troubling thoughts, Shane nearly crashed into Beau.

Beau braced his hands on Shane's shoulders. "Whoa, watch yourself."

"Sorry." With a shake of his head, Shane forced his mind back to the present. He heard laughter coming from Charity House's backyard, heard the sound of wagon wheels rolling along, the call of a bird, Beau's impatient click of his tongue. "Someone's in a rush."

"I have a lot on my mind."

Beau slapped him on the back. "I'm sure it's nothing an honest discussion between friends can't fix."

Shane cocked his head at that cryptic remark. "I'm afraid I'm not following you."

"Come have a cup of coffee with me. We need to talk." Beau punctuated his words with a measuring half smile. Shane had seen the look before, in the Charity House kitchen when he'd first asked Bella to become his assistant. Beauregard O'Toole, firmly ensconced in his role as protective big brother, wanted to discuss his sister.

And although Shane had searched out his friend for that very reason, he found himself reluctant to carry on with his mission now. "I have to check on my patients at Charity House first."

Beau was not to be put off. "They're in the middle of a baseball game. You won't be missed for a while yet."

Recognizing the hard purpose in the other man's eyes, Shane resisted the urge to rub at the sudden headache drumming behind his eyes. "I should let them know where I'll be."

"Already done. Now come, Shane." Beau gave him a look that was not becoming to a preacher. "It's past time we had ourselves a little heart-to-heart."

Shane had a quick impression of what a man felt like on his way to a firing squad. "Maybe we should go back to my office."

"We do this in my office today."

Beau took off toward his house. Shane had no other recourse but to follow. Or rather, no other recourse besides running away like a yellow-belly coward.

"We'll talk in my study," Beau suggested.

Trailing behind his friend, Shane removed his coat, all the while thinking hard. Something had spurred this meeting. And he feared he knew what. Bella. Him. Together, with *together* being the operative word.

One slim thought held his rising desperation at bay. Shane had remained above reproach in his behavior with his friend's sister. *More or less.*

As they filed into the study, Shane took in the dark paneled walls, the smooth leather chairs and the wide oak desk on top of rich-colored rugs. All that was missing was a sign that read No Girls Allowed.

Beau dropped into the chair behind his desk, and then kicked his feet on top, crossing his ankles over one another. Hands clasped behind his head, he shut his eyes and took a deep breath.

Clearly, the man was relishing this moment in his private retreat.

Unsure what Beau was about, Shane settled into one of the wingback chairs facing the other man and waited.

It didn't take long for Beau to open his eyes and settle his gaze on Shane. Although in a seemingly relaxed posture, he'd positioned himself in such a way that there could be no doubt this was not a casual get-together.

Shane sent up a fervent prayer for guidance. "What's on your mind, Beau?"

"Actually." Beau dropped his feet to the floor and leaned on his desk, pressing his weight on his forearms. "That's what I'd like to know."

Shane considered himself an intelligent man, but no matter how he mulled over Beau's words, he didn't understand the question. Was the man talking in some convoluted preacher code? Had Shane missed a portion of the conversation? "Speak clearly."

Beau's gold eyes glittered as he studied Shane in that thorough, patient way that had sinners spilling their guts.

"How's this for clear speaking," Beau said. "What's on your mind when it comes to my little sister?"

Shane reared back in his chair. "That was certainly direct."

"Are your intentions honorable?"

Shane fought a hard battle to keep his voice steady. "I have no intentions, honorable or otherwise." None he cared to share with her big brother, at least.

"Why not?"

"Pardon me?"

Beau settled back into his chair with a grin lifting the corners of his lips. "Why aren't you pursuing my sister?"

Shane drew in a hard breath. "Bella is my assistant. It would be inappropriate to *pursue her,* as you put it."

Could he sound any more pompous?

"Inappropriate. Hmm." Beau gave him a look just short of insulting. "But holding hands in church is altogether suitable?"

Shane's heart pounded with regret. He should have known that particular detail would come out at some point, but he'd been too stupid to prepare a defense.

"It was innocent enough." Shane stabbed a glance at the door. Maybe he could leave before this got ugly.

"Have you kissed her yet?"

Too late.

But…

Now wait…

If Shane wasn't mistaken, Beau's eyes danced with… delight?

"What is wrong with you?" Shane ground out. "You're Bella's brother. Aren't you supposed to be upset I've been chasing after your sister when I promised to protect her while in my care? Yet all along I've been thinking about…wanting to…that is…"

Shane gripped the arms of the chair and let his words trail off. His chest tightened at what he'd nearly revealed.

Despite Shane's telling admission, Beau continued calmly blinking at him, his gaze patient and unwavering as though he had all the time in the world to wait for Shane to collect his thoughts and continue.

Shane had nothing more to say.

At last, Beau broke the silence. "I just have one more question."

"Fair enough."

"Do you love her?"

Why lie now? Why turn this farce of a meeting into something uglier than it had already become? "Yes."

Beau muttered something under his breath about godsends and blessings, then added a little louder, "Then I return to my earlier question. Why aren't you pursuing her?"

"It's not that simple."

"Why not?"

"We… I… It… It just isn't." Shane shut his mouth. He was blathering like an idiot. But what was he supposed to say? He couldn't disclose the reasons for his reluctance to begin a personal relationship with Bella. To do so, he would have to reveal her liaison with the viscount. That wasn't Shane's secret to tell.

"She calls you Shane, you call her Bella. You hold hands in church. The way I see it, it's very simple." Beau said. "All I ask is that you court her properly."

Shane looked away from Beau's well-meaning advice. *Court her properly. Fight for her.* Bottom line, if Shane had any chance of happiness he had to stop waffling where Bella was concerned. He had to act. He had to—

The door burst open and in spilled the very subject of his thoughts. "Shane. I've been looking for you everywhere. There's no residency clause, no time restrictions. Don't you see? That's your answer. It's… Oh!" Her voice trailed off and she simply looked from one man to the other.

Shane rose and stared at Bella. He knew what he had to do. No more doubt. No more allowing the past to rule his actions. It was time he made some concrete decisions. No. It was time he did some proper courting.

Bella looked from one man to the other and then repeated the process two more times. They were two big, beautiful males. And the masculine backdrop of Beau's office only added to the strong impression they made as they stared at her.

The fact that these men neither realized nor cared how handsome they were made them all the more appealing. Without an ounce of vanity, they were a little too large, a little too confident and utterly terrifying.

Gathering her courage, her eyes connected with Shane's. "I'll come back later," she said.

"No." Beau rose from his chair. "I was just leaving. Shane has something he wants to say to you." He looked pointedly at Shane. "Isn't that right?"

Shane nodded.

Bella sighed. Obviously, something of monumental importance had been said about her.

More than a little agitated at the notion of her brother discussing her with Shane, she stepped to one side to make a path for Beau's exit.

But instead of looking at her brother as he approached, she kept her eyes on Shane. The intensity of his gaze reminded her of the first time they'd met when Ethan had cut his leg. Even then, before she'd known him, she'd sensed he was a man who made things better for those around him. She hadn't known he would change her life so dramatically.

Good thing she liked drama.

Through loving him, Bella had learned to think of another. To worry for another's well-being and happiness above her own.

Bella had found her life's partner in Shane. It was time he quit fighting her and accepted that fact.

Before exiting the room, Beau stopped beside her and squeezed her hand. "Be tough, Bella. Relentless, as you are with everything that truly matters to you."

As she stared into her brother's eyes she saw the truth there. He understood. Shane had revealed enough for Beau to know the situation. And now, he was telling her to battle for the man she loved.

And so she would.

Beau closed the door behind him with a soft click. For a long moment, Bella and Shane didn't move, didn't breathe. They were caught in some sort of odd moment in time, as if they were locked inside a photograph.

At last, Shane broke eye contact and looked at the satchel she carried. He lifted a questioning brow.

"I found your solution," she said.

"Yes?"

"I'll show you."

Glad for the distraction, she slid past him, pulling the papers out of the case as she walked. With a thump, she set Peter Ford's will on top of Beau's desk and gestured Shane forward. "Page six. Read the tenth line."

He slowly joined her, trepidation sparkling in his eyes.

"Trust me, Shane." They both knew she spoke of more than his father's will.

His steps faltered. Then he smiled. Really smiled. "Let's see what you found."

She took a shaky breath and turned the pages for him.

He bent his head over the will. She waited as his gaze flew down the page. And then his eyes stopped moving.

"Read it out loud," she suggested.

Glancing up, he cocked his head at her then lowered his gaze again. "This agreement is contingent on Shane Bartlett practicing medicine in New York City."

Impatience had her tapping her foot on the hardwood floor. "Well?"

He looked at her, looked back at the will. "I don't—"

"There's no residency clause. There's nothing specifically requiring you to live in New York City."

"Bella, darling, I can't practice medicine if I'm not in the city."

He'd called her darling. Oh, the dear, dear man.

"You could live here. Travel there four times a year."

He stood rigidly, with the unforgiving posture of a man who refused to yield. "Patients require day-to-day care."

"Then hire partners, doctors who will be there for the day-to-day care. With your father's money you could afford to hire several nurses, as well."

Shane swallowed a few times and she realized he didn't know how to respond.

"It's not a perfect solution, but it could work."

"We'll have to check the legalities," he said slowly. "And, of course, we'd have to find the right doctors. But if you're correct, I could have a clinic both here *and* in New York."

Her eyes lit up. "Oh, Shane. That's precisely what I was thinking."

His gaze locked on a point above her head. "Women like my mother would have decent medical care here and in my old neighborhood." A slow grin spread across his face. "My father would hate that."

"And best of all, you could afford to care for your sisters, as well."

"Thanks be to God."

Bella smiled. "The Lord has blessed you, Shane. Just like I knew He would."

Shoving the papers slightly away from him, Shane pierced Bella with one of his most intense looks to date. "Bella O'Toole, whether you're right or not, the real blessing in my eyes is that you cared enough to look for an answer."

She gave him a shaky smile, realizing no person in his life had cared enough for Shane. Not his mother and certainly not his father. "Of course I looked. I love you, Shane."

Blinking, he pulled her into his arms and held her close. "I love you, too," he whispered into her hair.

She flung her wrists around his neck and clung to him. "It's about time you admitted it."

His hold tightened. "Tell me you love me, Bella. I want to hear you say it again."

"I love you, Shane. With all my heart."

She felt him relax against her. Bella's pulse slowed to a lovely cadence, beating in perfect time with Shane's. *This* was where she belonged. *Oh, thank You, Lord.*

Slowly, deliberately, he released her. "We have a lot to talk about. Your past and mine will always be between us if we don't settle our differences now."

She tugged her bottom lip between her teeth and allowed herself a moment of hope. "I found a passage in Scripture that I think applies. It's from Luke, in the story about the woman who comes to wash Jesus's feet."

"One who is forgiven little loves little," he quoted from memory.

"Yes. And it goes without saying, a person who is forgiven a lot, loves a lot." She smiled. "You know, Shane, I have *a lot* of love to give."

"As do I."

They laughed. He took her hand in his, brought it to his lips. A wave of affection washed over her. She had found the man of her dreams. But the moment his mouth brushed her knuckles, a soft knock came at the door.

"Bella?" Hannah's lilting voice seeped into the room. "Are you in there?"

Shane released Bella's hand. "We'll talk later," he said.

Bella gripped his arm, a wave of desperation filled her. "Tonight? After we've finished seeing patients?"

"Of course." He smiled at her. "After *we* finish seeing patients."

"Does that mean you're hiring me back?"

He ducked his head. "I should have never fired you."

"I knew you'd see things my way."

"What can I say?" He winked. "I'm a reasonable man."

"Oh. I like reasonable men."

A grin flashed across his lips. "Come in, Hannah," Shane called out. "Before Bella has me promising her the moon and the stars and a rainbow or two."

Hannah popped her head through a small slit. Her gaze slid to Shane in silent apology. "Bella has a visitor."

At the softly spoken words, a sense of foreboding filled Bella. The same feeling must have passed through Shane, because he stiffened at Hannah's announcement.

Bella reached to Shane for support. "Who...who is it?"

In answer, Hannah handed her a small piece of paper with engraved lettering on it. "He gave me his card."

Reading the name, Bella's knees buckled. Shane reached out to steady her.

Tucked in the safety of his arms, she let the card flutter from her fingers. "It's William," she whispered. "He's come for me."

Chapter Twenty

Powerless to stop her life from spiraling out of control, Bella clung to Shane as he helped her catch her balance. When he set her away from him and left nothing but lifeless air between them, she thought, *Surely, this can't be real.* William couldn't be here. Not in her brother's home.

But he was.

And the look of defeat that flashed in Shane's eyes added to the reality of this horrible moment.

He started for the door.

Her hand shot out and stopped his progress. "Shane, no, don't go." *Help me, Lord. Help me to convince him to stay with me.* "I don't want this. I don't want him."

He dropped his head, took a deep breath and then lifted his flat gaze to hers. His eyes were so cold. So emotionless. But she knew he hurt. She could feel his pain in her own heart.

Oh, Shane.

"You should hear what he has to say. He's traveled a long distance for you."

"I didn't ask him to come."

"You did. By running away and ignoring his letters, you forced his hand." He cupped her cheek, his touch light and forgiving and completely at odds with the dark look in his eyes. "You have to finish what you started, Bella. You'll never know how you truly feel if you don't."

She ordered her voice to remain even, but her growing panic made her words come out shrill. "I don't need to talk to him to know how I feel."

Sympathy flashed in his gaze. "Nevertheless, you should take this opportunity to alleviate any doubt."

He was so calm, so in control. The flare of resentment surprised her and her reflex was to turn on him, but she shook it off. Shane hadn't done anything wrong. "Please. Don't leave me alone with William."

"Are you afraid of him?" Shane's eyes hardened with the look of a man protecting a woman he loved. "Will he hurt you?"

His concern cut through her anxiety. She wanted to reach up and cup his face. She wanted to kiss him and beg him to believe it was him that she loved. "No. Of course not. I—" She cut her own words off. How could she explain her real fear? How could she tell him she was terrified he might never come back once he walked out that door? "Shane, I—"

William's booming voice cut her off. "I will wait no longer. Bella? Bella!" He knocked hard on the door. "Are you in there?"

At the sound of the familiar voice, her stomach dipped and she looked frantically for an exit. There was only one door.

And Shane stepped toward it, away from her. "You must face your past, Bella. And you must do it alone."

"Shane, please."

Shaking his head, he took another step away from her. "She's in here," he called out.

The next second, William burst into the room.

Bella's pulse drummed in her ears as Shane melted into the shadows and William took another step forward.

Her first thought was that the viscount looked as handsome as ever, still tall and lean, with sharp, angular features and perfectly tailored clothing. But inside his expensive attire, William looked lost in his own image, like an actor playing an overrehearsed role.

Was this the man she'd nearly sacrificed her soul for?

As his gaze hunted for Bella, Bella's gaze strayed to Shane. He hadn't left the room yet. And although his features were curtained by the shadows, she knew he was standing ready to protect her if William crossed a line.

So caught up in staring at Shane, she nearly missed the moment when William's gaze found her.

With an exaggerated sweep of his hand he removed his hat and bowed to her. The gesture was so formal, so over the top, she wondered if it wasn't a bit calculated.

"Bella, my darling. I have found you at last."

An idle smile drifted along his lips and he reached out his hand in silent summons.

Tossing her head back, Bella refused his call. And again, she wondered what had attracted her to the viscount. Only months before she'd been desperate for William's love. Now, she felt nothing.

"I'll leave you two alone," Shane said into the silence.

Bella reached to him. "No, stay. Please."

He must have sensed her panic because his gaze softened and he gave her the look he used when his patients thought he might abandon them during a procedure. "I'll be right outside if you need me."

William straightened, his eyes fixed on a spot over Shane's shoulder as though Shane didn't warrant his full attention. "No need to fuss over her, my good man. Bella will be leaving with me shortly."

A ruthless look crossed Shane's face. "Bella will make that decision."

Before William could respond, Shane exited the room and shut the door behind him with a hard snap.

After months of separation, she was alone with William again. Her stomach rolled over itself in trepidation, but she kept her gaze steady. William held no more power over her. The relief that came with the thought nearly buckled her knees. She wanted to shout at him to leave at once. It was over between them, finished. But she restrained herself. A moment like this required a certain amount of dignity.

Unaware of her thoughts, William bowed over her hand and touched his lips to her knuckles. "You win, my dear." Tenderness and appreciation mingled in his gaze, but she knew better than to believe in him. He was only doing what he felt he needed to do in order to accomplish his goal.

She slipped her hand free. "What have I won, William?"

"Why, my dear, isn't it obvious?" He gave her the smile she once thought so charming but now appeared a little wicked. "You have won me."

"You?" Bella couldn't quite believe the arrogance of the man and a wave of impatience whipped through her. "What exactly do you mean by that?"

"I am a free man." Seconds ticked by before he added, "My wife is dead."

At the cold tone of his voice, a shiver iced over her skin. His wife was dead? Did he not miss the woman at all? "I am sorry for your loss."

He waved a dismissive hand. "She was always sickly. Her passing was a blessing in the end."

She thought she saw a flicker of something dark in his eyes, but then he smiled, putting the suave viscount back in place. Who was this man, really? Had she ever known him?

"I want you to come home with me, Bella. Back to London where you belong."

Where she belonged? Bella caught her rising gasp between her teeth and stared at him with a steady look. She had once craved to hear him say those exact words. But home was Denver now, not London. Home was with Shane, wherever that took them. "I can't go to London with you. I want more than the stage has to offer."

The satisfaction in his eyes put her on guard. "Then we are in agreement. Whatever you want, Bella, I will provide it for you." He ran his blue eyes over her in lazy thoroughness. "I want you with me and I am willing to pay for the privilege."

Unlike the last time he'd made his proposition, his words left her cold with rage. *This time around,* she heard what he wasn't saying as much as what he said.

"Go on, William." She clasped her hands calmly together. "Tell me what you're offering. You've come this far, you might as well expand on the details."

"I will give you the security you crave."

Holding firm, Bella waited for the rest.

Nothing more came.

"Is that all you're offering?" she asked.

His facade slipped, just a bit, making him look young and spoiled. *"Is that all?"* he repeated in an offended tone. "You will have carte blanche for the rest of your life."

She tilted her head, planted her hands on her hips. He looked like a child who was being denied a pretty toy that had caught his fancy. "You mean carte blanche as your mistress."

"As the love of my life."

His haughty attitude made her take a step back, but still, she persisted. She would force him to say what was on his mind, no matter how ugly the truth. "And if you tire of me?"

"You will be taken care of no matter what happens between us in the future."

Her knees wobbled again, but she locked them into place as understanding emerged. "You mean financially, of course."

"Of course. My solicitor has drawn up the contract." He grabbed her wrist and placed her hand to his heart. "Bella, Bella, can you not feel my heart pounding with love for you? Can you not believe I mean to take care of you for the rest of your life?"

She calmly pulled her hand free. "Am I to understand you are offering me security, but not in the form of marriage?"

Lifting his chin, he clasped his hands behind his back and drew in a long breath. "I can not marry an opera singer. It is simply not done. I have two sons, both with titles in their own right. I must take a wife of good family. But my heart will always belong to you, my love. I will simply find a woman to marry who understands this."

Bella's hand clutched at her throat. Her *bare* throat where she no longer wore William's condemning locket. She was free of him now, free of his filthy intentions. She would *not* feel shame over his sinful propositions any longer.

Before she could tell William exactly what she thought of him and his offer, Shane jerked open the door.

Beau shot in ahead of him, but Shane caught him by the sleeve and yanked him back. "This is my fight."

Her brother looked angry. Truly angry. But not as angry as Shane. Clearly, the men in her life were not going to allow anyone to hurt her.

"Fine, I will leave the matter in your hands," Beau growled. "But you better end this now. Today."

Shane's lips twisted in a sneer. "Count on it."

Bella had one second to take in her brother's answering glower before he slammed out of the room.

"Shane?"

"I'm sorry, Bella, but I won't allow history to repeat itself." His voice came out low and steadfast.

She almost missed his meaning, but then she understood. He loved her enough to ensure she didn't live his mother's life, even if that meant forcing William's hand. Who would have thought the caring doctor could be such a warrior at heart? "Oh, Shane, no, I don't need you to fight this battle for me. I have made up my—"

He cut off the rest of her words with a hard shake of his head. Like a knight guarding his lady-in-waiting, he set her gently behind him and then turned to glare at William. "Bella deserves nothing less than marriage. Offer it, or get out."

A range of emotions crossed the viscount's face, but the eyes that finally locked on Shane were sharp and measuring. "Who are you to demand this of me?"

Shane ignored the question. "You will find no woman better than Isabella O'Toole. She is kind, compassionate. Smart."

Bella cleared her throat. "Shane, you don't have to do this."

Shane patted her hand, and then shrugged away from her. "Yes, I do."

"I asked for your name," William demanded again. "Who dares to speak to me in this impudent manner?"

Their eyes locked and held.

"I am Shane Bartlett. Bella has been serving as my nurse these last few months."

"A nurse?"

Shane held up a hand at William's shocked declaration and took the opportunity to continue his litany of Bella's merits. "I have had the pleasure of working with Miss O'Toole in the sickroom. She's courageous, full of gentleness and joy and…" On and on and on he went.

Even Bella was losing track of all her fine qualities. And she wasn't one to sniff at a compliment. But with each new trait Shane presented on her behalf, William's face grew redder with outrage. If there had been a shred of doubt before, Bella no longer had to guess which man truly loved her.

And which man she loved in return.

Shane might be embellishing a bit—*a lot*—but she also realized he spoke from his heart. While William could only stare at him in growing disgust, a subtle air of disapproval floating out of his stance.

At last...finally... Shane wound down, ending with, "And, of course, she's beautiful."

"Is that all?" William asked, his tone droll.

"For a start."

"And if I don't propose marriage to this virtuous creature of perfection?" he challenged.

"I'll happily make Bella an offer myself."

"No. No. Can't have that." But William's face paled as he gazed at Bella. No longer the confident nobleman full of demands and bluster, he looked uneasy, a little ill and his breath came out in quick, hard bursts. "You have convinced me of what I must do."

Bella had never been more insulted in her life.

Shane, on the other hand, looked oddly triumphant. What? He was going to hand her over to William, just like that? Without a fight?

"Carry on." Shane wound his wrist in the air. "But make it quick, I have patients waiting."

William swallowed, his face looking green along the edges. "I'm getting to it."

Now Bella was *truly* insulted.

Seeming in no hurry to get to his "patients," Shane crossed his arms over his chest and hitched his hip against Beau's desk. He looked a little too pleased with himself, as though he was enjoying William's discomfort. "Get on with it, *my good man*."

"One can't rush an important matter such as this."

"It's four little words," Shane scoffed. "Can't be that hard to say. *Will you marry me?* See, I just said them myself."

William glared.

Shane grinned.

Bella sighed.

"Uh, gentlemen, I'm in the room," she reminded them. "Is anybody going to consult *me* on the matter?"

William continued scowling at Shane. Shane continued grinning in return.

And neither acknowledged Bella's question.

"Go on," Shane goaded. "Four little words and you win the girl for a lifetime."

William swallowed. Hard.

Shane's smile widened.

"Honestly." Bella interrupted the two. "I can make this simple for us all. I don't want to marry William."

They both ignored her and continued their ridiculous battle of wills.

As William's discomfort grew, Shane's confidence did the same. Bella suspected Shane was having a bit too much fun at the other man's expense. Clearly, William didn't want to marry Bella any more than she wanted to marry him. But the lofty viscount was too proud to admit that rather large detail in front of Shane.

She would have never suspected William to be so easily manipulated. Again, she wondered if she'd ever known the man.

Just when she thought the viscount would give up his pride and admit his true feelings, William surprised her. After muttering a rather nasty oath at Shane, he marched to Bella. With a final grumble under his breath, he snatched up her hand. "Bella, darling, will you marry me?" He spoke through gritted teeth.

Before answering, she drew her hand out of William's grip. Free of the contact, she actually felt her heart settle. "No."

"No?"

"I don't want marriage."

The look of relief on his face should have been humiliating, but his next words left her too cold for any emotion at all. "But you will consider—"

"Absolutely not." She and Shane said at the same time.

William looked at her then Shane scowled. "What's Bella to you, anyway?"

Shane stared at her for a long, agonizing moment. The intensity in his gaze took her breath away. "I love her. She is everything to me, second only to God."

The man had to work on his timing, but Bella could forgive the minor transgression. Shane had declared his love in front of William, who happened to be sputtering with indignation.

Bella sighed. The sooner she ushered the viscount out of the room, the better. He didn't belong in her world now, and she didn't belong in his. He'd know that if he'd give up a portion of his pride. "William, I appreciate that you traveled this far to find me. But I choose to stay here, with Shane."

William cocked his head, a frown marring his brow. "You're staying here? With *him?* You're not even returning to the stage?"

"God has called me to a different life, one with a higher purpose."

He looked at her as though she'd grown two heads. "As what, a nurse? You'd give up the stage to care for *sick* people?"

And then she knew the truth. William had never loved her. He had merely loved the idea of her. But he hadn't known her, and he certainly wouldn't recognize the woman she'd become. A woman of faith, who would spend her life praising God with her voice and honoring Him with her hands.

She didn't have to defend her decisions, not to this man. She doubted he would understand if she tried. *Has God not made foolish the wisdom of the world?*

"I'm happy here, William. This is where I belong."

She glanced at Shane. He smiled at her with encouragement. She wanted to rush into his arms, but he'd been right all along. She had to finish what she'd started back in London.

Head high, she focused once more on William. "Go home to your sons, Lord Crawley. Find a wife for yourself, one who will be a good mother, as well. I pray she's a woman who will make you forget you ever wanted a mistress."

He looked at her as though he was a man who couldn't run fast enough in the opposite direction. "So, this is it, then? The end?"

"Goodbye, William."

She held very still as William muttered a foul word, spun on his heel and left the room without so much as a farewell thrown her way. She felt a little empty as she stared at his retreating back, as though her parting with him had been anticlimactic, nothing but a boring ending to a mediocre play.

"Shane, I have a confession to make," she said as she continued staring at the space William had recently occupied.

"Yes?"

She turned to face him, let her love shine boldly in her eyes. "I wasn't completely forthright when I said I didn't want marriage."

His gaze turned inscrutable. "No?"

"Oh, I want marriage. As a matter of fact, I *deserve* marriage."

"Yes." He smiled. "Yes, you do."

She took his hand, pressed a kiss in his palm. "But I won't settle for just any man who comes along."

"That would be a disaster."

"Precisely. I have decided I want to share my life with a man willing to sacrifice his own happiness in place of mine, a man who thinks I'm kind, compassionate, smart and all the other things you said in my defense."

"I love you, Bella."

"I love you, Shane."

She lowered to her knees. "I have four little words for you," she said with a smile. "Will you marry me?"

Frowning, he knelt beside her. "Despite my unusual upbringing, I'm a traditional man, my dear. I'm supposed to ask the question."

"Then ask it, my love."

He cupped her face between his hands and kissed her on the lips. "Will you marry me, Bella O'Toole?" He kissed her again. "Will you be my wife?" He kissed her a third time. "And my partner in serving God?"

"I have just one word to say in response."

A muscle shifted in his jaw. "Is that one word *yes?*"

She gave him a firm nod. *"Yes."*

Epilogue

June 15, 1887, New York City, the Bowery, lower Manhattan

The day dawned clear and hot, magnifying the foul stench of unwashed bodies, rotting fish and stale whiskey. Bella wrinkled her nose as she walked alongside her husband. It wasn't what she would call the perfect fragrance to accompany a ribbon-cutting ceremony, but nothing could dampen her spirits now that this monumental day had arrived.

In a few moments, Shane would officially open the doors of the Bowery Medical Clinic to the general public. The small hospital was an exact replica of the one they'd launched six months ago in Denver, all the way down to the scrolled verse above the front door: *for we walk by faith, not by sight.*

God had provided far more than any of them could have accomplished on their own. And it seemed the more they gave, the more they received back in joy.

They were truly blessed.

Waddling alongside Shane, Bella felt like an overdressed, overstuffed cow. According to Hannah, seven months of pregnancy tended to do that to a woman. At least the morning sickness was gone. And yet, as Bella looked around her husband's childhood streets, bile rose in her throat.

The dark side of life was presented without any attempt to tone down the disreputable image. No decent man or woman would walk these streets at night. Even at this early hour, many of the concert halls and Dime Museums flourished with customers. Vulgar songs accompanied by wretched music spilled into the streets. The lodgings interspersed between the shady businesses were filthy beyond compare. Shane called the falling-down tenements "resorts for thieves." He would know.

The elder of Shane's two sisters, Drusilla, a pretty, blonde, round-faced sixteen-year-old spoke Bella's thoughts aloud. "Oh, Shane, how did you ever survive this place?"

Affection glittered in his eyes as Shane looped an arm over the girl's shoulder. "Simple. God protected me, my dear."

Drusilla grinned at him, sisterly adoration apparent in her eyes. "Well, I'm glad for that."

Not to be outdone, Elizabeth, the gregarious twelve-year-old and miniature version of her older brother, snatched at his other arm. "And now you've returned a hero."

He lifted a single eyebrow. "I wouldn't go that far."

"I would." She looked around her with keen interest, and a little sauciness kicked in her voice. "I think it's amazing you grew up here, no rules, no restrictions, no—"

"Food, at times," Shane reminded her.

"Of course." Elizabeth's eyes grew serious and she lowered her head. "I forgot that part."

Shane pulled her close and hugged her against him. "It's ancient history. And if I can help some of the children who live here now, well, maybe it was for the best. How would I know how to alleviate their suffering, if I hadn't experienced it myself?"

Blinking rapidly, she lifted her eyes to his. "I'm going to be a doctor just like you."

"I think that's a wonderful idea," Bella announced before Shane could offer his opinion on the matter.

Elizabeth turned her head. "You do?"

"I think you can do anything you set your mind to."

Elizabeth beamed. Emotion squeezed at Bella's heart. She loved this child dearly, just as she loved Drusilla. But most of all, she loved watching Shane interact with his sisters. Her handsome, serious-minded husband was more relaxed and definitely more affectionate because of his time spent with the girls. Yet another blessing to come from the ashes of Peter Ford's untimely death.

As soon as the legalities had been settled, Shane had sent for the girls. Thankfully, Drusilla and Elizabeth had grown to adore Shane in a very short amount of time. And Bella had won them over, as well. In truth, the girls had been desperate for real parents and now the four of them made a happy, albeit unusual, family.

Slowing her pace, Bella looked at Shane over the girls' heads. He winked at her. His code for *I love you.*

She blew him a kiss as they rounded the final corner of their destination. She froze midstep and gasped at the sight before her. Hundreds of people stood in line along the three blocks leading to 35 Bowery. "Oh, Shane, there's so many of them."

He blew out a long breath and studied the queue that snaked past brothels, beer gardens and flophouses.

"We'll do what we can," he said, looking more than a little stunned himself. "God will provide the rest."

"But it'll take a miracle," Drusilla cried in a shaky voice.

"God's specialty is miracles," Shane said with far more conviction this time. "Remember the story of the two fish and five loaves? If the Lord can feed the multitudes, He can certainly help us with this."

Drusilla slowly nodded. "I…suppose."

Taking a fortifying breath of air, Shane gripped Bella's hand and started forward. "By the grace of God we go."

Nodding, Bella took Drusilla's hand and Drusilla took Elizabeth's. As a unified family of four, they pushed their way through the throng.

Mr. Wilson and the young doctor Shane had recently hired stood behind a wide red ribbon that had been roped between two large columns in front of the clinic.

"I think it's wonderful you're using Father's money to open this hospital," Elizabeth said as they continued marching forward.

Bella couldn't agree more. Peter Ford's money was now funding medical care for the impoverished, including women much like the one he'd helped destroy. Had there been decent facilities sixteen years ago, perhaps Amanda Bartlett might still be alive.

It was a sad thought.

But this was not a day for sorrow. This was a day for joy. And celebration.

Much like he'd done in Denver, Shane escorted their

group up the front steps of the clinic. Smiling, he lifted the thick ribbon high enough for them to pass under it.

After giving a short speech, he handed Bella a pair of scissors, then wrapped his hands around hers. Together, they cut the ribbon.

A loud cheer lifted from the crowd.

Turning slightly, Shane returned the scissors to Mr. Wilson. "My wife, Dr. Marsalis and I will begin seeing patients in a few moments. In the meantime, will you take my sisters home?"

The solicitor nodded. "It would be my pleasure."

Both girls jammed their fists on their hips and placed stubborn, immovable expressions on their faces.

"I want to stay," Drusilla announced.

"Me, too," Elizabeth added.

Shane shook his head at them. "Perhaps tomorrow. Today will be too chaotic."

"Bella gets to stay," Elizabeth argued.

"*Bella* has done this before." Shane's lips flattened. "I won't continue arguing with you. My decision is final." His tone brooked no argument.

Knowing when to accept defeat, the girls relented.

Among hugs and grumblings and more hugs, Bella and Shane finally sent them on their way.

Before entering the building, Shane pulled Bella aside. "Thank you, my dear, thank you for being the best wife a man could hope to have." His ocean-blue eyes shone with emotion. "You are the love of my life."

A fresh spurt of joy tickled her throat. "Shane, I'm so proud of you. I love you so much."

Pulling her close, he ran his gaze down the long line of patients. "I thought I'd escaped this neighborhood. But God had a bigger plan in mind."

"You've come full circle, my love."

He kissed her on the nose and then set her far enough away to glance at her belly. Concern marred his features. "Are you sure you're up to this today?"

"Nothing could keep me away."

A smile lifted the corner of his lips. "I'm glad. I need you by my side, Bella. As my helper, my wife and my greatest love on earth."

She lifted to her toes and touched her lips to his. "Good thing I'm not going anywhere."

"A very good thing."

They laughed together.

"Hey," shouted a man from at least a half block away. "You gonna open them doors or not?"

Shane's gaze traveled down to the man speaking, then cut back to Bella. "Let's get to work, shall we?"

His words were the same ones he'd used when Ethan Scott had hurt his leg that first day she'd arrived in Denver. This time, however, Shane was asking Bella to assist him the rest of their lives.

Lord, thank You for giving me the courage to love this man, and to do the work You've planned for us.

She boldly held her husband's gaze and allowed a driving sense of purpose to shine in her eyes. "I'm at your disposal, Dr. Shane."

He kissed her on the lips. "A man never tires of hearing that from his wife."

This time, she kissed him. "Indeed."

Arm in arm, they stepped to the front of the line and ushered the first patient inside.

* * * * *

Janet Lee Barton loves researching and writing heartwarming romances about faith, family, friends and love. She's written both historical and contemporary novels, and loves writing for Love Inspired Historical. She and her husband live in Oklahoma and have recently downsized to a condo, which they love. When Janet isn't writing or reading, she loves to cook for family, work in her small garden, travel and sew. You can visit Janet at janetleebarton.com.

Books by Janet Lee Barton

Love Inspired Historical

Boardinghouse Betrothals

Visit the Author Profile page at Harlequin.com.

SOMEWHERE TO CALL HOME

Janet Lee Barton

And the Lord, he it is that doth go before thee;
he will be with thee, he will not fail thee,
neither forsake thee: fear not, neither be dismayed.
—*Deuteronomy* 31:8

To Tamela Hancock Murray and Tina James
for making a dream come true;

To all my LI and LIH author friends,
who have encouraged me to keep trying;

To the Bards of Faith and the OCFW chapter
for their encouragement and support;

To my husband, Dan, and my family
for their unending love and support;

And, most of all, to my Lord and Savior
for showing me the way.

Prologue

Ashland, Virginia
May 1895

Violet Burton sighed with disappointment as she left the mercantile. How could things have changed so much in such a short time? Only moments ago, on her way to the post office, there'd been a help-wanted sign in the store's window and another one in the milliner's shop. Evidently, she wasn't the only one seeking employment in her small hometown, for both positions were filled by the time she got through picking up her mail.

She walked along the main street, her gaze searching the windows of the businesses on each side of the street. When she spotted a sign in the café across the way, a flicker of hope nudged her to gather up her skirts to clear them from the dirt road and hurry across. However, just before she reached the door, the sign was yanked right out of the window. Violet's hope sank once more, but she entered the establishment anyway.

She walked over to the proprietor, who was putting

the sign under her cash box. "Good morning, Mrs. Wheeler. Has the position been filled already?"

The woman looked down at the floor and back up at Violet, her face a bright pink. "I'm sorry, dear. But I've decided I can't afford to take anyone on today."

It seemed an odd way to word the answer to her question, but Violet didn't feel she should press. Since her widowed mother's illness and death a few weeks earlier, she knew firsthand what it was not to be able to afford things. And if she didn't find employment soon, she'd be able to afford even less. Worst of all, she could lose her family home if she couldn't come up with the money to pay the mortgage her mother had taken out on the house as her illness progressed.

Violet nodded and sighed. "I understand. But if you should find that you do need someone after all, please keep me in mind."

The woman opened her mouth as if to say something, but seemed to change her mind, closed her mouth and only nodded instead.

Disheartened, Violet turned to leave, but just as she reached the door a thought came to her. She turned back and walked over to the woman she'd known all her life. Violet didn't want to put her on the spot, but she had to know. She kept her voice low and asked, "Mrs. Wheeler, by any chance, did Mr. Black tell you not to hire me?"

The older woman looked around to make sure none of her customers were within hearing distance before giving a curt nod. She motioned Violet closer and whispered, "He holds my mortgage, Violet. I can't afford to make him mad."

"I see." *All too well.*

"I'm sorry."

There were tears in Mrs. Wheeler's eyes, and Violet knew she was sincere. She reached out and patted her on the shoulder. "It's all right, Mrs. Wheeler. I don't blame you. Thank you for being honest with me."

Still, Violet felt the flush of anger flood her cheeks when she turned to leave, her stride strong and purposeful as she went outside and crossed the street to the bank. With each step she took, her outrage grew. If Harlan Black thought this was the way to win her heart, well, he had better think again!

"Miss Burton, how nice to see you," the receptionist said as she entered the building. "What can I do for you?"

"I'd like to speak with Mr. Black as soon as possible, Miss Bancroft." Violet tried to keep the irritation out of her voice, but she had a feeling she failed as the woman took one look at her and stood.

"I'll tell him you are here."

"Yes, please do that."

The receptionist hurried back to the banker's private office while Violet tapped her foot as she waited.

In a matter of seconds Miss Bancroft was back. "He'll see you now, Miss Burton."

"Thank you." Violet held her head high and marched back to the office.

Harlan Black stood at the door, a smug smile on his face. Violet supposed many women would find him handsome with his thick blond hair and gray eyes. He was always impeccably dressed and one could not fault his manners, but there was something about his sinister smoothness that made her skin crawl.

He bowed slightly. "My dear Violet. How nice to see you today—"

"You might not think it is so nice once I tell you what I have to say. And, I am *not* your 'dear.'" Violet swept past him and stood in the middle of the room, smoothing her skirts as she waited for him to join her. Then she pinned her gaze on the man.

"Please, take a seat, Violet, and tell me what has you so distressed." He motioned for her to take the chair across from his desk.

Violet chose to keep standing. "You and your deceitful ways of keeping me from finding employment so that I can pay off the mortgage on my home are what have me so upset. How dare you?"

Harlan's eyes narrowed, and the smile left his face. "Violet, dear, there is absolutely no reason for you to seek employment. I've told you I will forgive the mortgage, if only—"

"I will *not* marry you, Harlan Black. If my mind were not made up before, it certainly is now—after finding out that you've told the townspeople not to hire me." The very thought of marrying the man nauseated Violet. "I will pay off the mortgage to my home, even if I have to leave here to do it!"

Harlan raised an eyebrow and chuckled. "And go where? Think about it, Violet. I offer you freedom from debt and a life of comfort. No woman in her right mind would turn that down."

"Then I must have lost my mind, for I have no intention of marrying you. Not now, not ever!" Violet turned to leave, but Harlan beat her to the door.

He grabbed hold of her arm and pulled her near. His breath was hot on her face, and his nearness sent a cold shiver down her spine. "Don't be too hasty, my dear. I can make you happy. You know I can. You have two weeks until the next payment is due. I'll need your final word by then."

Bile rose in Violet's throat at his words and she willed herself not to heave as she jerked her arm away and yanked the door open. Never would she marry this contemptuous man. She'd lose the home she loved first—but not without a fight to keep it.

Chapter One

New York City
May 24, 1895

As the train came to a grinding stop in Grand Central Depot, Violet Burton's heart beat in excitement at the same time her stomach fluttered with apprehension. She stood, shaking out the skirts of her brown-and-beige traveling outfit before joining the other passengers in the aisle and following them out of the train. Pausing on the top step of the car, she fought the urge to turn around and seek refuge back inside. Perhaps she could ask the porter to buy her a ticket right back home. And then what?

Go back and marry Harlan Black? Violet shuddered. No. Never. Instead, she should be thankful her mother's old friend had come up with a solution to her problem. Violet took a deep calming breath and let it out. Once… twice…and again.

"Hurry it up, miss," a man behind her said. "Are you getting off or what?"

A woman beside him reached out and pushed Violet's shoulder. "Yeah, missy. You're holding up the line and we don't have all day."

Heat stole up Violet's face and her heart hammered in her ears as she gave her hand to the waiting porter and hurried down the steps and out of the way. She didn't know in which direction to look for Mrs. Heaton. There were more people here than she'd ever seen in one place, yet she'd never felt so totally alone in her life.

Mrs. Heaton had told her each railroad line had its own waiting room, baggage facilities and ticketing operation in the building, so Violet assumed it wouldn't be hard to spot her. But she'd been mistaken. She didn't know how she'd ever see her mother's friend among all the people coming and going from every direction.

"Your trunk and bags will be over at the New York Central baggage claim area, miss." The porter pointed across the way. "Over there, where all those people are gathered."

"Thank you."

He tipped his hat. "There's a waiting room there, too. I'm sure someone will be here to meet you soon, miss."

"Yes. I hope so." He'd been very helpful on the trip and she hated to see him turn away.

Violet tried not to panic. What was it Mrs. Heaton had said in her letter? She'd be there to meet her. But where was she? And what would she do if Mrs. Heaton didn't show up? Violet began to think she might have made the biggest mistake in her life by coming here. Her mother had always warned her about big cities, and Violet knew she would not be happy she'd come to New York City. Yet, she was certain Mama would not have wanted her to marry Harlan Black under any circumstances. Besides, she really had no choice.

She took another deep breath and looked around. The only way Violet could see how the name *Grand* could apply to this depot was its size. It certainly couldn't be considered a grand place to be—not with all the steam, smoke and ashes spewing from the locomotives, hovering overhead and condensing with the odors of people from so many walks of life. From the sweet scent of toilet water to the strongest perfumes, they all intermingled with the smell of unwashed bodies and sweat, pervading the huge room, making Violet more nauseated by the minute.

Grand Central Depot wasn't only the largest building she'd ever been in—it was also the busiest. No sooner had the train she'd just arrived on chugged away than another one arrived in its place. Passengers poured out of it, heading off in every direction. Some of the travelers looked as lost as she felt.

She glanced around again but there seemed to be more people than ever, many speaking languages she couldn't understand. There was all manner of dress, from elegant to almost threadbare. Men pulled out their watches to see if the time matched the huge clock in the depot while mothers tried to keep their children close to their sides. The noise level seemed to rise with each passing minute as Violet made her way across the room.

A man spit near one of the spittoons positioned all over the depot, but he didn't seem to have good aim as his spittle ran down the outside of the cuspidor and ended up on the floor beside the vessel. The sight, mixed with the smells, made Violet's stomach roll, and she picked up her pace.

Trying to tamp down her anxiety, Violet pulled a picture of Mrs. Heaton out of her reticule and looked at it once more, although she was certain she would recognize her old neighbor. Surely she couldn't have changed much in three years. She turned in a small circle, looking closely at each woman she saw. Finally, when she'd about given up hope, she saw a woman she thought was Martha Heaton hurrying across the building. The older woman waved, and Violet breathed a sigh of relief as her mother's good friend reached her.

"Violet? It is you, isn't it?"

Her eyes held such warmth Violet couldn't help but smile. "Yes, ma'am, it is."

Mrs. Heaton grasped Violet's hands in hers. "How lovely you are, all grown up. You look just like your mother when she was your age. You have her dark hair and blue eyes and even her coloring." Mrs. Heaton pulled her into a quick hug. "Oh, you bring back so many memories of my younger days."

The older woman's blue eyes sparkled, and her fading auburn hair was done up under a large hat that matched her afternoon dress of blue-and-green stripes.

"Thank you, Mrs. Heaton. It is good to see you again." An understatement to be sure. It warmed her heart to see the older woman's familiar face.

"I am sorry I'm a bit late." Mrs. Heaton shook her head and the green feathers on top of her blue hat bobbled to and fro. "Traffic is just awful today, and I'm so glad Michael came with me. Hopefully, it won't be so bad on the way home."

At the mention of her son, Violet looked over Mrs. Heaton's shoulder to see a man that looked very familiar, but so much…more, striding toward them. Dressed in a navy blue suit, a wing-collar white shirt and a blue silk cravat, his dark brown hair covered with a gray bowler, the young man she'd known back home seemed to have become a mature businessman. His warm brown eyes had an expression in them that made her wonder if he were as surprised at the changes in her as she was at his.

"Violet, how good it is to see you," Michael said, taking her gloved hand in his. "If Mother hadn't been talking to you, I'm not sure I would have recognized you. You've grown up since I last saw you."

If anything, Michael Heaton was even more handsome than Violet remembered. "I could say the same for you, Michael. It's so good to see you both."

"Mother has been looking forward to your arrival very much. She's been fussing over your room for days."

She slipped her hand from his and turned toward his mother. "Oh, you shouldn't have gone to any trouble, Mrs. Heaton."

"I've enjoyed every minute, Violet. I hope you'll like it and feel right at home."

Michael quickly took charge, and before Violet knew what had happened, he'd procured a man to fetch her bags and help carry them through the huge building. She barely registered walking across the marble floor and outside, as she dodged first one and then another person hurrying to or from the trains.

Michael helped them get seated in the hack waiting right outside for them, and once they were settled and he took his seat, Violet said, "Thank you for meeting me at the station. I'm not sure I would have known what to do otherwise." She shook her head and chuckled. "I've never seen so many people in one place. Or such hustle and bustle."

"The city can be intimidating at first. And for a

woman alone, I'm sure it's quite frightening," Michael said.

As the driver flipped the reins and steered his hack out onto the street and into the traffic, Violet could well believe the city would overwhelm her for years to come.

Once they were on their way, Mrs. Heaton turned to her. "I am so very sorry about your loss, my dear. Your mother was like a sister to me, and while I know your loss is greater than mine, I will miss her tremendously." The older woman patted her hand as tears gathered in her eyes.

Violet's heart warmed at her sincerity. "Thank you. She missed you sorely after you left. She looked forward to each of your letters, and I read them over and over to her when she couldn't read them herself anymore."

Mrs. Heaton dabbed at her eyes with the delicate handkerchief she pulled from her sleeve. "I'm so glad your mother and I stayed close through our correspondence. I know these last few months must have been grueling for you, dear, but I want you to know you have a place with me for as long as you need it."

Violet swallowed around the sudden lump in her throat. The very day she'd walked out of Harlan Black's office, she'd written a letter accepting Mrs. Heaton's offer to help in any way she could and telling her why. In the two weeks since, she'd been so consumed with getting ready for the move and getting out of town without letting Harlan suspect what she was doing, she hadn't had time to even grieve. The woman's kind words were like balm to her battered heart. "Thank you. I can't tell you how much your kindness means to me."

Mrs. Heaton gave a brisk nod, as if to dismiss the sad thoughts. "I'm just glad to have you here with us."

Violet began to relax. She was here among friends—even though she barely recognized Michael. Just seeing him stride across the depot toward her had taken her breath away. Sitting across from him now, she tried to keep from stealing glances at him as he and his mother pointed out different sights to her.

She wasn't even sure she saw half of all the sights since she closed her eyes each time another horse-drawn vehicle seemed bent on running them down, just before it stopped or turned on another street. She'd never seen so many different modes of travel in her life. Mrs. Heaton pointed out omnibuses, landaus and the trolley.

"Traveling in the city is a bit harrowing the first few times," Michael said. "But you'll get used to it."

"Thankfully, Grand Central isn't far from Gramercy Park, where our home is located. We'll have plenty of time to show you the sights and teach you the best way to get around, once you're settled," Mrs. Heaton said.

Violet wasn't sure she'd ever learn how to get around and was more than a little relieved when the hack pulled up outside a nice four-story brownstone on the corner of a quiet residential street. A small sign outside read Heaton House.

"We're home, dear," Mrs. Heaton said, patting her hand. "This is my boardinghouse."

Michael and the driver took Violet's baggage to the door, which was quickly opened wide by a young woman near her own age. She was slightly plump and wearing an apron and cap, her blond hair curling out from under it.

"I was getting worried, ma'am," she said as Michael and the driver brought Violet's trunk and bags into the foyer.

The foyer was wide and long, the floors polished until they gleamed. A long table with a vase of fresh flowers in the center of it and a holder for calling cards stood against one wall. There were several hat racks and coatracks on the opposite wall, and Violet assumed they got a lot of use when all the boarders were there.

"The traffic was quite heavy today, Gretchen." Mrs. Heaton took off her hat and put it on the rack. "This is Violet Burton, a dear friend from home and our new boarder. Violet, this is Gretchen Finster. She and her sister, Maida, help me out in the house and the kitchen Monday through Friday, and then on Saturdays and Sundays one goes home and the other stays to help with meals and the boarders' laundry. I don't know what I'd do without the two of them."

"How do you do, Miss Burton?" Gretchen's smile was welcoming.

"I'm fine, thank you." Now that they were out of the traffic and congestion, she felt much better. "It's nice to meet you, Gretchen."

"Come, let me give you a quick tour of downstairs while Michael and Gretchen take your bags to your room," Mrs. Heaton said.

"I'll see you later at dinner, Violet. I must get back to work for a while," Michael said.

"I'm sorry I interrupted your day, I—"

"I was glad to take some time to come greet you, and we're glad to have you here." He kissed his mother on the cheek and smiled at Violet before heading up the stairs with Gretchen following.

"See you later, dear."

"I'll try to get home early," Michael said just as he disappeared on the landing.

Violet forced her thoughts off Michael and back to Mrs. Heaton as the woman turned and pointed to the right of the foyer. "This is the front parlor, Violet. Some, if not all, of the boarders gather here most evenings before and after dinner."

The room was quite lovely and large, with a piano in one corner and at least two very comfortable-looking parlor suites covered in a plush burgundy color, along with several rocking chairs upholstered in a gold-and-burgundy stripe, stationed around the room. The draperies were of the same material as the rocking chairs. She would have liked to look closer at the paintings and portraits on the wall, the framed pictures on the tables, but there wasn't time before Mrs. Heaton led her across the hall to the dining room.

This room was attractively furnished, as well. There were the same drapes on these windows and a beautifully carved sideboard along the opposite wall. The lace-covered table was huge—it must seat at least twelve people, and Violet wondered if there were that many boarders. Next came the kitchen, and her stomach rumbled at the wonderful aroma coming from the large range. The room was large and sunny with plenty of cupboards and a large worktable in the center.

"We're having roast chicken this evening." Mrs. Heaton took up a pot holder and checked the contents of a large pan in the middle of the oven. There appeared to be at least two big hens in the pan. Mrs. Heaton seemed to determine all was well as she closed the oven door and motioned to Violet to follow her.

Across the hall from the kitchen was the back parlor. A bit smaller than the front parlor, it seemed cozy and inviting. It was decorated in greens and blues and was quite restful. "This parlor is more for reading or quiet conversation. Several of our boarders bring their callers here to visit with them. Gretchen or Maida are always glad to bring tea or coffee for our guests."

The next room, between both parlors, was Mrs. Heaton's private study. It was paneled with shelves reaching from floor to ceiling, packed full of books. "You're welcome to come see me here anytime, Violet. And the books are available for all the boarders."

Although she'd only gotten a glimpse of each room, the homey feel of the house comforted Violet. "It is quite lovely, Mrs. Heaton."

"Thank you, dear. I'll show you to your room now, as I'm sure you're longing for a rest after your trip." She led the way down the hall and it was then Violet noticed a telephone on a table in the curve of the staircase. Mrs. Heaton motioned to it as they passed by. "The telephone is for us all to use. Many times an employer will ring up to ask someone to come in early or change their schedule. And sometimes their families or friends need to contact them."

They continued up the staircase to the second floor. "All my lady boarders reside on the top floors. Michael and the gentlemen have rooms on the bottom floor. They may use the outside entry or come up through the kitchen stairs, but they are not allowed past the main floor. Most boardinghouses cater to gentlemen, but there is a great need for rooms to let for women and I wanted to help fill it."

She passed several rooms before stopping and opening a door. "I've given you a nice bright corner room. I hope you like it."

Violet smiled as she entered the room. Mrs. Heaton

was right. Sunrays glinted through the windows, splashing the lavender-and-yellow wallpaper and the striped bedcoverings of the same colors. It reminded her of her own room at home, only it was larger.

This room easily held a nice bedstead and armoire to match, an upholstered chair with matching footstool in one corner, a round table and lamp beside it. A writing table stood in front of one of the windows, and a small sofa set was grouped in front of the fireplace. It seemed to be a combination sitting room and bedroom, and Violet had no doubt she would be quite comfortable in it.

"Oh, this is a wonderful room, Mrs. Heaton. I'm certain I'm going to feel right at home here."

"I hope so, my dear."

"How nice of you to remember my favorite colors."

"It wasn't hard. I remembered how pretty your room was in Ashland. The bathroom is just next door, and you'll be sharing it with another young woman. I'll introduce you to her at dinner. Gretchen may finish helping you unpack, if you like. Then we'll leave you to rest awhile. Dinner is at seven but, of course, you may come downstairs anytime before."

Violet looked around and found Gretchen was hanging up her nicer gowns. "Thank you for what you've already done, Gretchen. I think I'll wait to unpack the rest. I must admit I am a bit tired."

Mrs. Heaton motioned to Gretchen, who immediately left the room. "I understand, dear. You try to rest. We only dress up for meals on the weekends—Saturday evenings, Sundays and holidays. All of the boarders work, and they are much too tired at the end of the day to follow society's rules for dress during the week.

A nice skirt and shirtwaist will suffice. If you aren't down by dinnertime, I'll send Gretchen up to fetch you."

"Thank you."

"You are quite welcome, Violet." Mrs. Heaton moved out into the hall and quietly shut the door behind her.

After all the noise and confusion, the sights, sounds and smells of the depot and then the ride to Mrs. Heaton's, Violet felt she needed some quiet time to take everything in. And she was more than a little nervous about meeting the other boarders. It certainly wouldn't hurt to get her bearings first.

For now, she was glad just to be at Mrs. Heaton's. She sank onto the bed and looked around the room once more. It did remind her of home. But would she ever have her family home free and clear from Harlan Black?

She'd paid this month's payment the day she walked out of his office. And she'd given her best friend the money to pay the next month's payment right before she left. Violet had barely had enough money left to get to New York City and live on for a few months. She must find work as soon as possible.

Once more she wondered if she'd done the right thing by leaving—but she'd worry about that later.

Michael found his mother in her private study, sitting in her favorite chair with her Bible in her lap and with her eyes closed as if she were praying. He had turned to leave when she called his name.

"Michael, come in, dear. I'm not asleep."

He took a seat in the chair opposite his mother's and put his feet up. "I didn't want to disturb you."

She closed her Bible and laid it on the table between them. "I'm through with my conversation with the Lord, at least for now. I was just taking a few minutes to talk to Him about our new boarder and asking Him to make Violet's transition to our home an easy one."

"I'm sure it's been difficult for her since losing her mother just a month ago, especially after finding her home was mortgaged and not being able to find work. Having to leave her home couldn't have been easy, and New York is very different from Ashland."

His mother nodded. "I'm so glad she came here. But I think she was a bit overwhelmed today. My being late to meet her train didn't help, but she was very gracious about it."

"We'll do what we can to make things easy for her, Mother."

"I know. We can begin tonight. I'm sure she's a little apprehensive about meeting everyone. She's grown into quite a lovely young woman since the last time you saw her, hasn't she?"

"Yes, she has." Michael hadn't been able to quit thinking of Violet all afternoon. He couldn't remember when thoughts of a woman had interfered with his work so much, and he didn't know quite what to make of it.

The sound of doors opening and closing signaled that many of their boarders were home from work, and his mother got up from her chair. "I'd better go see to the finishing touches for dinner."

Michael stood, as well. "Good. My mouth has been watering ever since I walked in the door."

"I figured as much. You might want to go to the front parlor and greet Violet when she comes down. And make sure our gentlemen boarders behave themselves."

"That I will do." Michael bent and kissed his mother's cheek. "She reminds you of Rebecca, doesn't she?"

His mother sighed and gave a quick nod. "She's the same age that Becca was when—"

He knew she couldn't bring herself to say the words. His sister had been missing for over three years now, and still they didn't know what had happened to her. "Is this going to be too hard for you…having Violet here, Mother?"

"Oh, no, dear. She does bring back memories of being in Ashland before Becca left to come here…but those memories are good ones and I welcome them."

Michael gave his mother a quick hug. "I'll be grateful that she's here then and do all I can to make the transition to the city easier for her."

"Thank you, son."

Michael watched his mother leave the room, hoping that she was right and that it would be good for her to have Violet here. She could use some joy.

Becca's sudden disappearance after she'd moved to New York City three years earlier had changed their lives forever. It'd been the catalyst for selling their home in Ashland, moving here and starting the boardinghouse. Thankfully, his father had provided for his mother well so that they could fulfill her wishes. She wanted to give safe haven to the people who lived under her roof, especially the young women. She wanted them to have a place they felt was home even while missing their own. And she wanted to make sure that their families would never have to hear that their loved one was missing, never to be heard from again.

Michael had been trained as a private investigator by the best. He'd worked for Pinkerton before opening his own detective agency, and now he made it his life's work to try to help his clients who had heard those same words—or others similar to them—and to follow each and every lead that might turn up about his sister.

That Violet was the daughter of his mother's best friend and their next-door neighbor was enough to make him want to watch her as closely as he would Becca, if she were here. Becca was several years older than Violet and while one wouldn't have called them best friends, he'd always considered them friends and had teased Violet as much as he had his own sister. He knew that if anything happened to Violet, his mother would blame herself, and Michael couldn't let that happen.

He stood and rubbed the back of his neck before heading down the hall to the front parlor. Their boarders were a good group for the most part, but after what his mother had told him about Violet, he wanted to be there to try to put her at ease among strangers.

"Why, Michael, how nice of you to join us early tonight!" Lila Miller, a young woman who'd been with them for nearly a year, left the side of Luke Patterson and headed in his direction as soon as he entered the parlor.

"Good evening, Miss Miller, everyone," he said, trying to make eye contact with each person in the room.

"To what do we owe this honor, Michael?" Lila asked. "You've barely been on time for meals the last few weeks."

He'd like to tell her that it was her company he'd been trying to avoid lately, but that was out of the question, of course. Michael didn't want to offend her. He just didn't like the way she fawned over him.

"I thought I'd greet our new boarder when she comes down."

"Oh?" Lila raised a narrow brown eyebrow. "She's here then?"

"She arrived this afternoon."

"And she's here now." Elizabeth Anderson, one of his mother's favorite boarders, entered the room just ahead of Violet. "Everyone, meet Violet Burton. I met her at the landing. She seemed a bit hesitant to come down, but I promised her that we'd all be on our best behavior. At least until we get to know her better."

The young woman who'd followed Elizabeth into the room smiled at everyone and said, "I took her at her word."

That brought chuckles from the boarders gathering around her, and Michael quickly crossed the room to her side. "Violet, I hope you've been able to get some rest?"

His mother was right. This was not the Violet he remembered. That one had been a young girl and, while pretty and sweet, this Violet was a fully grown woman and a lovely one at that. Her black hair was swept up on top of her head, and when her gaze settled on him, he was struck by how brilliantly blue her eyes were.

"I did, thank you, Mr. Heaton."

She hadn't called him Mr. Heaton back home. It'd only been Michael…and that in an exasperated tone when he'd been teasing her and Becca. He chuckled at the memory. Perhaps she was only doing it now because of the boarders, but he didn't like it. "Oh, come now, Violet. Surely as long as we've known each other, we can dispense with the formalities, can't we?"

She looked up at him and her smiled deepened. "I suppose we can… Michael."

But her smile didn't quite reach her eyes and the wary expression in them reminded him of all she'd been through so recently. Suddenly his protective instincts rose up full force, shocking him with their intensity. In that moment, Michael knew he'd do all he could to keep Violet Burton safe and to help her adjust to her new surroundings.

Chapter Two

"Dinner is served," Mrs. Heaton announced from the dining room. "Come along, everyone, we'll make the remaining introductions while we dine."

Michael held out his arm and Violet hesitated for a moment before taking it. This was Michael Heaton, after all, not a complete stranger. He'd been her neighbor for years and he was only escorting her across the hall to the dining room. Although he was several years older than Violet, she'd known him all of her life. And his teasing manner was just the same as it had been when she was growing up.

But Violet hadn't been prepared for the effect of his smile on her. The sheer force of it, with those twin dimples that hadn't been in evidence earlier that day, left her a little stunned and bewildered that she felt so drawn to him. She told herself it was because it was so good to see another familiar face in this strange city so far away from home, but she wasn't sure she was telling herself the truth. Her heartbeat hadn't slowed down since her gaze met his.

He led her across the foyer and into the dining room.

Pulling out a chair, he seated Violet while another of the boarders seated his mother at the opposite end of the table. Then Michael took his own place at the head of the table; his chair was adjacent to the one Violet was sitting in.

The brown-haired, brown-eyed woman who'd been standing with her hand on Michael's forearm when Violet came into the parlor had slipped into the chair opposite Violet, but her attention was solely on Michael.

Others who were in the parlor took their seats at the table, and Violet was relieved to see that, just as Mrs. Heaton had said, most of the ladies were dressed in skirts and nice shirtwaists. Mrs. Heaton had changed into a dark brown skirt and beige shirtwaist as well, and Violet felt as if she fit in with the navy skirt and crisp white shirt she'd chosen. It had a lace insert at the top of the bodice and she'd worn her mother's cameo, which made her feel a little dressed up, but not so much that she felt out of place. She let out a small sigh of relief.

Once everyone was settled, they all looked to Mrs. Heaton for direction.

"Michael, will you please say grace?"

"Certainly."

Violet bowed her head while he said a simple prayer of thanksgiving. She was touched that he thanked the Lord for her safe travel as well as for the food. Once he'd finished the prayer, he began passing dishes family-style with some help from Gretchen and Maida. The other boarders began to talk amongst themselves as the dishes were passed around, and Violet felt herself begin to relax.

Michael held the tray while she selected a piece of chicken, and then he handed it off to the man beside her while Gretchen and Maida helped keep the rest of the dishes moving around the table. The side dishes were creamed potatoes, peas, carrots and baby onions. The rolls were crisp and hot, and Violet was glad there were so many small conversations going on that hopefully no one could hear her stomach growl.

When all the dishes had made the round of the table, and Gretchen and her sister had slipped into their chairs, Mrs. Heaton introduced Violet to the other boarders.

"This is Violet Burton, our new boarder. She's a dear friend of the family and we're very happy that she's come to live here." She then motioned to the young woman on her right. "Violet, this is Julia Olsen, who works at Ellis Island. It's a busy job she has."

The auburn-haired girl smiled down the table at Violet. Her green eyes sparkled. "It's certainly an interesting one, too. I've many stories to tell."

"I look forward to hearing them." Violet took some potatoes and passed them down.

"The gentleman next to her is Benjamin Roth, who is a teacher," Mrs. Heaton continued with the introductions. "And across from you is Lila Miller, who works at Butterick."

Benjamin had blond hair and blue eyes. "Good to have you with us, Miss Burton."

"Thank you, Mr. Roth." Violet then smiled at Lila. "Butterick! Oh, wonderful! Their patterns certainly have made it easier for the home seamstress to make garments that fit," Violet said.

Lila gave a half smile and slight nod while Mrs. Heaton continued, "On your right is Luke Patterson. Luke writes dime novels."

"Dime novels?" Violet asked. She'd never met a real writer before. "How interesting."

Luke's blue eyes seemed to twinkle as he brushed his brown hair off his brow and smiled. "I think so."

Mrs. Heaton continued, "And next to him is Elizabeth Anderson, who works for *The Delineator*. She's also the young woman you'll be sharing a bathroom with."

"We met at the landing, Mrs. Heaton," Elizabeth said with a smile. She had blond hair and hazel eyes.

"And Elizabeth was kind enough to accompany me down to the parlor," Violet added. "I love *The Delineator*. Mother subscribed to it and we pored over it, looking at all the newest styles." She looked from Elizabeth to Lila and back again. "Isn't *The Delineator* owned by Butterick? Do you two work together?"

Lila gave a brief shake of her head, but Elizabeth explained. "Butterick does own the magazine. And we joke about being coworkers, but *The Delineator* has its own offices at Butterick Publishing Company on Thirteenth Street."

"I see." Violet liked Elizabeth. She was quite friendly and helpful. She wished she could say the same about Lila, who only seemed to smile for Michael's benefit.

Mrs. Heaton continued with her introductions. "Of course you've met Gretchen and Maida. We have another boarder, but he's out for the evening. You'll meet him tomorrow."

"It's probably better this way. The whole bunch of us at one time might intimidate Miss Burton," Luke Patterson said.

"I'm sure she can handle being around us all, Luke." Julia took a roll from the basket Mrs. Heaton passed her and handed it to Benjamin. "She's got to be a brave woman to move to New York City on her own."

Violet almost laughed out loud. If Julia could have seen her at the train station today, she might not think she was so brave.

"Violet will be able to handle this household with ease. I'm certain of it." Mrs. Heaton smiled at Violet and then looked around the table. "What we need to do for her now, though, is try to come up with places that she can apply for employment. Do any of you know of any openings?"

"What is it you are trained to do, Miss Burton?" Julia asked from down the table.

"Well, I can't say I'm trained to do anything. I can cook and clean. And I can sew, but I'm not sure I could call myself a seamstress. I've only sewn for my mother or myself." Suddenly, Violet realized she wasn't really trained for any kind of employment. She'd been groomed to be a wife, but that wasn't anything she wanted any part of at the moment—if ever. "I really don't know what kind of work I'd be best suited for...."

"Don't worry," Elizabeth said with a chuckle. "I most certainly wasn't trained to work for a magazine. Most of us have positions where we've been trained to do the job. I don't think *The Delineator* has any openings at present, but I'll check. I'm sure you'll find something, though."

"Lila, didn't you say recently that Butterick was needing help?" Michael asked.

Lila glanced over at Violet and chewed her bottom lip for a moment before looking back at Michael. Her smile brightened as she fluttered her eyelashes at him. "I believe they were needing help with folding and packaging the patterns or possibly with cutting them out. I know they hired one girl, but I can ask tomorrow if they still need help."

"Oh, would you, dear?" Mrs. Heaton asked. "I would think of it as a personal favor to me, if you would."

"As would I," Michael added.

"Then I will certainly ask." Lila batted her eyelashes once more.

"Thank you, Lila," Violet said. "That is very kind of you."

The other girl's smile dimmed somewhat as she glanced at Violet. "I'll let you know what I find out."

"Anyone else know of anything?" Michael asked.

"I have a friend who works at Tiffany Glass. They might not be hiring right now, but she says someone is always getting married and there are bound to be openings before too long," Elizabeth said.

"We can look at the classifieds in the morning paper, too," Michael suggested.

Several other ideas were mentioned as they ate their meal and Violet felt her hopes for employment grow. Surely in a city this large, she could find something before long. At least Harlan Black didn't have an influence here. He couldn't stop people from hiring her.

Coconut cake was served with coffee, and Violet enjoyed it while she listened to the others talk about their day. So far everyone seemed nice, but Violet couldn't help but notice that most all the women at the table seemed to hang on to every word that came out of Michael's mouth. And if Lila Miller batted her eyelashes at him each time he looked her way, she wasn't the only one doing so. Even with two other men at the table, Michael seemed to be the one who had the attention of every woman, and—much to Violet's dismay—that included her. She couldn't really blame them. Those dimples were hard not to watch for.

During the meal, Michael watched the interaction between the boarders and Violet. She listened more than she talked, and she seemed to be totally unaware that Luke and Benjamin were both taking in everything she did say. On the other hand, he hadn't missed the way the two men watched her every move.

A new woman in their midst was always of interest to the male boarders. Just as he supposed a new man would be to the females sitting at the table. But Luke and Benjamin appeared to be totally captivated by Violet. While he couldn't blame them—she was lovely and quite unpretentious—Michael felt a little out of sorts about the attention they were giving her.

He watched as Violet asked Luke about his writing and wondered, what would she think if she knew Luke sometimes did investigative work for Michael's detective agency? It was something few people knew about, which worked to Michael's benefit. No one would suspect one of his agents was the dime-novel writer living in his mother's boardinghouse. Violet seemed interested in Luke's writing—was she interested in him?

It shouldn't matter. Michael had made up his mind never to become interested in any of the women living in his mother's boardinghouse—an easy thing to do since he'd been burned once and was determined never to let it happen again. But Violet wasn't just a boarder. They'd lived next door to each other, and their mothers had been best friends. He couldn't ignore that connection. Nor did he want to.

He glanced her way as she spoke to Elizabeth, and realized how much she'd changed since he last saw her. She seemed to have lost the smattering of freckles that once graced her nose, and her skin was smooth and flawless now, but he found he missed those freckles.

It took some effort to pull his thoughts back to the present and he was glad to see that most everyone seemed genuinely interested in helping Violet find employment, with the exception of Lila. She didn't seem enthused about assisting in the search—at least not where she worked. He was certain she'd mentioned that Butterick was expanding and needed more help just a week or so ago, and he'd almost laughed at the look on Lila's face when he'd backed her into a corner so she had no choice but to say she would check on it. However, he wasn't totally confident that she would keep her word.

He'd had no reason to check the classifieds, so he didn't know if Butterick might have placed an ad. Hopefully they'd find something in the paper tomorrow, whether it be Butterick or some other place. It would make things easier if Violet found a position where one of the other girls worked. She'd be able to learn her way around a little faster if she had someone to go to work and come home with. But this was New York City, after all. Violet would find something. He was sure of it.

When everyone adjourned to the parlor, Violet excused herself saying she had unpacking still to do. That was the truth, but the real reason she felt the need to escape to her room was that she was quite overwhelmed by her whole day. It had been a very long one and she hadn't had time to let it soak in that she really was going to make her home in New York City, in this house, with these people.

Mrs. Heaton followed her upstairs. "Are you all right, dear?"

"I'm fine. I'm just—"

"Not used to all that conversation and everyone talking at the same time, are you?"

"No, ma'am." She smiled. The older woman seemed to have a knack for knowing what she was thinking. "But I did enjoy it. I think I'm just very tired tonight."

"I'm sure you are. I wanted to show you where the towels are kept and make certain you weren't feeling poorly." She pointed out the linen closet in the hall and got out a fresh towel and washcloth for Violet. "My room is just across the hall from yours, should you need me. Please remember, Violet, that you are like family to me and—"

"I thank you so much for that. Your hospitality is more of a comfort than I can tell you. But that being said, I need to pay you my first month's rent. It's fifty dollars, isn't it?"

"That's the fee, but I want you to wait until the first of July to pay me."

"Oh, no." Violet shook her head. "I can't let you do that, Mrs. Heaton."

"You have no choice, dear. I don't want you worrying about money until you have a paying position, which I'm certain you will have by then. You have enough stress trying to find employment and getting used to everything. Think of yourself as my guest at least until July. Then you'll be a boarder."

"But—"

Mrs. Heaton held up her hand and smiled. "Not another word about it, dear. It's final."

"Thank you. I am so blessed that you wrote me offering your help. I had no intention of ever leaving Ashland, but with Harlan Black making it impossible for me to find work, your letter seemed an answer to my prayers. I can't thank you enough."

"Your being here is enough thanks. You bring back happy memories to me of times past and I cherish them. As for Harlan Black... I do remember him as well, and I am glad you got away from that horrid man!"

"Oh, so am I." The very thought of Harlan sickened her.

"Do you think he'll come after you?"

Violet's heart plummeted to her stomach at Mrs. Heaton's question. Thus far, she'd not let herself think along those lines, but now she realized that same question had been lying at the back of her mind just waiting to torment her. "I don't know. I certainly hope not."

Mrs. Heaton placed a hand on her ample chest. "I am so sorry, Violet. I didn't mean to bring up unpleasant thoughts for you."

"It's all right, Mrs. Heaton. I'm just glad to be out of Ashland and away from him." She shivered again thinking of the last time she'd seen him.

"Well, never you worry, dear. He won't bother you here." Mrs. Heaton waved her hand as if to dispel the thought of Harlan. "Enough of this depressing talk. I'll let you have some time to yourself. Breakfast is from six to nine. It's set out on the sideboard in the dining room. We'll take a look at the classifieds and see if we can find some positions for you to apply for tomorrow. Good night, dear."

"Good night."

Violet heard the sound of the piano being played and voices singing "The Sidewalks of New York" as Mrs. Heaton went back downstairs. For a moment she wished she'd stayed with everyone. Then she reminded herself that there would be other nights and much more time to get to know the others. For now, she needed some quiet time.

Violet finished her unpacking and then took a long soak in the big tub in the bathroom. Once she was back in her room, she settled herself into the chair by the window and listened to the singing from downstairs. She loved to sing and would be happy to join them around the piano one day.

The music faded and she heard footsteps on the stairs, doors opening and closing down the hall and the sound of water running in the bathroom she shared with Elizabeth. She found she liked the sounds of life around her and knowing she wasn't alone.

As the house quieted, Violet opened her Bible and read several of her favorite Psalms. Then she said her prayers before turning in, thanking the Lord for giving her safe travel and for Mrs. Heaton and her offer. Exhausted as she was, Violet felt certain she would drift right off to sleep.

Instead, she remembered the conversation with Mrs. Heaton earlier and before long, her thoughts were in such turmoil wondering what Harlan would do when he found she'd left town that she couldn't sleep. She tossed and turned for what seemed like hours before flinging back the covers. Violet got out of bed and paced around her bed and back again.

Harlan was not going to be happy, that was for sure.

But would he try to find her? She prayed not. Still, afraid that he might look for her, she'd bought a ticket as far as Baltimore, then bought another one from there to New York City. She hoped it would be impossible for him to locate her, should he decide he must.

Violet stopped and pulled the curtain away from the window. Lights were still shining in some of the homes nearby and she could even see a light or two in the next street over. Somehow the light in the darkness comforted her, knowing others were up at this hour. Back home there wouldn't be a light shining anywhere this time of night, except for the taverns and the small police station. But this city was so large—surely Harlan would never find her here if he did decide to look for her.

She dropped the curtain and went back to bed. It wasn't going to do any good to worry about him. He'd either track her down or not. But he couldn't make her marry him. Worrying about him would serve no purpose; she'd just turn it over to the Lord and leave it in His hands.

The next morning Violet awakened to the sounds of doors opening and closing once more. She looked at the small clock on her bedside table. Six-thirty. She was used to sleeping a bit later than that on a Saturday, but she was eager to start the day.

Throwing back the covers, she hopped out of bed and hurried to the windows. The sun was up and it looked as if it were going to be a beautiful spring day.

Violet started to walk to the bathroom, but she heard water running. Elizabeth would be getting ready for work. She'd said she worked a half day today, and Violet was glad she hadn't hurried to the bathroom right away.

It seemed everyone had a job or somewhere to go except her, and she certainly didn't want to hold Elizabeth up.

The water stopped running, but Violet waited until she heard the bathroom door shut from the other side, signaling that Elizabeth had finished washing up. Even then she knocked just to make sure the bathroom was empty before entering.

Once she'd finished freshening up, she went back to her room to dress in a burgundy skirt and ivory shirt-waist. She put her hair up, twisting it up into a knot on top of her head in one of the current styles, and made her bed before leaving the room. By the time she arrived downstairs, some of the boarders she'd met the evening before were heading out the door and they wished her well in her search for employment.

"Thank you," she called as she waved goodbye and entered the empty dining room. She took a plate and began to fill it from the sideboard, choosing a couple of slices of bacon, some scrambled eggs and a biscuit. Just as Violet took a seat at the table, Maida, or maybe it was Gretchen, came in the room. On closer inspection, Violet decided it was Maida. She was a little taller and her hair was a darker shade of blond.

"Good morning, Miss Burton."

"Good morning, Maida." Violet knew she got it right when she was rewarded with a smile.

"Did you sleep well last night?" the maid asked.

"I did."

"Would you like tea or coffee this morning?"

"Tea, please."

Maida poured her a steaming cup from the silver pot on the sideboard. "Mrs. Heaton asked me to let her know when you came down. She'll be joining you soon."

"Wonderful. Maida, do you know where the morning paper might be? I'd like to look over the classifieds."

Mrs. Heaton walked into the room just then, the newspaper in her hand. "It's right here, dear. I've been looking over them for you."

Maida poured Mrs. Heaton a cup of tea and set it at her place at the table. "Would you like me to prepare you anything, ma'am?"

Mrs. Heaton glanced at the offerings on the sideboard. "No, thank you, Maida. There is still plenty here to choose from."

After Maida replaced the pot on the sideboard and left the room, Mrs. Heaton handed Violet the paper. "There are several positions you might be interested in, dear. If you see anything you want to apply for, I'll be glad to accompany you on Monday to put in applications. However, I hope you will let yourself rest this weekend. Besides, some of the other boarders might come back with news about openings in their companies this evening."

"That would be wonderful." Violet took the folded *New York Tribune* Mrs. Heaton handed her. "I'm sure I will take you up on the offer to go with me on Monday. I wouldn't have the faintest idea on where anything is located."

"I thought you might enjoy a ride around town today so that I can show you several of the places you might want to apply at on Monday—if you see anything that appeals to you."

Remembering the terrible traffic of the day before, Violet didn't exactly look forward to getting out in it again, but she did want to see the city. While Mrs. Heaton filled her plate, Violet looked at some of the circled entries. There were several requests for shopkeeper positions, a straw-hat presser—whatever that was—and an opening for a correspondent. Those were the only ones Mrs. Heaton had circled, but Violet's gaze skimmed the rest. A lady wanted a person to do writing for her at home; another wanted a companion, but that meant living at the residence, and Violet knew she wouldn't want to do that.

She liked being right here. When she'd awakened this morning, it'd been quite comforting to know that she was in the home of someone she was acquainted with, someone she could call a friend.

"What do you think? Do any of those positions sound good to you?" Mrs. Heaton took her seat at the table.

"I'm not sure appealing to me is the important thing," Violet said. "I need work, so most likely I'll accept any decent position I'm offered."

"Don't feel you must rush into employment, Violet. I'd prefer you take your time and find something you believe you'll be happy at. One good thing about the Butterick position is that you'd know someone who works there, and you'd have company for the trips to and from work."

"But we don't know if that is still open, do we?"

"You didn't see it?" Mrs. Heaton jumped up and came over to her. "Oh, dear, it's on the top of the next page."

She took the paper from Violet and turned the page. There, at the top, was circled: "Pattern cutter/ Pattern folder wanted. No experience necessary. Will train. Apply at 555 Broadway Monday through Friday, 8:00 a.m. to 4:00 p.m."

Violet looked up at Mrs. Heaton. "Oh, yes, I would like to apply there. They're willing to train me and that is exactly what I need."

"And once you are established here and meet more people, if this position isn't one you like, it will be easier to find another one. You'll know your way around the city and you'll have a résumé."

Violet couldn't help but chuckle. "You speak as if I already have this position. It may be filled by Monday."

"I don't think so. But we won't know until then. In the meantime, I'll show you around so that you can see where some of these places are. We'll be on our way as soon as we finish breakfast."

"Where is it you are off to so early in the day, Mother?"

Violet's breath caught in her throat at the sight of Michael striding into the room.

Even Mrs. Heaton seemed surprised to see her son. "Michael, I thought you left for work over an hour ago. What are you doing back home?"

"Good morning, Mother." Michael gave his mother a kiss on the cheek and grinned at Violet. "Good morning to you, too, Violet. I hope you slept well."

"I did, thank you."

"Michael, you haven't answered my question."

"I'm sorry, Mother. I did go to the office and I telephoned Butterick from there and found that they are indeed hiring, but they only take applications Monday through—"

"Friday." His mother laughed. "Well, I could have told you that!"

"How could you have known?"

"I read the paper this morning," she answered, waving it at him.

"So that is where it was!" He laughed. "I looked all over for it."

His mother grinned. "It was in my study. I'm sorry. It appears we're both anxious to find something for Violet."

Michael poured himself a cup of coffee from the pot Maida had left on the sideboard. He took his seat at the table and smiled at Violet. "Now that Mother has you here, she wants to make sure you stay."

"I have no plans to go anywhere other than out to find work," Violet said. "And I am very grateful to your mother for coming up with a solution for me."

"I thought we could take a ride around the city this morning so that Violet could get a look at some of the places she might want to apply at on Monday," his mother said.

"If you don't mind the company, I'll escort the two of you."

"I hate to take you away from your work—"

"We'd love to have your company," his mother interrupted. "I'll feel better if you are the one explaining the El and the trolley to Violet."

"Good. And there is no need to worry about taking me away from my work, Violet. I am fortunate in that I get to set my own work schedule."

"Then I thank you both. I'll just go freshen up and be ready when you are," Violet said.

Michael pulled out her chair for her. Although she'd

given in gracefully, he couldn't really tell if she was pleased or not that he'd be going with them.

"And I will talk to Maida about our dinner tonight," his mother said.

He pulled out her chair, as well. "All right. But there is no need to rush, ladies. I'll sit here and have another one of Maida's biscuits while I wait for you."

Although Michael could set his own hours, it wasn't often he took a day off from work, and he was going to enjoy it. He buttered a biscuit, plopped a spoonful of apple jelly in the middle and took a bite. Delicious.

He wasn't sure exactly why he'd decided to come back home this early. He'd telephoned Butterick when he got to his office because, for some reason, he didn't quite trust that Lila would ask about openings at the company. Still, he could have waited until this evening to tell Violet about it; she couldn't apply there until Monday, anyway.

However, knowing his mother as he did, he was sure that she and Violet would be out and about today. He really was a little concerned about Violet learning her way around the city—after all, it was his mother's suggestion that brought her here and there was no denying that made him feel personally responsible for her safety. He couldn't let anything happen to her.

"I'm ready, dear, and I'm sure Violet will be coming down the stairs any moment now. I do appreciate you checking into the Butterick position for her. I'm praying she gets it."

"So am I." For his mother's sake, if not for Violet's. "You like having her here, don't you?"

"I do," his mother answered. "Don't you?"

Michael hadn't expected that question, and he wasn't

really sure he could answer it right now. After all, Violet had only been here one night and her presence meant more responsibility for him. But his mother looked so happy this morning, he wasn't about to tell her any of that. So he chose to be as truthful as he could at the moment. "I want you to be happy, Mother."

"Thank you, dear. I want the same for you, don't you know?"

"I—" Footsteps could be heard crossing the foyer and Michael was glad. He took one last sip of coffee and stood just as Violet entered the room.

"I hope I didn't keep you waiting long," Violet said, pulling her gloves on and smiling at them.

She did have a beautiful smile. Michael couldn't help but smile back. "Not at all. Are you ready to see the city?"

"I am."

"Then, I'm at your service, ladies."

Chapter Three

Violet thought it was a beautiful day as they sauntered down the street to Third Avenue, where she assumed they'd find a hack to take them around the city. She couldn't help but be pleased that Michael had come home to tell her about the Butterick opening and wanted to accompany them today. But she didn't want to be a burden to either of the Heatons. She hoped she got the job at Butterick. At least that way, she'd have Lila to help her learn her way to work and back, and Michael and his mother wouldn't be worrying about her.

"Is it a long walk to the Butterick Company from here?" she asked.

"It could be done in around a half hour. But it would be much quicker to take the El or another mode of transportation," Mrs. Heaton said.

"We'll be traveling by the El today." Michael smiled down at her. "I want you to get familiar with the stops and comfortable with getting on and off at the right places."

While the sound of the traffic she'd witnessed the day before couldn't be heard from Mrs. Heaton's boardinghouse, as they got closer to the avenue, the sounds of horses' hooves and drivers yelling became more and more noticeable. When they reached the corner, Violet pulled up short and inhaled sharply. Somehow the traffic seemed even worse when one was on foot.

"What is it? Is something wrong?" Michael asked, his hand at her back.

Violet put her hand to her throat and expelled a deep breath. She shook her head, but there were no words for what she was seeing or feeling as she watched people from all walks of life hurrying along the busy thoroughfare, some even crossing the street, dodging the horse-drawn vehicles as best they could. And that had to be taking their lives in their own hands, because there seemed to be every kind of vehicle imaginable, and some Violet had never seen before, racing up and down the street. Then she heard a train and had to look up to see it. There, high above the traffic down below, was the El. Mrs. Heaton had pointed it out to her the day before. She didn't know whether to laugh or exclaim.

"It's the traffic, Michael," Mrs. Heaton said, grasping her hand.

"Of course it is. I'm sorry, Violet. I didn't realize—it is quite a change from Ashland, isn't it? But don't worry. One day you'll know your way around and the traffic will just seem normal to you."

Violet hoped so, as she tried to get her breathing back to normal. But she had to admit that as much as it all frightened her, there was something about all the hustle and bustle of this place that exhilarated her and had her heart pounding to keep pace with all the sounds around them.

Michael led her and his mother up to what she supposed was an entry to get on the train, which had stopped only a block away. He handed the man a coin for a ticket, then gave a coin to her and his mother and they did the same. Then they were allowed to go through a turnstile into an area where they waited in front of doors with glass windows until they were allowed to enter the train on the other side.

"Take a window seat, Violet. You'll see more that way," Mrs. Heaton said.

Violet sat down and Mrs. Heaton took the seat across from her. Michael sat down beside Violet. A conductor collected their tickets and, as the train took off, Violet couldn't keep an excited giggle from escaping as she looked down on the street below.

"It is quite something, isn't it?" Michael asked. "Seeing your reaction reminds us of our own just a few years ago. Mother and I were just as amazed as you are."

His words made Violet feel better, but she didn't have time to say so, as he leaned across her and pointed. "Look, there's City Hall on your left."

The train stopped just then for some of the passengers to get out and others to get on, and Violet got a good look at where the city government was conducted. Then the train was on its way again. They made a sudden turn and Violet slid closer to Michael. His nearness and the scent of his cologne were hard to ignore as she tried to right herself. Trying to compose herself, she pointed to the tallest building she'd ever seen. "What is that?"

"That is the Tower Building over on Broadway. It's thirteen stories high and is one of the tallest buildings in the city at present."

Violet was certain she wouldn't want to be on the top

floor looking down. She shuddered at the mere thought of it.

"We're on Sixth Avenue now and we'll get off at the next stop," Michael explained. "Butterick isn't far from here."

"If we have time, I'd love for Violet to at least get a glimpse of the Ladies' Mile," his mother suggested.

"The Ladies' Mile? What is that?" Violet asked as the train came to a stop once more and Michael and his mother both stood. Violet scooted out of her seat, shook her skirts and stood beside Mrs. Heaton in the aisle.

"Oh, my dear, the Ladies' Mile is blocks and blocks of the most wonderful shops and department stores. Some weekends the girls and I come down just to window-shop. Even if one doesn't buy anything, it's the place to go to know what is in style. Besides, several of the shops that need help are there, so it will be helpful if you know where they're located," Mrs. Heaton said.

Violet followed them out of the train and down to ground level again. Michael hired a hack and off they went once more.

"Aren't we going to show her Central Park, Michael? We've come this far."

"Perhaps we can go there tomorrow after Sunday dinner?"

"That is a wonderful idea. She can't see New York City all in a day, that is for certain."

As the Heatons talked over her, Violet began to believe she could live here the rest of her life and never see it all. Back on street level, in the traffic of a Saturday morning, Violet once again found herself closing her eyes from time to time as one or another vehicle seemed bound to run into them.

Michael was right. It wasn't far to Butterick on Broadway. Violet looked up at the building with the signs that said E. Butterick and Company. Ornate molding framed the windows and doors. The building was very nice, and Violet didn't think she would mind working there, but in her present circumstance she'd be glad to find any respectable position.

Michael pointed out all the El stops, but Violet had a feeling it would take a while before she knew exactly which one to take. He promised to draw her a map to keep with her, to make it easier for her to remember.

Mrs. Heaton pointed out Brooks Brothers, Tiffany's Jewelry and Lord & Taylor along with other stores on Broadway. Michael had the driver turn up and down several different blocks and, new as she was to the city, even Violet could tell when they got close to the Ladies' Mile.

Traffic slowed and became more congested. Carriages of all kinds, landaus, rockaways and phaetons moved slowly, giving them a glimpse of the ladies inside. That these women belonged to society was evident by the gowns they wore and the fact that many had liveried men driving them.

But there were others—everyday women dressed much like Violet and Mrs. Heaton—who were there, too. They were lined up, looking in the shop windows of Macy's, Le Boutellier Brothers, Hearns Department Store and Orbach's on Fourteenth Street. Violet remembered that Macy's and Hearns both had ads in the classifieds. She'd apply at them on Monday as well as Butterick.

Part of Violet wanted to be looking in the windows along with all of those other women, and the other part of her could not have been more relieved when Michael told the driver to take them back to the boardinghouse.

If anything, traffic was even more frenzied than earlier in the day, and Violet closed her eyes at more than one intersection. When Michael chuckled, she opened them to find him looking at her with a smile on his face.

"I'm sorry, Violet, it is just so entertaining to watch you try *not* to watch the traffic."

"I can't seem to help it. I fear a calamity is bound to happen at any moment, and I don't want to see it or be part of it."

"Oh, accidents do happen, and frequently. But most times they aren't all that serious." He grinned at her. "However, it might be best if you try *not* to shut your eyes, or pray that our driver doesn't shut his, as well."

Violet laughed with him. "Yes, I can see how that might help. I'll try, but I can't promise."

Just then, an omnibus careened around a corner and seemed to be heading straight for them. Violet scrunched her eyes shut tight and screamed.

After a much-needed nap, Violet woke refreshed and looking forward to dinner, in spite of feeling horrible about screaming in Mrs. Heaton's ear. When that omnibus had come straight toward their hack, she'd been certain it was going to topple them over. Thankfully, the Lord had been with them and, just in the nick of time, their driver had avoided the calamity.

The Heatons had assured her, over and over again, that they understood, and told her that if not for her scream, their driver might not have acted so quickly. Still, she felt a bit silly and embarrassed about it all.

Hopefully, it wouldn't be a topic of conversation at dinner.

She chose a gown of purple moiré that was several years old, but still in style. At least it had been back home. She only hoped it wasn't terribly outdated here in New York City.

After dressing her hair into a psyche knot, Violet turned this way and that in front of the standing mirror in the corner. The dress had an ivory lace inset in the bodice and a high collar and waistband of a darker shade of purple. It showed little wear, and, well, it would have to do. Even if she chose another gown, it would not be new.

After Mama had her stroke there'd been no money for new clothes, not even homemade ones, and Violet had no interest in them anyway. All she'd wanted was for her mother to get well. But that wasn't to be and, oh, how she missed her. Grief, sudden and sharp, threatened to engulf Violet, until she remembered the promise she'd made to her mother just before she had passed away.

Mama had been so alert for just those few moments as she'd grasped her hand and said, "Violet, now don't you give yourself over to grief once I'm gone. You've been a blessing to me and I don't know what I would have done without you. I want you to get on with your life. The Lord has great plans for you. I know you'll miss me, but I pray your days will be full of life and joy and living according to the Lord's will. When you start to give in to the grief, think of me in Heaven. Promise me, Violet, for I'm ready to go."

"I promise, Mama," Violet had said. Her mother had squeezed her hand, closed her eyes and slipped away.

Remembering how peaceful her mother had looked, Violet let one last sob escape before she wiped at her tears. They wouldn't bring her mother back, and Violet wouldn't have wanted her to suffer just to stay here for her sake.

She let out a huge sigh and nodded to herself. Enough of this—it wasn't what Mama would want. She would honor her mother's wishes and her promise to her. But, oh, how she wished she'd been with her today to see all the sights and hubbub of this city. It comforted her to think that maybe she saw it all from Heaven.

Hearing the sounds of the other boarders begin to make their way downstairs, Violet hurried into the bathroom to splash water on her face, trying to get rid of the telltale tears. She pinched her cheeks to give them color and took a deep breath before stepping out into the hall.

Violet hoped she wasn't overdressed, or underdressed, as she headed down to the parlor to join everyone. She was relieved to see that Elizabeth was dressed much as she was in a pale blue gown, and she put her worries about how she looked away.

"Violet, did you have a good day?" Elizabeth asked as she led the way downstairs. "I asked my friend about openings at Tiffany Glass, and as I suspected, there aren't any at present. Still, she said she'd let me know when one comes up. Evidently it's fairly often."

"Thank you for asking about it, Elizabeth. I did have a good day. I rode on the El for the first time and I know where several companies are that I'll apply at on Monday, including Butterick."

Elizabeth chuckled. "Riding on the El for the first time is an experience, but you get used to it very quickly. I'm so glad there is an opening at Butterick.

I'll be praying you get that position and then we can be coworkers, too."

They were both laughing when they joined the others in the parlor just as Mrs. Heaton called them to the dining room. Again, Violet found herself sitting adjacent to Michael and across from Lila.

After Michael said the blessing and began carving the large ham Gretchen had set before him, Mrs. Heaton introduced a new man at the table as John Talbot, a reporter for the *New York Tribune*. He'd been covering a charity ball the night before.

"Pleased to meet you, Miss Burton," he said. He was about her age and clean-shaven, with rust-colored hair and greenish-blue eyes. He didn't have the rough demeanor she'd thought a seasoned reporter might possess; instead, he looked like someone she could have gone to school with.

"Thank you, Mr. Talbot. I'm pleased to meet you, as well."

"How are you enjoying our city?"

"With her eyes closed." Michael chuckled and winked at Violet as he handed her a plate with a slice of ham.

His wink sent her heart into a little dive and dip and she felt color flood her cheeks, but she couldn't help but join in his laughter as she passed the plate down. "I'm not sure I'll ever get used to the traffic."

That brought laughter from all at the table and several nods of agreement.

"Oh...yes, well, that can take some getting used to. But it is easier with your eyes open," John said. "Did you apply for any positions today?"

"Not today, but I found several I'll apply for come Monday."

"Oh!" Lila put a hand over her mouth, then removed it to say, "I am so sorry. I forgot to ask if there are any open positions at Butterick today. We were very busy and it totally slipped my mind. But, I'll be sure to ask on Monday." She ladled a spoonful of scalloped potatoes onto her plate.

"No need to worry, Lila. There was an ad in the classifieds today," Mrs. Heaton said. "Violet is going to apply there first thing."

"Oh…" Lila nearly dropped the casserole dish she was passing down the table. "That's good. Maybe we'll be coworkers after all."

Violet didn't know if she meant it or not, but Lila did smile across the table at her. For some reason she didn't think Lila liked her very much. Then she told herself that she had no way of knowing that. Still, it didn't dispel the feeling she had that Lila wished she hadn't come to live at the Heatons' boardinghouse. Violet thought it might have something to do with Michael. Lila tried to catch his attention at every opportunity, and it was obvious that she was very interested in him, but so far he didn't seem to be giving her any more attention than he gave the other women. Violet hoped to become friends with all the boarders, but she wasn't sure it was going to happen with Lila. Only time would tell.

She was relieved when the conversation turned from her to the other boarders. She liked hearing about their days and the rest of the meal was quite enjoyable for Violet. Mr. Talbot entertained them with stories from the ball he'd covered the night before.

Up until now the names he mentioned were those

that Violet had occasionally seen in the newspaper, but none of their activities mattered much to her. However, they seemed to mean a lot to those around the dinner table. He was plied with questions about what the ladies wore, what was served and whom they talked to.

The conversation took them through a dessert of cherry pie à la mode and into the parlor afterward. This time Violet stayed for a while and, although she didn't join in on the conversations, she enjoyed listening and learning more about this city she would be calling home.

When everyone began heading to their rooms, Violet found herself going up the stairs with Elizabeth, Julia and Lila.

"What are you going to do tomorrow, Violet?" Julia asked. "If you don't have any plans, you are welcome to come home with me and have Sunday dinner with my family. Lila and Elizabeth are coming, and my mother always has plenty."

"Oh, thank you so much, Julia. But Michael and his mother mentioned something about showing me Central Park after church and Sunday dinner."

"Oh?" Lila arched an eyebrow and seemed to be waiting for an answer of some kind.

Violet didn't know what to say except, "I believe so."

"Oh, you'll love that, won't she, Lila?" Julia turned to the other girl. "We often go there as a group."

"I'd love to go with you all sometime." Violet was a little disappointed at having to miss the opportunity to get to know the girls better.

"Oh, there will be other times—don't you worry. We go on outings together quite frequently, don't we, Lila?" Elizabeth nudged the girl.

Lila gave a very brief smile. It was so quick, Violet was certain that had she blinked, she might have missed it.

On the other hand, maybe it was better that she couldn't spend the day with them. Besides, she'd had such a good time with Michael and his mother that she was really looking forward to the next day. "I'm sorry I can't go with you to meet your family tomorrow, but thank you for the invitation."

"You're welcome. There'll be another time," Julia said.

They'd reached the top of the stairs when Lila said, "Elizabeth, could you come to my room, please? I want you to help me pick out what to wear tomorrow."

"Of course," Elizabeth said before turning to Violet and Julia. "Good night, Violet. We'll see you tomorrow evening. I hope you have a wonderful time. Night, Julia."

"Good night, all," Julia said from her doorway.

"I hope you all have a wonderful time, too," Violet said. "Good night, Julia, Elizabeth and Li—"

"Come on, Elizabeth," Lila said, pulling the young woman into her room and shutting the door.

Julia smiled at Violet and shrugged. "Obviously, Lila is in a tizzy about something. Don't let her bother you. She's just like that."

"No. I won't. Good night."

"Good night." Julia yawned and shut her door.

Violet opened the door to her room more certain than ever that Lila did not like her. And she had a feeling she was the cause of whatever kind of tizzy Lila was in.

Violet joined the Heatons for church the next morning, and they introduced her to some of their friends and neighbors. She felt welcomed and it was good to be with friends on this Lord's day.

Since her mother's death, Violet had questioned the Lord as to why He'd taken her away, and then when she'd found out that Harlan Black held the mortgage to their home, she had even more questions on why the Lord would let that happen, causing her to leave the home she'd been raised in and her lifelong friends.

If the Lord had answered, she hadn't heard it yet. And deep down, much as she hated to admit it, she was afraid. Afraid that Harlan would come after her, afraid of this city that was so huge, afraid of being alone— afraid of so many things for the first time in her life.

She was truly thankful that she had Mrs. Heaton and Michael to turn to, that she had a place to stay. She was hopeful that she would find work in the coming week and would soon find the city not so strange and that she would begin to have the same confidence she'd felt in her hometown. She wasn't used to feeling vulnerable, and she didn't like it one bit.

A peace she hadn't felt in a long time settled over her as she sat between Michael and his mother, and the minister began his sermon. Taken from Isaiah, it comforted her for it said not to fear, not to be dismayed, that the Lord was her God and that He would strengthen and help her. That He would uphold her with His righteous hand. Violet wanted to believe it, but it'd been so hard in the past few months. Still, she would try to hang on to her faith, shaky as it seemed lately. She desperately needed to believe that the Lord was with her now.

Chapter Four

After a wonderful Sunday lunch shared by some, but not all, of the boarders—Julia, Lila and Elizabeth were gone of course—Violet was quite pleased that Michael followed through with his mother's suggestion to show her Central Park. He'd made arrangements to hire a surrey so that he could drive, and Mrs. Heaton had him help her into the backseat, insisting that Violet ride up front beside him so that she could see better.

Michael helped her into the buggy and then went around and hopped in beside her. Violet wasn't sure why she felt safer with him handling the reins instead of a paid driver, but she did.

They headed down the street to Fifth Avenue, and although there was traffic, Violet was pleased that it didn't seem quite as hectic as the day before. There were many people out and about, but the pace of the traffic was slower as they turned onto the avenue and headed north past Madison Square Park and the Fifth Avenue Hotel.

"Look, Violet."

Violet looked back to see that Mrs. Heaton was pointing to the left.

"There is Delmonico's. It is supposed to be one of the best restaurants in the city and, from what I hear, it is quite the place to see and be seen."

"Perhaps we'll stop there for dinner on the way home and see whom we can see and be seen by." Michael laughed and winked at Violet, who couldn't contain her chuckle—or the flush of heat that crept up her cheeks.

"Perhaps we should," Mrs. Heaton said somberly. But then she joined in the laughter.

They passed several large churches, including the Marble Collegiate Church and the Brick Presbyterian.

Michael pointed out the Waldorf Hotel, explaining that rumor had it that it had resulted from a family feud between William Waldorf Astor and his aunt, Caroline Astor. "William, the nephew, had always resented that even though he had more money than his aunt did, she held the social leadership of the family. So to spite her, he had his own house razed and the hotel built. It opened in '93. It must have provoked his aunt, because just last year she had a home built on down the avenue next to Central Park."

Mrs. Heaton took up the story from there, pointing to construction going on next to the hotel. "Now her son, John Jacob Astor IV, has had her old mansion next to the Waldorf torn down and is building a hotel of his own." She shook her head. "There is no telling how it will all end up."

"Probably not," Violet agreed although she knew absolutely no more than she'd been told about the families. Nonetheless, it was all very entertaining.

There were many carriages out and about on the avenue, and it was quite obvious when they passed those of great wealth. Their vehicles were larger and grander, for one thing. And many of them were open so that one could see from the way the occupants were dressed that they were of the upper echelon of society.

However, there were many others who appeared to be dressed as she and Mrs. Heaton were—still in their Sunday best, but far less elegant than the rich. Violet felt quite comfortable traveling in the company she was with.

They passed several more mansions and churches before Michael said, "This is known as Vanderbilt Row."

The mansions occupied a whole block, and Violet was so impressed at the size and the design of the elegant buildings, she had to remind herself to close her gaping mouth. There were balconied windows with intricately carved trims around the windows and between each floor, and moldings everywhere.

Michael leaned a little closer to Violet. "A far cry from what we're used to, isn't it?"

"Oh, yes." Violet shook her head. "I can't imagine living in anything that size or that grand. Why, one could get lost."

"I'm sure I would." Michael chuckled.

"Well, I think I much prefer my small family home in Ashland or your mother's boardinghouse to such opulence."

"Why, thank you, Violet," Michael's mother said from the backseat.

Soon they arrived at Central Park and Michael drove the surrey into it. They passed from the city into a tree-lined road that ran through the park until the scene before them opened up to a huge space, beautiful and unspoiled.

"It looks untouched, as if it's been here from the first," Violet said.

Michael shook his head. "Every bit of the park has been landscaped. None of it is like it was to begin with and, from what I've heard, that's a good thing."

As they kept riding, Violet was taken aback by the sheer size of it. "I had no idea it was this large or this beautiful."

They passed waterways and ponds, and at the north end there was a huge lake where she could see couples boating. There were trails leading off in all kinds of directions, and people walking, riding or sitting on park benches. The perfume of blooming flowers of all kinds permeated the air around them, and Violet sighed at the beauty of it all. She couldn't wait to spend a whole day here.

"There are outdoor music concerts this time of year, and, oh, the ice-skating in the winter is wonderful," Mrs. Heaton said.

"Ice-skating?"

"Yes," Michael said. "We'll have to go, if you're still here by then."

Violet wasn't sure what to say. She'd love to go ice-skating here, but her goal was to stay only long enough to pay off the mortgage on her home. She couldn't imagine living here for any longer.

"New Yorkers of every nationality and status love this park," his mother said, saving Violet from having to say anything.

"I can well see why," Violet agreed. "It is simply amazing right here in the middle of the city."

"It didn't start that way," Michael said. "At first, the wealthy were the ones who mostly took advantage of it and there was a lot of discussion on just whose park it was. But with the El and all manner of other transportation, it's easier for all New Yorkers to enjoy fresh air and sunshine these days, and now the park is enjoyed by anyone who can get to it."

"I'm glad," Violet said. It didn't seem right that only the wealthy should enjoy something so beautiful.

As they left the park and started back down Fifth Avenue, Michael said, "It's about dinnertime. How does Delmonico's sound? Should we see and be seen?"

"Oh, Michael, I was just teasing about that," Mrs. Heaton said. "Besides, I should get back and see about the boarders' meal."

"Mother, you know the boarders realize that our Sunday night suppers are whatever you, Gretchen or Maida decide to put out for them. Maida will take care of it and they will be fine."

"But it's expensive, Michael—"

"No buts. I may not be able to afford a mansion on Fifth Avenue, but I think I can manage to take us to Delmonico's. We're going."

Violet wasn't quite sure how she felt about it, but Mrs. Heaton seemed quite pleased, and she didn't have the heart to object and take the smile from her face.

Once at the elegant restaurant, they were shown to a table and given menus. Thankfully, the interior was dimly lit, because while a few other female diners were dressed in the manner that she and Mrs. Heaton were, most were dressed in gowns the likes of which Violet had never even dreamed of owning.

She felt a bit out of place, but if Mrs. Heaton did, it

never showed, and Violet tried to relax and enjoy herself. There were so many offerings on the menu, both in English and French, Violet wasn't sure what to order and asked Michael to choose. He chose lobster bisque to begin the meal of the Delmonico steak with asparagus and creamed potatoes.

Violet had never seen the evidence of so much wealth in her life from both the sights she'd seen on Fifth Avenue to the clientele of Delmonico's. Once the waiter left them alone, she said so.

"There is a lot of wealth in New York City, to be sure. But there is also great poverty. You just can't see it from here," Michael said. "You will, though. You can't live in the city for long and not become aware of it."

"That's true," Mrs. Heaton agreed. "It is a shame, but a fact that cannot be disputed."

"I think I'm glad I belong to neither group...although if I don't find work soon, I could certainly become one of the impoverished," Violet said.

"That isn't going to happen, dear. Neither Michael nor I would see you turned out on the streets."

"Oh, I didn't mean... I know I have a place to stay and I'll find work. What I meant was that I'm a lot closer to being poor than I am to being rich, and I don't think I'd like to be either."

Michael said, "I understand, and I must admit it is a great comfort to know that I have enough to enjoy my life, but not so much that someone would want to take it from me—or so little I'd want to take it from someone else."

"Michael! You'd never do that."

"I would not, Mother. But in this city, many do just that. I own a detective agency, Violet, and I've seen it all. Many who are poor will do most anything to survive, and some of the rich will do most anything to keep what they have."

On the ride home Violet couldn't remember ever having enjoyed a day more. The meal had been excellent, although she didn't want to even think of how much it must have cost Michael to indulge in that way.

"Thank you for such a wonderful day. I only wish my mother could have been here to take it all in."

"Oh, so do I, my dear," Mrs. Heaton said. "She would have loved being here with us all."

"Yes, she would have."

Violet's mother had told her that Mr. Heaton had left his wife and son fairly well off when he passed away. They weren't wealthy like the Astors and the Vanderbilts she was learning so much about, but she had a feeling they could have been living in a style above that of running a boardinghouse. Mrs. Heaton still didn't know what had happened to her daughter or even if she was still alive. And yet, she'd chosen to come to this city and reach out to others. That Mrs. Heaton chose to do that, to be there for young women who needed a place to feel safe, and that her son chose to support her in that endeavor, was proof enough for Violet that her sweet landlady sought to do the Lord's will in her life. And Michael seemed to do the same.

All she knew about Rebecca's disappearance was what her mother had told her. According to her, Rebecca had been talking about going to New York City for months before she actually did. Mrs. Heaton hadn't been happy about it, but Becca was determined and of age and there wasn't anything she could really do stop her from going. She'd evidently written to tell her mother that she was settled in a boardinghouse and would keep in touch. But that was the last they had heard from her. Finally after a couple of months with no answers from Rebecca, Mrs. Heaton received a packet with all her letters returned to her unopened with a note from the landlady saying that Rebecca hadn't lived there in over a month. Violet couldn't even imagine coming to this city without knowing anyone as Rebecca Heaton had done, and she was very thankful that the Heatons were here for her now.

Michael took his mother and Violet back to the boardinghouse before taking the surrey back to the livery and then walking back home. He helped his mother out first and then gave a hand to Violet to help her.

"I hope you enjoyed your day, Violet."

"Oh, I enjoyed every minute. Thank you for dinner, Michael. It was wonderful."

"I enjoyed it, too." He stood there looking down at her for a moment before clearing his throat and taking a step back. "I'll be back home soon."

But he watched her and his mother get to the front door before taking up the reins and heading out.

When she and Mrs. Heaton entered the house, Violet realized that if it didn't feel like home yet, it was beginning to feel very close to it. And once she thought about being alone back in Ashland, it felt even better to be here.

Several of the boarders were in the front parlor, including Lila. She didn't look the least bit happy, and Violet wondered if it was only her Lila wasn't happy to see.

"We were getting a bit worried about the three of

you, Mrs. Heaton," Lila said. "It isn't like you to miss Sunday night supper."

"I know, Lila. I'm sorry to have caused you concern, but Michael convinced me that Maida was perfectly capable of taking care of you all."

"Oh? And where is Michael?"

"He's gone back to the livery. He'll be along shortly," Mrs. Heaton answered. "We had a treat this evening. Michael took us to Delmonico's for dinner."

"Oh, my, Delmonico's?" Julia said. "What's it like? Who all did you see there?"

Violet found an empty chair and let Mrs. Heaton describe their outing. "Well, it is very dim in there so I can't be sure, but I think I saw Mr. and Mrs. William Waldorf Astor along with the Carnegies." She named several other people that Violet had never heard of, but the others in the room seemed to know exactly whom she was talking about.

More and more questions were asked, and Mrs. Heaton glowed recounting the people she thought she'd seen and the meals they'd ordered. Michael slipped into the room and listened to his mother's account of dining and grinned. Catching Violet's eye, he gave her smile. It was obvious that he was pleased his mother enjoyed herself so much. He was a good son.

Mrs. Heaton held everyone's attention from the beginning to the end of her report. "I hope you all get a chance to go there at least once. The interior was so elegant, and the food was truly delicious. I'm sure I'll not forget this day anytime soon."

"From your wonderful description, Mrs. Heaton, I feel I've just been there. I'm so glad you enjoyed yourself," Elizabeth said.

"Thank you, dear. I wish you all could have been there. It certainly wasn't something we planned."

"No, it was not," Michael said. "But if I'd known you would like it this much, I'd have taken you long before now."

"I'm glad you enjoyed it, Mrs. Heaton," Lila said. But the look she shot Violet seemed to say that she wasn't happy that Violet had been there with her.

Julia came to sit beside Violet. "I'm so glad you had a great day. How did you like Central Park?"

"It was wonderful. It's so beautiful and peaceful. I look forward to spending more time there soon. I hope you had a good time with your family."

"Oh, I did, thank you. I told Mama about you and she said you must come with me next time." She glanced over at Lila, who had made her way over to Michael and was talking to him. "I think Lila would rather have been with the Heatons and had you go with me."

Violet looked at the couple. Lila was leaning toward Michael and talking to him in earnest. Maybe there was more between them than she'd first thought. "Oh? Are they courting? I mean—"

"Not that I know of." Julia chuckled. "Lila might wish for that, but as far as I know Michael has never given her any reason to think that he might want to court her. He is very conscious of the fact that his mother runs this boardinghouse, and he behaves with the utmost propriety toward all of us."

Violet felt a relief she didn't quite understand. She had no claim on Michael Heaton. And she was determined not to let herself care about any man. Although Michael didn't know it, she'd had a childhood crush on him and he *had* broken her young heart when he got engaged to Amanda Cabot before his sister disappeared. Then there was Nick—she'd really thought he might become a beau, but when her mother had her stroke, he took off in a hurry, leaving her alone when she needed someone to turn to the most. Then there was Harlan, who tried to blackmail her into marriage. She saw no reason to trust any man with her heart.

Still, she was glad Michael wasn't considered taken by anyone. Especially Lila. But as she watched Lila bat those eyelashes at him from across the room, she knew the girl was trying as hard as she could to change that status.

"I just wondered."

Julia laughed. "It's quite understandable. We've all wondered the same thing."

"It is none of my business, really." And she wasn't sure why it seemed to matter so much, but it did.

Julia shrugged. "One can't help but wonder these things. Michael would be quite a catch. I don't think many women would turn his attentions aside."

"No. I don't think they would. He's very nice."

"Has he always been that way?"

Violet thought back to before he and his mother had left Ashland. Because Michael was older than her, they hadn't traveled in the same circles, but she had seen him and talked to him on many occasions. Although she'd been infatuated with him, he'd always been kind in a big-brotherly, teasing way, and if she were totally honest she'd missed running into him after he'd moved away. "Yes, I believe he always has."

"Somehow that doesn't surprise me. I think I'll call it a night. I hope you find a position you'll love tomorrow. And I'll say a prayer that you do."

"Thank you, Julia. I hope to have good news tomorrow evening."

"I look forward to hearing it." Julia stood and left the room after saying good-night to everyone.

Violet decided it was time to turn in, too. She wanted to be fresh for her interviews the next morning. She thought to slip out of the room unnoticed, but Michael called to her just as she got to the foyer.

She turned to him. "Yes?"

He quickly joined her in the foyer. "I hope you have a better feel for the city after yesterday and today."

"Oh, I do. And I thank you again for taking the time to show me around and the delicious dinner."

"It was my pleasure. I'll have a hack here to take you and Mother around to Butterick and the other places you'd like to apply at in the morning. What time do you wish to leave here?"

"Butterick's advertisement said to apply from eight to four. I'd like to be there by around nine anyway, if it isn't too much trouble and if the time is all right with your mother."

"If what is all right with me?" Mrs. Heaton joined them at the bottom of the stairs.

"To leave here about eight-thirty so that Violet can apply at Butterick first thing."

"Of course. I'll be ready."

"I'm sure that if I can hire a driver, I'll be fine. You don't have to go with me, Mrs.—"

"Oh, I want to. If we have time, maybe we can stop at a shop or two along Ladies' Mile after you make your applications. Besides, I want to celebrate with you when you get a position."

"I'd be glad to have someone to celebrate with, Mrs.

Heaton, and I hope we'll be able to. I can't thank you and Michael enough for all the help you're giving me."

"Oh, my dear, seeing this city through your eyes is enough, thank you. It's like seeing it again for the first time. I can't remember when I've had a better time than I've had today. It has been a very long time."

Violet's heart swelled with gratitude that this woman had invited her to New York City and that she and her son had been so kind and willing to help her. Much as she missed her mother and her home, she felt blessed to have friends like these.

"I—"

"Violet, wait." Lila caught her attention as she sashayed across the foyer and joined her and the Heatons. "I just wanted to wish you well tomorrow. You'll probably be meeting with Mr. Pollard or Mr. Wilder. They are both very nice men and I'm sure either of them will give your application good consideration. You can give me as a reference if you like."

Violet wondered if she looked as surprised as she felt at Lila's sudden change in attitude. "Why, thank you, Lila. That is very nice of you."

"Yes, well, I hope you come home with good news tomorrow."

"Thank you. So do I."

"I think I'll turn in now," Lila said with a big smile. "Good night."

"Good night." Violet watched Lila head up the stairs. She couldn't help but wonder if Lila was putting on an act for Michael and his mother. Then she felt guilty for thinking such a thought. She shouldn't be so judgmental.

"Well, I—that Lila never fails to surprise me," Mrs. Heaton said as Lila disappeared at the landing.

Violet felt a little better that Mrs. Heaton seemed as surprised as she was at Lila's change in attitude. But Michael's expression was unreadable, and it was hard to tell what he was thinking about the other woman.

Chapter Five

The next morning, Violet dressed to apply for work in a blue serge skirt and white shirtwaist. She thought back over the evening before as she twisted her hair up into a knot and pinned it at the back of her head. She was still a little stunned at Lila's offer to help her get a position. The young woman's whole attitude toward her seemed to have changed so suddenly. One moment Violet thought Lila was glaring at her, and the next she was wishing Violet well and acting as if she would be pleased if they were coworkers. Acting. That's what it all seemed like. For, deep down, Violet still felt that the other woman didn't like her at all.

She pinned her mother's cameo to her shirtwaist. But what if she was wrong? Perhaps she had misjudged Lila. If so, she needed to pray about it and ask the Lord's forgiveness. It would be nice if she and Lila could become friends, perhaps not best friends, but good enough that Violet could think the other girl didn't dislike her as she'd been doing the past few days.

She took one last look in the mirror and said a silent prayer that she'd get a position today—and asking for forgiveness if she'd been wrong about Lila. Leaving it in the Lord's hands, she left her room and hurried downstairs. Most of the boarders had left for work, and Mr. Talbot was just getting up from his place at the table when Violet entered the dining room.

"Good morning, Miss Burton. I hope you have good results from your job hunt this morning."

"Thank you, Mr. Talbot. I hope so, too." Violet smiled at the man. "I hope you have a good day."

"Thank you." He slid his chair back under the table and left the room.

Violet fixed herself a plate of strawberries and pancakes, with a small slice of ham on the side. Just as she set her plate on the table, Gretchen came in the room.

"Good morning, Miss Burton. Did you have a good weekend?"

"I did, Gretchen. I hope you did, also."

"May I get you some juice or tea or coffee?"

"Tea, please."

"Mrs. Heaton said she'd be taking you around to put in applications today and that you'll be eating lunch out. I wish you well with your interviews." Gretchen poured her tea and brought it to her.

"Thank you. I am hopeful that I'll have good news to share this evening."

Gretchen bobbed her head up and down, her curls bouncing out from under her cap. "I'll pray that you do."

"I appreciate your prayers on my behalf. I know that is the best help I can have."

Just as Gretchen left the room, Mrs. Heaton entered from the foyer. "Violet, dear, I trust you slept well."

"I did, thank you. I didn't think I would, thinking about today. But the Lord saw to it that I slept like a baby and I didn't lie awake worrying about what today would bring."

"I'm hopeful it's going to bring you a job." Mrs. Heaton laid the folded paper down beside Violet's plate. "The Butterick position is still open, and there are a few more I've circled that might be of interest to you."

Violet skimmed the classifieds while Mrs. Heaton filled her plate and brought it to the table. Along with the Butterick opening, there was also a new opening for a typist that Mrs. Heaton had circled and one for a receptionist at a bank.

The older woman poured her tea and brought the pot to the table, warming up Violet's cup. "What do you think?"

"Well, I don't know how to type—"

"Oh, that might make a difference. But should you wish to learn, typing, along with other clerical skills, is offered at the YWCA and several business schools in the area."

"Really? That's very good to know."

"Yes. There are so many positions opening up in that field of work that the YWCA felt it was a need they could fill."

"Should I not be able to find employment this week, that might be something I'll consider looking into."

"Hopefully you'll find something today. But if not, we can find out more about what the YWCA offers." Mrs. Heaton pulled an envelope out of her pocket and slid it to Violet. "This is a letter of recommendation, Violet. It may not be needed, but just in case."

"Thank you, Mrs. Heaton. I—"

Mrs. Heaton held up her hand in a manner that Violet had come to realize meant "say no more." "You're more than welcome, dear. I just want to help in any way I can. But we must hurry with our breakfast. The hack driver will be here soon."

Violet took Mrs. Heaton's suggestion and they finished their breakfast in a companionable silence until Michael surprised her by entering the dinning room.

"Mother, I took a call for you. Mrs. Wentworth wanted to remind you of the meeting today."

Mrs. Heaton gasped. "Oh, dear, I forgot all about that meeting. And it is important I be there. Oh, Violet—"

"It's fine, Mrs. Heaton. I'm sure the hack driver will take me wherever I ask him to and back home. Please don't miss your meeting on my account."

"Oh, but I—"

"Mother, there is no need to miss your meeting. I'll be glad to accompany Violet on her job search."

"Michael, you gave up a day of work last week, I can't let you—"

"Violet, Mother will miss the meeting if you don't let me. Besides, I've been working much too hard lately and it will be good for me to take another day off."

Mrs. Heaton chuckled. "He's right on both accounts, Violet. So, what's it to be? Do I miss my meeting and deprive Michael of a much-needed day off?"

Violet shook her head at the two of them. "You two are a pair for sure. Thank you for the offer, Michael. I believe I'll take you up on it."

"Good. The hack should be here any minute now."

The hack he'd hired did show up right at eight-thirty, and Violet couldn't deny that she was a bit relieved not to have to find the places she'd be applying to alone. Nor could she deny that she was happy to have Michael's company once more.

He helped her into the hack and sat down beside her. "Where would you like me to tell the driver to go first?"

In spite of Lila's offer to help the night before, Violet still had a feeling that she did not want her working at the same company—no matter what she said around the Heatons. Because of that, she asked Michael to have the driver stop at the bank that'd advertised for a receptionist first.

"I thought you wanted to start with Butterick first."

"Well, I have no real experience, and surely being a receptionist won't take a lot of training. I believe I could handle greeting people without too much trouble."

"I'm sure you can do anything you set your mind to, Violet. If you want to start with the bank, that is what we will do." He gave instructions to the driver and it seemed no time before they pulled up in front of a very imposing building.

"Would you like me to accompany you?" Michael asked.

"I think I'll be fine, but thank you for the offer."

"I'll just wait here, then. Good luck, Violet."

"Thank you." Violet hurried inside, but her confidence quickly deflated once she found that they were only looking for someone with several years' experience.

"I'm sorry, Violet. Didn't they state that in the advertisement?" Michael asked when Violet returned and told him what happened.

"No. But I suppose I should have known."

"I don't know how you would have without them saying so."

"Thank you for being so kind, Michael."

The next stop along the way was at Hearns Department Store, where she was treated much more kindly and told that they would get back to her, as did Macy's when she put in her application there.

"I'm sure both places will be ringing you up on the telephone by the time we get back home, Violet," Michael said. "But why don't you try Butterick next?"

Violet agreed. She couldn't very well tell him that Lila didn't seem too happy about them possibly working together…not after she'd acted as though she'd love it just the night before. Her hopes starting out this morning had been dashed, but she might as well get it over with. If her earlier interviews were any indication of how this one would go, Lila wouldn't have to worry about it.

By the time the hack arrived at Butterick and Company, Violet was so nervous she wished she hadn't eaten that morning. Her stomach felt as if a hundred butterflies had been taken captive and were all trying to escape at the same time.

"I'll wait here for you, Violet," Michael said. "You'll do fine, I'm sure."

"If this is like the others, you won't have to wait too long," Violet said as Michael helped her out of the hack.

"I'll say a prayer all goes well."

"Thank you, Michael," Violet said. "It helps to know that I have you and your mother praying for me. Gretchen said she would be praying, also."

The knowledge that she had people talking to the Lord on her behalf suddenly calmed the flutters in her stomach, and Violet felt at peace as she entered the building.

A young woman about Violet's age was sitting at a

desk and looked up as she entered. Violet assumed she was the receptionist and walked up to her.

The young woman smiled. "Good morning, miss. What may I help you with today?"

"I'd like to apply for the position advertised in the paper, please."

"Of course. Your name, please?" The young lady motioned to another young woman and had her come forward.

"Violet Burton."

"Miss Rogers, this is Miss Burton. She would like to apply for employment. Mr. Wilder is taking interviews today. Would you take her to his office, please?"

"Of course. Come this way, Miss Burton."

Miss Rogers led her up a staircase to the second floor. "Don't be too nervous, Miss Burton. Mr. Wilder is very nice and we do need help."

Her kind words helped keep Violet calm as she followed the woman down the wide hall. At the end of the hall, Miss Rogers knocked briskly on a door.

"Enter," a male voice said.

Miss Rogers opened the door and led Violet inside a room that was paneled in beautiful hardwood, with windows that looked out onto Broadway. There were two people there, a man and a woman. The man sat behind the desk and the woman in one of two chairs in front of the desk. "Mr. Wilder, Miss Carter, this is Miss Burton and she's come to apply for the cutting/folding position."

Mr. Wilder stood as Violet and Miss Rogers came farther into the room. "Pleased to meet you, Miss Burton. Take a seat and we'll talk."

Violet wasn't sure what she was expecting, but it

wasn't a talk. Still, she took the seat Mr. Wilder motioned to, and was encouraged a little by the smile Miss Carter gave her as Violet took the chair beside her and Mr. Wilder sat back down.

"You may go, Miss Rogers. Miss Carter will show Miss Burton out when we are finished."

"Yes, sir." Miss Rogers smiled at Violet before taking her leave.

"Now, Miss Burton, what makes you want to work at Butterick?" Mr. Wilder asked.

What to tell him? How much should she tell him? Violet set up straighter in her chair and cleared her throat. "Well, sir, I'm new to the city and I need work."

"Where are you from, Miss Burton?" Miss Carter asked, her pencil poised above a stenographer's pad.

"I'm from Ashland, Virginia."

"And why did you decide to move here?" It was Mr. Wilder asking this time. Perhaps they were going to take turns.

"My mother passed away recently and, to be honest, I have family debts to pay and there was no work to be found in my small hometown." Violet grasped her shaking fingers together. Her nervousness was threatening to come back much quicker than it went away.

Miss Carter looked at her in a sympathetic manner. "And why did you decide that Butterick is a place you wanted to apply to?"

Violet laughed and she wondered if she sounded as anxious as she felt. "Butterick is a familiar name to me. I love the patterns and *The Delineator* magazine. My mother and I spent many an hour poring over the pages of it, looking at the patterns and—"

"You are a seamstress, Miss Burton?" Mr. Wilder asked.

"Not a professional one. Just a home seamstress who loves your patterns because they make it possible for the everyday woman to make clothing for her family that actually fits them well."

Mr. Wilder leaned back in his chair, placed his fingertips together over his chest and rocked back and forth. He had a huge smile on his face. "That is music to our ears, Miss Burton."

"Indeed, it is," a voice from behind Violet said. She turned to find an older man sitting in a chair in one corner of the room. He was dressed in a black suit and sported a long white beard. He stood and walked toward them. "I'm Ebenezer Butterick, and I believe you've just found yourself a position at Butterick and Company, Miss Burton."

Violet looked from Mr. Butterick to Mr. Wilder and then to Miss Carter. All three were nodding and smiling. "But...but I don't know if I am qualified for the work and—"

"Most everything we do here can be learned, Miss Burton," Mr. Wilder said. "And I have a feeling you already know what you need to, to work here."

A wave of relief washed over her at his words.

"And we do like to help those who need work, and we love to hire those who understand what it is my wife and I started out to do when this company was formed in '68," Mr. Butterick said. "You are hired, Miss Burton. Miss Carter will help you fill out all the information we need from you and you can start tomorrow at eight o'clock sharp. You'll be shown how our operation works and then we'll start you working."

"Oh, I—" She remembered the letter Mrs. Heaton had given her and pulled it out of her reticule. "I do have a letter of recommendation from my landlady. She used to be a neighbor of ours and—"

"The fact that you are willing to give us a letter of recommendation and are concerned that we might want one is enough, Miss Burton." Mr. Wilder waved away the letter. "You are hired."

"Oh…thank you so much!" Violet didn't know what else to say. She'd never thought to be hired so quickly— especially after her earlier interviews. She could only give credit to the prayers that Mrs. Heaton and Gretchen were saying on her behalf, for she knew she did nothing to get hired on her own. *Thank You, Lord, for answered prayers.*

"You are quite welcome, Miss Burton," Mr. Butterick said. "I've pretty much retired from the daily overseeing of things. But Mr. Wilder and Mr. Pollard are doing a fine job of taking care of the business. However, I'm glad I was here today, to be in on your interview."

"I'm glad as well, sir."

"Come this way, Miss Burton," Miss Carter said.

Violet stood and followed her. But just before they left by a side door leading to another office, she turned back. "Thank you again!"

"You are quite welcome, young lady," Mr. Butterick said.

Violet fought the urge to run back into the room and hug the man. She couldn't believe it. She had a job at Butterick. She would be able to pay off the mortgage on her home. Violet couldn't wait to share the news with Michael.

Chapter Six

Michael jumped out of the hack as soon as Violet came out of Butterick. She didn't try to hide her smile and he grinned at her. "You got the job, didn't you?"

"They hired me. I start tomorrow, Michael." She placed a hand over her hammering heart.

"Oh, Violet, that's great news. I've been out here praying that you would be hired, but never did I dream that you would find out today, especially not after—" Michael stopped speaking and looked at Violet apologetically.

"My earlier interviews today." Violet smiled and said the words for him. "It's all right, Michael. I was thinking the very same thing. I'm finding it hard to take in, but it's true. I really have work. I still can't believe it! But they were so very nice, and Mr. Butterick himself told me I was hired!"

"From what Lila has told us, I thought he was retired now."

"I think he is. But evidently he comes in from time to time to see how things are going and today was one of those days. I didn't even realize he was in the room until he spoke up from behind me."

Michael chuckled. "I'm sure that surprised you."

"Oh, it did!"

"You must have impressed him as one who will work hard and do your best for the company."

"I'm not sure about that. I think he might have had some sympathy for me with my mother's passing and all."

"Well, for whatever reason you were hired, I am sure they'll never regret it."

"I certainly hope not."

Michael helped her back into the hack and took his seat beside her. "You know, Mother probably isn't even home yet, and I'm taking at least half a day off. Why don't you let me take you to lunch to celebrate?"

Violet loved his suggestion, but she didn't want to impose on his time any more than she already had. "Oh, Michael, you don't have to do that."

"I know I don't, but I'd like to. Unless you don't want to—"

"Oh, I'd love to have lunch with you, Michael. And I must admit I'm in the mood to celebrate."

"Well, then. That's what we'll do. And you'll be doing a lot of it this week. Mother loves to have something to celebrate."

Michael leaned forward and said something to the driver, but Violet couldn't understand what he said. And it really didn't matter where they went, she was just glad to get to spend more time with him.

The hack moved out into traffic, and the route he took was one Violet hadn't seen before. Of course, as large as New York City was, she doubted that she'd ever see it all. Still, she loved looking at the buildings, seeing all the hustle and bustle on the streets.

Michael turned to her. "You know, Violet, now that you have a job, I must admit to not knowing a lot about why you came here to find employment instead of staying in Virginia—not that we're not glad you did, but—"

"Your mother didn't tell you?"

"Not really, only that you needed to come here and find work to pay off the mortgage on your family home because you couldn't find employment there. When I asked why, she said it was your story to tell. And if you'd rather not tell me, that's all right."

Violet shook her head. She was impressed that Mrs. Heaton hadn't told even Michael all about Harlan. Since she was staying at his mother's and he'd been such a help to her, she felt she owed it to Michael to tell him what had happened.

"No, I don't mind. I just thought you knew. I couldn't find a position in Ashland because, well, the banker who holds the mortgage to my home made it impossible for me to find work."

"Why would he do that? Seems to me he'd be helping you and not trying to hinder you."

"One would think so. But he had other plans. He thought that if I couldn't find a position at home, I'd give in and marry him. Said he'd forgive the loan if I did."

"He tried to blackmail you into marrying him?"

"Why, yes, I suppose that is what he did. But I couldn't bear for him to..." Violet shuddered, remembering that last time she'd talked to him.

"Violet, he didn't try to— He didn't hurt you did he?"

"No. Other than grab my arm and try to convince

me. But I must admit I wonder what might happen if he ever finds out where I am."

"He doesn't know?"

"Not that I know of. And I hope not. I went to some lengths to keep him from knowing."

"I see. And who is this banker? What's his name?"

"Harlan Black. Do you remember him?"

"I do. I'm glad you turned his offer down, Violet."

"Yes, so am I. Now I just want to get that mortgage paid off so that I can have my family home back free and clear."

Suddenly, a crash was heard up ahead, and their driver brought the hack to an abrupt stop, jostling her and throwing her against Michael.

"Are you all right?" Michael asked as he gently helped her sit back up.

Violet nodded and Michael turned to the driver. "What is it? What's happened?"

"I'm sorry, sir, but it seems there has been an accident up the street." He stood to get a better look before turning to Michael. "Could be a while. Looks like there's been a pileup of vehicles in the intersection."

"Oh, dear. Is anyone hurt?" Violet asked.

"Don't look like it, ma'am. But traffic is piled up ever which away. Don't you worry none. I'll get us around it all." He sat back down and quickly turned the horse to go back the way they'd come. Then he took a detour along one of the side streets, turning the hack this way and that into areas Violet knew she hadn't seen.

She noticed that the area seemed to be more residential than commercial, yet there were buildings, not homes, up and down the blocks. When their driver stopped at the next intersection she asked, "What are these buildings, Michael? It looks as if people live here."

"You're right. They do. These are apartment buildings and multiple-family residents. Some are two-and three-family dwellings along here and some much larger. On farther down there are what we refer to as the tenements, where many immigrant families live. There is much crowding together there and the living conditions for so many have been atrocious."

Violet craned her neck to look down the street as their driver took the hack into the intersection and turned once more. Soon they were in what must be the middle of what Michael had called the tenements. Violet could see all manner of trash piled up in front of many of the homes. And the smell was… Violet prayed she didn't gag before they got out of the area.

She saw young children playing in the streets, even in the trash, and some just standing on the street corner. Two little boys in particular caught her eye as they stood, holding hands and looking sadder than any children should.

"Oh, Michael, look at those two little boys."

"Stop, driver," Michael said. He motioned to the two little boys to come closer, and at first they started to move forward and then they stopped. Their eyes were big and blue and looked as if they'd been crying.

"They're afraid to come near," Violet said. She pulled some coins from her reticule and held them out so that the boys could see, but they shook their heads. Then she dropped them on the street and Michael told the driver to be on his way.

Violet turned in her seat to watch the two little boys as they hurried into the street and gathered the coins.

She waved and, after a moment, they waved back with the most wistful expression she'd ever seen in their eyes. Surely there was more to do there. She watched until the driver turned down another street and she didn't think she'd ever forget the look in their eyes.

"Driver, get us out of here—now," Michael said when he turned down one more wrong street. "Surely you could have found another way to go!"

"Sorry, sir! I took a wrong turn up there for sure. We'll be out of here soon." The driver flicked the reins and the hack picked up speed as he did as told.

"I'm sorry, Violet. You need to know this way of life exists here, but I never wanted you to see it like this. I know it's nothing like you've seen back in Ashland." Michael sighed and shook his head. "Sadly, this is as much a part of the city as the mansions we passed the other day are."

Violet could see the sorrow in Michael's eyes as he went on, "It is absolutely horrible what some in this city endure. But with the publication of Jacob Riis's manuscript called *How the Other Half Lives,* many have been fighting to change things for the poor."

"I'm relieved to hear that. I can't imagine living in those conditions." She'd really had only a glimpse of it, but it'd been enough to throw her imagination into high gear and now she felt she must know more.

"The reality of it is heartbreaking. And sometimes, I wonder if Becca could have been caught up in… If she might be—" Michael broke off and shook his head.

"Michael? Surely you don't think Rebecca could be living in that kind of…" Violet didn't even know how to continue the thought. Didn't want to.

"I simply don't know, Violet."

His voice was hoarse and his eyes so sorrowful, Violet wished she'd kept her mouth shut. "I'm sorry, Michael."

As if it were too painful to talk about, he shook his head. He continued as if his sister hadn't been mentioned. "With the right people finally in office, things are changing, thank the Lord. Since Mayor Strong was voted into office last November, real effort is being put into cleaning up the streets and helping to make living conditions somewhat easier for those who must live in such crowded spaces. But living in the tenements is nothing like what you and I are used to, Violet. The streets have been much worse than you see now—filled with rubbish, trash...so much so that vehicles could barely get down them. It's a shame what the city allowed."

"It's that bad?" Violet asked. Her heart broke for those children and the people living in such dire conditions as Michael described. The overcrowding, the filth and disease they were forced to live with. What she'd seen was bad enough; she hated to think of it being worse.

"Yes. Of course, it is a big city and I suppose it is to be expected. And I'm hopeful that with Theodore Roosevelt, the new police commissioner in charge of fighting the crime in the city, the crime rate will come down. Much has been done since the elections, but more must be accomplished." Michael sighed. "So much more."

Hearing that things had been even worse than what she'd seen, Violet could only nod in agreement.

"Do you have that book you mentioned, Michael? May I borrow it?"

"I do. It's in Mother's study, and of course you may borrow it."

Curious as she was about the tenements and those that lived in them, Violet felt even more blessed that she had the Heatons to turn to in this city and she was eager to get out of this area of it.

As they made it back to Fifth Avenue, Violet breathed a deep sigh of relief. But the comparison between the tenements they'd passed through earlier and the wealth in this part of the city—not to mention the conversation about Rebecca—was almost more than she could take in. Violet tried to put the sights she'd seen in the tenements out of her mind and concentrate on celebrating her new job. Besides, she didn't want to spoil Michael's plans.

Michael took Violet to one of his favorite restaurants not far from his office. It catered to both men and women, so he felt sure Violet would feel comfortable. He tried to keep the conversation on lighter things.

He owed it to her. He hadn't meant to put a damper on her day by bringing up the reason for her move to the city, but he had. He had managed to bring up hurtful memories for her—to think any man had treated her that way had him clenching his teeth.

And then—how they'd ended up in the part of town they had was beyond him—but it had only served to diminish her joy in finding a job even further…and brought up memories of the sister he couldn't find. He couldn't believe he'd opened up and confided his fears to Violet. He rarely talked about Rebecca to anyone anymore. Maybe it was because she'd been open with him—or maybe it was simply because she knew Rebecca and no one in this city did. But the fact remained that he'd managed to make her smile disappear and he wanted it back.

"Would you like to help me surprise Mother, Violet?"

"Surprise her?" Violet leaned her head to the side and smiled at him. "What do you have in mind?"

"Well, I feel sure she would have wanted to take you to the Ladies' Mile to celebrate your good news—did she mention it?"

"She might have. But it's all right, Michael. I'll get to go another day."

"Why don't you let me take you?"

"Oh, Michael, I've imposed enough on your time. I'd never ask you to take me to the Ladies' Mile." She giggled. "But thank you for the offer."

"You haven't imposed on me. I believe it was my suggestion to take you and Mother around the other day, and I know it was my suggestion to go with you today. And you're right to assume I might be a bit uncomfortable visiting most of the shops in the Ladies' Mile. But we could go to Macy's. It has most everything anyone—man, woman or child— might need or want. Would you like to go there?"

"Michael, really you don't have to—"

"Actually, I could use a new cravat, and you could help me choose one." He'd gotten her to smile again, but now, his goal seemed to be to get her to let him take her to Macy's. "Please."

Violet's laugh was light and melodious. "Well, if you put it that way, I'd be glad to go to Macy's with you, Michael."

"Let's go, then."

He pulled out her chair. As they headed out of the restaurant, he couldn't ignore the admiring glances

Violet received from the men at other tables. But she seemed oblivious to them and he smiled. She truly was like a breath of fresh air in this city.

He hired a hack to take them to Macy's and once inside, watching Violet's expression as she saw all that was offered in the store, Michael couldn't remember when he'd enjoyed shopping so much.

And Violet did help him choose a new cravat—a red one no less. He wasn't sure where he'd wear it, but she seemed to like it. "It will look wonderful with the black suit you wore on Sunday or the gray one you have on now," she said.

He was flattered that she remembered what he wore and once he'd made his purchase, he turned to her. "Now, what would *you* like to look for?"

"Oh, I don't need anything right now, but I do like browsing. I've never seen so much merchandise in one place in my life."

He laughed. "No, it's not like anything back home, is it?"

"Do you miss Ashland, Michael?"

"Sometimes I miss the times I lived there. But nothing there is the same now and I've come to love living here in the city. It took a while, but now I feel this is home. What about you? Do you plan on going back to Ashland or—"

"Oh, it's still home for me. And, of course, once I pay off the mortgage, I'll be returning."

Her words didn't really surprise him, though they did seem to put a pall on his mood. He knew the whole reason she was here was to earn enough money to get her home paid off. But he was going to have to warn his mother against becoming too attached to Violet so that she didn't take it too hard when she did leave. And he couldn't let himself enjoy her company too much for the very same reason.

"Well, you don't have Macy's back in Ashland, so you might as well see what it has to offer. We'll take a tour so that if something should catch your fancy, you'll know where to find it when you come back with Mother."

"All right. I'd like that."

They spent the better part of an hour going from one floor to another, browsing in the book department, the jewelry department and on to the fine-art and china department. Then Violet turned to him. "One truly could spend a whole day here and not see it all, I'm sure."

"Mother says the same thing, and I can tell you that you haven't seen anywhere near half of it yet."

"Well, I've taken up enough of your time for today, and I really need to make sure that my clothes are ready for work. I suppose we should be going."

Michael had a feeling Violet avoided browsing the women's department for fear of embarrassing him, and he had to admit he appreciated her thoughtfulness. Still, he almost hated to leave. It was the most time he'd ever spent with Violet alone and he'd thoroughly enjoyed getting to know her better.

By the time they returned to Heaton House, Violet's heart felt lighter than it had since she learned Harlan Black held the deed to her home. Now she had hope that she could pay off the debt against it. And even if she stayed here, she would have a home to keep in her family as part of a dowry if she should ever—

Violet caught her breath. Where in all the world did

that thought come from? She had no need for a dowry, nor did she want to have need of one. She'd been disillusioned by Nick and then Harlan and wasn't sure she could trust any man. All she wanted now was to have her family home free and clear of the likes of Harlan. What she did with it could be decided when that was accomplished.

She'd had a wonderful time with Michael, seeing a side of him she'd never known. She'd enjoyed lunch and the shopping trip and she'd been surprised at how easy it was to open up to Michael about Harlan and her fears. Maybe it was because she had known him a long time and she trusted him and his mother. After all they'd done for her, how could she not?

Violet kept busy for the rest of the afternoon, and by the time she started downstairs that evening, she was confident she was ready to start work the next morning. She'd pressed and brushed her clothing, deciding exactly what she would wear each day. She was nervous, to be sure, but excited, too. She looked forward to beginning this new phase of her life more than she'd thought she might.

Michael asking her if she would be returning to Virginia had given her a lot to think about. She was a bit bothered that the thought of returning home didn't fill her with joy, but told herself that it was because she had no family living to return to. She did love her home and she wanted to keep it, but she wasn't quite so certain that she would be happy to leave here when the time came. Violet sighed. Now was not the time to be worrying about it all. She needed to be thankful that she had work and would be able to keep her home.

"Violet, wait!"

Violet stopped her descent and turned to see Elizabeth hurrying down the stairs.

"How did your interviews go today? I've been praying off and on all day."

"Thank you for asking and especially for praying for me, Elizabeth. The first one didn't go well at all. The next two said they'd be in touch with me."

Elizabeth sighed. "I'm so sorry. I thought for sure that you would have several and come home with a position."

"But I did come home with a position." Violet smiled at her new friend.

"You did? Oh, I am so happy. Where are you going to work?"

"The fourth interview was at Butterick. And I got the position. I'm still finding it hard to believe that I start tomorrow. It seems we'll be coworkers now…just like you and Lila."

They were both laughing when they stepped into the parlor.

"What is so funny?" Ben asked.

Violet was just about to announce her good news when Michael came into the room and announced, "Mother says dinner is ready, everyone."

There seemed to be a mass exit from the room, but Violet stayed put as Michael walked over to her. "Mother was quite pleased that I took you to lunch and shopping, Violet. Thank you for making me the son she can be proud of today."

Violet laughed. "She's proud of you every day, Michael."

"That may be, but she was quite pleased and surprised that I'd thought of it."

"So was I. It was very nice of you, and it made the day even more special for me." She took the arm he held out and let him lead her across the foyer and seat her at what had become her place at the table.

Ben seated Mrs. Heaton. When everyone else had taken their seats, she looked to her son. "Michael, will you say grace, please?"

Everyone bowed their heads as he thanked the Lord for the day and the food and for Violet's good news. He'd barely finished with an "Amen" before everyone started asking questions.

"What good news?" Lila asked from across the table. "You found a job?"

"Did you find a position?" Luke leaned forward from down the table.

"I did. I applied at Butterick this morning and it looks like we'll be working together, Lila."

The other girl looked a little stunned, and Elizabeth rushed in to fill the silence. "It appears we have another 'coworker,' Lila. Or at least you really will." Her chuckle drew laughter at the running joke between the two women and even Lila managed a giggle—if it did seem a bit forced.

Everyone else congratulated her heartily as Michael began serving the main course and Gretchen began to pass the side dishes around.

"When do you start?" Lila asked as she took the bowl of creamed potatoes and served herself.

"First thing tomorrow morning."

Lila surprised Violet once more by saying, "I usually leave at seven-thirty. If you're ready by then we can go to work together."

Maybe there was hope for a friendship with Lila.

Her change of heart from the evening before seemed genuine. "Thank you, Lila. I'll be ready."

"That's nice of you, Lila," Mrs. Heaton said from the other end of the table.

"Well, there's no sense in her going by herself when we can keep each other company on the way." Lila looked back to Violet. "Did you give me as a reference? If so, I wasn't asked about you."

"They didn't seem to need any references," Violet said. "They didn't even take the nice letter Mrs. Heaton gave me."

"Hmm, that's odd. Who did the interview?"

"Mr. Wilder and Miss Carter both interviewed me. But Mr. Butterick was there, too, and he seemed to have the final word."

"Oh!" Lila seemed a bit surprised as she continued. "Well, how nice. I—"

"I'm sure it's a relief to know that you have employment," Luke interrupted.

Violet was glad of the interruption. She wasn't sure she wanted to hear what Lila was going to say next. "Oh, yes. It is."

"We're all very happy for you, Violet," Elizabeth said.

"Thank you. I feel blessed to know I have everyone's good wishes and prayers." Looking around the table, Violet realized she was among friends, and she sent up a silent prayer, thanking the Lord above for Mrs. Heaton and her boarders.

Chapter Seven

Michael watched as everyone congratulated Violet on finding work. He'd been pleasantly surprised by Lila's offer to accompany Violet to work, even though he'd been hoping she would. Had she not, he'd been prepared to suggest it.

What he hadn't been prepared for was the relief he felt that Violet had gotten the position, which meant that she would be staying with them. She'd never given any indication that she would go back home, but he'd wondered if she might if she didn't find something right away. Many who came to New York City did just that if they couldn't find employment quickly. He was glad Violet wouldn't be one of them, because his mother seemed to have perked up considerably since Violet's arrival and he wanted to make sure she stayed that way.

He had to admit he liked having Violet around, too. But he and his mother had to keep in mind that she would be leaving at some point. Her only reason for coming here in the first place was to find a job to be able to pay off her family home and go back to Virginia. And Michael had no intention of moving back to

Ashland. His life was here in the city now. If his sister was still alive she was out there somewhere, and he'd never find her if he left. Besides, his mother's life was here, helping other young women. So he'd best keep reminding himself that Violet's stay here wouldn't be permanent. It wouldn't be wise to let himself become too attached to her.

"Did you go on other interviews, Violet?" Julia asked.

"Yes, I did. The first three came up empty, and I was sure Butterick wouldn't be any different. But I was hired before I left."

"Oh! I thought perhaps they'd telephoned you to let you know you had the position."

Violet looked lovely—her face was flushed with color and her eyes sparkled. She looked as relieved as Michael felt about her getting the position.

"Well, actually, you did receive a telephone call this afternoon. Gretchen remembered to tell me just before dinner," his mother said. "There seemed to be no hurry to let you know, with you getting the position at Butterick. It was the personnel director at Macy's asking that you come in and have another interview tomorrow. Gretchen told her she'd give you the message."

"Thank you for letting me know, but you were right that there needn't be any hurry to tell me. I'm quite pleased that I was hired by Butterick."

"And I'm so glad you and Michael celebrated your good news by going to lunch and Macy's, since I didn't get to go with you," Mrs. Heaton said.

"Oh? Michael took you around?" Lila raised a thin eyebrow and looked at Violet. "That must have been a real treat."

Michael had a feeling Lila wasn't very happy about the time he and Violet had spent together. And in spite of the fact that she seemed to be trying to befriend Violet, he didn't feel any of it was genuine. But at least he wouldn't have to worry about Violet finding her way to work and home alone, and for that he was thankful.

"Oh, it was—at least after Violet had an unexpected tour of the tenements," Michael said.

"How did that come about?" his mother asked.

"There was an awful accident and our hack driver was trying to avoid the worst of the traffic, but I think he went entirely the wrong way about it. Needless to say, Violet saw that mansions and wealth are not all this city is made up of. It is something one needs to know. I just hadn't planned on her seeing it all up close yet."

"But after that we saw the other side of life," Violet said. "I couldn't believe the size of Macy's. I've never seen so much merchandise in one place. Do society women really need all of that finery?"

All the men at the table chuckled, including Michael.

"They seem to think they do," John Talbot said with a laugh.

"Well, you would know, covering all the society goings-on as you do," Elizabeth said, cocking her head to the side.

John only smiled at her. As always, there seemed to be an undercurrent between those two, and numerous times in the past few months Michael had caught them stealing glances at each other when they didn't think the other was looking. He couldn't help but wonder if Elizabeth was sweet on John or if it was the other way around, but they'd certainly make a nice-looking couple if they ever became one. At least John wasn't hanging on to every word that came out of Violet's mouth as Luke and Ben were.

Michael didn't like the attention the two men were giving Violet tonight any more than he had the first night she arrived. Not one bit. He told himself that it was because he felt responsible for her…as he always had his sister, Rebecca. But that didn't ring true either and, deep down, he knew it. There was something about Violet, something—

"Michael, what are you so deep in thought about down there?" his mother asked.

"I'm sorry. I was just woolgathering, I suppose." He laughed and hoped he'd thrown his mother off track. She was very good at reading him, and he wasn't ready for a barrage of questions he didn't have the answers to.

Being on time the next morning was not a problem for Violet. She woke just after dawn and was in and out of the bathroom before she heard anyone else stirring. She took time dressing with care, at last feeling confident she was dressed in the same manner as the women she'd seen at Butterick the day before. She'd chosen a gray-and-black-striped skirt and a crisp white shirtwaist with a black ribbon trim. She tied her mother's cameo with a black ribbon and wore it around her neck.

Violet made her bed and took one last look at the room she'd come to feel was almost like home before hurrying downstairs to join the others for breakfast. She was pleased to find she'd made it down before Lila this morning in particular, and that Michael was still at the table when she entered the dining room.

"Good morning, everyone. Now I really feel as if I belong, seeing you all here this morning."

"Good morning, Violet," Michael said, adding his voice to the others around the table.

He smiled, flashing those dimples, and Violet tried to ignore the way her pulse raced as she hurried to the sideboard and began to fill her plate with bacon, scrambled eggs and a muffin.

Michael stood to pull out her chair and once he took his own, he slid a piece of paper to her. His fingers brushed hers as she took it, sending a spark of electricity straight up her arm to the vicinity of her heart, taking her breath away. She quickly looked at Michael and was relieved that he didn't seem to notice as he began to explain the map he'd drawn.

"This is the map I told you I would make for you. Just in case you and Lila should get separated at some point. This will show you where the El and trolley stops are." He pointed them out to her on the map while she tried to get her breathing back to normal. "None are far apart, and you should be able to get back home by yourself easily enough."

"Thank you, Michael." Violet sounded a little breathless to her own ears but he didn't seen to realize the effect his brief touch had on her, and for that she was extremely thankful. "I'll keep it with me until I know my way around by heart."

"If it isn't clear to you, let me know, and I'll do my best to make it easier for you to read."

"I'm sure it will be fine." She was touched that he'd remembered his promise to her. And she felt a little less nervous knowing she'd have the map with her at all times.

"Are you nervous this morning?" Michael asked.

She let out a shaky sigh. "I have to admit that I am."

"I'm sure it will all go well for you," he said.

"Having a case of nerves is normal for the first day," Elizabeth assured her. "You are already doing better than I did on my first day at *The Delineator.* I was afraid to eat anything, and by noon I was starving. But I'd forgotten to take my lunch with me! Thankfully one of my coworkers shared hers."

"Oh. I hadn't thought about what to do about lunch," Violet said.

"No need to worry, dear." Mrs. Heaton came in from the kitchen to hear her last words. "Gretchen packs a very nice lunch for all the boarders. She puts them on the table in the foyer. Just pick one up when you leave. I look forward to seeing how your first day goes this evening. I'm sure all will go well, but I think everyone is nervous that first day."

"Thank you all for your encouragement. I must admit that this is one *first* I'll be glad to have over with." Violet smiled around the table and her eyes came to rest on the woman she'd come to think of as family.

"Well, good morning, everyone!" Lila said as she entered the room.

Somehow Lila's greeting didn't seem to match the expression on her face. She looked a bit out of sorts as she went to the sideboard. Violet joined the others in greeting her. "Good morning, Lila."

"Are you ready for today? I warn you that it will be a busy one," Lila said as she took her seat across from Violet.

"Good. That means I'll get the first day over with quickly," Violet said, grinning at the other woman.

"Hmm. I suppose you are right," Lila answered. "Actually that's one thing I like about working there. Most days go by very fast."

Violet was glad to hear it. Not that she minded working. She was looking forward to making her way in this city. But she was beginning to enjoy the company of the other boarders more each day, and she looked forward to hearing about their days and getting to know them all better.

Michael slid his seat back and stood. "I suppose it is time to go. I hope you have a really great first day, Violet."

The smile he gave her made her heart beat faster and do a little flip that she tried to ignore, but those dimples were just too hard to avoid. "Thank you, Michael."

He was on his way out the door when he turned back. "And, Lila, thank you for seeing to it that Violet will know her way to and from work."

"Why, you're welcome, Michael. I'm glad to do it." For the first time that morning, Lila's smile seemed genuine as she batted her eyelashes at him.

Violet had no doubt that Lila was attracted to Michael, but did he feel that way about her? Suddenly she felt a little sick to her stomach. She quickly put it down to nerves about her first day of work and chided herself for wondering if there might be something going on between Lila and Michael. It wasn't any of her business anyway. But the thought didn't sit well with her. Not at all.

Violet was more than a little relieved when they arrived at Butterick and Company. Although Lila had smiled a time or two, she'd barely spoken to Violet once they left the boardinghouse, and Violet wondered if she would ever feel comfortable around the other young woman.

Lila had hurried her along, saying they must rush or they'd be late when they got to the trolley stop. But it turned out that they waited about five minutes before the trolley arrived and there were several others waiting with them.

Violet had expected to ride the El as she and Michael and Mrs. Heaton had, but she found the trolley ride quite interesting. At this time of the day, she was sure that most of the men and women were on their way to work just as she and Lila were. She enjoyed wondering what kind of jobs they held and if they'd all get off at the same stop. But each time they came to a standstill, one or two got off and several more hurried to get on.

Perhaps it was all the stopping and starting, but for some reason the traffic didn't bother Violet quite as much today. Maybe she would get used to it, after all.

When they arrived at Butterick, Miss Carter was at the base of the stairs. "Good morning, ladies. Traffic must not have been too bad this morning. You're right on time."

"Good morning, Miss Carter," Lila said before Violet had a chance to say anything. "Traffic wasn't nearly as awful as usual."

Her tone was much more exuberant than it had been that morning. Perhaps Lila was the kind of person who needed time to wake up and get her thoughts together in the morning. Violet didn't know her well enough to be sure.

"Violet and I live at the same boardinghouse. I've taken her under my wing to show her how to get here and back home," Lila informed Miss Carter.

"That's good of you, Lila. It's always nice to have company on the way to work and home."

"I really appreciate it," Violet said. "Everything seems so different to me."

"I'm sure it does, just moving to the city and away from what is familiar." Miss Carter smiled at her. "Well, let's get started. I'll show you around and then assign your work duties and introduce you to your supervisor."

Lila was still standing listening to what Miss Carter had to say. The older woman turned to her. "Lila, dear, you may go on to work now."

"Yes, ma'am. I'll look for you when the lunch bell rings, Violet. Good luck!" With that she pivoted and headed in the other direction. Something about her demeanor made Violet wonder if Lila and Miss Carter didn't quite get along.

"Have you and Lila become good friends?" Miss Carter asked as they watched her walk away.

"I don't think you could call us that. At least not yet. But we do reside at the same boardinghouse. She was kind enough to tell me I could use her as a reference when I applied for the position, but I forgot to mention it yesterday."

"You made a fine impression on your own, Violet. I'm not sure a recommendation from Miss Miller would have done as much as just talking to you did." Miss Carter smiled and motioned for Violet to follow her up the same stairs she'd climbed the day before.

For the next half hour Miss Carter gave her a quick tour, showing her where the designers and pattern makers worked. They watched for a while before going out into the hall once more.

"The templates are then sent to the cutting room,

where they're placed on a stack of tissue paper and cut out. The markings are then transferred to each piece by hand. The pieces are identified by letters marked on it with small holes. Once that is done, the pieces are sorted, folded together and labeled with an image of the garments and brief instructions."

"I never realized just how much work went into making the patterns I've come to count on," Violet said.

"It is a lot." Miss Carter chuckled. They went down another floor and entered a room where seamstresses were working on different outfits, and then they entered another room where artists were sketching the finished products that were placed on mannequins.

"This is where the drawings you see in *The Delineator* and other magazines come to life. After the sketches are finished, some are done in pen and ink and others are colored in for templates to make into prints that are then put into the magazine."

Miss Carter led Violet around the room so she could get a good look at what was being done. She'd never imagined how many steps it took to get a pattern made and to be able to show it in a way that made her and her mother think that an outfit would look good on them.

Everyone she met was very nice and Violet looked forward to getting to know them all better.

"Come along. We'll go to the cutting and folding room and get you started." Miss Carter led her to a huge workroom. "This is where the cutting and folding operations take place. As you can see, it takes a lot of people to keep up with it."

Violet looked at the floor below and saw both men and women at work. She saw that most of those doing the folding were young women of about her age, including Lila, who looked up and gave her a wave before whispering to the girl next to her.

Violet followed Miss Carter down the stairs and into the room where she introduced her to Mr. Hanson, the floor supervisor. "Mr. Hanson, this our newest employee, Miss Violet Burton."

Mr. Hanson sported a dark brown beard and mustache, and he had a nice smile. "Pleased to meet you, Miss Burton. How do you like what you've seen of our operation?"

"Oh, I am quite impressed. I never dreamed of how much work it took to make a pattern. I'm looking forward to working with everyone."

"Now, that is the kind of attitude we like around here. I'm sure you are going to fit right in, Miss Burton."

Violet was beginning to feel that she might.

Chapter Eight

Michael had watched the clock all day, wondering how Violet's day was going. She'd seemed quite nervous this morning, and he'd prayed that she'd come to feel at ease in her new surroundings. It was well-known that Mr. Butterick was one of the kindest, more generous men in the city. He gave much to the poor, in particular to needy children, and his company had always had a reputation for treating its employees well.

He gazed out the window of his office and jangled the coins in his pocket as he watched the traffic on Third Avenue. He'd felt a restless energy all morning—one would think he was the one starting a new job today instead of Violet.

In spite of the fact that there were times when she looked very vulnerable and Michael had wanted to ease her fears about the city, the traffic and her decision to move here, Violet Burton was a strong woman. A weak woman would not have made the decision to leave all she knew and move to New York City to find a way to keep her family home instead of entering into a loveless marriage.

After Violet had told him about what Harlan Black had tried to do, he was certain she could take care of herself. After all, she'd decided to chance losing her inheritance rather than marrying the likes of Black. Still, it infuriated Michael that the man had tried to blackmail Violet into marrying him.

He clenched his fists, wishing he could get ahold of Black. Michael remembered Harlan and his reputation. There weren't many in Ashland who liked the banker. He misused his position in town to get what he wanted, and it didn't matter to him if others had to suffer. But he did have a reputation as a ladies' man. In fact, at one time Michael had feared Becca might be attracted to him, but that was before she'd left to come here. At least she hadn't come under his influence. And neither had Violet. He was thankful for that.

Still, Black held Violet's inheritance in his hand, and Michael didn't like that one bit. One of the things that bothered him was why Mrs. Burton had had any need to go to Black for money in the first place. His mother had said that she thought Mr. Burton had made provisions for his wife and daughter in his will. She'd been under the impression that while they might not have been well-off, they had enough money to provide for them in the manner they'd been accustomed to.

Evidently it had been much on his mother's mind, because just this morning, she'd mentioned that she wondered if Harlan Black had made Mrs. Burton believe something other than the truth about her money situation.

As always, when he heard something like that, Michael wanted to know more, get to the bottom of it. Maybe he should send one of his men to look into things in Ashland. Yes, it might be time to do just that. It was certainly something to think about.

That Violet had turned down Black's offer showed him that *weak* was not a term that applied to her. Even so, a strong woman could be naive in ways. This city was far different from their hometown. But after yesterday, she must realize there was a darker side that hid behind all the mansions, the businesses on the Ladies' Mile and the beauty of Central Park. The dangerous side that had swallowed up his sister. He couldn't let that happen to Violet. *Wouldn't* let it happen.

The noise of traffic seemed to intensify and Michael looked down to see that an omnibus had hit a street vendor's wagon. It didn't look as if anyone was seriously hurt from what he could tell three stories up, but he hoped traffic was better today and that no omnibuses came close to running into the streetcar Violet and Lila rode to work in.

Michael chuckled, remembering Violet's reaction to the near accident on Saturday. To give her credit, had it not been for her scream, they might well have been in a horrible accident. All in all, except for that near calamity, it had been the most enjoyable weekend he'd had in a very long time. And he'd enjoyed yesterday even more. He hoped Violet had enjoyed it as much as he had.

He decided to take off a little early so that he would be sure to be home when she and Lila returned. As soon as he let himself into the house, the aroma coming from the kitchen assured him that his mother planned a special dinner to celebrate Violet's first day of work.

That she was becoming attached to the young woman was obvious. Violet was a link to their hometown, to the woman who'd been his mother's best friend and even to

Rebecca, in his mother's mind. He couldn't blame her because he felt much the same way—only different—and definitely not brotherly.

Since the disappearance of his sister, Michael hadn't given much thought to his personal life. He'd been more concerned with helping his mother and trying to find his sister. And for propriety's sake, because of his mother's business, he'd made a conscious decision not to let himself become interested in any of the women boarding with her.

But Violet Burton could very well be the exception. If the amount of time he spent thinking about her was any indication, she already was. Since the moment he'd first seen Violet all grown up, there had been something about her that drew him to her. He wasn't comfortable with it, tried to ignore it—to no avail, but there it was. He enjoyed being around her. Already, he looked forward to seeing her each morning and evening.

And yet he had no intention of falling in love with her. Violet was going to return to Virginia when she got the mortgage paid off. She'd said as much. She had no intention of staying in New York City. And just as he wanted to warn his mother not to get too attached to her, he had to tell himself the same thing. Besides, after Amanda broke their engagement, refusing to postpone the wedding until he had a chance to look for his sister, he knew that not many women would accept his commitment to finding his sister or even helping his mother. There was no sense setting himself up for disappointment again.

Still, Violet was a family friend and he wanted to help her in any way he could. And he was curious to know how her day had gone.

Michael made his way down the hall, peeking into his mother's study only to find it empty. He headed to the kitchen. His mother was icing a three-layer coconut cake, and she looked up with a smile when he entered the room.

"Michael! You're home early today, son."

"I am." He joined her at the worktable and stuck a finger in the icing bowl before bringing it to his mouth. "Mmm. Love coconut cake."

His mother playfully slapped at his hand when he went for another dip in the icing. "You didn't know I was making this, so that isn't why you came home early."

"You're right. Actually, I wanted to see how Violet's first day went."

His mother chuckled. "I understand. I've been a bit nervous for her all day. I'm sure everything has gone well—still I'm anxious for her to get home to find out."

At the sound of the front door opening, Michael's heart seemed to do some kind of funny little jump and twist and he decided that *anxious* described how he felt perfectly. It was all he could do to let his mother hurry to the foyer before him.

"How did your first day go?" his mother asked as soon as she spotted Violet.

Michael didn't need to hear the answer. He could tell from the look on Violet's face. A deep sigh of relief left his lungs before she answered.

"It was wonderful. Everyone was so friendly and kind. I'm sure I'm going to like working there."

"Oh, yes," Lila said. "Violet is going to fit right in."

From the conflicting tone in Lila's voice and the almost smile on her face, Michael couldn't decide if she was being sarcastic or sincere.

"Lila was very kind to introduce me to everyone she could when we took lunch," Violet said, turning to smile at the other girl. "Just knowing someone there helped put me at ease."

Her words went a long way to convincing Michael that Lila was being genuine.

"I'm so glad everything went well," his mother said. "I was sure it would, but it's good to hear that I was right to plan a dinner to celebrate your first day. I remembered that coconut cake is one of your favorites and I'd best get back to icing it. You girls have plenty of time to freshen up."

"I believe I have the beginning of a migraine," Lila said abruptly. "If I'm not down for dinner, please don't be concerned. I think I might need to lie down and close my eyes for a bit."

"Oh, I'm sorry, Lila," Michael's mother said. "Would you like me to send you up some tea?"

"No, thank you." Lila turned to the stairs.

"I'll be sure to save a plate for you and a big slice of cake for later if you don't come down to dinner."

Lila said nothing as she began to climb the stairs.

"Is there anything I can get you?" Violet asked. "A cool cloth?"

"No. I just need some quiet and a dark room. I'll be fine." Her voice trailed off as she reached the landing.

"I hope she feels better soon. Does she have these headaches often?" Violet asked.

Mrs. Heaton shrugged. "Occasionally. But she usually recovers quickly."

"I'm sure she'll be fine," Michael said. Lila had

looked more irritated than in pain, and he had a feeling that she didn't like all the attention Violet was getting. She'd acted much the same way when one of the other girls was getting more attention than she was.

"I hope so. Is there anything I can do to help in the kitchen, Mrs. Heaton?"

"No, dear. Dinner will be in about an hour and a half. You have time to relax and rest."

"Oh, I don't think I can rest. My mind is still in a whirl." Violet gave a light laugh. "There is so much going on at Butterick it's hard to take it all in. But I have much more appreciation to what goes into making the patterns to make it easier for the home sewer."

"Maybe you should go sit in the garden for a bit. It's very relaxing out there this time of day. I've got to go finish icing the cake." She started back to the kitchen and then turned back. "Michael, why don't you show Violet the garden? It's a nice place to relax."

Michael surprised himself by saying, "I'll be glad to, if you want to see it, Violet?"

"That would be nice," Violet said as Michael took her elbow and led her through the hall to the doors at the end.

"Mother's pride and joy is the garden. It is very small, but she's done a lot of work getting it just the way she likes it." He opened the door and let Violet go through first.

"Oh, it is beautiful." The air was sweet smelling from the roses and all the other flowers in bloom. It felt much cooler here than anywhere else she'd been that day.

Michael led her to a small bench and waited until she sat down before joining her. "I'm glad your first day went well."

"I am, too." Something about the way he was looking at her had her feeling warm and…fluttery. Michael was such a handsome man and very considerate of others. How could a woman's heart not beat a little faster when his attention was turned on her?

She told herself that he was just acting as any old friend would, being happy for her, as she continued, "I must admit I was very nervous. I hope I can live up to their expectations. I was so surprised when they offered me a position as a seamstress instead of the pattern folding."

Michael leaned a little closer and grinned down at her. "What? You're going to be a seamstress? You aren't going to be working alongside Lila in the pattern room?"

Violet tried not to think about how deep his dimples were up this close. She shook her head. "No. I don't think she's very happy about it, and I can understand how she might not be. I expected to be folding patterns right along with her, but after lunch I was summoned to the office and told that one of the seamstresses was leaving to get married. They asked if I would be interested in taking her place since I was familiar with sewing from their patterns."

"Violet, that is very good news for you. It pays better than the pattern folding, I'm sure."

She nodded. "It does, and I'm so glad. I think I'll be able to make an extra payment to the bank every other month or so. I just feel bad for Lila. And I'm a little apprehensive. I tried to tell them that I am not an excellent seamstress, but they said that since they target the home seamstress, that is exactly who should be making their sample wardrobes."

"Mother is going to be so excited for you. And so will the other boarders."

Violet sighed. "All except for Lila. I feel so bad—"

"Don't worry about Lila. You didn't seek out the position and, besides, I'm pretty sure Lila doesn't know how to sew."

Violet jumped up from the bench as an idea came to her. "Maybe I could offer to teach her to sew, so that next time an opening comes up she could apply for it."

"That would be nice of you."

She let out a sigh and shook her head. "But I don't have my sewing machine with me."

"I'm sure Mother would loan you hers."

"Or maybe I could have Beth, my friend from home, send me mine."

"Either way would work. But don't be surprised if Lila doesn't take to your suggestion. She might not really want to learn. Or she might not want to—"

"Learn from me?" Violet finished for him.

Michael shrugged. "One can never tell how Lila is going to react to an idea. But it's very kind of you to want to make the offer."

"No, it's more selfish than anything. I'll feel better if I do. She was kind enough to introduce me to several coworkers today and, well, I might feel the same way if I'd been at the company first. In fact, I'm sure I would."

Violet saw no need to mention that Lila had barely spoken to her on the way home—or even on the way to work that morning. She might have known Michael and his mother longer than Lila had, but Lila had been living in their home longer than she. At this point Violet had no idea how close any of them were.

"That's understandable. Still, if she doesn't know

how to sew, she wouldn't have gotten the position anyway. Try not to blame yourself for her attitude."

Violet had to ask, "How long has Lila lived here?"

"She's only been with us about eleven months."

"Oh. I thought she'd lived here much longer."

"No. Although sometimes it feels as if she has been here much longer."

Violet couldn't tell how he felt about Lila, and she told herself once more that it wasn't any of her business anyway. Still, she wished she knew. "I suppose I'd better go freshen up for dinner. Hopefully, Lila will feel better and come down."

"Mother will send something up if she doesn't. Don't worry about her. She'll be fine."

Violet was sure she would be, but today's events weren't going to make it easier for them to become friends. And she might have to accept that they never would be. But it would make living in the same house much easier if they could get along.

They parted at the staircase. Violet had just reached the landing when Julia came out of Lila's room and hurried to give her a hug. "I heard about your wonderful news," she whispered. "I am so happy for you."

"Lila told you?"

Julia steered Violet down the hall away from Lila's room.

"How is her headache? I feel so bad—"

"Don't you feel that way for a minute. You thought you were being hired to be a pattern folder. You had no way of knowing they would be in need of a seamstress. But you can sew and Lila can't. For whatever reason you were asked to take the position, just rejoice and thank the good Lord for the blessing. That's what I'd do."

"Oh, thank you, Julia. I needed to hear those words. I do hate that Lila is upset, but I'm so very excited to begin my new position!"

"Good! You should be. Hopefully Lila will get a promotion one day soon. But don't blame yourself if she doesn't. Now, let's freshen up and get downstairs. I can't wait to see what Mrs. Heaton has prepared for your first-day-at-work celebration—it's bound to be delicious. She's so great to make all 'first days' special."

"She's a wonderful woman. I'm so thankful she suggested I come to New York when I couldn't find work at home."

"Well, I'm thankful she did, too. I'm glad you are here, Violet. So is everyone…" She grinned and shrugged. "Well, all except for one, maybe. It's impossible to please everyone, you know."

Julia was right. If Lila was determined to dislike her, there was nothing she could do to make her change her mind. Mrs. Heaton had put a lot of effort into this celebration dinner and Violet wasn't going to let Lila's attitude ruin it.

The table was set with the Sunday china, and as Michael pulled out her chair for her, Violet realized how much she was coming to look forward to dinnertime. She loved hearing him say the prayer before meals, and that he thanked the Lord for her quick promotion touched her heart.

As Michael began passing dishes around, there was a family feel to sharing meals with these people she was coming to know. Everyone seemed truly happy about the way her day had gone and wanted to know all about her new position.

"I would think that would be a more interesting position than the one you applied for," Elizabeth said. "How fortunate that you know how to sew."

"I am very thankful that I do. And the fact that I'd been using Butterick patterns to make mine and Mother's clothing the last few years seemed to help."

"I'm sure it did," John said. "Any company wants to have an employee who likes what they sell."

The dinner Mrs. Heaton served was one of Violet's very favorites and it made her feel even more at home than ever. Had her mother been alive, she would have prepared the exact same thing. Dinner was filet of beef with mushroom sauce, creamed potatoes and peas along with other side dishes. The dessert was a huge coconut layer cake.

"Thank you so much, Mrs. Heaton. Everything is delicious." Violet tried not to think of Lila missing out on it. Was she sulking? Violet sighed inwardly at her thoughts. There she went again—judging others. It was possible the other woman really did feel bad for reasons other than jealousy. She shouldn't be jumping to conclusions.

"I love it when someone has something to celebrate on a weeknight," John Talbot said. "It feels like a holiday."

Elizabeth added, "We're blessed that Mrs. Heaton considers most pieces of good news a reason to celebrate."

"So, Violet, how did it come about that you've become a seamstress instead of a pattern cutter or folder?" Luke asked.

Violet explained about the young woman she'd been replacing getting married. "Evidently, from what I was told, openings come up quite often in all departments for that reason."

"They come up often in all businesses. I suppose there are some women who keep their positions once they are married, but I haven't known many," Julia said. "And, were I to get married, I don't think I'd want to work. Of course there are women who must take care of their families for various reasons and I would hope they would be able to find work, should they need it."

"Times are changing," Mrs. Heaton said. "There are many more opportunities for employment for women now that were not available when I was young. I was blessed in that I married for love, but I knew young women who weren't so fortunate. Their fathers arranged marriages for them or they felt forced to marry any available suitor. You have many more choices, particularly in this city. But you must always be aware of the dangers, too."

"Yes, we know. And we're all thankful to you, Mrs. Heaton. You've given us a safe haven and you watch over us so well," Elizabeth said.

"Even with my rules about not going out at night alone or without one of our male boarders accompanying you?"

"Even with those," Julia said. "I think that's part of why I feel so much at home here. I know you would give me the same advice my mother would. And I have no desire to go out by myself after dark."

"There's not one of us who objects to keeping you ladies company any evening." Luke grinned and winked at Violet.

"That is true," Michael said, capturing Violet's gaze. "Anytime."

The look in his eyes as his gaze met hers had a warm flush creeping up Violet's neck and cheeks.

"Why don't we all go to a concert at Carnegie Hall—" All conversation stopped as a loud series of knocks on the front door interrupted Michael.

Maida hurried to see who was interrupting their dinnertime. Then Michael and his mother were called to the door. The pocket doors were shut for but a few minutes and then Gretchen was summoned to the foyer. From the looks on the other boarders' faces, Violet was certain she wasn't the only one wondering what was going on.

Chapter Nine

Everyone was waiting in silence when Michael opened the pocket doors once more. In fact, no one spoke until he and his mother had taken their seats.

"What is it, Michael? Has there been some kind of trouble?" John Talbot asked.

"No, at least not for any of us. Only for the young woman we're taking in for a while." Michael understood the intensity in John's voice. He wanted a big story to break. One that could get him out of covering those high-society festivities that he disliked so much. If he could break a big story, he could work for any newspaper in the country. But it had to be the right one, and John was always on the lookout. This wasn't it, unless one took a look at the bigger story—the overcrowding of the tenements, the corruption that couldn't be completely eradicated.

"I'm sorry about the interruption, everyone," Mrs. Heaton said. "I knew we were going to gain another temporary boarder, but I wasn't expecting her quite so soon."

"A temporary boarder?" Violet asked.

Michael could see the confusion in her eyes as his mother tried to explain.

"Yes. Sometimes we take in someone who needs a safe place to stay just for a while, until they can go back to the home they've left or move on to another more permanent place. I give them a room on the third floor. Anyway, Mrs. Clara Driscoll, who lives a few streets over and works for Tiffany Glass, asked her landlady, Mrs. Owens, to see if we could take in one of her girls for a short time, as there was no room at her boardinghouse."

"And of course you said yes," Elizabeth said. "That's one of the things we all love about you, Mrs. Heaton. You are always willing to help out those less fortunate."

"Thank you, dear."

Michael's mother cleared her throat before going on and he knew Elizabeth's words had touched her deeply…along with the problems of the young woman they'd just taken in.

"You all know not to mention this to anyone, of course. This young lady has been treated very badly where she's been living." She sighed and tears came to her eyes. "It seems her brother-in-law kicked her out of their tenement and she had no place to go. Clara says she's a hard worker and will help to find her a more permanent place. For now, though, she needs encouragement and the peace of knowing she's safe."

"How sad," Violet said.

"I'm sorry that I haven't gotten around to explaining all this to you, Violet."

"I'll explain to Violet later, Mother."

Mrs. Heaton took a deep breath. "Thank you, Michael. For now let's get on with our meal. I'll have something sent up to her after she's settled in her room."

"Oh, Mrs. Heaton, if you are needed upstairs, please don't give me another thought. We're nearly finished with our meal anyway. Thank you very much for making it so special."

"I'm not leaving until we have the cake. Michael, please bring it to me. And, Julia, would you be a dear and get the dessert plates, please?"

Michael and Julia hurried to do as requested. Once the cake was in front of her, his mother cut large slices and sent them around the table.

"Too bad Lila didn't feel like joining us," Elizabeth said. "Coconut cake is one of her favorites, too."

"She won't miss out," Michael said. "Mother will send a plate up to her."

"I already did—all except for the cake," Mrs. Heaton said. "But she sent it back down. I'll leave it in the kitchen in case she changes her mind, and I'll make sure there's a slice of cake for her."

"If she doesn't want it, I'll be glad to take her piece of cake so it doesn't go to waste," Benjamin said.

Everyone laughed at that. It'd been mentioned on more than one occasion that with men in the house, there wasn't much food that went to waste. From what his mother told him, Michael knew it was true. But she always took that into account and he was certain there would be plenty left for both Lila and the new boarder. And he was pretty sure Lila's appetite would be back before the evening was over—in fact she'd probably be starving by then. He had a feeling that migraine was only a ruse to keep from celebrating with Violet.

* * *

Violet joined the others in the front parlor after dinner, but her thoughts were on the young woman the Heatons had just taken in. What must it be like to be kicked out of your home…even if it was a tenement? Thoughts of the area she and Michael had wound up in made her shudder. But still, it was home to many. It was all they had. And to be forced out… Where did one go from there?

It appeared they could possibly come here. Violet had known there were rooms on the third floor and that Gretchen and Maida stayed in two of them, but she really hadn't thought about the other empty rooms. Nor did she know how many there were. But she was pleased to know that the Heatons reached out to those in need. Much like they did her, only in a different way.

Mrs. Heaton went upstairs right after dessert to see about the young woman they'd taken in and Michael seemed to have disappeared. Violet wondered if it had anything to do with their new boarder. Everyone else was there, except for Lila, who still hadn't made an appearance.

Violet wondered if she should go check on her. She'd just decided to do that and had excused herself when Maida met her in the foyer.

"Miss Burton, Mr. Heaton would like to talk to you, if you have time for him. He is in Mrs. Heaton's study."

If she had time for him? Violet couldn't imagine ever not having time for Michael Heaton. "Thank you, Maida." Violet headed down the hall to the study. She knocked lightly on the door frame and was pleased to be greeted with Michael's smile.

"Maida said you wanted to talk to me. If I've come at a bad time—"

"No, you haven't. Please, come in and take a seat, Violet. I didn't forget that I would try to explain about our temporary boarders to you. Would you like me to have Maida bring us some tea?"

"No, thank you. I'm still quite full from supper." She took a seat in one of the chairs by the fireplace. "And please don't feel you have to explain. It's really none of my business."

"Oh, but it is. You live here, and while most of our boarders know Mother takes people in from time to time, they don't know everything. But Mother and I want you to know what it is we do here besides take in boarders."

Michael took the seat on the other side of the fireplace. "It's been a busy evening. We were expecting this new boarder, but we didn't know exactly when she would arrive. There's been trouble in her family for a while now, but evidently things escalated last night and her brother-in-law insisted that she move out of the apartment she'd been sharing with her sister and him and their children."

"How sad." Violet's heart broke for the woman upstairs.

"It's a story we hear often. Families all crowded into a small apartment, with little income to provide for everyone." He shook his head and looked into the fire. "Tempers flare and relationships are sometimes damaged forever. This may be one of those cases."

"I hope not."

"So do I." Michael's gaze turned to her once more.

"But to explain about how we came to take in temporary boarders—"

"Michael, you don't have to explain to me. This is your home. You have the right to do whatever you want with it. And I am the last person who would have a problem with you helping others less fortunate. Your mother came to *my* aid. It does not surprise me at all that she would do the same for others."

"It is a little different with you, Violet. You're a family friend and you've become very special to mother and…" Michael paused and chewed his bottom lip. He shook his head and continued, "I cannot thank you enough for moving here and becoming part of this household. Your presence has made my mother very happy. Since Becca's disappearance, she's poured herself into this house and helping others. But with each passing year, much of the hope of finding my sister has disappeared, and, well, you've brought joy back into my mother's life. I am so glad you are here."

"Why, thank you, Michael. But it's I who am blessed to be here."

Michael smiled and shook his head. "Shh. I'm trying to thank you for what your being here means to my mother. And I'm getting off track. I'm supposed to be telling you how this all came about."

"I just assumed it was because of Becca's disappearance that your mother decided to open the boardinghouse."

"And you'd be right in that assumption. From the first, Mother's goal has been to provide a place for young women to live where they could feel at home and safe." Michael got up and began to pace and Violet could tell it was hard for him to continue. She waited in silence, not knowing what to say.

Finally, he continued, "When it became obvious that Becca wasn't coming home, we came here and went to the boardinghouse where the last letter we'd received had come from. But it was only to find that she'd lived there just a week before disappearing. She'd never given them our address to contact us, if something happened, never even—" He shook his head and sighed.

Taking his seat once more, he looked at Violet. "It's been very hard on both Mother and me. Not to know where she is, for the few leads we had go nowhere. Still we look for her, but I'm not sure we'll ever get the answers to all the questions we have."

The sorrow in his voice had Violet blinking back tears as she reached out and touched his arm. "I'm so sorry, Michael."

"I pray you'll never have to know the feeling." His hand covered hers and he squeezed it before letting go. She quickly moved her hand back to her lap, her pulse racing up her arm and straight to her heart at his touch.

"So, Mother decided to move here and open a boardinghouse. I wasn't going to let her do it alone, so I came, too. She's comfortable with the number of boarders we have, but she's always wanted to have room for those in dire need, if only for a night, a week or a month or so. It took a year before she began to make the connections that let others of the same mind know she was willing to help in that way."

"How was she able to get the word out?"

"There are several boardinghouses in the area and many all over the city. She met the owners and let them know that she keeps some rooms available for such a need. In my work, I've come to know several police-men, firemen, others who came into contact with young women who needed help, and I let them know. After a few months, we began to get calls from boarding-house owners who had no room and knew someone who needed a place for a night, then we'd have a knock on the door from a policeman or fireman who'd run across someone in real need for a temporary place to stay to get away from a situation…somewhere safe until they could decide what to do."

"What wonderful work you and your mother are doing, Michael. If there is any way I can help, please let me know." Violet paused. "After seeing only a small part of the other side of the city, I've not been able to get it or the little boys we saw out of my mind. I realize I've lived quite a sheltered life in Ashland."

"I understand. I realized the same thing. It is quite a shock at first—to know there is poverty at such high levels just blocks from here. Does it make you want to go back?"

"I don't like it. But no, it doesn't make me want to go back—at least not until I have the money to pay off the mortgage on my family's home. However, it does make me feel selfish for feeling sorry for myself. I never had to live in those kinds of conditions. Never had to worry about my next meal or having a roof over my head. Oh, I worry about not being able to keep my home…but if that happens, I'll be able to work and stay here. I wor-ried about finding work, but I was blessed to find it so quickly. I've never had to live in squalor. I'd like to help in some way, if I can."

"You have the heart of my mother and the others who want to make a difference. And I'm sure you'll be able to. There are all kinds of opportunities and ways to help, Violet. We just wanted you to know how we came to the point that we take in more than just our regular boarders. You'll find there is a group of people working to help in many ways. We can't do it all, and there will always be more problems than we can solve, but we try to do our part, one person at a time."

Violet had never felt prouder to know this man than at that moment. "Thank you for explaining it all to me. I see now why this house feels like a home. It holds much love for those who come to it."

Long after Violet went upstairs, Michael sat in his mother's study thinking about their conversation. Violet had a huge heart and he could tell she was sincere in wanting to help others. Well, she'd have plenty of opportunity in this house. And his mother would be thrilled to have her help.

Perhaps it was a good thing their hack driver had taken a wrong turn the other day. Although Violet just saw the tip of the iceberg, she at least knew for certain that New York wasn't all mansions and fancy shops. And she'd find out more the longer she lived here.

There were many who didn't want to see or even hear about those less fortunate. Sadly, a few of their boarders were like that. Lila came to mind. She was much too self-absorbed to care much about others.

Her actions this evening were a prime example. She might have had a headache, but he'd seen her act that way before and he was pretty sure that Lila was just plain jealous of Violet and didn't want to be part of her celebration tonight. If she had any idea how transparent she was, she'd see that her attitude was what actually made people less inclined to want to spend time with her. Lila wouldn't want to know about the temporary boarder. She would barely acknowledge her existence once she joined them downstairs.

She and Violet were total opposites, and it was no wonder that Violet was getting most of the attention Lila craved. Violet cared about the others in this house, how their day went, what was going on in their lives.

Michael had never felt about a woman quite the way he did about Violet. On one hand, it was as if he'd known her all his life, which he had. On the other, it was as if he was getting to know her for the very first time and he was aware of her presence in a way that made him feel more alive than ever. Not even his ex-fiancée, Amanda, had made him feel the way Violet did.

He wondered if he should have told her that he'd sent someone to Ashland to try to find out where her attorney had gone and to try to find out what Harlan Black was up to. He'd talked to his mother more about the Burtons' finances and she was quite sure there would have been no need to take out a loan. Not unless something had happened that her best friend hadn't told her.

It was enough to see what, if anything, could be found out. There would be time enough later to let Violet know if something turned up. Until then, he would just be glad that she was here and had a job and wouldn't be thinking about going back home.

The relief he felt when she'd said she didn't want to go back just yet had surprised him in its intensity. He didn't want Violet going back to Ashland. Certainly not until he knew what Black was up to. Truthfully, he didn't want her going back at all. He told himself it was for his mother's sake, but to be honest, he wanted her to stay right here where he could get to know her better. For him, it was a big admission to make. And he wasn't ready to make it to anyone but himself.

Violet half expected to meet the temporary boarder the next evening, but when they sat down to dinner Mrs. Heaton announced that she'd returned to her family. It saddened Violet to know the woman had gone back so soon. Would anything have changed by then? How would she be treated?

"I don't know why you bother yourself with these people, Mrs. Heaton." Lila shook her head. "All the trouble you go to for one night."

Violet opened her mouth to come to Mrs. Heaton's defense, but the older woman quickly came to her own.

"Sometimes, in some instances, that is all that is needed to bring clearer thinking and for things to get better," Mrs. Heaton said. "And sometimes it is too soon. In this case, I feel it was. But all I can do is offer a safe place for however short or long a time is needed and pray it helps."

"Still—"

"We knew we wouldn't be able to help everyone who came here for a night or a week or longer when we began to open our home to those in need," Michael said. "But if we can help a few, then we've done what we set out to do and what we feel the Lord has called us to do."

Violet's heart warmed at his words. He and his mother would be here for those in need no matter what the objections from others.

"And it is very noble of you to want to help. But—"

"Lila, you're fortunate you've never been in the position some of the young women who come to us have found themselves in. Mother has her reasons for opening her home to regular boarders like you and they are as important as her reasons for taking in those who need help immediately. But if you are unhappy here with what we do…"

It was no surprise to Violet to hear Lila backtracking. "Oh, no, of course I'm not. Who wouldn't love living here?"

"Good," Michael said. "I'm glad that is settled."

Conversation quickly turned to small talk as if everyone wanted to change the subject, and Michael turned to Violet, speaking in a voice meant only for her ears. "It's been a beautiful day and I wondered if you would like to take a walk later. There's something I'd like to show you I think you'll enjoy."

At this moment she wanted nothing more than to get away from Lila and her sulky silence and resentful stares. "I'd like that very much."

"Good. But I'd like not to have to go with the others. We'll head out once everyone has gathered in the parlor, if that's all right with you?"

Violet nodded as her heart flooded with warmth that he wanted to spend some time with just her. But when she took a sip of water, her eyes met Lila's over the rim of her goblet and she knew the other woman wanted to know what they'd said to each other.

It was doubtful they'd ever become friends, but Violet was determined to keep trying—if for no other reason than for the Heatons' sake. She wondered what it was Michael wanted to show her but wasn't sure it mattered. It would be good to get out of the house for a bit.

Once dinner was over, she hurried up to her room to freshen up and have a reason not to join the others in the parlor without a lot of questions. When she came back downstairs, she was pleased to see that the parlor doors were closed and Michael was waiting for her at the front door. She felt like a child slipping out of the house with him, but she knew she was safe in his company. He'd never harm her.

He pulled her hand through his arm and they headed down the street. "I don't know why we haven't shown you Gramercy Park yet, but it dawned on me today that you might want to know we have a park nearby for those days when you feel you must be outdoors. Mother's garden is wonderful, but it is small. It was she who suggested that you might need an outing."

"Your mother reads people very well. I love being at Heaton House, but I must admit that there are times when it's—"

"Too much noise—too many people?"

"Considering it was just Mother and I for the last few years, at times it does seem a little overwhelming. I'm sure I'll get used to it, though."

"I hope so. Mother would be very upset if you left us."

Violet couldn't help but wonder how he would feel, but couldn't bring herself to ask, so she changed the subject. "Is Gramercy Park large?"

"Nowhere near as large as Central Park and only residents can get in." He flashed his dimples at her. "I feel the same way you do—I'm glad that everyone in the city can go to Central Park and I feel they should. But it's nice to have an oasis in the middle of this neighborhood we live in."

They turned a corner and Violet didn't need Michael to point out the park to her. She could tell from the trees and the iron gate that surrounded it. As they neared the entrance she could smell the roses and see all manner of blooming flowers. "Oh, Michael, it's lovely."

"It is. Come see it all." He pulled out a key and unlocked the gate, leading her through to a walking path. "See, it's not really large enough for the whole city to visit, but it's—"

"Wonderful." As they strolled around the paths, Violet felt herself relax. She'd always loved being outdoors and, much as she liked the city, she'd missed just walking outside to lean against the porch rail to hear the birds sing and watch the squirrels at play. "Thank you for bringing me here."

"You're welcome. Would you like to sit awhile?" He pointed at a nearby bench.

"I'd love to." She sat down and sighed at the beauty around her.

Instead of sitting, Michael stood and propped a foot up beside her. He looked down into her eyes. "You've seemed a bit somber this evening. Are you all right?"

"I'm fine. I've just been wondering about the temporary boarder and praying that things are better for her today."

"You have a heart like my mother, Violet. There is no way of knowing about the young woman, but our prayers are joining yours. We had to accept that we wouldn't be able to help everyone who came to us a long time ago."

"Oh, I realize there is no way you could. I just admire what you do. I'd like to be able to help people in that way."

"You are helping."

Violet shook her head. She wasn't doing anything.

Michael's touch on her chin as he lifted it to look into his eyes stilled her thinking and sent her pulse racing. "As I said before, just having you here has helped my mother more than I can tell you."

"But it's not the same. Besides, I'm the one being helped."

"It's helping another person, Violet. In whatever way we do it. I can't thank you enough for what your presence in our home has done for my mother." His thumb grazed her cheek and then he suddenly dropped it. "Would you like to walk some more?"

Violet gave a quick nod and swallowed hard. She might not be quite as safe in Michael's presence as she first thought. Oh, he'd never harm her, of that she was sure. But she wasn't so sure of her heart. That could be another matter entirely. And she couldn't allow herself to have feelings other than friendship for him. Besides the fact that she was disillusioned with men in general. Violet was beginning to like feeling independent and making her own way. For now, falling in love simply wasn't in her plans.

Chapter Ten

By the time Violet and Lila got home from work on Friday, it was apparent Lila was only going to talk to Violet when she felt she had to and that seemed to be whenever Michael or his mother were around or when one of the supervisors at Butterick was nearby.

Violet tried not to let it bother her. Surely Lila would get over her anger one day. The only thing she could think of to do was offer to help Lila to learn to sew, and that only if she could get her sewing machine shipped there.

She was sure Mrs. Heaton would loan her sewing machine to her for that purpose, but Violet didn't want to tie it up if she didn't have to. Besides, she could make her own clothing if she had her own machine here.

So, she'd written to Beth on Wednesday evening to let her know about her position at Butterick, to tell her all about what she'd seen of the city and to ask if she could have her papa crate up the sewing machine and have it shipped to her. She'd inquired as to the amount it would cost to send it beforehand and sent the money to Beth, as well. Hopefully, she'd hear from her friend soon and once she knew the machine was on its way, she'd see if Lila wanted to learn to sew. Other than that, she didn't know how she could help their relationship.

It was wonderful to have two days off to look forward to, and when Elizabeth knocked on her room before supper to ask if she was going to Central Park with the rest of them the next day, she was pleased she was included even if Lila might not want her to go.

"I would love to! I didn't know you were all going."

"Oh, I'm sorry. Didn't Lila mention it to you? We decided on it last night after you went upstairs, but she said she'd tell you today."

"No, Lila didn't say anything about it." But she hadn't said more than a few words to her since Tuesday.

Elizabeth closed her eyes and blew out a breath. "I'm sorry, Violet. I'll be sure to let you know when we plan something from now on. Anyway, we're going to leave here around eleven and take a picnic. I told Mrs. Heaton about it this morning, and she said she and Michael might join us."

They headed down to the parlor together. "What should I wear tomorrow?" Violet asked.

"It's getting really warm out, but of course it's cooler in the park than anywhere but on the water this time of year. Just wear what you'd wear to work and as cool a material as you have."

"I can't wait. I only saw Central Park driving through that one time and now we'll get to picnic there."

"Mrs. Heaton said she'd have fried chicken prepared and lemonade, and I'm sure there will be a cake. There always is when we picnic. I can't wait for you to go skating with us in the winter. It's so much fun," Elizabeth said.

"What's so much fun?" Michael asked as they entered the parlor. He walked over to them with a smile.

"Skating in the winter. Sledding, too, for that matter."

"Don't forget sleighing. I love it most of all," Mrs. Heaton added as she came into the room.

Lila still hadn't shown up when Mrs. Heaton called them to dinner, but she slipped into her seat across from Violet right before Michael said the blessing. She barely got her head bowed before Michael began praying.

"Father, we thank You for this day and for our many blessings. We ask You to be with all around this table and keep each one safe, and we ask You to bless this food, Father. In Jesus's name we pray. Amen."

Michael began carving the ham his mother had set in front of him and passing plates down before Gretchen began passing side dishes around.

"Just in case some of you have not heard the news, we're all planning on going to Central Park tomorrow and taking a picnic, as well. Please be ready to leave by eleven o'clock," Michael said.

"I can't wait," Violet said. "I've been looking forward to going again."

"I forgot to tell you about the outing, didn't I?" Lila acknowledged with a shrug. "Oh, well, I was sure someone here would tell you. It appears I was right."

Michael found he was looking forward to showing Violet more of Central Park. She'd get to see and experience it so much better on foot. So many of them were going, they'd arranged for an omnibus to pick them up. As everyone gathered and got in the vehicle, he was a little put out to see that Luke had taken a seat next to Violet before he had a chance to.

He really was taken aback a bit by the quick surge of jealousy that rose up inside him. He'd never had quite this kind of reaction to any woman, not even Amanda, and that fact alone told him he'd begun to care more about Violet than he'd intended to.

But as she answered his smile with one of her own, taking her attention away from Luke for at least a moment or two, his heart quickened and he realized he'd begun to look for her smile, to try to elicit it.

"Michael," Lila said as she sat down beside him, sitting a little closer than he was comfortable with. "It's a beautiful day for a picnic, isn't it?"

"Yes, it is." He scooted over to put some space between them but Lila moved even closer, keeping only a pencil's width of room between them. She leaned nearer. "Violet seems to be fitting in at Butterick very well."

"Oh? Do you see much of each other?"

"Not as much as we would have if she'd stayed in the pattern room. But she seems happy." She nudged him and motioned to where Violet was laughing at something Luke had said to her. "She does look happy."

Yes, she did. But was it because of working at Butterick or was it Luke making her look that way? Just then she looked over and caught him staring at her and he watched a warm color steal up her neck and cheeks as she smiled back at him. For that one moment he felt it was only the two of them in the bus. Lila and Luke both seemed to fade into the background. Then Lila spoke his name and Violet broke eye contact and looked down before Luke claimed her attention once more.

Lila grabbed Michael's arm, but before she could gain his attention fully, John nudged him from the seat behind them. "Michael, have you had a chance to find out any more about the matter we discussed the other night?" John asked. "Remember, the break-in on Irving Place?"

"A little," Michael said, glad to have someone other than Lila to talk to. "I'm not sure there's a story there."

"There might be." John shrugged. "You never know."

"That's true. And one day, you're going to get that big story, my friend. Of that I have no doubt."

"Thank you, Michael. It helps to know someone believes in me."

"I'm not the only one who does, John. It'll happen. You try to stay on top of everything and you care about this city and the job you do. It'll happen when the timing is right."

"Timing has a lot to do with it. Part of my problem is that there are so many of us out there trying to get a story. And whoever gets the scoop first is the one that breaks in. My goal is to be the one who will break a big story first one of these days."

"I understand." And he did. Michael knew what it was to hunt for something so hard you were sure you had it—only to find that you didn't. He'd followed more leads than he wanted to think about trying to find his sister. He knew his mother had almost given up on them ever finding her.

And from the amount of leads he received now, perhaps they should. But every once in a while he'd get a new tip and there was no way he couldn't follow it, even if he was sure it would lead to another dead end. He knew he'd follow any lead he found for as long as it took to find Becca, or for as long as he was alive. He couldn't stop trying to find his sister.

* * *

Violet hadn't expected such a strong reaction to seeing Michael and Lila sitting so close. Nor had she ever had her heart feel as if a knife had punctured it, but that's exactly how it felt to see Lila leaning so close to him.

To Michael's credit, however, he had tried to put some space between them, but if Violet had learned one thing about Lila, it was that she was very persistent, especially when it came to Michael.

She'd tried to ignore them and pay attention to what Luke was saying to her, but when she looked up it was to find Michael's gaze on her. She could feel the flush of color flooding her cheeks, but she found she couldn't tear what she had intended to be a quick glance away. At least, not until Lila called his name and grabbed his arm again.

And then she couldn't keep from looking over again when she heard Michael talking. She saw that it was John he was speaking to and not Lila. Lila didn't seem the least bit happy with that turn of events, and it was written all over her face.

The omnibus came to a stop and she was relieved that they were at Central Park. Her attention certainly hadn't been on the ride over. The park was even prettier than she remembered. A few days made a big difference this time of year, and it seemed there were twice as many flowers in bloom as last time.

She was so busy looking around she didn't realize that Michael was walking beside her, holding a huge basket. He smiled when she looked up and those dimples seemed deeper than ever, causing her heart to skip a beat or two.

"Michael, I didn't know—"

"Whom you are walking beside? Or even quite where you are." He grinned, bringing out those dimples again. "That's why I fell into step beside you. I didn't want you getting lost."

His dimples were definitely playing a game of hide-and-seek today, and Violet's heartbeat was having a hard time keeping up with them. "And you do know where we are going?"

He led her through a hedge and followed some of the others, who seemed to know where they were going. "I believe we are going to claim a spot for our picnic and then everyone will take off in different directions. Some will go to the lake to canoe. Others will rent a bicycle, and others will just take a stroll through the gardens. Think about what you want to do, okay?"

"It all sounds good to me, but I suppose I can't do it all in one day."

"Well, you could, but you wouldn't get to enjoy any of it to its fullest. Remember that you live here now. We can always come back, you know."

She did live there now, and the city was beginning to feel like home to her. Michael had said they could come back…did that mean he wanted to come back with her? Maybe his sitting by Lila meant nothing. After all, Luke sat down beside her before Michael got on the omnibus. And it was Lila who'd sat down by him.

"Michael, Violet, we're over here," Mrs. Heaton called, waving to them.

Violet saw that she'd found a grassy spot under a nice-size tree that would give shade for the time they were there. She followed Michael over and helped his mother spread a huge quilt over the ground. There were several baskets to be unloaded, and everyone helped. By the time it was all laid out, Violet wondered how they could possibly eat it all.

She wondered how many chickens had been fried early that morning so that it would be ready for the picnic. There were also sandwiches made with minced ham mixed with a touch of mustard on thin white buttered bread. They also had potato salad and boiled eggs along with pickles and olives and pickled peppers. There were two cakes, chocolate and a yellow pound cake, to round out the meal.

Violet thought that maybe she should decide to go for a stroll after eating. She was pleased when Michael followed her to a spot under the tree beside his mother. It was cool under the tree's branches, and Violet couldn't remember a prettier setting for a picnic.

"I'm so glad we've had such a beautiful day for our picnic," Mrs. Heaton said. "I love this time of year. We come out here quite often in the spring and summertime. But it is truly beautiful in the fall and winter, too."

"I can't wait to see it then," Violet said. She tried to picture the trees with no leaves, the bushes bare and snow all over everything. But today the sun was bright, the sky blue and a light breeze made a perfect day for a picnic. She'd have to take Mrs. Heaton's word for the other seasons until she could see it for herself.

The park was a wonderful place to just sit under a shade tree and watch people—much different from Grand Central Depot. Instead of looking harried, these people looked relaxed and eager to enjoy the day.

There were people dressed in their Sunday best and others more casual, as Mrs. Heaton's group was. Others were dressed in what was most likely the best they had. But all seemed to be having a wonderful time.

"What is that language those people next to us are speaking, Michael?" Violet had never heard it spoken before.

He leaned his head to the side and listened. "It's Italian."

"Mmm." Violet smiled as she watched the family. There was a lot of gesturing and laughter and she'd love to know what they were talking about.

Just a few trees away, there seemed to be a group that could well have come from any of the homes she'd seen on Fifth Avenue. She could tell the walking costumes the ladies had on were of the finest materials and custom-made. The gentlemen were dressed much the same as the men in her group, but again, their clothing seemed to be custom-made. They appeared to be having a good time, but no better than the Italian family to their left.

A couple bicycled by them and then another. It looked like such fun. She'd only been on a bicycle one time and for few wobbly moments and she'd enjoyed it very much. She couldn't help but notice that one of the women was wearing a bicycling costume. She wondered if that pattern was one Butterick made. She'd like to make one for herself one day.

Out in the middle of the grassy area, children were playing, flying kites and chasing one another. Violet could have sat there and watched those around her for the rest of the day, but Michael stood just then and held a hand out to her. "Come on. There's a lot to see and do. Have you decided what you'd like to try first?"

"I'm not sure. What are your recommendations?"

Violet turned to look down at Mrs. Heaton. "Would you like to go with us?"

"No, dear, thank you. You'll be able to go much faster without me. I think I'll just sit here and enjoy watching people."

"I think I'll join you, Mrs. Heaton," Elizabeth said.

Lila seemed to have appeared out of nowhere. "Why don't you come canoeing with me and Julia, Violet?"

"I'm going to show Violet around some, Lila," Michael said. "Then if she wants to go canoeing or bicycling, we'll do that."

"Thank you for inviting me, Lila," Violet said.

Lila only shrugged and walked away.

Julia smiled. "We'll have plenty of time to bicycle together. There is a lot to choose from. You have a nice walk."

Violet sighed. She knew Julia wasn't upset with her, but Lila obviously was. "Perhaps I should have gone with Lila. That's the first time she's asked me to do anything with her."

She didn't think for one moment it was because the other girl wanted her company. Lila's motive was much more personal than that. Violet had come to realize Lila didn't like it at all when Michael was giving his attention to anyone besides her.

"Sorry if I misspoke, Violet. If you wish to go—"

"Oh, no, Michael, I didn't mean I'd rather go with her. It's just—" she shrugged her shoulders "—I don't think she likes me very much."

"And you have very good manners and wouldn't want to disappoint me." Michael grinned down at her.

"Well, there is that." Violet smiled back at him and took the arm he offered. She didn't want to disappoint him in any way. And she would much rather see Central Park with Michael than spend the afternoon with Lila anytime. "Let's go."

Chapter Eleven

Michael had never enjoyed Central Park more than he was right then, with Violet. She loved watching people out on the lake. There were all sizes of rowboats, from those for two people to the kind that held Julia, Lila, John and Ben. They waved when they passed by and he was glad when Violet didn't seem disappointed not to be with them.

"I believe I'd like to be rowing my own boat, although I've never done it before," Violet said.

"It's quite fun. Of course, it does take some strength."

"Are you saying I'm weak, Michael Heaton?" Her eyebrow shot up, daring him to do so. Oh, how he'd missed that look. She'd always been a bit feisty as a child and he was glad to see she still had some feistiness left in her.

He laughed. "Oh, no. I wouldn't dare do that. But I'd love to take you rowing. You can even have your own oar."

"All right then, let's do that."

"Let's do." It would be nice to have her out on the water, just the two of them. He loved his mother's home, but sometimes it was very hard to find a quiet place for two people to talk without someone barging in on the conversation.

In only a few minutes, he'd helped Violet into her seat and taken his own. He explained how to hold the oar and what to do, going from one side to the other, although he'd be the one doing most of the rowing.

As he lowered his oar, she did the same. Mimicking his movements, she held her own as they floated over the water and into the middle of the lake. They passed the larger canoe that held their friends and waved once more as they headed across to the other side of the lake. People were standing or sitting all around the edge watching the boats glide over the water.

"Oh, this is fun. And it's so much cooler on the water, too."

"The light breeze is helping today. You're doing very good."

"Thank you. I must admit, however, that my arms are getting a bit tired. Guess I'm not quite as strong as you." She grinned and dipped her oar in the water again.

"I think that's how the Lord wanted it to be, don't you?"

"I suppose it is. I really don't want to be as strong as a man—not physically, anyway."

"You are a strong woman in every other way, Violet. You've been through a lot."

"So have you and your mother."

"Want to stop for a while? I can row us or we can sit still for a bit and float."

"That would be nice."

They pulled their oars in. "I should warn you that

you may be very sore tomorrow. The first time works muscles you might not have used in a while."

"Or ever?"

"Now, that only you would know." Michael chuckled and looked a little closer at her. He grinned and reached out to touch the tip of her nose. "Your freckles are back."

Violet giggled and rubbed her nose. "Must be this time out in the sun. I don't think I'll ever be rid of them."

"I hope not. I've missed them—I'm glad to see them again." Her smile warmed his heart.

"Thank you. I'm not sure I feel the same way, but I'm so glad we came today. I love this park, the lake, all of it." She looked around and sighed.

"I think all New Yorkers feel the same way."

"It is so quiet and peaceful, as if the city has disappeared and yet it's right there." She raised her arm and pointed all around them. She didn't mention that her arm was already beginning to hurt, but he saw the slight wince as she put it back down.

Michael hoped she wasn't too sore tomorrow. "And that's what draws everyone. It is a wonderful place to relax and think, knowing that there is more to life than the hustle and bustle of the city."

"Do you think you'll ever move back to Virginia?" Violet asked.

"No. Our lives are here now. What about you?"

"Oh, I don't know. I want to keep my family home because it is my inheritance, I suppose. But I must admit that I like it here. And I know I haven't had my fill of this city."

Michael breathed an inward sigh of relief. "I'm glad

you like it here. And I'm glad you don't plan on leaving anytime soon. Mother and I would both miss you. We're just getting to know you again."

"Thank you, Michael. I can't begin to tell you what it's meant to me to have your mother's and your support at this time. I do have some friends in Ashland, but no family now, and it will never be quite the same to me there. When Harlan made it impossible for me to stay there unless I married him, I felt I had no choice but to leave."

"Black is a cad of the first degree. I'm glad you didn't accept his terms, Violet." For more reasons than he wanted to go into at present. Michael wondered if it was time to tell her he was looking into Black's business dealings with her mother. He just wasn't sure what to do. He'd not heard back from his agent yet and there really wasn't anything to report.

He picked up his oar and Violet started to do the same. "You don't need to help, you know. These canoes are fine for only one to row."

"Then I'm going to plead female weakness and let you do it."

"Thank you for making me feel stronger."

"You're welcome."

He rowed them around the lake. As they got closer to the bank they'd left from, he saw Elizabeth waving them in. When they got close enough to hear her, she said, "Hurry! There is a family fight going on right next to where we had our picnic. Luke is there, but—"

The boatman held the canoe steady while Michael helped Violet out. They all took off in a run toward the picnic spot. By the time they got there, a brawl was in progress. Violet and Elizabeth hurried to Mrs. Heaton's side. Michael stepped into the fight just as two police-men showed up and pulled the man who'd evidently been causing all the problems off Luke.

"What's going on here? Heaton, what started this?"

Michael knew both officers from working with them on cases in the past. They were good men and would get to the bottom of things.

"I don't know. I just arrived."

"I can tell you, Officers. This man tried to harm that young lady and his wife tried to pull him away." Michael's mother pointed from one to another of the women as she spoke. "He tossed his wife aside and the other gentleman was coming to the women's defense."

"It this true, miss?" O'Malley, the officer Michael knew best, asked.

"This is a family affair, Officer," the man that Luke had been fighting with said as he was being handcuffed. It was obvious they were Irish from his accent. "It's not your business."

"'Tis our business when it's out here in public," O'Malley said. He turned to the two women and Michael's mother. "We need to ask you a few questions, ladies. We can do it here or at the station."

"Oh, please, here, Officer," the woman with the man said. From the looks of her she was expecting a child.

"I can tell you what it's about," the man yelled. "My wife's sister owes me rent money, is what this is all about."

"Ma'am—" Officer O'Malley broke into the conver-sation. "Do ya owe rent to this man?"

"No, she doesn't," the man's wife said.

"Ma'am, do you be wishin' to press charges against this man?" Officer O'Malley asked the sister.

The man's wife shook her head and said, "Please, no, Kathleen."

The woman she'd called Kathleen looked at the two little boys who'd come running up and hidden behind their mother's skirts.

"Aunt Kathleen, please don't let them take Papa to jail." The boy peeked out from behind his mother and added his plea to hers.

Michael knew what she was going to say. He'd seen it happen too often not to.

"Ma'am?" Officer O'Malley prodded.

"No, Officer. I won't press charges—at least not this time." She looked at her brother-in-law, who'd turned a hateful glance her way.

"You give either of these woman cause to call us and they won't have to press charges. We'll have you in the clinker before they have a chance to decide," the officer said as he took the cuffs off the man. His wife hurried over to him, pulling him off in the opposite direction as the officers, her young boys following.

"Thank you, Officers," Michael said.

"Yes," Luke said, rubbing his jaw with one hand and shaking each officer's hand with the other. "I'm certainly glad you all showed up when you did."

The younger woman, who'd begun to follow her sister's family, turned and ran back to where they were. "I thank you for comin' to our aid."

"You get in touch if he roughs you or your sister up again," Officer O'Malley said.

"I will." The young woman turned to Mrs. Heaton. "I'm sorry we ruined your day."

His mother handed the woman one of the cards she'd had printed up for anyone she felt might need a safe place. "You keep this. If you ever need to, you come to us again."

The young woman looked down at the card and nodded. She slipped it in her pocket. "Thank you. I will."

Michael looked at Violet, who had tears in her eyes as she watched the young woman leave.

"Those little boys…they're the ones we saw in the street that day. Aren't they, Michael?" she asked, a tear escaping and running down her cheek.

Michael wanted to pull her into his arms to comfort her, but pulled a handkerchief from his pocket and handed it to her instead. "I'm sorry to say, I believe they are, Violet, and their aunt is our last temporary boarder. The one who stayed only one night."

The ride back to Heaton House was a somber one. Violet couldn't get the image of those little boys out of her mind. That they'd had to witness their father acting in such a way as Mrs. Heaton had described and beg their aunt not to send him to jail. And what about once they got out of sight? How did he treat those women— or his children, for that matter?

The question was still in her mind late that afternoon as she sat in Mrs. Heaton's garden and enjoyed the air sweetened by her roses. Her mother had loved roses, anything flowering. She missed her so much. But she thought it might be even harder if she'd stayed in Virginia around so many memories of the last few months when her mother was in so much pain. Violet's sigh was ragged as she wondered if the ache ever went away.

She heard the back door shut and wiped at her eyes. Tears weren't going to bring her mother back, and she reminded herself of her admonition to live her life and not to grieve. But she was finding that it was much harder to do than to say.

"Violet? Are you out here?" Michael's voice found her at the back of the garden.

"I'm here." She headed toward the house.

They met in the middle and she found that he'd brought her a glass of iced lemonade. "Gretchen said she thought you were out here. We thought you might like this about now."

"How thoughtful of you, Michael. Thank you." Violet hoped he couldn't tell she'd been crying as she reached out for the glass he held out to her.

Michael led her back to the bench, and they both sat down to enjoy their lemonade.

"Is your mother resting?"

"She's napping. Something she doesn't do very often. I think this afternoon bothered her more than she let on."

"I'm sure it did. It was very hard to see those little boys so upset. I pray things get better for that family soon."

"So do I. There is so much hurt out there…." He looked up at the sky and sighed.

"Michael, do all of the boarders know about Becca and why your mother decided to open her boarding-house?"

"Some do, but not everyone."

"Do you still have hope that you'll find her?"

"Some days I wake up hopeful and others…" He shrugged and sighed. "But I try to let Mother only see the hope."

"Do you get many leads anymore?"

"Not near as many as I'd like, and none in a while.

I don't know. It would help if I knew what she'd been doing before, who she was with, what made her leave in the first place."

His voice sounded raw with sorrow and Violet felt to blame. "I'm sorry, Michael. I shouldn't have brought it up. I didn't mean to bring you painful memories."

"No, Violet. Don't be sorry. Actually, it feels good to talk about Becca. Mother and I don't talk about her disappearance much anymore. I think we're both afraid to bring each other sorrow. But the need to talk about it is sometimes still there, even after all this time."

"I must admit that I don't know why Becca decided to leave and come here in the first place. I've always wondered about that."

"That's our problem. We don't really know why either. Oh, she'd always been independent and more than a little feisty and it was no surprise that she wanted to be in charge of her life. But her decision to move seemed to come out of the blue. Mother and I both tried to talk her out of it, but she seemed almost desperate to get away."

"And once she was here? Did she keep in contact?"

"She wrote, giving us an address where she was going to be living, and said she would write more soon. But days went by, then weeks. Finally, Mother insisted that we come here and make sure she was all right."

Michael rubbed his temples as if he had a headache, and Violet waited for him to continue. "But as you know, she'd left the boardinghouse."

Tears sprang to Violet's eyes. How devastating that must have been for both him and his mother. Wanting to comfort him, Violet reached out and touched his hand. "I'm so sorry, Michael. I wish I knew something that could help you."

He turned his hand and squeezed hers. "Thank you, Violet. I wish you did, too. But knowing I can talk to you about this helps more than you know."

"I'm glad." His words touched her heart and his touch sent her pulse racing.

"I suppose we should go inside. It's about dinner-time and Mother likes us to be on time," Michael said.

Violet moved to stand and Michael stood, too, pulling her up with him. She slipped her hand from his. "Please feel you can talk to me anytime."

"Thank you. I can't tell you how much good this has done me. Just going over it all from the beginning again has helped."

As they headed toward the house, Violet thought she'd seen a side of Michael very few others did, and she felt they'd created a bond she would cherish always.

They entered the foyer just as Lila and Elizabeth came down from upstairs. Not wanting to hear what Lila might have to say about them being in the garden together, Violet quickly took Michael's glass from him. "I'll just take these to the kitchen."

"Coward," Michael whispered. He grinned down at her and gave her a wink no one could see but her. It was as if he had read her mind and understood, and her heart turned to mush.

Chapter Twelve

After supper the next evening, Violet was surprised when Gretchen handed her a letter from Beth. "This came in the mail for you today."

"Thank you, Gretchen." Violet hurried to her room and slit the envelope open with her mother's letter opener. She unfolded the stationery and dropped down onto the settee to read it.

> *Dear Violet,*
> *It was so good to receive your letter! I miss you so much, but I'm so happy you found a good position at Butterick and you are happy at Mrs. Heaton's boardinghouse. Is Michael still as handsome as ever?*

Oh, yes, he was.

> *Papa and I have already crated up the sewing machine and he'll put it on the train tomorrow. I'll be making your payment soon. Papa is going to go with me just to make sure Harlan Black*

doesn't give me any problems. He's been asking about you everywhere. Wants to know where you are and everything. But don't worry. We aren't going to tell him.

The very thought of Harlan still made Violet nauseous, even this far away.

I've sent you a long letter in with the sewing machine. You answer back soon, okay? Just don't put your name on the outside of anything. I'll be sending things to you addressed to Mrs. Heaton, so be sure and tell her. The postal clerk, Mr. Tyler, is a friend of Papa's and he said Harlan was in there asking if we'd had anything from you. Take care of yourself, Violet. Much as I miss you, I'm relieved you aren't here. That man seems obsessed with finding you. He wants more than your home, Violet. He wants you.

Violet shuddered.

Now don't you start liking the city so much you don't ever want to come home. If you have to stay gone too long, I just might have to come see that city for myself.

Violet hated that her friend had to deal with Harlan Black. Maybe after Beth made the next payment, he'd realize she was going to pay off the loan and accept that he wasn't going to get her home or her.

In the meantime, she needed to let Mrs. Heaton know

about the sewing machine coming to her and any letters that might follow.

She found her in her study having a cup of tea. "Why, Violet, dear, how nice to see you. Sit down." She motioned for Violet to take the other chair in front of the fireplace. "Would you join me for some tea?"

"I'd love to, if you have enough."

"I always have a big pot and extra cups brought in this time of night. Sometimes Michael joins me and once in a while one of the other boarders." She poured a cup and handed it to Violet.

"Did you come to chat or is there something on your mind?"

"Well, I just received a letter from Beth Edwards, my best friend back home," Violet said. "Do you remember her?"

"I remember the Edwardses. They are very good people. What did Beth have to say? I hope she and her family are doing well."

"They are. She wanted to let me know that she's sent my sewing machine, and I wanted to let you know to expect it."

"Oh, good. I'll be looking for it."

"She also told me Harlan Black is trying to find out where I am, and that she would be sending things for me addressed to you. I'm glad that when I sent the letter to Beth, I just put your name and address on it and sent it to her mother."

"That was very clever of you, Violet," Michael said from the doorway. "I'm sorry. I wasn't trying to eavesdrop, but I didn't want to interrupt you."

"It's fine, Michael. You might as well know, too."

"So Black is trying to find out where you are?"

"It appears so. Beth thinks he's obsessed with finding me now."

"He has that type of personality."

"I thought I should let you know in case he shows up here one day," Violet said.

Michael shut the study door and leaned against it. "I guess it's time I told you I sent one of my men to Ashland trying to find out what we can about what your family finances were when your mother passed away."

"Oh?" Violet wasn't sure what she thought of that. "Why?"

"Mother has some concerns about your property, and they made sense to me."

"What concerns, Mrs. Heaton?"

"Violet, dear, I remembered that when your papa died, your mother said you two were fine. That he'd left you with a home paid for and with enough money to live in the manner you'd been accustomed to. And I can't understand why your mother would have needed to put your home up as collateral for a loan when it sounded as if she had a nice bank account."

"And we both know how Harlan works. We became concerned he's been up to something unethical. We just don't know what yet," Michael said.

"You know, I wondered the same thing, but then Harlan showed me the papers after Mama passed away."

"You only then found out about the house being mortgaged—when your mother died? Is that when Harlan came to you about the loan?"

"Yes. And as I told you, he offered to forget it if I would—"

"Marry him." Michael nodded. "Something isn't right here, Violet, and I'm going to get to the bottom of it. Hopefully before too long. Isn't Mr. Atwood your family's attorney?"

"He is, but he's been ill and I think he went to Arizona because of his asthma." Violet blew an errant strand of hair off her forehead. "I tried to get an address before I left, but his office was closed and his wife went with him. I should have asked around more, but I was afraid word would get back to Harlan and I didn't want him to know what I was doing."

"It's all right, Violet," Michael said. "We'll get to the bottom of it all. My agent is there now. I'll let him know what you've told us and he can go from there and try to get an address for Atwood."

"I hope you aren't upset we've taken it on our own to find out what is going on, Violet," Mrs. Heaton said. "It's just that your mother was my dear friend, and I can't get rid of the feeling Harlan is up to no good."

"Oh, no, ma'am. I'm thankful you care and relieved you know what is going on."

"Good. I'm glad you know what we've done," Michael said. "I didn't want to tell you because I didn't want you worrying about Harlan without reason. Now I want you to be on guard at all times. Should Harlan learn where you are, he could well show up here."

Violet closed her eyes at the very thought. She heard movement in the room and opened them to find Michael sitting on the footstool in front of her. He reached out and touched her chin.

"Violet, rest assured I will *not* let Harlan Black harm you. I won't."

She released a shaky sigh. "I don't want him to bring harm to anyone here. Perhaps I shouldn't have come to New York."

"This is exactly where you should be, and it's where you belong now," Mrs. Heaton said. "You're family to us and you're safe here."

"I'm glad this is all in the open. I'll let you know when I hear anything. You be sure to let us know whatever you find out from your friend back home. Agreed?" Michael smiled, bringing out those wonderful dimples.

"Agreed."

"Good. Now let's finish this pot of tea and talk about happier things. How are you liking your job?"

By the time the teapot was empty, Violet felt much better. It was a relief to know Michael was aware of what was going on in Virginia. And that he cared enough to send someone there to try to find out what Black was up to. She tried to not to think about the fact that Harlan was trying to find her. But she had to admit she felt safer now that Michael knew, too.

She said her good-nights and took her leave, nearly running over Lila just outside the door. "Oh! I'm sorry, Lila. I didn't see you. Were you waiting to speak to Mrs. Heaton or Michael? They are both still there."

"No. I, ah, I was just on my way to the kitchen to see if there was any dessert left over from dinner," Lila said. "Want to come with me?"

Violet tried not to show how surprised she was at the invitation. "No, thank you. I just had tea with Mrs. Heaton. I think I'll call it a night."

"All right. See you tomorrow."

"Good night." Violet headed to the staircase, but when she looked back, it was to see Lila still outside the study. Was she waiting for a chance to talk to Michael alone? Was there something going on between the two of them?

* * *

Later that evening, Michael knocked on Luke's door. He was thankful he had an agent living in the house, even if he worked for him part-time. Just the fact that he was here gave Michael a peace of mind, knowing that his mother could call on him anytime Michael wasn't around.

"Yes? Who is it?" Luke called out.

"It's Michael, Luke."

"Come on in."

Michael opened the door to find his friend seated at his desk in front of his typewriter. "Looks like you're writing. I'm sorry to interrupt, but I need to talk to you."

"No, it's fine. I'm at a good stopping place." Luke pecked a couple of keys and turned around. He motioned for Michael to take a seat. "You have my undivided attention."

Michael quickly explained about Violet and the letter about Harlan Black. "I wanted you to know, in case he should show up here looking for Violet."

"I'm glad you told me. I've always wondered why she couldn't find work in Ashville. It makes sense now. This Black guy sounds a little…"

"Obsessed?"

Luke nodded. "Yes, that's the word."

"I think he is. And that's what worries me. I'm going to send Jim to Ashland to see what he can find out. I'd send you if it were any other case, but I need you here more. I certainly don't want to leave Violet and my mother vulnerable at home, where they feel the safest."

"No, of course you don't. I wouldn't either. And you know you can count on me."

"I do. And I'm thankful for it."

"But, as far as we know now, Black doesn't know where Violet is, does he?" Luke asked.

"Not yet. But it may only be a matter of time until he does. He's asking questions everywhere."

"Sounds as if he's determined to find her. I hope Jim can find out more for you soon, and if there is anything at all else I can do, let me know."

"You know I will." Michael stood. "I'll let you get back to it. What's this story about?"

"Oddly enough, it's about a banker, a woman and dirty dealings."

"Doesn't take place in Ashland, does it?"

Luke laughed. "No, it takes place down in Texas. The sheriff saves the day and gets the girl."

Both men chuckled.

"That's the way it should be," Michael said. "I'm glad it has a good ending."

"All this will, too. You'll see."

"I hope so. Good night."

"Good night, Michael."

Violet's sewing machine arrived on Thursday and was waiting in the foyer when she and Lila got home from work. As usual, Lila had barely spoken five words to her that day, but one look at the crate and curiosity got the better of her. "My goodness, whatever did you order, Violet?"

Mrs. Heaton joined them in the foyer. "I'll have Michael or one of the men bring it up soon as one of them gets home, Violet."

"Thank you, Mrs. Heaton." She turned to Lila. "I had my sewing machine sent to me."

"Whatever for? Don't you sew enough all day at Butterick?"

"Well, I can't sew for myself there. And… I thought that you might want to let me teach you to sew so that if another opening comes up in the sewing room, you could apply."

For once, Lila seemed speechless.

"You don't have to. Some of the others may want to learn—"

"You'd do that for me?" Lila asked as if she couldn't believe Violet's offer.

"Why, of course. But you don't have to decide right this minute. You can think about it."

"I will. I… Thank you," Lila said.

As she went on up the stairs, Mrs. Heaton and Violet both stood there watching her. This time, it was Violet who felt speechless. They were still staring up when Michael came in the door.

"Mother, Violet, is something wrong?"

Mrs. Heaton chuckled and Violet giggled.

"I don't think so. Something out of the ordinary just happened, and I think we're both wondering if we imagined it," his mother said.

"Well, if you both witnessed the same thing, then it probably happened. What was it?"

Mrs. Heaton stood on tiptoe to whisper, "Lila thanked Violet for something."

"She actually said the words?"

"She did," Violet said.

"What for?"

"Violet has offered to teach her how to sew so that the next time an opening comes up, she'll be qualified."

"That is very nice of you, Violet. Especially considering the cold shoulder she's been turning to you ever since you moved in."

"Thank you. But I really don't mind at all. I'll ask the others if they'd like to learn, too."

"Can you get the crate upstairs by yourself, Michael? Or would it be easier for you if it were in the little parlor, Violet? That way if someone wants to be sewing they wouldn't always have to use your room."

"Oh, that would work better, if you are sure you don't mind."

"I don't mind at all. It isn't used that much, and when it is, it's mostly by you girls. Go ahead and put it back there, Michael. I know just the spot for it."

Ben walked into the foyer just then and heard the last of the conversation. "Need some help?"

"I wouldn't turn it down."

Together, they uncrated the sewing machine, and Violet was pleased to see that there wasn't a scratch on it. The two men easily picked it up and took it to the back parlor where Mrs. Heaton instructed them to put it under a south-facing window where there was plenty of light.

"That is a perfect place for it, Mrs. Heaton. Thank you."

"You are quite welcome. If you have many wanting to learn, we'll bring mine in here, too."

"Do you need anything else?" Michael asked.

"No. Thank you for your help, Michael and Ben," Violet said.

"You're quite welcome," Michael said. "I'll go get rid of the crate. It'll make good kindling for the winter."

"Glad to help. See you at dinner," Ben said, giving a wave as he walked out the door.

"And speaking of that, I'd best go check on our meal," Mrs. Heaton said.

Violet stayed in the room for a few minutes. Seeing the machine her mother had taught her to sew on, the one she'd made many of Violet's clothes with, brought warmth to her heart. Of all her mother's possessions, it was this sewing machine that held many of Violet's best memories—it and the sewing box she'd always had with her. She'd kept her pins and buttons and all kinds of trims in it. Violet could remember reading to her mother while she mended a tear or did the hand sewing of trims on her outfits. She wished she'd asked Beth to send it, too.

She sat down on the tapestry-covered stool that had been packed with the sewing machine and rubbed her hand across the shiny black machine. Somehow, just having it there gave her some peace.

Violet remembered many of the frocks she'd made on that machine in the past few years. Then of the ones her mother had made for her, the last being a gown for her senior commencement. And…she remembered her papa standing in the doorway smiling as her mother talked and sewed at the same time. That was back before he'd died from influenza.

Odd, she hadn't thought about her papa's smiles in a long time, but now she remembered how he'd looked at Mama. How had she missed the look of love in his eyes at the time? She was glad to have the sewing machine here. It brought back long-forgotten memories of a happier time.

Michael hoped Lila learned to sew soon. Evenings were getting a little boring for him. He didn't know exactly when or how it had happened, but he'd come to realize that he looked forward to seeing Violet first thing at breakfast each day and at dinnertime and after, more each day. But the "after" had been cut short by the sewing lessons.

The past few weeks had been a whirl of activity, with the women disappearing into what had become the sewing parlor after dinner Monday through Thursday. Violet said they'd picked those days so that they could be free on the weekends. The women had all decided to keep each other company, with those who didn't have a desire to learn to sew reading or just chatting with each other. But that meant the men had only themselves for company.

They'd taken to reading, playing chess and talking politics after dinner, waiting for the ladies to join them, if only for a little while. But they were all getting just a bit tired of each other's company. It was music to Michael's ears to hear the ladies coming down the hall that Thursday evening, and particularly to hear Violet's voice. He could recognize her from anywhere in the house now—and it never failed to lift his spirits.

"It's about time," John said. "Are you ladies ever going to get through with these lessons?"

"Actually, we just about are," Violet said. "At least I'm nearly through teaching. The girls have made several outfits now and they know how to follow Butterick's directions very well. The rest is just practice."

"Oh, I know I need more help, if I'm ever to get promoted, Violet," Lila said. "Please help me with at least one more gown."

"I'll be here whenever you need help. But now it's

time for you to gain confidence without me standing over your shoulder."

Michael was proud of the firm way Violet handled Lila. She'd gone out of her way to help the woman, but she shouldn't have to give up all her free time.

"Violet's right," his mother added. "You girls will learn more from just sewing on your own than anything. We know you know how to read the directions and to do as they say. You know how to adjust the patterns, how to do about anything that will come up in the patterns' instructions. And both of us are here if you have any questions."

It appeared that Lila had no choice but to accept that she'd be responsible for how adept she became at the sewing machine, and she didn't look very happy about it. But there really wasn't a lot new about that.

Although in the past few weeks, she had seemed easier to be around. She was nice to Violet, nicer to everyone in fact, but Michael couldn't shake the feeling that it was a ruse. He just wasn't sure why. Violet was trying to help Lila out of the kindness of her heart, and she'd done nothing to hurt the woman. Still he didn't really know what Lila was thinking so maybe he was jumping to conclusions. He hoped that was the case and that Lila truly did want to be Violet's friend.

Nevertheless, he was quite happy that Violet wouldn't be spending all her evenings in the back parlor. He'd missed her company more than he wanted to admit.

"Well," Luke said, "I, for one, am glad to hear we'll have you ladies as company again."

"So am I," Ben added. "We're getting a little sick of each other, to tell the truth."

"Yes, we are. We've missed your company," Michael said, his gaze resting on Violet.

"Well, it's good to know we've been missed, isn't it, girls?" his mother asked. "Let's celebrate by going to get an ice cream soda."

Chapter Thirteen

Violet loved charades and was having a great time watching Luke try to get his idea across to everyone on Friday evening when Mrs. Heaton came and whispered, "I hate to interrupt your fun, but Michael asked if you would come to the study. He needs to talk to you about something he's found out."

Michael had been called to the telephone just as dinner ended and hadn't been seen since. Much as Violet was enjoying herself, she'd wanted Michael to join the game and was disappointed when he didn't. Besides just wanting to spend time with him, Violet realized it must be important for him to say he was working and then ask to see her.

"Of course. I'll go now." Everyone was having such a good time; she didn't think anyone noticed when she left with Mrs. Heaton. They entered the study to find Michael sipping a cup of tea from the pot he'd had Gretchen bring them.

"Please get a cup of tea first and then we'll talk." Violet and his mother did as he suggested and took seats in the two chairs in front of the fireplace. Michael made sure the door was closed and took a seat at his mother's desk.

"I have news for you."

"News? About Harlan?"

"Yes. Just as your friend said, he is trying every way he can think of to find you, and, apparently, now he's got some idea you're here in the city. He's already thinking about sending someone to find you."

Violet's breath caught in her throat. "But why? I've kept up my payments and—"

"He doesn't want your payments, Violet. He wants your property. Mostly, though, from what you've told us and from what your friend has said, I think he wants you. But try not to worry. The man he's thinking of sending is the agent I sent to find out what he was up to. He went into town as a former Pinkerton agent who was interested in opening his own agency. Black went to him a few days ago and hired him to try to find you. But with my man working for him, it gives us time to come up with a plan to prove Black is up to no good."

"But how are we going to prove anything? Mr. Atwood isn't there and—"

"The good news is my man gave me an address for Mr. Atwood. And I'm sending another man out West to meet with him."

"Wonderful, Michael. I'm sure Mr. Atwood can shed some light on all of this," Mrs. Heaton said. "He must know what is going on."

"I am so glad you know where he is." Violet breathed a sigh of relief. "Surely he'll know how our finances were before he left."

"I believe he will. I just need your approval to talk to him about your situation."

"Of course you have it, Michael. Do you really think he can help us?"

"I do. I think he's the only one who really knows what your mother's finances were before he left town. And I believe he might know what Black is up to and why."

"Thank you for trying to get to the bottom of it all."

"I think it's very good news," Mrs. Heaton said. "And I believe the Lord is at work in that Black hired Michael's man to find you."

Violet was sure it must be. She prayed it was.

"I'm going to leave you two to talk it over. Thank you for including me and letting me know what's going on. I've got to talk to Gretchen about tomorrow's menu, but I'll peek in on the charade game so our boarders won't become too curious about my calling Violet out."

Michael took her place in the chair next to Violet. He took one of her hands in his. "I'm sure this news has upset you, Violet, and I'm sorry. But I felt you needed to know the latest developments."

"I'm glad you told me, Michael. My only worry is, what if you can't find Mr. Atwood? What if he's gone somewhere else?"

Michael looked her in the eye. "Violet, please try not to worry. I am not going to let Black get to you. I'm not going to let him hurt you. I just wanted you to know what's going on and assure you we are going to get to the bottom of it all."

She took a deep breath and let it out. "Thank you, Michael. I'll try not to worry, and I will pray about it. I know you'll do all you can to help me. But I don't want you or any of your men hurt either. Harlan Black has always given me the shivers. I don't like him, I don't trust him and I—"

Michael's fingertips on her lips silenced her. His touch was light and gentle. Her breath seemed to be lodged in her throat. "Don't worry, Violet. I won't let Black hurt you. I promise."

His touch had her wanting him to pull her into his arms, and Violet forced herself to put some distance between them. She got up from her chair and walked over to the window. "I'm not so afraid of him as I am sickened by him, Michael." She could still see the look in Harlan's eyes when he'd grabbed her arm and pulled her close, demanding that she marry him. The repulsion she felt was as strong now as it had been then. She shook her head to get rid of the vision. "I just hope we can settle things so he won't foreclose on the loan Mama took out."

Michael came to stand beside her. He tipped her face up toward him and looked into her eyes. Violet couldn't help but compare the two men. While one left her cold, this one took her breath away with his nearness.

Michael's large hand cupped her cheek. "Oh, he's not going to foreclose, Violet. We'll come up with something. Don't worry. Harlan Black isn't taking your home away. He's not taking anything that belongs to you. I'll see to it."

Michael's gaze settled on her lips, and Violet found herself wishing he would kiss her. The thought alone shocked her. She'd never felt that way about any man, but right now, at this moment, she wanted to feel his lips on hers.

As if he had read her mind, his head dipped down

and his lips captured hers, softly, gently…and she responded.…

A soft knock came at the door but Violet reacted as if a cannon had gone off, jumping back and putting a hand to her lips. Had he really kissed her or had she imagined it?

The door opened before Michael got to it and when his mother entered, Violet breathed a sigh of relief it was only her and not Lila or one of the other boarders.

"The boarders asked for hot chocolate of all things this time of year. Gretchen is making it now, but I thought I'd see if you two might want some, too."

"I don't," Michael said. "Isn't it a little warm for cocoa?"

"I think so, but that's what they asked for. What about you, Violet?"

"No, thank you. I think I'll pass this time. I'm going to turn in. I'll see you both in the morning." She turned back to Michael. "Thank you for letting me know what you found out."

"You're welcome. I'll update you again after I've met with Jim Moore. Sleep well."

"Thank you. Good night." The intensity in his eyes when their gaze met sent another warm flush up her neck as she hurried out the door.

If Mrs. Heaton noticed anything different about her, she didn't say anything. But Violet knew something had changed in the past few moments, and she was certain it was written all over her face.

"Violet seemed a bit flustered, son. Is she all right?"

Michael didn't think she could be any more flustered

than he was and he hoped his mother didn't pick up on that fact. "I think so."

He hoped so—if he hadn't put panic in her heart by kissing her. But she had responded, he was sure of it.

"Are you all right, Michael?"

His mother looked at him closely. The last thing he wanted was for her to start asking questions he didn't want to answer. "I just want to make sure she's safe from Black. I'm going to put a man out to follow her, just to make sure she is."

"Did you tell her?"

"No, not yet. I've got to write Atwood and get someone on the earliest train I can tomorrow. I hope he'll have some answers for us."

"So do I. I am certain Violet's father had provided for them. I just don't see how it could be possible a mortgage would have had to be taken out on the house. It doesn't make any sense to me. I do hope once everything is settled in her favor, as I'm sure it will be, Violet will decide not to go back."

Michael's heart twisted at the very thought she might decide to and he knew he'd do whatever he could to keep her in New York now.

"She seems happy here, Mother." At least she had—if he hadn't ruined things tonight. "Surely she won't want to go back. But if she thinks she does, we'll just have to persuade her to stay."

His mother smiled at him. "I was hoping that's what you were going to say. You know, Michael, it's about time you thought about starting a family of your own. I wouldn't object if you made Violet part of this family one day."

"Mother—"

"Oh, dear, I think I hear Lila calling me," his mother said as she hurried out the door.

Michael had a feeling she didn't want to hear what he'd been about to say and he was relieved he didn't have to say anything at the moment. Because if he hadn't been thinking about marriage before, he certainly was now.

Violet's goal was to get her home back free and clear and then go back to Virginia. And he couldn't go back there to live. The only hope he had of finding his sister was here in the city. Amanda hadn't understood his need to be here—he wasn't sure any woman could—and he didn't need any more heartache. So any thoughts of marriage needed to be done away with. His life was here now.

He'd go find Luke. He needed to fill him in on what was happening with Harlan Black. Michael was glad he'd let Luke in on what was going on. With Black, one never knew what he might decide to do next. It helped to have Luke around to talk to and know he could count on, should Black show up here. Michael would sure like to have all of this settled as soon as possible—for all kinds of reasons.

Violet hurried up the stairs, hoping not to run into Lila or any of the boarders. She needed time to herself—time to think about what Michael had told her about Harlan Black and what might happen because of it.

But first and foremost in her mind was what had happened in those last few minutes in the study. The kiss they'd shared. And how she felt about it. Her heart was beating so hard she could feel it in her ears, and her fingers were trembling so badly she could barely unlock her door. Once inside, her legs seemed to turn to jelly before she reached her settee and sank down on it.

She leaned her head back and let out a sigh. Michael had taken her by surprise. Now she didn't know what, if anything, to do about it. She'd never thought to have strong feelings for Michael or any other man at this point in her life. Her goal was to get her home back, not give her heart away. After Nick and Harlan, she'd had enough disillusionment. The best thing for her to do was to concentrate on the reason she'd come to the city in the first place. And it wasn't to fall in love. And in fact she was enjoying the feeling of independence living here in New York City gave her. But somehow this man she'd known all her life as a friend seemed to be quickly working his way right into her heart as something more.

How did it happen? Violet forced herself off the settee and hurried into the bathroom to get ready for bed before Elizabeth came up and needed it. She tried to put the earlier events out of her mind, but as she looked in the mirror, the pink of her cheeks and the glow in her eyes brought the touch of his lips to mind once more and she splashed her face with water, trying to erase the telltale signs of how much she'd been affected by those few moments.

All she did know was the last few minutes in the study had become much more important to her than what Michael had called her into the study to talk about. She wasn't really worried about Harlan Black. Not after Michael's promise to protect her.

But she was concerned that somehow she'd never get her home back, and that remained of utmost importance to her. Her father had worked hard for what they had…sometimes to the extent of leaving too much for her mother to take care of, to Violet's way of thinking. Still, they had a nice home and her mother had loved every inch of it. The last person she wanted to have it was Harlan Black.

Violet finished her toilette and went back to her room. She turned her bed down, thinking about her home. While Mrs. Heaton's house now felt like home to her, the one she was raised in was full of her childhood memories.

After her mother had passed away and Violet found her mother had taken a mortgage out on it, she'd blamed her father, wondering what he'd done with the money. But if what Mrs. Heaton thought was true, then maybe he *had* provided well for them. If so, Violet had been wrong to blame him.

Her head still reeling from the events of the evening, Violet sighed and opened her Bible to Proverbs. Tonight it seemed to speak to her confusion. In chapter three, verses five through six, it said, "Trust in the Lord with all thine heart; and lean not unto thine own understanding. In all thy ways acknowledge him and he shall direct thy paths."

Well, she understood nothing tonight. Not how it happened that Michael had kissed her. Not what would happen if Harlan Black came to New York, nor if she'd ever return to her family home. And she was beginning to wonder if she'd misjudged her own father.

Violet slid to her knees and prayed. "Dear Father, please help me to understand what is or isn't happening between Michael and me. To know what You would have me do about my family home. Please direct my

path and help me to do only Your will. In Jesus's name,
I pray. Amen."

She put her Bible up and slipped beneath the covers,
feeling at peace. She might not know what the next day
would bring, but the Lord did and she'd rely on Him to
guide her through it.

With thoughts of the kiss he and Violet had shared
fresh in his mind, Michael lost no time writing a letter
to Mr. Atwood the very next morning and assigning a
man to get it to him. It was imperative that he contact
the attorney as soon as possible because they'd only be
able to put Harlan Black off for so long.

If Black was sending someone to find Violet, he must
be afraid Atwood knew things Violet didn't. At least
Michael was hoping that was it and that her home really was free and clear of debt.

Once that was done, he went to Grand Central to
meet Jim's train. At some point, Jim would have to let
Black know he'd found Violet, and when he did, Michael was sure Black would act on the news. It was entirely possible he would show up at the boardinghouse.

When the younger man got off the train, they shook
hands and went to pick up his luggage.

"It's good to be home," Jim said. "I don't think I
like small-town living much. And I don't like working for a man like Harlan Black, even if I'm only pretending to. Half the town seems to owe him something
and he doesn't let them forget it. He's not a good man,
Michael."

"I know. Thankfully I didn't have any dealings with
him, but I know many of the people in town think he
should be run out of the state."

They stopped for lunch at a café just down from Michael's office so Jim could go into more detail about what he'd found out. The restaurant was full of men who worked in the area. After they'd given their order for the day's special of beef and fried potatoes, Jim filled him in. "The man seems to make a practice of keeping his clients in debt in one way or another. Once they're late on a payment, he adds so much interest over time that it becomes near impossible for them to catch up. And he uses the fact that they owe him to get them to do things for him, tell him things about other clients."

"You think that's how he found out Miss Burton might be here?"

"I only know it could be."

"Any idea why he hadn't already hired someone to come find Violet?"

Jim shook his head. "He tries very hard to act as if he is a benefactor instead of a crooked banker, and even though most people know what he is, they don't know exactly what he's up to. He appears to be an upstanding citizen and makes sure he's in church every Sunday, but I think it's all for show. You should hear the language he uses when he is angry. Just as we figured, he didn't want to go to anyone in town and that's why he came to me."

"Did he give you any timetable to get back to him?"

"He wants results as quickly as possible."

"And you are to collect money from Miss Burton?"

"No. He just wants me to make sure she is here. In fact he told me not to let her know anything. He just wants to know her whereabouts for now. He seems almost obsessed with finding her."

"From what I know of him, I'm not surprised."

"I didn't figure you wanted me to argue with him, boss."

"You're right. I don't want him getting suspicious of you. How did you come up with an address for Mr. Atwood?"

"It was pretty easy. I asked around town for the names of good lawyers and was told Atwood was the best and that even though his office is closed now, he will be returning in a few months. One of his good friends said I could write him if it was important and gave me the address." Jim grinned at him. "Don't worry, boss. Harlan Black doesn't know I was asking about him."

Michael certainly hoped not. The last thing they needed was for Black to get suspicious. "That's good to know. I'll keep you here as long as I can, but I'm assuming Black is wanting you to telegraph him with what you find out."

"Yes, he does. I'll try to put him off as long as I can."

"We'll figure out what to do. Where are you staying?"

"He thinks I'm staying in some fleabag hotel, if the traveling money he gave me is any indication. But I'm staying at my apartment."

"Good," Michael said. "I'll know where to find you."

"I'm glad I don't have to work for Black…not for real anyway and not much longer, I hope."

"I'll get you back here to stay soon as I can." Michael wanted things with Black settled. The sooner the better.

Violet was glad to see Monday come. She hoped keeping busy would take her mind off Michael and what to do about her growing feelings for him. If she could quit thinking about him and his kiss, that would be even better, Violet thought as she worked the pedal on the sewing machine. He'd only meant to comfort her, she was sure of it. The kiss wasn't because he cared for her in any romantic way. And she couldn't let herself begin to think that he might. It would only lead to heartache.

She sighed in exasperation and tried to put all thoughts of him out of her mind as she worked on one of the bicycling costumes. If it turned out well, she might make one for herself. It'd be nice to go cycling in Central Park one day.

"Violet," Harriet, the girl working on her left, called to her. "Did you hear?"

"Hear what?"

"One of the girls just got engaged!"

Apparently it was true, because by midmorning all the talk at Butterick was about another seamstress who had announced her engagement and impending marriage. As soon as Violet heard the news, she hurried to talk to Mrs. Waters about Lila having learned to sew.

"But do you think she's talented enough to work in the sewing room, Violet?"

"Well, I think so. I taught her, and while I wouldn't say she loves it, she is quite adept at it. I believe she would love to work up here."

"She has been with us for a while. I suppose we could promote her and see how she does, since you recommend her. I'll talk to Mr. Wilder and Mr. Pollard about it."

"Thank you." Violet was glad to have the decision out of her hands. She'd taught Lila to sew and asked Mrs. Waters to give her chance. Now it was all in the Lord's hands and whatever happened, she hoped she could quit feeling guilty that Lila hadn't been promoted before.

By midafternoon, Lila was being shown around the sewing room and told to think about whether or not she wanted to make the move.

"One does have more freedom to talk in the pattern-making room," Mrs. Waters said. "Up here, it's mostly the sound of the sewing machines you'll be hearing. But there's a feeling of accomplishment in seeing a beautifully finished garment."

"Yes, ma'am, I'm know there is. And folding patterns can get quite boring after a while," Lila said. "I really don't think I need time to think about it. I would love to work up here."

Mrs. Waters smiled. "I'm sure you will. We all do. Still, I'll give you this evening to think about it. If you are still sure about it tomorrow morning, the position is yours and you'll start this coming Monday."

"Oh, thank you, ma'am," Lila said.

"It is Violet you need to thank. She's the one who recommended you."

Lila turned to Violet and her smile looked almost genuine. "Thank you, Violet."

"You're welcome. I think you'll like working up here."

"Oh, I'm sure I will."

Violet had no doubt that Lila would like the pay and being out of the pattern room. What she wasn't so sure of was how they'd both like working in such close proximity to one another. She wasn't sure about that at all.

The next night, as she did for all her boarders, Mrs. Heaton had a special meal prepared for Lila in honor of her promotion. She'd made her favorite meal of ham and mashed potatoes and peas, along with coconut cream pie for dessert.

Lila seemed genuinely happy for the first time since Violet had come to stay. For once everyone's attention was on her.

"We're all so happy for you, Lila. I hope you like it in the sewing room," Julia said.

"I like the pay much better, I know that much. And truthfully, folding patterns is a very boring job."

"I imagine it would be. It was so nice of Violet to teach you how to sew so that you could qualify for this new position," Elizabeth said.

Lila glanced over at Violet and smiled. "Yes, it was. I can't thank Violet enough for recommending me for the position."

"You are welcome, Lila. It helped that you wanted to learn. And I think Butterick likes to promote from within, if they can. I'm just glad that you wanted to learn so that you could apply for the position when it came along."

"All the women down in pattern folding are very envious that I was promoted," Lila said. "I'll miss a few of them, but I won't miss that position at all."

"Maybe you could teach one or two of them to sew, like Violet taught you," Mrs. Heaton suggested.

"Perhaps," Lila said, but she didn't seem very enthused to Violet.

"That would be nice." Michael smiled at her. "I'm sure it is very rewarding to help someone move up at their workplace."

Violet was glad that Lila had been moved up, but she still wasn't sure how well she would like having her in the same department. Hopefully it would all work out fine.

She had a feeling that while Lila was thankful that she'd learned to sew, she wished anyone but Violet had taught her. Oh, she'd thanked her on the way home and again at dinner, but her manner had been a bit stiff and forced.

Other than that, they hadn't talked any more about it. Lila had burst into the house and announced to one and all that she had finally been promoted to seamstress, as if it were a position she'd been qualified to have for a very long time.

Of course, anyone living at Mrs. Heaton's boarding-house knew that it'd only been a short while since she'd learned to sew, but Lila seemed to have forgotten that part of it all. No matter—Violet could quit feeling guilty because she'd been given the seamstress position right off. She'd done what she could to help Lila and now that they were both on equal footing at Butterick, hopefully, Lila would be easier to be around from now on.

She had been nicer overall since Violet had taught her to sew, but that wasn't saying a lot. Still, anything was an improvement on the outright distaste she'd shown to Violet since she'd first come to live at Mrs. Heaton's.

Violet was still convinced that Lila's dislike of her was because she was an old friend of Michael's. As she watched Lila trying to capture his attention this evening, she was even more certain that the woman wanted Michael for herself. And deep down, Violet knew that what bothered her most of all was not really knowing how Michael felt about Lila.

Chapter Fourteen

Once dinner was over, Michael knew he'd need to move quickly before Violet went upstairs or joined the others in the parlor. "Violet, may I speak to you a moment?"

"Of course," Violet answered.

Michael could see that Lila wanted to hang back, but he turned his back to her so that she wouldn't hear what he was saying and bent down to whisper in Violet's ear. "Would you like to take a walk in Gramercy Park?"

Her eyes seemed to light up as she smiled at him. "That would be very nice. Thank you."

"I'll let Mother know where we're going and meet you back here in ten minutes, all right?"

She nodded and hurried up the staircase while he went in search of his mother. He made it back to the foyer just as Violet came back down, and he swept her out the door fast as he could so as not to draw notice that they were leaving.

"I feel like a kid trying to slip out of the house without letting anyone know," he said as he took Violet's elbow and steered her down the walk. It wouldn't surprise him if Lila called out the door for them to wait for her. She was getting increasingly hard to avoid.

"Has something happened with Harlan that you need to talk to me about?" Violet asked as he unlocked the gate to the park.

"No. You just looked a little frazzled and I thought you might enjoy some quiet time in the park."

"You read me almost as well as your mother does, Michael. This is just what I need."

"Good." He drew her hand through his arm as they strolled through the garden. He loved coming here. There were always others from the neighborhood, but not too many at one time, and there were areas where one could find a quiet spot and sit and relax. Being here with Violet, knowing she loved it as much as he did, made it even more special, and he knew he'd never be able to come by himself again without thinking about her. He led her to the bench they'd sat on when he'd shown her the park for the first time.

"It's beautiful out this evening," Violet said. "I love the way lights in the houses around the park come on one at a time here and there this time of day. The lights shining down make me feel safe."

Michael wanted to be the one who made her feel safe. Had he failed in that respect? "Violet, are you worried about Harlan coming after you?"

"Not really. But I don't know what he's going to do as time goes on."

Michael turned to her and tipped her chin up with his thumb and forefinger. "I'm not going to let him get to you here. We're going to get to the bottom of everything and take care of Harlan for you."

"I know. I just wish we could get word soon."

"So do I. And I feel that we will but I know the waiting isn't easy."

"At least my job keeps me busy."

"How do you think it will be working with Lila in the same department?"

Violet gave a little chuckle and shook her head. "That I don't know. But at least I don't feel guilty for being given a seamstress job before her."

"You had no reason to feel guilty. And you taught her to sew so that she'd get this job."

"I'm glad she did. Hopefully it will make life easier on all of us."

Michael didn't have the heart to tell her that their home had been full of tension from Lila for one reason or another ever since she'd moved in. He didn't have much hope that it would change just because she got promoted. Maybe for a day or two, but then it would be something else she'd be upset about.

"Well, if it doesn't, it won't be your fault. It seems that Lila brings a lot of her distress on herself."

"That's sad."

"It is. I just don't want you worrying about her. You've done a lot for her even if she doesn't appreciate it."

"Thank you, Michael. And thank you for bringing me here tonight. It's just what I needed."

Michael was glad, but not only for Violet's sake. Sitting here with her made him realize just how much he'd needed to have even a few minutes with her just to himself. He was beginning to think of this park as their special place.

* * *

On Wednesday morning, Michael was pleased to have a letter from Mr. Atwood, saying he wanted to meet with Michael at his earliest convenience to discuss Violet's predicament with Harlan Black and discuss what could be done about him. He planned on coming to New York City before going home to Virginia for that very purpose and would be arriving on Friday.

At last it seemed that they'd be able to find out what Black was up to. From reading between the lines of Mr. Atwood's letter, Michael was pretty sure his opinion of Black wasn't much better than Michael's.

He met with Jim Moore that afternoon and found that Black was pressing to know what he'd found out.

"I've tried to stall as much as I can. I told Black that I haven't been able to see Miss Burton going in or coming out of the boardinghouse and finally had to remind him that he had told me to make certain that I didn't make anyone suspicious about his trying to find her."

"What did he say to that?"

"He gave me more time."

Michael nodded. "Good. Hopefully, he won't insist that you return to Virginia until after we've heard what Mr. Atwood has to say. I'm counting on whatever information Atwood has will help us come up with a plan to help Miss Burton keep her home."

"She's very well thought of in Ashland. I've met her neighbors and they all want her to come home."

"How'd you find that out?"

"I said I was interested in her house—asked if they knew if it was for sale or not. Every one of them said they hoped she came home soon."

Violet going back home was the last thing Michael

wanted, and he prayed that she felt the same way. Oh, maybe she'd want to go home for visits, but he hoped that she thought of New York as her home now. At least he knew she did love some things about the city. The thought of living in this city without Violet here too was almost enough to make him think of moving back to Virginia. But he couldn't just up and leave his mother here to do the work she did by herself either.

And that was another problem. Violet had given his mother a new outlook on life. It was as if she'd helped to fill that hole in her heart from the loss of Becca. Not that Violet would ever take his sister's place in his mother's heart. But she'd made a place of her own there and his mother would miss her terribly if she left.

"Miss Burton is a wonderful woman. I can see how they would feel that way. She's been a real boost for my mother. I hope she decides to make the city her home and just keep the place in Virginia for visits or maybe even sell it."

"Maybe after this is all settled, she'll be free to make a decision," Jim said.

"Hopefully so." Who was he trying to fool? There was only one decision Michael wanted Violet to make—and that was to stay here. And it had nothing to do with the good she could do in the city, or even how much his mother cared for her. Deep down, Michael knew that wanting Violet to stay here had much more to do with the place she was claiming in *his* heart than anything else.

Over the next couple days, Violet tried not to think about Harlan Black or what might happen if he showed up. That was the last thing she wanted. If anything bad happened to Michael or his mother or anyone else in this house because of her, she wouldn't be able to forgive herself.

"Why don't we plan a visit to the Ladies' Mile this weekend?" Julia asked as she passed the breadbasket.

Her idea was a welcome interruption of Violet's thoughts. "Oh, I'd love to. I've been wanting to see more of the shops."

"We haven't been back down there, have we?" Mrs. Heaton asked. "We've been quite busy, though."

"Yes, we have." Violet could hardly believe she'd been living in the city for over two months now. Time had sped by, with learning a new job, teaching the girls to sew and trying to learn her way around.

"Well, let's go this Saturday. We can go right after breakfast and have lunch at one of the restaurants down there," Mrs. Heaton said.

"What are we doing to do?" Ben asked. "I don't think I want to go shopping."

"Ben, you men can surely entertain yourselves for a day," Julia said. "I mean, we do know you don't always consult us when you want to do 'men' things."

"That is true. I've wanted to check out a new exhibit at the Museum of Natural History. Any of you want to go with me?" Luke asked.

"I might," Ben said.

"I'm not sure what my plans are yet," Michael said. "I'm hoping to meet with someone from out of town on Friday, but I don't know exactly when we'll finish our business."

Violet wondered if it could be Mr. Atwood that Michael was meeting with. Oh, she hoped that was the case. And if it was, she was sure that he would let her know. The thought that he might ask for her to come to his mother's study again brought thoughts of the last time they were together there and the breath caught in her throat. She had to stop thinking about that night and the kiss they'd shared. She had to. He'd only meant to comfort her, she was sure of that. But he'd done much more. He'd made her want him to kiss her again, and she didn't have any idea what to do about it.

"You men can do whatever you wish," Mrs. Heaton said. "We'll be back for dinner, but we're going to have a great time showing Violet all that the Ladies' Mile has to offer."

Luke gave a mock shiver. "How you can all stand to spend hours looking at the latest frippery is beyond me, but I hope you all enjoy the day."

"Oh, never fear. We'll enjoy ourselves," Elizabeth said. "It's been quite a while since we had an outing like this. And it will be even more fun showing it all to Violet."

"I can't wait. Michael and I only went to Macy's the day we celebrated my getting hired at Butterick."

"We won't get to see it all even in a whole day," Mrs. Heaton said. "But you'll certainly find out why there is such an attraction of the mile."

Violet remembered so many things about the day she and Michael celebrated her new job at Butterick. The lunch and getting to know each other better were highlights of the day. But what she remembered most was running upon the tenements and those two little boys who looked at them so wistfully—the same ones they'd seen at the park. To go shopping after that had been a stark reminder of the differences in society, and it'd been almost overwhelming to Violet.

She hoped she could enjoy the outing on Saturday, but after all that had happened at the park, she thought those differences might be more glaring than ever.

Michael was glad everyone had plans for the day, for he was to meet with Mr. Atwood at noontime. He'd arrived the evening before, but asked to have a good night's sleep before they met—unless the need was urgent. Michael was relieved to be able to tell him that as far as he knew nothing was urgent at the moment.

Now, as he picked up the older man at his hotel and they took a rented hack back to the boardinghouse, Michael could tell that his illness and the trip had been hard on him. "Mr. Atwood, sir, I can't tell you how much I appreciate your willingness to help Miss Burton out."

The man might look frail, but his handshake was that of a much younger man, firm and strong. "No need to thank me, Michael—if I may call you by your first name. And, please, call me Nigel. I've felt guilty for getting sick and not being there to take care of the Burtons' business when I heard Mrs. Burton passed away. I didn't even know she had until a month or so ago. It was then that I knew I needed to get back to work."

"Still, I know it wasn't easy to go out of your way to come up here."

"Better than for Black to see us together. He'd be sure to put two and two together and I fear that could cause even more problems for Miss Burton."

"That is the last thing I want for Violet."

"I feel the same way. How is your mother doing?"

"She's doing quite well. She'll be pleased to have you to dinner this evening. She and the women boarders have gone on an outing—which worked out very well for us today. The men took off in different directions and we won't have to worry about interruptions. I think you'll be more comfortable at my home than you would be in my office."

"I've learned to try to be comfortable in most situations and places, Michael. But I'll take you up on your hospitality."

"Good. I've asked our housekeeper to make us a nice lunch and my agent, Jim Moore, will be joining us. That way, we'll all have the same information to assimilate."

"That makes good sense," Mr. Atwood said. "I'm sure we can come up with a plan to put an end to Black's dishonest dealings. It's about time he was found out."

"That is what I think, too."

They'd no more arrived at the boardinghouse than Jim Moore showed up. Michael made introductions as he led them to the dining room where Maida had set the table for three and was ready to serve them as soon as they were seated.

Michael waited until she served them lunch before getting down to business. "So, you have knowledge of Black's underhandedness?"

"I believe I do. At least where it concerns the Burtons. I know that there should have been no reason at all for Mrs. Burton to take out a loan on her home."

"Then my mother was right. She said she was certain that Mr. Burton left Violet and her mother well enough off to live the life they'd been accustomed to. Not that it was one of luxury, but they should have been able to live debt free."

"Your mother is exactly right. Mr. Burton worked long and hard to provide for his family, and he was very determined to leave them a good inheritance. His place had been paid for long ago. And there was ample money in the bank to take care of their needs and more. Even Mrs. Burton's illness."

"Then what do you think happened? How could things have turned so bad?"

"I don't believe they did. I think that Harlan Black saw an opportunity to pull the wool over their eyes, and once I was gone and Mrs. Burton got sick, he did just that."

"So how do we prove it?" Michael handed a basket of crusty rolls to Mr. Atwood.

"I know a judge that will make sure we can go through the bank records, once I give him my records and documentation." He took a roll and buttered it as he continued, "Mrs. Burton's doctor will help, too. I know there is no way Doc Malone would have charged her so much that she'd have had to put her place up for a loan. Did Violet say if she asked the doctor about his charges?"

"No. I'm not sure she thought to. Violet is a very trusting person. I think she just believed Black."

"Yes, she is that. I don't know how Black got to her mother, but I do have an idea why he's after that property and possibly even Violet herself."

Michael sat up straighter in his chair and took a drink of water to wet a throat that had suddenly gone dry. "What would that be?"

"Back in the day when I was young, Harlan Black's father had it bad for Violet's mother. She'd have nothing to do with him and he couldn't stand it. When Burton won Grace's heart and married her, Harlan Senior went on a drinking binge that lasted over a week."

Atwood popped a piece of bread in his mouth and Michael waited until he'd chewed and swallowed for him to continue.

"Once he found out that Burton was going to build his new bride a home where it stands today, Harlan Senior tried to overbid him. The seller didn't like Harlan any more than anyone else in town did and wouldn't change his mind to sell to Burton. Harlan Senior went on another drinking binge and ended up married to Harlan Junior's mother. She was a good woman. Didn't deserve a man like Black."

"How would Harlan Junior know about all of that?"

"Oh, the whole town knew his papa still carried a torch for Grace. I think somehow Harlan Junior thinks that if he can get the land and Violet, he will have somehow won the prize for his father."

"Is his father still alive?"

"Oh, yes, he is. I'd have thought he would have drunk himself to death by now, but he's still with us. Wouldn't surprise me if he put the whole idea into his son's mind."

"From being around him, I wonder if he was warped by his papa's obsessions? He seems to have a lot of his own," Jim Moore said.

"I'm sure he does. He's just like his father was when he was that age. I'm glad Violet got away from him when she did. Now we just have to make sure he doesn't get to her."

That had become Michael's worst nightmare, and he had no intention of letting it become a reality.

Maida cleared the table and brought in dessert. Michael didn't feel much like eating anymore, but he waited until the other men finished before suggesting, "Let's have coffee in my mother's study. I don't want to take a chance of anyone overhearing our plans should the boarders return sooner than expected."

"Don't worry, Michael. We'll come up with a plan and put a stop to Black's best-laid ones. He's not going to get away with his scheme."

As they made their way to the study, Michael could only pray that Mr. Atwood was right.

Violet had never had a day quite like the Ladies' Mile outing. She'd forgotten just how congested it'd been the day Michael and Mrs. Heaton had driven her around. That had been bad, but today the crush of women on the streets and in the stores was almost unbelievable. Of course, she was in the crowd instead of a hack and found that made a huge difference.

Once one got past the women window-shopping outside the stores, it was even worse inside. The clerks couldn't seem to move fast enough for their customers and there were women lined up to make purchases, ten deep in some places.

The first store they went in was Macy's, and although she'd been there before with Michael, Violet was glad to go again. They'd made such a quick trip that day and she'd still been reeling from seeing the tenements and from excitement over finding employment, she hadn't really had her mind on shopping. Not that she planned to buy anything today, but it was fun to see what was on display. It appeared that everything a woman could think of, and more, was offered in these stores.

They looked at ready-made clothing from bicycle dresses, which seemed all the rage at the moment, to ball gowns that most only hoped to one day have reason to wear.

To be sure, Ladies' Mile was an accurate name for the area. The only men Violet saw were a few clerks and the many drivers of the various vehicles waiting for their owners to return. It was not hard to tell the very rich from everyone else, for they seemed to have someone by their side to hold their packages, to do their bidding. They were dressed in the most fashionable gowns of the day, custom-made in the best materials and trims, and wearing jewels that Violet had only seen the likes of behind cases in the jewelry store back home. And those were nothing like the diamonds, emeralds and rubies she saw on the necks of some of the women in this store.

From one department to another, then one store to another—Hearns Department Store, Le Boutellier down the street from Macy's—women coming from all walks of life shopped together. If one of the not so wealthy had to wait for one who was to be waited on, no one seemed to mind, being a bit awestruck by the wealthier woman.

But it wasn't until Violet returned from purchasing a lacy handkerchief in Le Boutellier, so delicate she couldn't resist, that she realized she'd been standing next to one of the Vanderbilts.

"Violet, do you have any idea who you were standing next to?"

She turned to look at the woman who was still being waited on. She was elegantly dressed, bejeweled and wearing a hat Violet was sure Mrs. Heaton would love. She turned back to Elizabeth and shrugged. "Should I?"

Julia laughed. "No, there is no reason you would. At least not until you live here a little longer and know all the Vanderbilts." She leaned closer and whispered,

"That is Edith Vanderbilt Shepard, Margaret's middle daughter."

"Oh!" Violet turned to look at the woman once more. The woman turned just then and saw Violet looking at her. She gave a short nod and a small smile as she swept by the group. For a moment Violet wondered if she was expected to curtsy, and then chided herself for the thought. This was America, which didn't have royalty. But, the way people got out of Miss Vanderbilt's way it was hard to tell.

"Violet, the look on your face is priceless!" Lila pointed at her and laughed.

"I'm sure you looked the same the first time you came to the Mile," Elizabeth said. "It's very intimidating to visit the first few times. And even more daunting to run into American royalty."

"You are joking, right?" Violet said.

Elizabeth laughed. "Of course I am. But here in New York, many consider the Vanderbilts and others of their wealth in that way."

"They set the style for the elite in the city. So it never hurts to keep up with what they are wearing so one can stay in fashion," Lila said. "I'm sure even the people at Butterick stay abreast of what the wealthy are wearing here in the city."

"Oh, I'm sure they do," Mrs. Heaton agreed. "They are in the fashion business, after all. In fact, I would imagine they know what is in style even before the Vanderbilts show up in a designer gown. They have people at all the European fashion shows."

"No wonder the clerks take such a long time with them. They've probably been told to. The longer they stay in one store, the more others want what they buy," Violet said.

"Well, I'm ready to move on," Mrs. Heaton said. "Let's go get some lunch before we shop any more."

"Yes, we must make sure we have enough energy to make it through the afternoon," Julia said. "We've barely started."

Violet's feet were hurting already, and she wasn't sure what they could possibly find in any other store different from what they'd already seen, but she was going to enjoy the outing with the others even if she had to soak her feet for hours just to be able to get them in her boots for church the next day.

By the end of the day, they'd seen more ladies' clothing and adornments than Violet would be able to remember, much less where she'd seen an item, if she should recall it. All she really wanted was to get out of her shoes and soak her feet—providing she could get them off. But she felt like patting herself on the back for she'd only thought of Michael about once every half hour today—wondering what he'd been doing and how his meeting had gone. She couldn't wait to get home and find out.

Chapter Fifteen

When they arrived back to the Heatons', Violet was more than pleased to learn that Mr. Atwood was there and would be taking dinner with them. They got back just in time to freshen up before dinner, and she hurried down to the parlor to greet him, only to find he wasn't there.

But Michael had sent word by Maida asking Violet to come to his mother's study to meet with an old friend and she hurried down the hall and gave a light knock on the door.

Mr. Atwood greeted her before she could say a word, coming to take her hands in his. "Violet, dear, I am so sorry about your mother. I didn't get word about her until a month ago. Had I known, I would have contacted you with the details of your father's will immediately."

His sincerity brought tears to her eyes. She was so happy to see that while it was apparent that he'd been ill recently, as he'd lost weight since the last time she saw him, he seemed on the road to recovery. "I should have made more effort to find you. I was just so confused that there was a mortgage on the house, and then I couldn't find a job."

Mr. Atwood patted her hand. "I assure you that I am much healthier than I appear, Violet, and I'm determined to get back to Ashland and get to the bottom of whatever it is that Harlan Black has been scheming."

"Then you think he has not been telling the truth, as Mrs. Heaton does?"

"Oh, I am certain of it. And I'm very glad that Michael contacted me about Black. Don't you worry. We are going to get to the bottom of this and put an end to his dirty dealings as soon as possible."

"I knew I was right. And I can't wait to hear more about it," Mrs. Heaton said. "But we need to continue this later. The boarders are waiting for me to call them to dinner and I don't want to stir up their curiosity any more than necessary."

"We'll talk later, Violet. Mr. Atwood has helped us form a plan, but we want to get your opinion before we put it in action," Michael said, taking her arm to escort her to the dining room.

They headed down the hall as Mrs. Heaton called everyone to dinner. She'd had Maida prepare roast chicken and dressing in honor of their guest. She introduced him as a friend of her and Violet's families from back home, and everyone was very cordial to him.

Mr. Atwood had been given a seat adjacent to Michael's mother, and he turned to her after the introduction. "Mrs. Heaton, I can tell you that you are missed greatly by my wife and the ladies in the Ashland Women's Club. Edith said to tell you so."

"Thank you, Mr. Atwood. Please let Edith and the others know that I miss them, too. I'd love it if you'd bring her back for a visit sometime. There is much to see and do in the city and I'd love to show you both around."

"I'll tell her. Don't be surprised if she writes you accepting your invitation."

"That would be wonderful."

Dinner conversation revolved around the ladies' outing and Luke and Ben's trip to the Museum of Natural History. John had missed out on that because he'd been covering a fund-raiser that the Carnegies were holding that afternoon.

"Nigel, you should hear some of the stories John can tell," Mrs. Heaton said. "He covers their parties and fund-raisers and all manner of things the rich do in this town."

"Is that right?" Mr. Atwood said. "Please tell me a few stories to take home to my wife. There aren't a lot of high-society doings where we live."

John obliged and entertained them through dinner and dessert with tales of the events he'd been to and covered for the newspaper.

Mr. Atwood was still chuckling when they excused themselves to have a private chat in the back parlor. "I hope to get to visit with you all more on my next trip, but for now I hope you will forgive me if I take these old friends off to myself for the evening."

He'd quickly gained favor with the boarders and they were all quite gracious in being left to their own devices for the rest of the evening.

Violet breathed a sigh of relief that finally she might find out if there was a way to keep Harlan Black from trying to take her family home.

* * *

Out of hearing of the others, Michael had asked Luke to join them in his office, too. While he waited for him to show up, he finally let Violet know that he'd told Luke about Black in case he came looking for her.

"Luke works for you?" she asked.

"He is a writer, just like he told you. But sometimes he does work for me and right now it makes me feel much better just knowing that he's here when I can't be."

"I see." She nodded but still looked a little confused when Luke slipped in the door.

Luke looked at Violet and then at Michael. "Does Violet know you've told me—"

"About Black and that you sometimes work for me?"

"Yes, I do, now," Violet said.

"Good." Luke nodded. "I'm glad."

"So am I." Michael let out a huge breath and smiled at Violet. He was relieved she finally knew about Luke. "I didn't like keeping it from you, Violet. But I didn't want you to start worrying about Black any more than necessary."

"I understand, Michael. But since you've told me, does that mean I might have reason to worry more now?"

"I hope not. We're going to do all we can to see that you are safe. You know that, don't you?"

"I do."

Michael nodded. He hoped he was worthy of her trust in him. "Now, I want to update you on what's going on while Mr. Atwood is still here and can fill in anything I might forget. That way everyone will know our plan." He watched Violet closely as he and Mr.

Atwood explained everything and how they hoped it would pan out.

Michael could see the hope in Violet's eyes and he prayed that it all would work out the way they hoped it would. "We'll let you know what we need you to do, should he show up here, Violet. And I'm sure he will come to the city once Jim lets him know that you are here."

"When I get back home and talk to the judge and we get our part of the plan together, I'll let you know," Mr. Atwood said. "I feel I let you down by not being there with you when your mother passed away, Violet. Rest assured I will be here for you from now on."

"Oh, Mr. Atwood, I don't blame you. You couldn't help getting sick any more than my mother could."

"Her illness came on very fast, didn't it? I know she was fine when I left."

Violet nodded. "Yes. One day she seemed perfectly all right, and the next she was having horrible stomach pains. Even Doc Malone didn't know what the problem was but he did all he could to help. And then, a few weeks later, she had the stroke."

"I'm so sorry, Violet. Before the stroke, did your mother tell you she'd taken out a mortgage on the house?"

"No, sir." Violet shook her head. "I didn't know that until after her funeral. Harlan came by to offer his condolences and tell me what she'd done."

"Hmm." Mr. Atwood rubbed his chin and let out a sigh. "None of it makes any sense and I'm going to find out what he's been up to."

"Thank you. But why would he say such a thing if it wasn't true?"

Mr. Atwood explained the past to her as he had done to Michael. "I believe he somehow thinks that if he can win you and gain the land, he will be avenging his father for past hurts."

"But why would it matter to him, especially after all these years?"

"Well, that I don't know."

"And when did he decide to do it?" Violet asked.

"Did he ever make any advances to you before your mother died?" Michael asked.

"Well, yes, he did. He asked me to a church picnic a year or so ago. I told him no. And then he asked me again a month or so before Mama became ill."

"I wonder if maybe he told his father and that brought up his past with your mother?" Mrs. Heaton asked.

"And he was bound and determined not to lose you like his father lost your mother," Michael suggested.

"But why would anyone want a life with someone who didn't feel the same way about them?" Violet asked. "That just doesn't make any sense to me."

"Nor to any of us in this room. But the Blacks don't like to lose at anything," Mr. Atwood said. "And it appears that Harlan Junior is determined not to lose you."

"How can you lose something you never had? I never gave him any encouragement."

"And that is probably what made him even more determined to win you." The thought of Harlan getting anywhere near Violet made Michael sick. He thanked the Lord that she'd had sense enough to spurn his attentions and get out of town.

"Well, that will never happen," Violet said, her gaze resting on him as if she was trying to reassure him in some way. "I'd never marry the likes of Harlan. I must take after my mother when it comes to the Blacks. He makes my skin crawl."

"Yes, well, I'm sure you do take after your mother in more ways than that. And I'm certainly glad you do," Michael said. "Your instincts are very good, Violet. Trust them."

He watched Violet flush the most delectable shade of pink. He wanted this thing with Harlan Black settled. There were other things he wanted to take up with Violet, and her feeling about another man wasn't one of them.

On Sunday, Mr. Atwood had joined them for church and the sermon seemed one meant for them all. It was about how one should not worry about tomorrow, that today had enough worry of its own, that had her turning it all over to the Lord and asking Him to protect Michael and Mr. Atwood as they tried to discover what Harlan Black was up to.

As they'd left church, Violet felt more peace about the situation with Harlan Black than she ever had. Both Michael and Mr. Atwood had assured her they were on top of it all and that had helped, but it was knowing that the Lord was in control of it all that really calmed her. She'd been able to fully enjoy going to lunch with Michael and his mother and Mr. Atwood before they took him to catch his train back to Virginia.

At quitting time on Monday, Violet was surprised when Lila told her she'd be coming home later.

"I made plans with an old friend who used to work for Butterick. He started up his own pattern company several months ago and he asked if I'd have an early dinner with him since we both have something to celebrate. He's probably going to try to get me to work for him."

"You wouldn't quit Butterick after just getting a promotion, would you?"

"No, of course not. At least not until I know how his company is coming along."

The man showed up just then, but Lila didn't make any introductions. She simply said, "Please let Mrs. Heaton know that I'll have an escort to get me home if I'm not there before dark."

"Yes, I will."

"Bye!" Lila waved and took the arm of the gentleman as they headed in the opposite direction Violet was going.

It seemed odd that Lila had never mentioned her friend before now. Violet didn't think she was romantically interested in the man—not the way she acted around Michael. But truthfully, she knew very little about Lila. From what she'd heard from the others, no one else knew much about her either.

Violet headed toward the trolley, thinking it would get her home faster and she was more familiar with its stops, since that was the way she and Lila traveled back and forth to work, most days.

She looked in her reticule, just in case, to make sure she still had the map and directions Michael had given her weeks before. As long as she had it, she wasn't overly worried about getting back to the boardinghouse.

Once on the trolley, she felt a new kind of independence. It was the first time she'd ever traveled anywhere in the city alone. She knew she wouldn't want to go anywhere alone after dark, but it was a relief not to have to put up with Lila's up-and-down emotions. Or her total silence.

Violet took a deep breath and expelled it. It was quite nice to relax on the way home. She looked around and noticed that many of the people on the trolley were the ones she traveled with most days. A new gentleman had begun to ride the same trolley a few days earlier and she'd wondered about where he worked and lived. He nearly always got on the trolley when she and Lila did, and he got off at the same stop in the mornings. But afternoons, when the trolley stopped just down from Mrs. Heaton's, he stayed on it. She couldn't help but wonder if he had a second job somewhere. Not that it mattered, really. It was just something to think about as she and Lila traveled back and forth. Only today, she couldn't help but wonder if he was one of Michael's men. The thought that he might be, did make her feel safer.

She felt a sense of accomplishment when the trolley stopped and she got off and walked home. She almost wished Lila would have somewhere to go every afternoon. This had been the most peaceful ride home she'd had since beginning work at Butterick.

They were just finishing up dinner when Lila came home. Her eyes were bright with excitement, and Violet couldn't help but wonder what had brought that about.

Nor, it seemed, could anyone else.

"Good evening, everyone," Lila said, slipping into her seat at the table just as Mrs. Heaton began cutting into the chocolate cake that was a favorite of the boarders. "I see I'm right on time for dessert. I was hoping I'd make it."

"We're glad you made it, dear," Mrs. Heaton said. "You should have asked your escort to join us."

"Oh, I've been with him long enough today."

"You look as if you enjoyed yourself. Where did you go for dinner?"

"We went to that new little café down the street from Butterick. The food was pretty good. Mostly we were celebrating my new position and his new company. Of course he's trying to get me to come work for him, but I only told him I would think about it."

"But Lila, you just got a promotion. Surely you aren't going to quit Butterick now," Elizabeth said.

"I'm not planning on it, but you never know." Lila took a bite of cake and chewed before continuing, "At this time it probably wouldn't be the smartest thing to do. But he's got some great ideas and I'd like to help him if I can. The day may come when I do go to work for him."

Violet bit the inside of her mouth to keep from saying anything. Part of her wanted to let Lila know what she thought of her even considering changing companies after she'd just been promoted. But there was another part of her that would be almost relieved if she quit Butterick. She knew she needed to pray about her attitude, but as time went on, Violet wasn't sure she liked Lila any better than Lila liked her. So maybe she'd better reserve judgment and leave it all in the Lord's hands.

"He also asked me to keep an eye out on others who might be willing to change companies. His starting pay is more than Butterick—"

"But he's only been in business a short time. How can he possibly compete with Butterick and the other large pattern companies?" Luke asked. "That doesn't make sense unless he came into some kind of inheritance to start up his business."

Lila shrugged. "I didn't ask. But it is a growing business and there should be plenty of room for new pattern companies, don't you think?"

"Quite possibly," Julia said. "Still, I would much rather work for a well-known company than one just starting out. But it will be your decision to make, Lila."

"True. And I'll let you all know if and when the time comes that I make it."

"My goodness, Lila, one would think you were talking about being a department manager instead of a seamstress position."

"Well, maybe I am." Lila smiled and looked over at Violet. "You might think on it, too, Violet. Being a department manager would pay really well."

"I like what I'm doing a lot, Lila. I don't think I'll be going anywhere else for employment. I like the people at Butterick. Why would I want to leave?"

"Well, that will be your decision eventually, I suppose. But you might want to keep an open mind."

"Thank you for your advice, Lila. I will keep an open mind, I can assure you."

Chapter Sixteen

The next day, no one was more surprised than Violet when she was called into the offices of Mr. Wilder and Mr. Pollard and offered the position of assistant supervisor of the sewing department.

"But, Mrs. Waters does such a wonderful job."

"And it is for that reason that we want an assistant for her. She works very hard and has said that she is thinking of turning the reins over to a younger woman with more energy," Mr. Pollard said.

"Why, Mrs. Waters has more energy than anyone in the sewing room," Violet said.

"She certainly expends much energy. We think it may be that she is just tired, and we don't want her to leave. We've discussed it with her and she's said she would stay if we get her an assistant and she can have a little more time off. She also recommended you for the position."

"Oh, but I'm so new to the company—and, well, I'm sure there are several women in the department that have much more experience than I do and have been here longer."

"Not really," Mr. Wilder said. "And those who do have the experience aren't much younger than Mrs. Waters. According to her, the others don't show the same regard for the work they do that you do."

Violet was touched by the other woman's high opinion of her. But, oh, how she dreaded Lila's reaction to her getting yet another position higher than hers. She would be livid. And they lived in the same boardinghouse. Violet began to shake her head. "I'm not—"

"Please think it over, Miss Burton. I know there will be some resentment from some of the younger women," Mr. Pollard said. "They are going to try to make your job very difficult. But you are the one we want and the only one Mrs. Waters is willing to stay on and train, as she says. Should things get too bad, I expect you to come to us so that we can take care of it. Just think about it and let us know tomorrow. Agreed?"

"Yes, sir." Violet couldn't help but smile. She worked for some very nice people and they'd been good to her. She owed them the courtesy of thinking it over. "I'll let you know my decision tomorrow."

"Good, we hope you decide to take the position, Miss Burton," Mr. Wilder said. "You are the kind of person we like working for us. We look forward to talking to you tomorrow."

"Thank you, Mr. Wilder, Mr. Pollard."

Violet left their offices unsure of what to do next, other than to think on their offer and pray hard about it. It was a wonderful opportunity and she knew it. She didn't want to turn it down, but she knew Mr. Pollard was right. It wouldn't be easy. Still, it hadn't been easy to leave her home and move to New York City either. But she'd done it. It wasn't easy to think that she might lose her home, but she was doing all she could to be able to make those payments— unless it was proved that Harlan Black was a crook and her mother hadn't needed to take out that loan. Until then, she had loan payments to pay and this promotion would make that much easier.

"Where have you been? Are you in trouble?" Lila asked when Violet got back to the sewing room.

"No. I'm not in trouble. I—"

"Violet, could you come here, please?" Mrs. Waters called from her glass-enclosed office doorway.

"Well, if you weren't before, I'm sure you are now," Lila whispered. "Mrs. Waters isn't going to be happy you were gone so long from your machine."

Violet didn't miss the smirk on Lila's face as she got up and hurried over to her supervisor's office, thankful for the interruption.

"Yes, Mrs. Waters?"

"I just wanted to see if you accepted the position I know you were offered. I'm hoping that you did."

"Oh, Mrs. Waters, I am so grateful for your recommendation, but I don't know what to do. I don't have near the experience I feel I'd need to be an assistant to you."

"Violet, you have all the experience you need. I'll be training you to be a supervisor while you take a great deal of pressure off me. I can't think of a better arrangement—at least for me. You didn't turn it down outright, did you?"

"No, ma'am. I am to give an answer tomorrow."

Mrs. Water sighed. "Oh, I'm glad. Please say yes, Violet. I'm not quite ready to retire yet, but I can't keep going at the pace I have been. I truly need help, and you are the only one in the department that is young enough, trustworthy enough and that I like well enough to work with in that capacity."

"I promise you I will truly think about it and pray on it. I do want the position, Mrs. Waters. I just am not sure…" Violet hesitated. "There are women out there who are going to be very upset and—"

"Oh, I know. I remember well when I was given this position. I had some trouble from some of the other girls. That is to be expected anytime one is promoted over another, I suppose. And some will try to make things hard for you. But it is a good promotion, Violet. Look at it this way. If you take the assistant job, you will one day be qualified for my position. And even should we both leave at some point, another position has been created. You will have helped with that."

That was something to think about. "Thank you, Mrs. Waters. It has helped to talk to you."

"Good. Just know that I'll be praying that you take the position." She looked at the clock on the wall. "Looks like it's quitting time. You go do that thinking and praying and I'll see you in the morning."

"Yes, ma'am. Thank you." Violet felt like hugging the woman for wanting her to take the position and for recommending her. But she was sure Lila and all the other seamstresses were curious enough about their meeting and she didn't want to make it worse. She didn't have a clue what she was going to tell Lila as it was, but from the look on her face, Violet knew she'd better figure something out quickly.

As soon as the quitting bell rang, Lila ran up to her and asked, "Did you get in trouble?"

"No, Lila. Why would I? I didn't do anything wrong."

"Well, I certainly wouldn't get away with being gone as long as you were this afternoon. Is someone getting fired or quitting?"

"Lila, I really can't say."

"Violet, I thought we were becoming good friends. Why won't you tell me why you were gone so long today and what you and Mrs. Waters were talking about?"

Somehow, Violet had a hard time believing that Lila considered them good friends. She'd never given any indication before that she wanted to be friends at all. "Thank you for your concern, Lila, but I'm not at liberty to say what our talk was about."

"I see," Lila said. "Well, I'm not going to be riding home with you today. I'm meeting my friend again. Will you tell Mrs. Heaton?"

"I'll be glad to. Have a good time."

Lila only gave a brief wave and hurried off.

Violet breathed a sigh of relief that she would have a peaceful trip home. She needed some time to herself for she had much to think about.

After dinner Violet went in search of Mrs. Heaton. She knocked on the door of the study and said, "Mrs. Heaton, do you have a minute?"

She was surprised to hear Michael's voice. "Come in, Violet."

She entered and looked around, but Mrs. Heaton wasn't there. "I'm looking for your mother. Do you know where I might find her?"

"She said she was very tired and went on up to bed. Is there something I can do for you?"

He was sitting in one of the chairs by the fireplace, an open Bible in his lap.

"Oh, I'm sorry. No, that's all right. I don't want to interrupt your Bible reading."

"You aren't. I've just finished my reading for tonight. Come join me for some tea." He didn't wait for Violet to accept, but poured her a cup and handed it to her instead.

"Thank you." Violet took the cup and sat down in the other chair.

"What can I do for you? Is something wrong?"

"No, not really. I just need some advice and I know your mother will tell me what she really thinks." That was one of the things she loved about Mrs. Heaton. She felt she could come to her about anything—with the exception of her growing feelings for her son.

"I'd be glad to listen, if it's something you can talk to me about. What is it that's happened?"

"Well, it's nothing bad. It's quite the opposite, in fact. I've been offered a promotion—"

"Another one? That's great news, Violet. Mother has always said Butterick was the best place for you. What is it they want you to do?"

"They want me to be the assistant supervisor of the sewing department."

"Oh, that is quite a step up. But you don't seem terribly excited or happy about it."

"Oh, I am, or at least I want to be. But I know that I'm going to have some resentment in the department. I can't blame anyone. I might feel the same way if I'd been at a business for as long as some have and a new person came in and got promoted over me. I don't imagine I'd like it either."

"Well, I suppose there might be some who won't be

happy about it, but it is that way in any business, Violet. You aren't thinking of turning it down, are you?"

"I'm not sure. I want to take it, but, oh, Lila is going to be so upset."

Michael shook his head. "You taught her to sew so that she could get the promotion to the sewing department, Violet. You can't live your life worrying about Lila's reaction to your good news."

"I know. And Mrs. Waters has said she needs me. Mr. Wilder and Mr. Pollard seem to think she will resign if she doesn't get some help soon. And from what she said, I believe she might."

"Well, then, if you are considering feelings, you might want to think about what it would mean to her if you don't take the position."

"Oh, I have. She's been so good to me, and as far as I can tell, everyone in the department thinks highly of her. But she did say that when she got promoted, she had some who resented her, too."

"It didn't stop her from taking the position, did it?"

"No, it didn't. I suppose it shouldn't stop me either." Violet took a sip of tea and made her decision. "I'll let them know I'll be happy to accept the promotion first thing tomorrow."

"Good. I think that's exactly what you should do and I'm sure my mother would tell you the very same thing."

Violet smiled. "I think you're right. Thank you, Michael." Her heart slammed against her ribs at the smile he gave her and her pulse began to race at the sight of those dimples.

"Still, I don't want to make it hard on everyone living here," Violet said, giving a small smile. "I feel the tension between Lila and me pours over to everyone."

Michael shook his head. "Well, you're wrong. Everyone living here knows Lila and her moods. No one is going to blame you for those. Enjoy your good news, Violet. Lila can get another migraine if she doesn't want to celebrate with us. You do know Mother is going to want another celebration dinner, don't you?"

"I'm sure she will, but it's not necessary."

"It is to her. Thank you for giving Mother something to look forward to, once more."

"Oh, Michael, thank you. She's a very special lady and I can see why my mother counted her as her best friend. She's become very dear to me, too."

And you've become very dear to me. If he thought about Violet once a day, he thought of her a thousand. In fact, she was on his mind from morning 'til night and beyond. He had only to get a glimpse of her to begin thinking about the near kiss they'd shared. He was sure that Violet only thought he'd been trying to comfort and assure her that he wouldn't let Black get to her, and he'd told himself that was the reason he'd kissed her. But he knew that his yearning to kiss her now had nothing to do with comforting her. It went much deeper than that.

"I have some news for you." Michael dropped into his mother's vacant seat and took it on himself to pour Violet another cup of tea. He wanted to keep her there as long as he could. It seemed way too long since they'd had any private time together.

"What is it? Has Mr. Atwood found out anything?"

"Not yet, but he's getting closer. He says it won't be long now." He filled her in on what Atwood had passed on to him. "Just pray that our suspicions turn out to be right. I'll let you know as soon as I know more."

"Thank you, Michael. I appreciate all you are doing to try to find out the truth of my family's finances."

"No need to thank me, Violet. I hate to see someone taken advantage of. Speaking of which, Lila has taken advantage of your good nature. She got her promotion only because of you. Don't you let her take the joy out of yours."

"I'll try not to. I've got to give them an answer tomorrow. She knows something is up and she wanted me to tell her, because we're good friends and all."

Michael's laughter startled her and she felt her lips twitch in response. Finally, she couldn't contain her giggles as he continued to laugh.

"It is funny, I suppose," Violet said when she got her giggles under control.

"You could say that. Anyone who's sat at the same table with the two of you would think so, too. No one in this household would ever think that you and Lila were good friends. Through no fault of yours, Violet. It's very hard to think of Lila being good friends with anyone."

"Perhaps. But maybe it is a good friend she needs." That thought had just come to her and she couldn't help but wonder if that was part of Lila's problem. Maybe she simply didn't know how to be a friend because she'd never really had one.

Michael looked thoughtful. "Maybe you are right. But she doesn't make it easy for anyone to be good friends with her. She's too busy thinking about herself."

What he said was very true. Lila didn't seem to care enough about anyone else to be interested in what was going on in their lives. Violet wondered if maybe that was because Lila hadn't had anyone care about what was going on in hers. Maybe she'd been too hard on her.

As if he read her thoughts, Michael said, "Violet, are you trying to blame yourself for all of Lila's problems now? You know, Lila hasn't changed into what she is just since you moved in. She's been the way she is for at least as long as she's been here."

"Not so much blaming myself, but wondering if there is something I can do to help her. I suppose all I can do is try to be a friend to her."

"I hope your efforts aren't for nothing, Violet. You have the biggest heart of anyone I know besides my mother."

Violet shook her head. "There is no way I compare to your mother, although I would love to help others as she does. And don't for a moment think that Lila's attitude doesn't get as tiresome to me as it does to you."

"And yet you still want to help her."

"I feel sorry for her at times. I can't help it. It's just hard for me to believe that anyone would want to be moody and hard to get along with, and—"

"Hard to like? I'm sorry, Violet. I don't mean to hinder your willingness to try to be her friend."

"I know you don't."

Michael wanted to explain. He had a bad feeling about Lila's intentions. He couldn't believe that she really wanted to be friends with Violet—much less good friends. He'd seen the way she looked at Violet when she thought no one was watching. "I just don't want you to get hurt."

Color flooded her cheeks as his gaze locked on hers. "Thank you, Michael. It means a lot to know that you want the best for me. I don't really expect to be great friends with Lila. If I'm honest, I don't want to be. We don't have much in common. But I do feel the Lord wants me to try to get along with her, to try to be a friend. We'll see if she truly wants to be friends or not. The first test will be when I tell her I've been offered a new position."

"We'll see if she will celebrate with you or not."

"Yes. We will."

Michael stood in his mother's study waiting for Violet and Lila to return home from work the next afternoon. He hoped she'd had a good day because he had some disappointing news to report to her. Earlier in the day, he'd received a long-distance call from Atwood that it was taking a little longer than they'd expected to get access to the records he and the judge needed. Plus he was trying not to let Black know he was even back in town. Michael sighed. He wanted this to be over with for Violet's sake—and for his own.

He heard the front door open and several of the boarders arriving back home at the same time. Michael hurried out of the study and down the hall to the foyer just as the door opened once more and Violet and Lila entered. He could see the storm clouds in Lila's eyes, but she managed a smile to all who were in the foyer.

"Guess what, everyone? We have another celebration to look forward to. Violet received another promotion! She's been made assistant supervisor over the sewing room. It's a brand-new position made just for her!"

Her voice sounded loud and a little brittle to Michael's ears, but at least she didn't run upstairs claiming to have a migraine like the last time. Of course, she'd taken the moment from Violet, but Violet didn't seem to mind. In fact, he was sure she didn't. Violet didn't feel as comfortable being the center of attention as Lila did.

"Congratulations, Violet. Mother has dinner going as we speak."

"I love celebrations." Julia gave Violet a hug. "I am so happy for you! I know you will make a wonderful supervisor."

Michael wished he felt free to give Violet a hug. It'd been much too long since he'd held her close, and he wondered if she even remembered that he had. But as her eyes met his, color flooded her cheeks and his chest tightened. Maybe she did. Of course that could be wishful thinking on his part, but he hoped he was right.

Violet was swept upstairs with the other girls wanting to know all about her new position and he was left to go let his mother know that Violet had officially been promoted. He'd tell her about the conversation from Atwood later when he could talk to her privately. The prospect of having a few minutes alone with Violet put a spring in his step as he went to find his mother.

Chapter Seventeen

Chapter Seventeen

Lila did join them for dinner, but Violet couldn't say she celebrated with her. Still it was more than she'd expected and everyone else made up for Lila's broodiness.

When dinner was over and everyone went their own way—Lila heading up to her room for a change—Violet thanked Mrs. Heaton for the trouble she'd gone to.

"I loved doing it, dear," she said. "I can't tell you how happy I am about your promotion and that you've given me so many things to celebrate since you've been with us."

Violet leaned over and kissed her cheek. "You are so dear to me. I will never be able to thank you enough for all you've done for me. I can't think of anyone my mother would want me to have turned to than you."

"Oh, my—"

"Excuse me, ladies," Michael interrupted. "But, Violet, I've heard from Atwood today and I've been hoping for a chance to talk to you without fear of interruption."

"Of course. Where would you like to talk?"

"Why don't we go to the park?"

"I'd love to."

"You children go on. Enjoy the evening. It's a beautiful one," his mother said, waving them away and heading toward the kitchen.

They slipped out the door unnoticed and with relief on Violet's part that Lila wasn't watching every move they made.

Once at Gramercy Park, they strolled to the bench she'd secretly come to think of as "theirs." Michael waited until Violet sat down before joining her. She missed his hand when he removed it from her elbow as she sat down, but when he joined her on the bench, she caught her breath at his nearness.

Trying to ignore the rapid beating of her heart, she asked, "What did Mr. Atwood have to say? Have they been able to find any records that could free up my property?"

"No, not yet. Evidently, it's been a little harder than they thought it would be to get in without Black finding out. And it's not been easy for Atwood to keep undercover so that Black doesn't know he's in town."

"I can see how that would be a problem. I'm sure that Mr. Atwood has clients who want to speak to him as much as I did."

"Well, it's going to take a bit longer that he thought, but he says it will get done. He's staying with the judge—that's where he telephoned me from. His wife and the judge's are good friends and so no one is the wiser when she comes to visit him. She came in early to get the house and office cleaned and ready for him while he came here. Now everyone is asking when he'll be home and she's had to tell them that they'll know when she does. So far everyone seems to accept that he'll be there before long."

"That's good, I suppose?" Violet asked.

Michael nodded. "We hope so. But evidently Mrs. Atwood has had several visits from Black wondering when Mr. Atwood will be home and that tells them that they need to come up with the records as soon as possible before he does something with them. My agent has heard from Black, too, and he wants an immediate accounting of what he's found out about you. Things will be happening fairly fast once Mr. Atwood and the judge get hold of the bank records, but until then, all we can do is wait."

"Well, if not for your quick work in finding Mr. Atwood, we still wouldn't be this far along. I'll just need to pray for patience," Violet said. But, oh, how she wanted it all settled.

The bells on a nearby church rang the hour, and Michael stood up and gave her his hand. "I suppose we should be getting back to the house."

"I suppose we should." Although she hated to go back—she really had begun to think of Gramercy Park as *their* place and she loved being there with Michael. Violet rose a bit too fast and lost her balance. Michael's arms circled her to try to steady her and she caught her breath at his closeness. "Thank you. I—"

"I must have tugged you too hard. I'm sorry." Michael took the blame for her clumsiness.

"No, I just—"

He reached out and tucked an errant strand of hair behind her ear, looked into her eyes and smiled. "One day soon, Violet, we're going to talk about something other than Harlan Black or Lila. One day soon we're going to talk about us."

Violet's pulse quickened at the tender look in his

eyes, but she was caught off guard by his words and didn't know what to say. She only knew that she couldn't wait for that day to come. She managed a nod and Michael pulled her hand through his arm once more, covered it with his own and escorted her home.

The boarders decided to continue celebrating Violet's promotion by going to Central Park on Sunday. This time they were taking the trolley and Michael intended to sit by Violet, if one of the other men didn't beat him to it, and he was going to make sure they didn't. It had taken all the willpower he had not to kiss her the other night in the park. And it was getting increasingly hard not to tell her how he was feeling, what he was thinking. Ever since his mother had mentioned it was time he made a life of his own he'd been thinking about what it would be like to be married to Violet, to call her his wife.

Since Amanda, he'd never thought that way about any other woman. Never let himself because he wasn't sure he could trust his heart to another one—not after his failed relationship with Amanda. And yet Michael knew Violet was nothing like his ex-fiancée. He'd come to realize that his relationship with Amanda wasn't what it should have been from the beginning. Neither of them had loved each other enough. Truth was, he hadn't been the same since he kissed Violet. And what had been meant to comfort her—at least that's what he'd told himself—had brought him nothing but turmoil. Every time he saw her, he thought of the kiss and how it had felt to hold her.

"Are you ready?" Violet asked, interrupting his thoughts as she came down the stairs.

"I am. Did you sleep well?" Michael held his arm out to her and they joined the others as they headed out the door to catch the trolley.

"I did, thank you."

As the group made their way to the trolley stop, Michael was glad he'd made sure that he would be sitting beside Violet. He'd not been quick enough last time, but this time he dropped right down beside her and felt a cocky sense of pleasure when Luke frowned in his direction before grinning, shrugging his shoulders and taking a seat beside Julia.

Michael had a feeling Luke suspected he cared a lot for Violet from some of the remarks he'd made lately, and he saw no reason to let him think otherwise.

John sat by Elizabeth and Ben had no choice but to sit beside Lila. It was just the eight of them today. His mother had decided to stay home and rest after her busy day on Saturday, promising them a good meal when they got back.

It promised to be a beautiful day, with the sun high in the sky and a light breeze to cool the heat. Once at the park they all discussed what they wanted to do. Michael only knew he wanted to be able to talk to Violet in private and rowing on the lake seemed to be the best way to accomplish that.

"Our boating time got interrupted last time. Want to go out again?" he asked Violet. She looked beautiful in her summery outfit of yellow-and-white lawn.

"I'd love that."

"Well, I want to go cycling," Lila said. "Anyone up for that?"

The rest of the group agreed to rent bicycles and they set a time to meet back up before heading home.

Michael caught the look Lila gave him and Violet before she linked arms with Ben and he hoped that Violet didn't see it. Lila was not happy and her anger seemed aimed at Violet.

Oh, he had a feeling it was partly because of him. He'd have to be blind not to know that Lila had hoped he cared about her—even before Violet got there. But he'd made sure not to give her, or any of the other women boarding with his mother, any indication that he was interested in them. More for his mother's sake than his, but he truly hadn't been interested in any woman romantically...until recently. And in spite of his determination not to care about another woman, Violet had captivated him from the beginning and he could no longer deny that his feelings for her had been growing since the day she came to stay with them.

He felt bad that he hadn't been able to hide his attraction for Violet as well as he'd thought he had and had caused Lila to dislike Violet. And yet, he didn't think Violet had any idea how he felt about her. And he certainly didn't know how she felt about him. But it was becoming more important each day for him to find out. Only he didn't know how to go about it.

For now, he'd enjoy his time with Violet and hope that by the end of the afternoon, he'd have an inkling of how she felt about him. She seemed happy that he'd sat beside her and pleased that he asked to take her rowing.

Now, as they headed out to the middle of the lake, she looked more relaxed than he'd seen her since the last time they were out on the lake together. He loved looking at her watching the people on the shore, those who gathered at the plaza, those who were strolling along the lake and others out on the lake just as they were.

"You seem deep in thought." Michael smiled as he dipped the oars in the water. "What are you thinking?"

"Oh, about how nice it is out here in the middle of the lake. It's so beautiful and peaceful."

"What else?" He smiled as he rowed the boat across the water.

"How glad I am I accepted your mother's invitation to come to the city. I can't think of anywhere better to be than here, today. To see the sky and feel the space. I do love coming to Central Park."

So did he. And he could think of nowhere he'd rather be than in that rowboat with Violet.

"I'm glad you like something about the city." He was more than glad. If she could begin to think of New York City as home, perhaps she'd want to stay even after she got her house back.

"Oh, I like many things about it. In fact it sometimes surprises me how I've come to love this city—in spite of how much I wish there wasn't a need for the tenements and that life wasn't so hard for the people living in them."

"I know that feeling well," Michael agreed. "I hope that one day we'll see life get better for those who are living in the tenements. I know there are many trying to make life better for the poor. I pray that we'll see the children there now grow up to become respectable citizens helping things get better for those less fortunate than they are and that it will continue that way."

"Oh, Michael, that would be wonderful. But do you really think—"

"Sadly, no. I know better. There will always be tenements here. There will always be the destitute among us. I just hope there are less of them in time."

"Yes, so do I. And I pray about it. I just wish there was something more I could do to help."

As she'd actually admitted that she loved the city he thought maybe now he might add one more thing. "You know, I realize that your goal is to get your home back free and clear, but I hope you consider keeping it as a summer home and staying here in New York. Mother is going to feel lost without you."

Violet looked sad, and Michael changed the subject as he picked up the oars and dipped them in the water, down, up and down again. "Enough talk about things we don't have control over. We can pray about all that and do what we can to help. But for now, let's enjoy the rest of the afternoon. Fall will be here before we know it. I think you will like it here then, too. And after that there is winter and ice-skating and sledding and sleigh rides."

"It all sounds wonderful. I can't wait to see the seasons change. There is still so much of the city I haven't seen yet, but every day I seem to find out something new."

"I was thinking you might enjoy going to Carnegie Hall to a concert one night. Would you like to?" He felt the need to introduce her to other things to love in the city.

"I've never been—we talked about it, remember? But we never planned anything. I'd love to go, Michael."

"Good. I'll find out who's performing and when and we'll try to set a date." He could think of nothing he'd enjoy more than to spend an evening out in Violet's company.

"Wonderful. I look forward to it." Her smile dove

right into Michael's heart. He cared about this woman. Could she begin to have feelings for him, too?

Violet's heart did a funny little dive and she tried to ignore her racing pulse at the knowledge that Michael seemed to want to spend more time with her. Could she begin to hope that he had feelings for her, too?

When he'd said he was glad there were some things she liked in the city, she'd realized that there was much she liked about the city and that there were people she'd come to care deeply about. Mrs. Heaton was like family to her, and she was so thankful the Lord had nudged her to suggest Violet to come to New York after her mother passed away.

She also had come to care about most of the boarders and she liked being around them. She hadn't really realized how lonely she was and how much she could enjoy being in others' company until she'd moved here. Life was never boring at Heaton House.

But what she'd also come to realize she could no longer deny to herself was that she cared deeply for Michael Heaton. And that caused her some amount of turmoil. He'd never found anyone after Amanda. Did that mean he'd never gotten over her? They had shared a kiss, but she was sure it was only to comfort her, and there'd not been another.

And he'd only told her that his mother would be lost without her here. Nothing about how he might feel. Maybe he only felt brotherly toward her?

And that was the last thing she wanted. Yet he'd said they needed to talk about them one day soon. Could he care for her the way she cared for him? And even if he did—after her experiences with Nick and Harlan, she still wasn't sure she could trust her heart to him or any other man. But she wanted to. With all her heart.

She told herself she couldn't even think about it until after things were settled with Harlan Black. When she'd come to New York, her goal had been to get the mortgage paid off on her home and get it back free and clear. And she'd intended to go back to Virginia.

And do what? Get a job, if she could find one? Hope for a beau to come along—although he'd have to be a stranger moving to town for she knew the others and most were already married and starting families. And those that weren't, well, she couldn't see herself with any of them.

Then she'd be watching her friends marry and start their own families and she'd become the town spinster. No, that wasn't the life she wanted. She wanted more. So much more.

But if Michael didn't feel the same way about her that she felt about him, she wasn't sure she could stay here. She was almost certain she could not.

Chapter Eighteen

The next few weeks seemed to drag as they waited to hear from Atwood. The longer it went with no news, the deeper Violet's spirits seemed to sink, and Michael wanted nothing more than to take her in his arms and tell her how he felt about her. But he held off, wanting things settled about her home and Harlan Black before he did. Only then would she know what she truly wanted to do—go back home to Virginia or stay in New York City. And only then would he feel he could find out for sure if there was a chance that she cared for him the way he did her.

In an effort to raise Violet's spirits, Michael suggested that they all take in a concert at Carnegie Hall. He would have preferred it be only him and Violet, but at this point he didn't trust himself to keep how he felt about her to himself if they were alone for any length of time.

Everyone seemed up for the outing, and Michael made sure he sat beside Violet.

Violet was quite impressed with the music hall. "Oh, Michael, it's lovely." She looked all around at the tiered seating, the red plush seats and the private boxes at the top of the hall as the Philharmonic Society began to tune their instruments. "Thank you for suggesting we come here this evening."

He leaned close to her ear, taking in the sweet scent of her hair. "*You* look lovely tonight, and you're welcome. After all that's happened lately, I felt you needed an outing." He smiled and made a little motion for her to look at his mother and the others. Their excitement was obvious as they looked in every direction and chattered about the people they recognized from the society pages of the newspaper.

"Look at that box up there, Violet," his mother whispered and gave a little nod in the direction she was talking about. "It's the Vanderbilt box. And over there is the Astors'."

Michael chuckled at his mother's excitement. "Actually, I think we all needed this."

Violet nodded and turned back to him. "I think you're right."

Their faces were so close it took his breath away and he could hear Violet's quick intake of breath and see a delicate flush of color flow to her cheeks.

Being so near to Violet sent Michael's heart soaring—just as the notes being played soared to the top of the ceiling. From that moment on, Michael couldn't distinguish his heartbeat from the instruments being played, until the last note sounded and he looked into Violet's eyes. The look in them had his heart flying higher than any note he'd heard that night.

It was a magical evening, sitting together, enjoying another first for Violet in this city, and Michael hoped there would be many more—some he and Violet could enjoy without the company of others. What was he thinking? More time with Violet wasn't what he needed. He cared about her too much already and once she got her home back free and clear, she could easily decide to go back to Ashland and take his heart with her. Not to mention what her leaving would do to his mother.

His chest constricted at the thought of Violet going back to Virginia. But the choice had to be hers, and he couldn't pursue a relationship with her until he knew her decision. And even if she decided to stay in the city, he needed to pray for direction.

Michael was getting more impatient by the hour, but finally on Friday morning the telegram he'd been waiting on from Atwood was delivered. Thankfully, Violet hadn't left for Butterick yet, and he sent Gretchen to find both her and his mother and ask them to meet him in the study.

Once they were both there, Michael wasted no time. "It appears we are about to get to the bottom of Harlan Black's shady dealings."

"Finally!" His mother sank into her chair and looked up at him expectantly while Violet stood speechless.

"I had this telegram from Mr. Atwood first thing this morning. This is what he says. 'We have the goods. Put plan into action. Rumor has it Black is leaving for the city in a few days. Must work fast, but make sure you get in after dark. Will meet you at the Edwardses' home tonight.'"

"Tonight?" Violet and his mother asked at the same time.

"Yes. I'm going to send Jim and another agent on

ahead of us so that they'll be in place before we get there. It looks as if your worries about keeping your home will soon be over with, Violet."

"Really?"

"Yes, really." Her smile lit his heart and he truly was happy that things would soon be settled for her. He only hoped she wouldn't decide to move back once everything was cleared up—especially after being back home again. But it would be much easier to get Black behind bars there, on his turf, than here in the city.

"I don't know what to say," Violet said. "I'll be so glad to get to the truth and have this behind me. I can't thank you enough."

"So will we all, Violet," Michael said. He was more than ready to get it behind them for personal reasons of his own. Until things were truly settled, he didn't feel free to tell Violet how he felt about her.

"When do we leave?" his mother asked.

"Mother, there is no need for you to go with us. It might get dangerous, and I don't want you in harm's way. It's bad enough that Violet has to be there. If I could take care of it all myself, I would."

"I'm going, too. I don't want to wait here worrying about the two of you. As you always tell me, Maida and Gretchen can take care of the boarders, and it's not like there won't be men in the house to protect them all. Besides, I think I'd like to see some of my old friends and invite them personally to come for a visit."

"But, Mrs. Heaton, if it's dangerous—"

Michael's mother's hand went up and he and Violet exchanged a glance. They both knew not to argue with her when she did that. She'd made up her mind and she wasn't going to change it.

"All right then. We'll leave as soon as Violet gets home from work and can get packed. I'll make arrangements for the first evening train. That way it will be dark when we get there as Mr. Atwood instructed. If everything goes according to our plan, by tomorrow evening we should be celebrating."

Michael prayed as he went to find Luke and let him know what they were doing.

Violet was happily surprised when the train pulled into the station to find Beth and her father waiting for them.

Beth hurried up to her and hugged her. "Oh, Violet! I'm so glad you are back!"

Michael and his mother got off from the next car and were quickly taken to a surrey where Mr. Atwood's wife was waiting. "Oh, Martha, it's about time you paid us a visit, I can't tell you how much I've missed you!"

Evidently Mr. Atwood and the judge had coached the two women on how to act and what to say to throw any suspicion their arrival might cause.

Violet went in through the front door of the Edwardses' home and was greeted like a long-lost daughter by Beth's mother, just before Michael and his mother were escorted down the alleyway and into the house by the back door. Once they were all inside the Edwardses' home, where the shades were drawn tight, there was a collective sigh and some nervous laughter.

Both Mr. Atwood and the man Violet presumed to be the judge greeted her as a dear friend and granddaughter.

"Violet, Michael and Mrs. Heaton, this is Judge Bancroft. Do you remember him?" Mr. Atwood asked.

"Of course, I do," Mrs. Heaton said.

"I know I've heard the name, but I don't believe I've had the pleasure. I'm pleased to meet you, Judge," Michael said, holding out a hand to the older man. "Thank you for being willing to help with this case."

The judge shook his hand. "You're welcome, son. When I heard what Atwood thought Black was up to, I was determined to see if we could put together an airtight case against the scoundrel." He turned to Violet. "And you, young woman, do you remember me?"

"I do. Mama thought very highly of you, Judge."

"Thank you for letting me know that, Miss Burton. Your parents were well-thought-of in this town. I'm sorry that scoundrel Black has caused you even more grief after the loss of your mother."

"As you can see, the judge is as determined to put a stop to Black's shenanigans as we are," Atwood said. "And we have all the proof we need, right in here." He patted a briefcase. "Violet will have her land free and clear by tomorrow this time."

Violet prayed that was so. She'd done a lot of thinking about what she would do if they could prove that Harlan had been lying and there was no mortgage on her home. She still wasn't sure exactly which way she would go with it, but she did know that if she had money once all was said and done, she wanted some of it to help those in need someway. But things were still up in the air, and she was afraid to make a solid plan until she knew for sure her home was hers—and after that, she hoped she'd find out how Michael felt about her.

After the wonderful meal Mrs. Edwards had prepared for them, they went into the parlor to discuss the final plans. Everyone would have a part to play. Mrs. Heaton would be spending the night with Violet in her home because Michael and his men would also be staying there—in case Black showed up that night or first thing the next morning before Mr. Atwood and the judge got there. If that happened the alternate plan could go forward.

The judge and Mr. Atwood had even involved the police, and the chief informed them that they had a patrolman watching Mr. Black to make sure he was nowhere around when they went over to the Burton home. A policeman would also take Jim's place first thing in the morning when he went to let Black know that Violet was back in town.

Michael had a feeling Black would know long before that, but at least they seemed to have all possibilities covered. Mrs. Edwards and her daughter had stocked the kitchen for the next few days. Once Violet showed them around so that Michael could decide where to place his men, they all adjourned to the kitchen for coffee and the three-layer chocolate cake that Mrs. Edwards had provided. They went over the plan one more time.

And while Michael couldn't wait for it all to be over with, he prayed that once Violet knew she didn't have a mortgage to pay off, that she really didn't have to work for a living, she'd still want to stay in the city. He didn't want to lose her. Not now—not ever. She'd stolen his heart without lifting a finger to do so.

However, Michael wasn't sure his heart was what she wanted, and he hadn't been able to tell her how he felt yet. Just as soon as this was all settled, he intended to. He wasn't going to lose her without a fight.

But first he had to make sure she stayed safe, to make sure that Black didn't get to her.

When Violet awoke the next morning, she lay in her bed listening to the sounds of the house she'd grown up in, just as she'd done numerous times before. But something was different. The house she'd been born in, grown up in, no longer felt like home to her. Thinking back, she realized it hadn't felt the same since her mother had passed away. There had been a different feel to it as soon as her mother had been laid to rest.

And now, after living in New York City, Violet wasn't sure she would ever really feel at home here again. Wasn't sure she wanted to. New York and Mrs. Heaton's boardinghouse had become home to her. Oh, she knew that if she moved back here, she would eventually feel differently, but more and more she realized that just as her home felt different, so did the town.

It was wonderful to see Beth and her parents again, but Violet couldn't really think of anyone else here that she was eager to see, to spend time with or even that she missed. And yet, she knew she would miss most everyone at the boardinghouse if she came back. Being an only child, she felt as if she almost had siblings now, with the family atmosphere of Mrs. Heaton's home. Not to mention that there was so much more to do and see in the city.

Violet flung her covers off and got out of bed. She could find many more reasons not to leave New York City, but deep down she knew that the real reason she didn't want to move home was Michael. He'd become so much a part of her life, so much a part of her heart, that she couldn't imagine even a day without seeing him. Didn't even want to. But did he feel the same way about her? *Dear Lord, I pray he does and that I'll know for sure soon.*

She hurried to get ready for what the day would bring and prayed again that it would bring truth out into the open and that it would all be settled soon so that she could move forward with her life.

Mrs. Heaton had slept in Violet's mother's room, and Violet tiptoed past her door so as not to waken her. Violet had planned to cook breakfast for everyone, but as she got closer to the kitchen, she smelled coffee and her heart melted at the sight of Michael standing at her mother's range, frying bacon. He must have heard her footsteps for he turned and smiled, those dimples deep and captivating.

"Good morning, Violet, I hope you slept well."

"Good morning, Michael. Actually, I did sleep pretty well. I didn't know you could cook."

"My mother insisted I learn years ago. It's been a long time since I have, but I don't think I've lost my knack for it, if I do say so myself." He forked the bacon that was done just the way Violet liked it onto a plate. "I don't think my biscuits will be as good as Maida's or Gretchen's, but I think they'll be edible."

Mrs. Heaton entered the kitchen just as Michael took the biscuits out of the oven. "I am so glad I taught you to cook, son." She kissed him on the cheek and turned to Violet.

"Violet, dear, didn't you say you hoped to find your mother's sewing box? When I got into bed last night, I kicked my slipper under the bed and when I went to retrieve it, I found the sewing box under the bed."

"Under the bed?" That was odd. "I can't imagine

why Mother would have put it there, but I am so glad you found it. Of course, she hadn't felt like using it for weeks before she passed away. Maybe she put it beside the bed thinking she could get to it when she felt up to it."

"I'm sure that was it. Anyway, I just wanted to let you know it is here."

"Thank you so much." Violet fought the urge to go get it and look through all the things her mother kept there. To bring back good memories. Maybe she'd feel more at home here if she could.

"We can't tarry long over this wonderful breakfast I made," Michael said. He grinned as he put the biscuits and bacon on the table. "Simple but good, I hope. Anyway, I sent Jim to get breakfast out. Didn't want him teasing me if this was bad and I wanted Jim to be able to contact Harlan first thing to keep him from showing up here before we're ready for him."

"I don't think I'll ever be ready for him. But I so want all of this settled." Violet opened her biscuit and spread butter on it. She took a bite and closed her eyes. "Mmm, you do know how to cook, Michael! These are as every bit as good as Gretchen's and Maida's."

"Thank you." Michael grinned as he handed her the plate of bacon.

"Yes, it's always been quite a relief to me to know that if the girls couldn't come into work, Michael could help me in the kitchen," Mrs. Heaton said. "He always loved helping me when he was young. And I don't think it hurts any man to know how to feed himself."

A knock on the back door startled them all. When Violet started to get up to go see who was there, Michael waved her aside, letting her know that he'd go.

But it was only Mr. Atwood and the judge showing up as planned.

"Looks like we got here just in time, Judge," Mr. Atwood said. He put his briefcase down and helped himself to a biscuit.

"We just ate breakfast, but those do smell mighty good. I think I'll have one, too," the judge said. "Must be a case of anticipation of closing a case that has us so hungry."

"Soon as we finish here, I guess we'd better take our places, just in case Harlan decides to come calling on Miss Burton earlier than is deemed appropriate."

"Well, he'd better not, but I wouldn't put it past him," Mrs. Heaton said.

Violet took a deep breath. This was real. They'd talked and planned the best they could, and now it was time to put those plans into action. A shiver of apprehension slid down Violet's spine and for the first time she felt nervous. She sent up a silent prayer that it would all work right, and hopefully, Harlan Black would be behind bars before nightfall.

Chapter Nineteen

Violet found it hard to keep still as they waited for Harlan to show up. The judge and Mr. Atwood were playing a game of chess in the front parlor; Mrs. Heaton was trying to keep to the kitchen in the back—although she'd already been up front several times to check on everyone and see if they needed anything. And Michael was just inside the front door, out of sight, but a reassuring presence to her. His men and the local police chief were hidden around the sides of the house.

"Violet, if you keep pacing back and forth you are going to make Black think you are waiting for him when he shows up," Michael said softly. "Why don't I have Mother make you some tea? Is there a magazine or paper around you can read while we're waiting?"

Violet stopped in her tracks. Michael was right. Harlan might think something was brewing if she were out here pacing when he arrived. "I'm sorry. I'm just so nervous."

"That's understandable, Vi, but it's going to be all right."

Did he realize that he'd called her Vi? Or how it

warmed her heart? She'd never had a nickname before and no one had ever called her Vi. That Michael was the only one made it sound even more special to her.

"The Lord is with us. Never forget that, Vi." Michael continued to try to calm her.

"Thank you, Michael. I needed that reminder. I really did."

"Violet, dear," Mrs. Heaton whispered from over her son's shoulder. "Why don't you sit down and look through your mother's sewing box? Maybe there's something in there to mend and you can keep your hands busy, instead of your feet, while we wait." She handed the white wicker sewing box to Michael and he handed it to Violet. "You are making us all nervous, dear."

Violet took the box. "Thank you."

"Yes, thank you, Mother," Michael said. "But please go back to the kitchen and make something. *You* are making me nervous."

Everyone chuckled as his mother smiled and patted him on the cheek before heading back to the kitchen.

Violet took the sewing box and went to sit in the porch swing her father had put up for her mother.

She opened the basket and looked inside. There were spools and spools of thread, packets of needles, a pattern—Butterick, of course—and as she dug down to the bottom she found a packet. Violet opened it and found cards and notes...sweet loving ones from her father to her mother.

Violet pulled out one more envelope. It was crumpled, and Violet smoothed it out to find it addressed to... Mrs. Heaton, in her mother's handwriting. But the flap wasn't sealed.

"Violet, stay there and try to stay calm." Michael's voice came to her softly from behind the screen door. "Black is coming up the street now. Don't worry. I've got you covered from all sides. Just be yourself."

Violet's mouth went dry as she swallowed, and all she could manage was a nod. She stuffed the packet into the box and put the lid back on. Only then did she look to the street to see that Harlan Black was almost at the front walk.

She stood, smoothed out her skirts and waited for him.

Harlan reached the front walk and stopped. He took off his hat and waved it. "Miss Burton, you *are* back. I'd heard you were and came to see if it was true."

"As you can see, it is, Mr. Black."

"I'm glad. Will you be staying?" He hurried up the walk to the porch, but stopped at the first step.

"For a few days, at least."

Harlan came up the steps. "And what brings you back to town? Did you get homesick?"

"I just wanted to come home and check on things and take care of some business."

"Oh? What kind of business?"

Violet wanted to tell him it was none of his, but that wouldn't get them where they needed to be. "Well, I was coming to see you later this morning."

"Oh?" Black leaned against the porch railing and smiled. "Why did you want to see me? Have you—"

Violet couldn't bear to have him ask if she'd changed her mind. "I want to see the paper my mother supposedly signed putting our home up for collateral on the loan."

Black pushed away from the rail and moved a little

nearer to her. "I showed it to you. Don't you remember? Why do you want to see it now?"

"I was mourning my mother at that time and you know it. I didn't look at it that closely and I'd just like to see it again."

"You don't believe her signature is real?" He took a step closer.

"I just want to make sure it is hers. I can't understand why she would have put our home up when my father left us enough—"

"No. He didn't."

"I believe he did."

"Well, you're wrong."

"No, she isn't, Black." Mr. Atwood appeared at the door. "I know for a fact that Mr. Burton left this family well-off. Why don't you come in, Mr. Black?" He held the door wide. "We have some things to straighten out."

"Mr. Atwood! The rumor mill said you'd be back soon. Glad you are better, but I don't believe we have a thing to discuss. Mrs. Burton asked me to take care of things since you were gone."

"I think you are lying, Black," Mr. Atwood said.

Harlan turned to leave, but by then Michael's men had come around the side of the house and stood ready to stop him. Jim Moore was one of them.

"What is going on, Moore? Have you set me up?" The hatred in Black's eyes was evident for anyone to see as he looked for an escape route.

"You could say that," Michael said, coming out of the house and standing right behind Violet. "But I'm the one he works for."

Violet could see the fear on Harlan's face. "Heaton. I should have known you'd be mixed up in all of this. I'll have you all arrested!" Harlan's eyes looked wild and Violet wasn't sure what he was going to do.

"I don't think so," Judge Bancroft said, slipping out the door and moved to stand beside Michael and Mr. Atwood. "Mr. Black, why don't you come in and talk this over with us? It's not going to do you much good to run at this point."

"What have you got in there? A whole army?" Harlan yelled.

"We just want to ask you a few questions, Mr. Black. It appears you've been doing some creative bookkeeping. Come on inside. Or, if you'd rather, we can do this down at the police station."

Violet was fearful for everyone as Harlan made to slip a hand to the inside of his jacket. Did he have a gun?

"I wouldn't try that if I was you, Black," Michael said.

"It's not worth it, son," Mr. Atwood said. "You can't change the past. You are in enough trouble. No need to make it worse."

Harlan looked from one man to the other for several minutes before he slipped his hand inside his jacket and pulled out a gun, pointing it straight at Violet. "I don't think you want to pressure me just now."

But Michael quickly pushed her behind him and then dived for Harlan, pushing his arm away and wrestling him down, managing to knock the gun from his hand. Harlan dived after it and Michael grabbed him before he could get to it. Michael threw the gun to Jim Moore just before Harlan's fist caught him in the eye.

Michael gave as good as he got and it took Jim and the other agent to pull them apart. Then everything seemed a blur as Jim Moore stopped Michael's fist from crashing into Harlan's face once more. "It's done, Michael."

By then the chief of police and the other agent had handcuffs on Harlan and had yanked him to his feet. Michael looked at Violet, and she could see that his eye was turning black already. But there was a gleam in his eye as he looked at her and smiled. She smiled back and his dimples deepened as he winked at her. He was all right. Her heart slammed against her chest. Only then did Violet feel that she could breathe again. *Thank You, Lord.*

"Let's talk," the judge said, opening the door wide.

"Maybe it will help you to hear what we know," Mr. Atwood said once everyone was seated in the parlor. "I know what Mr. Burton left his wife and daughter, and it was a home and land, free and clear of debt, and a tidy sum in the bank. But somehow you left Mrs. Burton, and then Violet, under the impression that they were near penniless."

"I never—"

"Yes, you did. You went so far as to convince Mrs. Burton that she needed to put her home up as collateral so that there was enough money in her account to pay for her medicine and the doctor."

"You are making this all up."

"No. I'm not. We've checked your records and we know what Doc charged."

Harlan laughed. "You're bluffing."

"He's not bluffing," the judge said. "I was with him. We've seen all your records."

"You broke in and—"

"We had a search warrant. It was all legal and above-board. Your actions, however, have not been."

Mr. Atwood drew out papers showing that the bank account in Violet's mother's name was still intact and in fact had money in it. "What were you planning on doing? Persuading Miss Burton to marry you, get her house, land and bank account for yourself? And for what reason? To show your papa that you were a better man?"

It was at that moment that Harlan Black broke. "He never loved my mother. Always wanted Violet's mother, right up until she died. He never stopped loving her. And he never loved me. Never wanted me. I wanted to show him that I could have it all. But Mrs. Burton didn't want me to come around and try to court Violet. Didn't want to give me a chance because of him! I knew I had to do something. When she got sick, well, I tried to convince her that she had money troubles and the only way out was for me to give her a loan, putting up the house for collateral. I knew she wasn't long for this world, so I even promised to leave Violet alone."

He looked at Violet. "But she yelled at me and told me to get out of the house. She was real agitated. And then she collapsed. She wasn't ever the same after that. Couldn't talk or anything." He looked at Violet and then down at the floor.

Did he have any remorse at all? He'd probably helped cause her mother's stroke. Violet closed her eyes and willed herself not to throw up. The pity she'd begun to feel for him changed to repulsion.

"So you forged her name on the papers and told Violet she'd signed them?"

Harlan raised his head and grinned. "She believed me."

"Because she was in mourning, not thinking straight, and I wasn't here to tell her different and to look into it for her," Mr. Atwood said.

"And if you'd waited to come back, you old coot, I probably could have convinced her to marry me by now. Especially now I have someone in the Heaton House working for me."

"What are you talking about? Who is working for you?" Michael asked.

"Not your agent, if that's what you think. No. It appears there is someone who wants Violet away from you as much as I do."

"Lila," Violet whispered. "But how—"

"Miss Lila Miller got in touch with me a few weeks ago. Let me know right where you were. I bought a train ticket and was going to leave on Monday. We had everything set up so when you came out of Butterick she could say she'd met a friend and leave you to catch the trolley on your own. And I'd be there waiting for you." Black grinned at Michael. "And you'd never see her again. But you ruined all my plans by coming here before I could leave town."

His arrogance had Michael on his feet and grabbing his collar. "You are scum, Black. You always have been and it doesn't have anything do to with your father."

There was loathing in Black's eyes when he looked at Michael and sneered. "Your sister didn't think so, though. No, she didn't think I was scum at all. I remember one night—"

Michael drew back his fist and only the fast action of his men stopped him from giving Harlan Black exactly what he had coming to him.

* * *

It had been a long day, both heartrending and happy. By nightfall, Violet had seen Harlan Black arrested for fraud and the inheritance she'd never realized she had reinstated to her. Her home was really hers, and she had money in the bank and never had to worry about paying Black one more cent. She even had the means to be able to help some less fortunate than her.

They'd had dinner with the Edwardses that evening, and afterward Violet, Michael and his mother relaxed on her front porch before going in to pack for the trip back to the city. She and Mrs. Heaton shared the swing and Michael was in one of the wicker chairs.

He looked pitiful, his eye swollen, black-and-blue and looking worse by the minute. Her heart swelled with love for this man who'd fought for her today. He'd won—though he looked a bit worse for it. But it could have turned out so differently. He could have been shot and killed. She shuddered at the very thought.

Just thinking about how close he'd come to losing his life on her account made Violet tremble.

"I'm so glad this is all over and we're headed home," Mrs. Heaton said. "I loved Ashland when we lived here, but I don't want to move back. I might feel differently if your mother was still alive, Violet, but not now."

At the mention of her mother, Violet finally remembered the letter her mother had written and never mailed. She reached into the sewing box she'd left on the swing, dug out the letter and handed it to Mrs. Heaton.

"I have something for you. I found it when I was out here earlier today, but it was about the time Harlan showed up and so much has happened since then, I forgot until now." She handed it to Mrs. Heaton.

Mrs. Heaton took the packet from her and turned it over. She opened the flap that had never been sealed and pulled out another envelope with a letter wrapped around it. Her quick intake of breath told them that she was surprised. She swallowed hard. "This envelope is addressed to your mother and it is from…" She sighed deeply and her eyes were full of tears as she continued, her voice shaky, "It's from Becca!"

She ran trembling fingers over the writing before opening the letter from Violet's mother and reading out loud. "'Dear Martha, I received this from Rebecca a few days ago. I don't know that anything in it will help you and Michael to find her, but I pray it does. I have a suspicion that Harlan Black had something to do with her disappearance, but I have no proof of anything. Just that he makes the hair on the back of my neck stand on end. He's made it known that he wants to court Violet and I'm going to let him know just how I feel about that—in no uncertain terms. Please let me know you received this, I—'"

Mrs. Heaton turned the paper over and looked at Michael and Violet. "That's it. She stopped in midsentence." She handed the letter to Violet.

"Maybe she got interrupted or just didn't have the energy to finish right then. She never told me about it and it's dated only a few days before her stroke." Violet handed the short note to Michael. His mother opened the envelope containing Becca's letter and began to read. "'Dear Mrs. Burton, I know I've been gone a long time without being in contact. But I wanted to write and ask you to let my mother know that I am all right. I've heard she and Michael moved, but I don't know where they are. I hope that you do, so that you can forward this to her. But I do not want her to know where I am because she never wanted me to move away, and, well, I fear seeing me now would bring her more heartache. I just want her to know that I am all right. Please tell her I love her. Sincerely, Rebecca Heaton.'"

Michael's mother looked up at him, her eyes swimming in tears. "Oh, Michael, this means our Becca is alive. She's really alive."

Violet brushed at her own eyes as she watched Michael hug his mother, unshed tears making his eyes bright.

"I know this doesn't mean we'll ever find her, Michael, but—"

"I'll try to renew the search, Mother, I—"

Mrs. Heaton shook her head. "No, son. You've done all you can to that end. Follow leads if you get them, but I don't want you to feel you can't have a life until you find Becca. I can rest easier just knowing she's alive, and I know that if we're meant to find your sister, the Lord will see to it that we do."

Michael nodded. "I'll continue to pray that we do, Mother. And you know I'll never give up looking for her."

"I do. But I want you to have a life of your own. You gave that up once. I don't want to see you do it again." Mrs. Heaton held the letter close to her heart. "I believe I'll turn in now. I'm ready to go home."

Chapter Twenty

Michael opened the door for his mother to go back
inside and then turned to Violet. "I can't begin to tell
you how much the letter you found means to Mother
and me. It's given us hope that Becca is alive and that
one day we *will* find her. Or she'll find us."

"You really aren't going to give up just because that
letter said she didn't want to be found, are you?" Violet asked.

"No, of course not. But—"

"But what?"

"I won't let the search for her turn into the obses-
sion it was at the beginning. Mother is right. I did do
that once, although I know now that it worked out for
the best."

"What do you mean? Are you talking about your engagement to Amanda?"

"I am. She wasn't willing to support my search for
my sister in any way and she called off the engagement
when I decided to move to New York City."

"I knew the wedding had been called off, but I didn't
know why. I'm sorry, Michael."

"I'm not. At least not now." He'd never loved Amanda the way he loved Violet. What he'd felt for Amanda had been more of an infatuation, until he'd realized what kind of woman she was. "I decided a long time ago that if I ever gave my heart to another woman, it would be one who supported my need to try to find my sister. But it would also be someone I loved so much that I would make sure that whatever I was working on would come second to her needs. I didn't feel that way about Amanda and she didn't feel that way about me, or what I had to do. Maybe I was too fixated with finding Becca, but—"

"She's your sister. I can't believe that Amanda couldn't understand that you had to search for Becca. I'd do anything I could to help you find her."

And she would. Michael knew it as sure as he knew he loved her. This was the one woman who could and would stand by his side no matter what—if he was blessed to have her return the love he felt for her. But this was her home and she just had it returned to her. He had to ask.

"Violet, now that you have your home free and clear and an inheritance—do you know what you're going to do? Are you going to move back here?"

"I don't know what I'm going to do. But I can't leave my position at Butterick without giving notice so that they can name someone to replace me. And I'm just not sure…" She shook her head. "I've got a lot of thinking and praying to do, Michael."

He joined her on the swing and put it into motion. "The decision must be yours. But just so you know—" he reached out and cupped the side of her face with his hand "—while you're praying, I hope you stay in the city."

He heard her catch her breath and he dipped his head, his lips touching hers for a brief moment—only until she responded and then he deepened the kiss. He loved this woman. *Please, dear Lord, let her decide to stay in New York City.*

He raised his head and looked into her eyes, wanting to tell her how he felt, wanting to ask her to marry him. But she looked exhausted and his head had begun to throb. Now wasn't the time to press. It could wait until they got back home. Maybe that was the place to tell her how he felt. At least she was going back with them. He'd be thankful for that.

"Please just think about it, and we'll talk when we get back to the city?"

She nodded. "It's been a long day and you need to get some rest. Can I get you some ice or a cool rag to put on your eye?"

"No, I'll get it when I go in. I'm just going to sit here for a while, though."

She got up from the swing. "All right. I'll see you in the morning, then."

"Night, Violet."

"Good night, Michael."

Violet tossed and turned most of the night. What was she going to do? Move back here or stay in the city? She loved Michael with all her heart—and he'd fought Harlan for her. But did that mean he loved her, too? He'd kissed her and said he wanted her to stay, but was it for his mother's sake or his own?

She pounded her pillow and turned over. *Dear Lord,*

*please help me to know what to do. Help me to know
how he feels about me. I don't know if I can stay in the
city only for Mrs. Heaton's sake, much as I love her.
If Michael doesn't love me, I don't think I'd be able
to continue living at Heaton House. Please show me
what to do.*

Finally, once she heard Michael come inside and shut
the door, she drifted off to sleep.

The next morning they joined the Edwardses at
church. Michael seemed to sport his black eye with
pride. All Violet knew was that she was extremely proud
of him.

Then, after a wonderful dinner with Beth and her
family, Mr. and Mrs. Atwood, the judge and his family, Violet waved goodbye to her friends as she and Michael and Mrs. Heaton boarded the train to go back to
New York City.

They took their seats on the train, Michael beside
her, and Mrs. Heaton sitting across from them, talking
to an old friend across the aisle who was going to visit
her son's family in the city.

Now, as the locomotive began to move, Michael
smiled down at her and said quietly, "Are you all right?
Sure you want to return to the city?"

"I'm fine now. And I'm happy to be going back. I
have a job to return to. And I've realized that with no
family in Ashland, there really is nothing holding me
here now. Beth will be more than happy to come visit
me in the city."

Michael's dimples deepened. "I'm glad. I wasn't sure
if you were feeling sad to leave."

"No. I'm better than I've been in months. I know
that what I suspected about Harlan was true and I'm

relieved to know that he's going to pay for his deeds. I can't thank you enough for being the reason for that, Michael." His eye was black and blue and purple now. Just looking at it made her hurt for him. She wanted to say so much more, but now wasn't the time or place.

Mrs. Heaton's conversation with her friend ended and she turned her attention back to them.

"I still can't believe Lila was working with Black, giving him information about Violet. How did she know about him anyway?"

"I don't know." Michael rubbed his temple.

"I ran into her in the hall coming out of your study one night. I have to admit I wondered if she might be eavesdropping, then I felt bad for thinking it. But it was the night we talked about Harlan."

"Now that you mention it, I caught her coming out of your room one night. She said she'd been returning a shirtwaist you'd loaned her. I believe it was right after your sewing machine arrived."

Violet inhaled quickly. "The letter Beth sent—when I went up to read it later that night, it was on the floor. I just assumed I'd knocked it off the bedside table, but—"

"Most probably, at least at one or the other time, and maybe in both instances, Lila found out enough to contact Black. I knew she was a scheming young woman, but I never thought she'd turn on someone living in our home," Michael said.

"I am so sorry, Violet. I knew she was jealous of you, but she was always envious of anyone getting more attention than she was." Mrs. Heaton shook her head. "If I'd had any idea that she would turn on you, try to put you in harm's way, I would have told her to leave."

"Oh, Mrs. Heaton, please don't blame yourself. I

knew Lila didn't like me, but I never suspected she'd go to such lengths to get rid of me." Her heart filled with love for Michael and his mother. "I'm sorry I've caused you so much trouble."

"You've given us much joy, Violet. The only ones who've caused problems are Black and Lila. We've taken care of one, and the other will be taken care of as soon as we get home. It's time Lila learned her actions have consequences," Michael said.

Violet looked at Michael's bruised face and shuddered. He could have been killed. He was right. She just wished Lila had taken a different path in her life.

Violet could feel the tension radiating off Michael as he opened the door of his mother's home that afternoon. Gretchen met them just inside, as if she'd been on the lookout for them. She opened her mouth to speak, but before she could say anything, Michael said, "Gretchen, please tell Lila I want to see her in Mother's study right away."

Gretchen began wringing her hands and shaking her head. "She's not here, Mr. Heaton. She's gone."

"Where is she, do you know? Is she with some of the other boarders?"

"No, sir. She must have moved out all of her things in the middle of the night. When she didn't come down for Sunday dinner, Elizabeth went to check on her and there was nothing in her room except for a letter to Mrs. Heaton and one addressed to Butterick. Nothing else. We don't know where she went."

By then Elizabeth, Julia, Luke and John had joined them in the foyer.

"I'm so glad you're home, Mrs. Heaton." Elizabeth

had several letters in her hand and handed them to the older woman. "Lila started acting odd as soon as she found out you all had gone to Virginia on Friday, and she was jumpy as a cat all day yesterday, but we couldn't get her to tell us what was wrong and she went to bed early last night."

"We don't know when she left," Luke added. "Our best guess is that it was after everyone went to bed last night or first thing this morning before anyone was up."

"Let me read her letter," Mrs. Heaton said. "Maybe it will shed some light on why she left. If not, I believe we can. Let's go into the parlor."

Violet sat down on one side of Mrs. Heaton and Michael sat on the other while she silently skimmed Lila's script. Then she handed it to Michael. "You tell them, son."

Michael nodded and began to read: "'Dear Mrs. Heaton. I've been called home suddenly and couldn't wait until you returned from your trip. I don't know when I will be able to return, so I must resign from Butterick. Please have Violet give them the letter I've addressed to them. I thank you for your kindness to me and I ask you to give Michael my regards. Please tell everyone else goodbye for me. Lila'"

Michael sighed and looked at Violet. "Obviously she had a feeling we'd find out what she'd done and got out of town before we could confront her with it. I think I'll send one of my men to her hometown, but I don't think she's been called home suddenly."

"No, neither do I," Luke said.

"What is it? What has Lila done?" Elizabeth asked.

By the time they'd explained everything to the board-

ers, Gretchen was there to tell them dinner was ready
and they moved from the parlor to the dining room.

Violet could understand that Elizabeth and the other
women might miss Lila, but when she voiced as much,
Elizabeth put that thought to rest.

"Well, much as I hate to admit it, it took a lot of energy to be polite to Lila most days. It wasn't easy to be
a friend to her," Elizabeth said. "I'm sorry she betrayed
you after all you've tried to do for her, Violet. I can't
say I'm sorry to see her go."

"True," Julia added. "I knew she resented Violet, but
I never thought she would go so far as to try to put her
in danger. I admit I'm glad she's gone, too."

"It will be a lot more peaceful around here," Luke
said. "Lila liked to stir things up on a daily basis. It's
a shame she couldn't appreciate the friendship you ladies tried to show her."

Angry as Violet was at Lila, she pitied her at the
same time. Now she could only pray that the woman
would find the Lord and turn her life around.

It was later that evening before Violet and Michael
had a chance to talk to one another in private. So much
had happened so quickly that Violet's head was still
spinning. Coming home to the city was part of it. Violet had known that she was glad to be coming back, but
when she had walked through the doors of Mrs. Heaton's boardinghouse, there was no longer any feeling
as if it was *almost* home. Now it *was* home to her, and
when the boarders welcomed them back she knew that
she was in New York City to stay. She might not stay
in this house, depending on how Michael felt about her,
but she didn't want to move back to Ashland.

Michael had asked if he could speak to her after dinner and visiting with the boarders, telling them about all that had happened and Lila's part in it. Violet was more than happy to oblige. She had much to thank him for. And she secretly hoped that they might have that talk about them, the one that Michael had said they would have "one day."

When the gathering began to break up, Violet went to Mrs. Heaton's study where Michael had asked to meet her. She was a little surprised to see Luke there, too. But Michael smiled at her and motioned her to come in.

"Luke is blaming himself for not keeping Lila here."

"I'm so sorry about Lila's part in all this, Violet," Luke said. "If I'd had any idea I would have watched her closer."

"Why, Luke, it's not your fault. None of us suspected she even knew who Harlan was."

"Still—"

"Luke, I should have called home that night. It's my fault that she left before we got here," Michael said. "I thought she'd be here when we returned."

"Well, if you haven't decided who to send to her hometown, I'd sure like to go," Luke said. "Maybe she'd just think I came looking for her as a friend. She doesn't know I work for you."

"I was going to ask you to do just that. But I don't think she went home."

"I'm sure she didn't. But I'd like the chance to find out what I can."

Michael nodded. "You have it."

"Just be careful, Luke," Violet said. "She's not to be trusted."

"I know. I'll be careful. Now, a bit of advice to the two of you."

"Oh? What advice is that?" Michael asked.

"Quit wasting time and tell each other what everyone else in this house already knows."

Michael raised an eyebrow and smiled. "And that would be?"

"That you are in love with each other. It's pretty obvious to everyone but the two of you."

Violet could feel her face flush as she and Michael glanced at each other.

"I'll leave you to do that in private," Luke said.

"That'd be nice of you." Michael grinned.

Luke chuckled on his way out the door, and Michael's arms encircled Violet before it clicked shut.

His cheek had been changing colors by the hour and Violet couldn't stop herself from reaching out to touch his face now that they were alone. But, afraid that her touch would hurt, she quickly pulled her hand back. "I'm so sorry you got hurt. But you saved my life, you know, in more ways than one."

Michael waved his hand to dismiss her thanks and then brought it down to grasp the fingers she'd lowered. "I'm glad it all turned out well. After Mother voiced her fears, I knew something wasn't right, and there was only one thing to do and that was to get to the bottom of it all. But as for saving a life…" He paused before bringing Violet's fingers to his lips and then laying them against his cheek. He looked deep into her eyes and released a deep breath. "I think it was my life I saved, for if anything had happened to you, Vi, I don't think I would have been able to forgive myself."

"Michael, no. Don't even talk like that."

Michael pulled her into his arms and put his head against hers. "Violet, it is well past time that we talk about us. I can't begin to tell you how I felt when Black pulled that gun on you. I thought for sure my heart would never beat again."

"Oh, Michael—"

His fingertips sealed her lips as he shook his head. "Please let me finish."

Violet nodded and he removed his hand to pull her closer. "I know I'm probably doing this badly, but after coming so close to losing you, I don't want to wait one more minute before telling you how I feel about you, Violet. Luke is right. It's time. I love you with all that I am and I can't tell you how relieved I am that you don't want to go back to Ashland. I want you to stay here and…if there is any way you think you could learn to love me, too, I—"

"Michael." Violet's hand reached out and she gently touched his cheek once more. "I think I began to fall in love with you from the moment I walked into the parlor that first night. I've loved you for a good while now, and I've only dreamed that you might come to care for me, too."

Michael tipped her face up to his. "It seems we should have had this talk long before now. And I won't let another moment go by without asking you to marry me. Will you be my wife, Vi?"

Violet's heart flooded with happiness and love for this man. "Oh," she breathed, "yes, Michael, I will be honored to marry you."

"I love you with all my heart, Vi." Michael's head dipped and Violet stood on tiptoe as his lips grazed hers.

Suddenly, she realized that she finally had somewhere to call home. And it wasn't in Virginia. It wasn't New York City or even Heaton House. Home for Violet would always be right here in the circle of Michael's arms.

Epilogue

Heaton House
December 20, 1895

Violet couldn't believe her wedding day was finally here. Michael had wanted to marry right away, but to please his mother, who wanted to give them the wedding she'd never been able to plan for her daughter, they agreed to a December 20 date. After all she'd done for her, Violet was more than glad to grant her request.

And it'd worked out fine; it gave them time to find a home of their own only a few blocks away. Michael had given her permission to work until they started a family and Butterick had reciprocated by providing Violet's wedding dress.

It was from their winter line, made of ivory satin and lace, and Mrs. Waters had made it for her. Violet felt beautiful in it, and as she stood at the landing at Heaton House, she thanked the Lord for the blessings He'd bestowed on her.

Now, Violet took a deep breath and held her bouquet with trembling fingers to her heart as Elizabeth straightened her skirts from behind.

"Just wait until Michael sees you," Elizabeth whispered. "He's going to fall in love all over again."

Violet smiled just thinking of her husband-to-be. Michael would be all she'd ever hoped for in a husband. He was loving and kind, affectionate, honest and strong. Best of all, he loved the Lord as much as she did.

"I hope so. Because I think I fall in love with him more each day," she whispered back.

She and Michael were going to spend a few days in her home in Ashland and try to decide whether to keep the house or sell it, then they'd return on Christmas Eve just in time to celebrate with Mrs. Heaton—Mother Heaton—and the boarders who'd been so happy for the two of them. The plan was to have everyone over to their house for New Year's.

As the "Wedding March" began playing in the parlor below, Elizabeth gave her a quick hug and started down the stairs before her. Violet's heart hammered against her ribs with each step she took as she followed her maid of honor down the stairs, into the foyer and on into the parlor.

She almost forgot to breathe as she saw Michael waiting for her, standing with Luke, his best man. They were in front of the Christmas tree his mother had made sure was up and decorated for this day. Garlands graced the mantel and the windows, and Violet couldn't think of a better setting for a wedding.

Michael looked regal and so very handsome standing there in his tuxedo, the expression in his eyes touching her heart, drawing her to him, past their friends from Ashland, Mrs. Waters and several of her coworkers and

Michael's agents, too. Then there were Julia, John and Ben—the boarders she'd come to think of as family—and even Gretchen and Maida dressed in their finest and ready to serve the guests after the ceremony. How blessed they were to have so many friends.

She stopped beside Michael's mother and placed a kiss on her cheek as she handed her a flower from her bouquet. Then she took her place beside Michael and they turned to the minister.

Her fingers trembled holding the bouquet and only Michael's gaze kept her steady as they said their vows in front of the people they loved. They both promised to love and cherish each other for the rest of their lives and she handed her bouquet to Elizabeth before Michael slid the ring that'd been her mother's on her finger.

"I pronounce you husband and wife," the minister said. "You may kiss your bride, Michael."

Michael pushed back the veil and tipped Violet's face up. "I love you, Vi. Today, tomorrow and forever."

Violet barely got out, "I love you, too," before her new husband claimed her lips in the sweetest kiss she'd ever known—the very first one as Mrs. Michael Heaton.

* * * * *

WE HOPE YOU ENJOYED THIS BOOK!

Love Inspired® SUSPENSE

Uncover the truth in these thrilling stories of faith in the face of crime from Love Inspired Suspense. Discover six new books available every month, wherever books are sold!

LoveInspired.com

LISHALO2019

SPECIAL EXCERPT FROM

Carolyn Wiebe will do anything to protect her late sister's children from their abusive father—even give up her Amish roots and pretend to be Mennonite. But when she starts falling for Amish bachelor Michael Miller, can they conquer their pasts—and her secrets—by Christmas to build a forever family?

Read on for a sneak preview of
An Amish Christmas Promise *by Jo Ann Brown, available December 2019 from Love Inspired!*

"Are the *kinder* okay?"

"Yes, they'll be fine." Uncomfortable with his small intrusion into her family, she said, "Kevin had a bad dream and woke us up."

"Because of the rain?"

She wanted to say that was silly but, glad she could be honest with Michael, she said, "It's possible."

"Rebuilding a structure is easy. Rebuilding one's sense of security isn't."

"That sounds like the voice of experience."

"My parents died when I was young, and both my twin brother and I had to learn not to expect something horrible was going to happen without warning."

"I'm sorry. I should have asked more about you and the other volunteers. I've been wrapped up in my own tragedy."

"At times like this, nobody expects you to be thinking of anything but getting a roof over your *kinder*'s heads."

He didn't reach out to touch her, but she was aware of every inch of him so close to her. His quiet strength had awed her from the beginning. As she'd come to know him better, his fundamental decency had impressed her more. He was a man she believed she could trust.

She shoved that thought aside. Trusting any man would be the worst thing she could do after seeing what Mamm had endured during her marriage and then struggling to help her sister escape her abusive husband.

"I'm glad you understand why I must focus on rebuilding a life for the children." The simple statement left no room for misinterpretation. "The flood will always be a part of us, but I want to help them learn how to live with their memories."

"I can't imagine what it was like."

"I can't forget what it was like."

Normally she would have been bothered by someone having sympathy for her, but if pitying her kept Michael from looking at her with his brown puppy-dog eyes that urged her to trust him, she'd accept it. She couldn't trust any man, because she wouldn't let the children spend their lives witnessing what she had.

Don't miss
An Amish Christmas Promise *by Jo Ann Brown,*
available December 2019 wherever
Love Inspired® books and ebooks are sold.

LoveInspired.com

Copyright © 2019 by Jo Ann Ferguson

LIEXP1119

Looking for inspiration in tales
of hope, faith and heartfelt romance?

Check out **Love Inspired**® and
Love Inspired® **Suspense** books!

New books available every month!

CONNECT WITH US AT:

Facebook.com/groups/HarlequinConnection

 Facebook.com/HarlequinBooks

 Twitter.com/HarlequinBooks

 Instagram.com/HarlequinBooks

 Pinterest.com/HarlequinBooks

ReaderService.com

Love Inspired®

LIGENRE2018R2

SPECIAL EXCERPT FROM

Can a mysterious Amish child bring two wounded souls together in Cedar Grove, Kansas?

Read on for a sneak preview of
The Hope *by Patricia Davids*
available December 2019 from HQN Books!

"You won't have to stay on our account, and we can look after Ernest's place, too. I can hire a man to help me. Someone I know I can…" Ruth's words trailed away.

Trust? Depend on? Was that what Ruth was going to say? She didn't want him around. She couldn't have made it any clearer. Maybe it had been a mistake to think he could patch things up between them, but he wasn't willing to give up after only one day. Ruth was nothing if not stubborn, but he could be stubborn, too.

Owen leaned back and chuckled.

"What's so funny?"

"I'm here until Ernest returns, Ruth. You can't get rid of me with a few well-placed insults."

She huffed and turned her back to him. "I didn't insult you."

"Ah, but you wanted to. I'd like to talk about my plans in the morning."

Ruth nodded. "You know my feelings, but I agree we both need to sleep on it."

Owen picked up his coat and hat, and left for his uncle's farm. The wind was blowing harder and the snow was piling up in growing drifts. It wasn't a fit night out for man nor beast. As if to prove his point, he found Meeka, Ernest's big guard dog, lying across the corner of the porch out of the wind. Instead of coming out to greet him, she whined repeatedly.

He opened the door of the house. "Come in for a bit." She didn't get up. Something was wrong. Was she hurt? He walked toward her. She sat up and growled low in her throat. She had never done that to him before. "Are you sick, girl?"

She looked back at something in the corner and whined softly. Over the wind he heard what sounded like a sobbing child. "What have you got there, Meeka? Let me see."

He came closer. There was a child in an Amish bonnet and bulky winter coat trying to bury herself beneath Meeka's thick fur. Where had she come from? Why was she here? He looked around. Where were her parents?

Don't miss
The Hope *by Patricia Davids,*
available now wherever
HQN™ books and ebooks are sold.

HQNBooks.com

Copyright © 2019 by Patricia MacDonald

Looking for more satisfying love stories
with community and family at their core?

Check out **Harlequin® Special Edition**
and **Love Inspired®** books!

New books available every month!

CONNECT WITH US AT:

Facebook.com/groups/HarlequinConnection

 Facebook.com/HarlequinBooks

Twitter.com/HarlequinBooks

 Instagram.com/HarlequinBooks

Pinterest.com/HarlequinBooks

ReaderService.com

**ROMANCE WHEN
YOU NEED IT**

HFGENRE2018